"I TRUST YOU,"
KARPOV TOLD IRINA.

She said nothing, cautioned him to be silent.

"Your hands," Karpov said. "I knew them so well. Long, gentle. I know what pleasure they gave me. They'll inflict pain now. But in the end I'll be a better man. At the mercy of your hands. Almost medieval, isn't it, Irina? A laying on of hands."

She was candid with him. She told him Colonel Dort had visited her and had ordered the operation. "He needs you. He's lazy and incompetent, and he wants you to wind up the Levitch matter. I told him you could be back at work in two weeks, and there is every chance you'll be cured."

"Or changed?"

"There will be no change in your personality. The operation has one purpose. To relieve you of seizures. It is not a mind-altering process. You will be your old self."

"I believe you." He took her hand.

The operation took somewhat less than two hours.

KARPOV'S BRAIN

D0978344

KARPOV'S BRAIN

Gerald Green

A PERIGORD PRESS BOOK

BANTAM BOOKS
TORONTO · NEW YORK · LONDON · SYDNEY · AUCKLAND

KARPOV'S BRAIN

*A Bantam / Perigord Book / published in association with
William Morrow and Company, Inc.*

PRINTING HISTORY

*Morrow / Perigord edition published May 1982

Bantam / Perigord edition / June 1984*

ISBN 0-553-24352-7

Published simultaneously in the United States and Canada

---

*Bantam Books are published by Bantam Books, Inc. Its trademark,
consisting of the words "Bantam Books" and the portrayal of
a rooster, is Registered in U.S. Patent and Trademark Office
and in other countries. Marca Registrada. Bantam Books, Inc.,
666 Fifth Avenue, New York, New York 10103.*

PRINTED IN THE UNITED STATES OF AMERICA

H   0 9 8 7 6 5 4 3 2 1

For Marlene

Karpov's Brain

1

AT MID-MORNING, under a sky charged with metallic frost, they began to gather. Cold and vulnerable, shabbily dressed, they shuffled on the sleet-glazed pavement in huddled groups, their breath creating wispy clouds. They exchanged gossip, studied documents, glanced nervously at the turnout of KGB men who stood to the left of the columned synagogue scribbling notes and taking photographs.

A hundred feet away, in a black Zhiguli, Karpov and Malik watched them in silence. Karpov lit a Marlboro, offered none to Malik, exhaled a stream of smoke.

Bastard, Malik thought, *with his American cigarettes and Scotch whisky. Always carrying sacks of oranges and bananas, boxes of chocolates to his mistresses.* And the smart cut of his British warm, his London suit, his snap-brim black Borsalino. He wondered—as he had since the telephone call that morning from Karpov—why an assistant chief of the Second Directorate should bother with the routine surveillance of a mob of ratty Jews.

Karpov rubbed his left temple and his left eye. Malik had heard stories about him—neurotic, flighty, brilliant. They

1

tolerated him in the high echelons at Dzerzhinsky Street because he got results. Half of Karpov's life as spy, enforcer and policeman had been spent in the West. His English, his French and his German were flawless. He knew vintage wines and how to play bridge. But there was said to be a screw loose in him—a wild erratic strain. Rumors about exotic foreign women, sexual adventures. No one else in the organization got away with as much as Karpov. Yet he survived.

The people outside the synagogue moved as if underwater, mist-shrouded. Hunched, apologetic, they didn't belong in the Soviet Union, Malik thought. *Why not let all the kikes out? The whole stinking crowd. Open the gates, load them on trains and planes, let them crawl or swim to their Zionist desert. And let the Arabs finish them off.*

"Hitler did us a favor," Malik said. "If he'd finished the job, they wouldn't be here to bother us. Why should we have to worry about them?" He glanced at Karpov for a reaction.

Karpov yawned. He rubbed his left eye, turned a white-toothed grin on the younger man. The teeth were milk-clear and even. Malik had heard that Karpov had had them covered in some ingenious way by a dentist in San Francisco. The teeth unnerved Malik.

"How are you on jokes?" Karpov asked.

"About Yids?"

"Stories about our leader."

Malik smiled wanly. One had to watch one's every move, every reaction with Karpov. The cynical son of a bitch was all guile. "I'm afraid I haven't much of a sense of humor, Andrei Borisovich."

"No humor? A subdirector of the Jewish Department of the Fifth Chief Directorate with no sense of humor? Your department is the laughingstock of the KGB. Laugh, Anatoli Malik! Laugh! Look at them! Are they threats to the state? Traitors, spies, defamers?"

"I think so. Yes."

"You *think* so. What do you think of this? Some old Jew in Magnitogorsk was sentenced to ten years at hard labor last week for calling Marshal Ustinov an idiot. Two years for slandering him and eight years for giving away a state secret."

"Ah, oh. A Jewish joke."

"Not really. I changed it to a Jew. It could have been a

farmer in the Ukraine or an Uzbek machinist. You don't think it's funny?"

"Only if you do, Major Karpov."

"I see you were warned about me. The unpredictable Karpov. Full of wild ideas. But a genius. Malik, I'm just an efficient policeman. You can laugh if you wish."

"Whatever you wish me to do. In the old days, I suppose, both of us could be shot for telling such jokes."

Karpov ignored him. "New statue of Andropov in the Tretyakov Gallery. It's a bust with two fat breasts. One peasant asks another, what are the tits for? The other says, one breast shows all the good things Andropov gives to the people of Asia. The other shows the good things he gives to the people of Africa. So the other peasant asks, so how does he give good things to the people of the Soviet Union? *Idiot*, the first peasant tells him, that's why they made the statue from the waist up."

"I'm not sure I understand, Comrade Major."

"God, I enjoy the look of pain on your peasant face, Malik. You're part Ukrainian? Sentimental, a romantic?"

Why in God's name, Malik wondered, *did he bother looking at my dossier? So I have a Ukrainian mother. So what? Does he think this gives him an edge?*

It was a relief to Malik when Levitch appeared in the crowd outside the Moscow synagogue and Karpov's attention focused on the Jewish leader. As usual Levitch made his entrance followed by a group of foreign journalists. Malik could see his own photographers taking stills and motion pictures. Abram Levitch was the star of their continuing film. Without the Little Yid their films would be dull and repetitious. A parade of sheep-faced troublemakers, too dumb to give up their game, to abandon their primitive faith, forget about their doomed Israel and weepy relatives.

Levitch, a joyful man, added zest to things. He didn't weep. He never looked unhappy. Malik could see him laughing, handing out sheets of yellow onionskin to the journalists, chatting with his coreligionists. He was kidding the nearest KGB photographer, Gorchakov, who was clicking away as if recording an Olympic event.

"Levitch, Abram Moiseivich," Major Karpov said. "Uncrowned king of the refuseniks. What is wrong with your department, Malik? Why do you let him get away with so much?"

"In terms of the Soviet Constitution, Andrei Borisovich, he hasn't done anything illegal yet."

"Find something."

Karpov studied Abram Levitch. A man of middling height, broad-chested, bareheaded in the chill March wind. A shock of curling reddish-brown hair, high forehead. And that unmistakable soft look that many Jews had—round dark-brown eyes, a short round nose, a wide, active mouth. *They talk too much, think too much, analyze too much. Not like our good, silent, stolid, trusting Slavs. No wonder Stalin had to shoot the big-shot Jews who made the revolution.*

In his foreign posts, Karpov had read everything he could lay his hands on about Trotsky. He had developed a sneaking admiration for him. *There was a Jew for you!* Brilliant, ingenious, courageous. Looked like a wispy poet or an intellectual schoolteacher—but hard as a diamond and with as many facets. What would an idiot like Malik say—or any of those KGB hoodlums taking photographs—if Karpov told them that Trotsky-Bronstein organized the Red Army, developed ingenious military strategy, beat the guts out of the White Guards, the Fascists, the whole howling mob of Czarists, reactionaries and imperialists? No wonder Stalin had to brain him.

But Levitch was no Trotsky, Karpov could see. A bit of a clown. Joking with his admiring coterie of journalists. Waving pudgy hands, hugging fellow Yids, exchanging tales of woe with a show of good humor.

"Who are they?" Karpov asked.

"Who . . . ?"

"The people who came with Levitch."

"Jews."

"I know they're Jews, Malik. The journalists."

"Three Americans and an Englishman. A West German, a Frenchman."

"Their names?"

"The tall man with the yellow beard is Floyd Hanson. World News Association. Speaks hardly any Russian. He's been in Moscow only a month. The husky man in the light-blue ski cap is Anthony Parente. An Italian-American with a Chicago newspaper. He's been under high-level surveillance.

He has embassy connections. The American woman is here on a temporary visa. The tall Englishman, Cardwell, is one of ours."

"They seem to adore Levitch."

He must be joking, Malik thought. *Or is he taunting me, playing me like a perch on a light line?*

"He speaks fluent English," Malik said. "Always kidding around, always here with his lousy petitions. Parente invites him to his house two and three times a week. They feed him, give him a place to sleep. He's even looked after Parente's children when the American and his wife go to the Bolshoi or the movies."

"Where did Levitch learn English?"

"He taught himself. From books. He was a mathematics teacher. When he was fired seven months ago, he started studying English so he could talk to the journalists. His French isn't bad either."

"And I gather he has learned a lot of Hebrew."

The bastard knows everything I'm telling him, Malik thought. *He's testing me.* It gnawed at him: Why was Karpov here?

"During the last raid on his apartment—it's not really his; it belongs to Chaim Slesik, the tall guy with the beard, standing in back of Levitch—in the raid we confiscated crates of Zionist propaganda. We took Hebrew books, grammars, dictionaries. He's convinced he'll be in Israel someday. He also figures if he wants to be a real Yid, he's got to speak the language."

"He must speak it well." Karpov stretched. "Last year, when some American Jews were here, they held a Passover feast at Slesik's house. Am I right? Don't look upset, Malik. Levitch got a bunch of his friends together. A rabbi from Milwaukee ran the ceremony. The whole affair—wine, matzo, a lot of praying and medieval magic. Right?"

"I was new in the Jewish Department then, Andrei Borisovich. But, yes, it's in his file. They also had a celebration of some kind in December, that holiday when they burn candles."

"It is called Chanukah. Did you get a report?"

"We had a man with them. One of their own reports to us. Not much happened. They pray, they sing, they eat. Nothing of a criminal nature."

"And his wife? Quite beautiful, as I recall."

"Comrade Karpov, it's difficult keeping tabs on her. The

Mossad keeps her well protected in Haifa. She's got a big mouth. She's going to Washington next month, then the United Nations. The Pope, Mitterand. As if we were doing anything wrong in keeping these troublemakers in their place."

Karpov lit another cigarette. "A Hebrew queen. What was her name?"

"Sonya Varvansky. She calls herself Sarah now."

Karpov scrutinized the shuffling damp group outside the columned building. It was always full on Saturdays. On Jewish holidays it was packed, crowds of people in dark clothing outside, weeping, talking, making plans, exchanging letters.

He could see Levitch embracing an elderly couple. He was making them laugh. The reporters kept jotting notes on their pads. An English television cameraman arrived. Gorchakov and two other KGB agents chased him. There was a scuffle. His camera was seized. Film was yanked from the magazine, unrolled in a long tan helix.

"Whose orders?" Karpov asked.

"Your department's, Andrei Borisovich. Colonel Dort said—"

"We may have to change them. It's no secret Jews do this every Saturday. Maybe we should let some newsreels out. Show the world how tolerant we are. I have to confess Levitch has a fascination. Why is he so happy? Do you think outsiders sympathize with him?"

"Not at all, Comrade Major. Look at the United Nations. The Jews are hated. The world knows what they are. Scum, liars. The Arabs know. The Socialist people know. The Third World knows. I've always felt that's the useful thing about keeping Yids in their place. Nobody cares."

Malik laughed throatily, hawked an oyster onto the frost-filmed street. "Imagine, Levitch's wife going to see the Pope. Who does she think wrote the first book on how Jews should be handled? Christians! Catholics! And all that crap about Babi Yar they keep blubbering about. As if they were the only ones who suffered, and as if it were the first time people killed kikes."

Karpov's pale-green eyes glinted. He smiled at Malik, bared his dazzling American teeth, a reproach to a land of steel molars, tin bicuspids. "Really, Captain Malik? Babi Yar? A Ukrainian would know all about that, wouldn't he?"

"My people died there also," Malik said sullenly.

"I suppose so. And a hundred thousand of the Chosen People? With your Ukrainian relatives pulling triggers for the SS?"

"That is unkind, Comrade."

Malik swallowed nervously, and wondered: How did he get away with it, this dandy, this schemer? *And what the hell is he doing here anyway?* Levitch was nothing more than a pain in the ass. A pest, a whiner. His wife had been permitted to emigrate; he had been turned down. Did that give him the right to go around defaming the Soviet Union, handing out his onionskin slander, arousing all the other Yids who were happy to spend the rest of their lives as Soviet citizens?

Malik began to point out others in the group around Levitch. The tall man, suggesting a Jewish Don Quixote, was Slesik, a computer technician, formerly one of the leaders. He was dying of cancer and had appointed Levitch his successor, Malik said. A young couple, in identical fur hats, were Marfa and Fyodor Bakofsky. They had once been technicians at the Moscow Hospital. Now they were unemployed—"unreliables." God knows how they lived.

As Malik identified people, the American Parente, the bulky man in the blue-and-white knitted cap, came to the aid of the British cameraman. There was some minor shoving. Parente was big and menacing but was no match for four KGB agents, Malik knew. Yet the American stood his ground, shoved one man aside and defended the Englishman.

"Get your hands off me, you *muzhik* prick," Karpov heard Parente shout.

"The Italian-American," Malik said. "He should be expelled. A hooligan, a savage."

"Nonsense. I think I once met Parente in Washington. A lot of noise. His boorishness makes us look better, Captain. Teach your underlings to use tact and flattery with him."

One of the KGB men came to the car and saluted. He looked startled when he saw Karpov's cold green eyes, the chiseled features. Like Malik, he wondered what Karpov was doing observing the weekly gathering outside the synagogue.

The watchdog gave Malik the sheet of paper, glanced nervously at Karpov and returned to his post.

Karpov took the sheet, slightly wet from the misty air, and read.

> *Irina Cohen, 53, formerly a lathe operator in
> Minsk, denied permission to emigrate to Israel, af-
> ter ten requests. No charges have been raised against
> Cohen, mother of two and the widow of Genrik
> Cohen, a hero of the battle of Leningrad. . . .*
>
> *Moishe Byalikoff, 22, student at Kiev University,
> five times denied permission to emigrate to Israel,
> charged, without evidence, of anti-state activities
> and slandering Mischa Lemka, assistant director . . .*

Karpov gave the onionskin to Malik. "For your files,
Comrade. Dangerous people. Enemies of the state. Have you
heard about the American diplomat, who is at an international
gathering at the UN, and asks, 'Why is there not enough
bread in the Soviet Union?' "

Malik shook his head.

"A Frenchman says, 'What is *why?*' A German says, 'What
is *not enough?*' And the Russian asks, 'What is *bread?*' "

"Forgive me, Comrade Major, but you really aren't here to
tell jokes. I'm curious as to what brings you to the synagogue.
Am I not doing my job? Are you dissatisfied with the Jewish
Department? I have a right to ask. You didn't come here on a
Saturday unless you had a good reason." There was a childish
whine in Malik's voice.

"Quite right. And here it is. The green Volga sedan."

"I see it."

"And in a second you will see the reason I am here,
Malik."

The door of the car opened. A slender, erect man, his long
gray hair fluttered by the wind, got out. He wore a fur-
collared brown parka, rough corduroy trousers and brown
boots.

"My God," Malik said. "Zolkin."

"Yes, Zolkin."

The tall man raised his arms in greeting. It was a consciously
theatrical gesture. There was applause from the Jews. Levitch
and a few others came forward.

"Since when?" Malik asked. "What the hell is Zolkin doing
here?"

"You're a policeman, Malik. You should have the answers.
Professor Mikhail Ivanovich Zolkin. Former director of the
Soviet Academy of Natural Sciences, internationally known

biologist, inventor of the Zolkin vaccine. A close friend, over the years, of Comrades Malenkov, Khrushchev, Andropov, and Brezhnev. Recipient of every major decoration awarded by the motherland. Look at him, the ungrateful toad."

Malik was aghast. "It's that bastard Levitch. He sucked him in. Comrade Major, why didn't we throw him out when he asked us to?"

"He needed educating."

"Educating, yes. Look what he's done. He's educated Zolkin."

Karpov rubbed his left temple, grimaced. "Double the surveillance on Zolkin. Tap his phones. Open his mail. No obvious harassment, Malik, nothing crude. But let him understand we are not pleased with his philo-Semitism, his friendship with people like Levitch."

"I can't imagine what they have in common, Comrade Major."

"Fluency in English and misguided counterrevolutionary zeal. I want a full report on this new alliance. Suggestions as to how we can go about destroying it in the nest."

His headache intensified. Karpov popped a phenobarbital tablet. He considered lighting a third Marlboro, then remembered that his physician had warned him tobacco was bad for *migraineurs*.

He ordered Malik out of the car. "Zolkin seems to have gone astray. Let him truly understand we don't like his new associates."

"What about Levitch?"

"Make him unhappy."

Tony Parente and the new reporter, Floyd Hanson, were no less surprised than the KGB agents to see Zolkin's seamed face. He was, after all, one of the best-known Russians in the world. True, he had often spoken out in favor of dissent and liberalized conditions. He had signed petitions, written letters, traded on his fame and his old friendships with Communist leaders to get favors done: a poet released from jail, a scientist allowed to join his family in Canada, a job for a teacher. *But this?*

Parente studied the haggard, smiling face. One hell of a man. Years ago Mikhail Zolkin had been a party member. A showcase for the West. Professor Zolkin. International conferences, speeches to fellow scientists, articles for American scientific journals. Now he earned a living by tutoring, a favored occupation for those approaching the status of unpersons. It would have taken little, Parente knew, for Zolkin to get back into the good graces of the commissars, the policemen and the politicians. But he was a proud and brave man. There was no turning back for him.

"Boy, this is a story," Hanson said to Parente. "First time here for him?"

Parente nodded, gestured to Hanson to follow him. A generous man, not given to the normal rivalries of journalists, Tony Parente often acted as adviser and guide to the new boys in town. He felt a little sorry for Hanson, with his cornfield innocence, his lack of Russian. "Follow me, Flerd," Parente said. "Don't ask questions, just listen."

Delighted, Hanson clomped behind Parente. They joined the circle of cameramen and photographers taking pictures of Professor Mikhail Zolkin. In Hanson's mind, history and drama were unfolding. Zolkin had been a world-famous face, a presence, a conscience. Now Hanson saw him clear and plain and he was exhilarated. Zolkin's suffering seemed to inspire those surrounding him: Jews, reporters, ordinary Russians. (The last, Hanson would learn, were unhesitant in their public damnation of Jews; Zolkin was another matter.)

The Americans could hear the voices rising from the Jews, who now moved toward Zolkin, smiling at him, trying to touch him.

"What are they saying?" Hanson asked.

Parente was jotting notes on a copy pad. "They have a new friend, a powerful friend. He's a real man, a hero of the Soviet Union. Nobody can hurt them if Mikhail Zolkin is on their side." Parente studied the strange, almost religious, scene. "I wish the poor bastards were right."

Several reporters and three men with videotape cameras pushed their way through the crowd around Mikhail Zolkin. He was shaking gloved hands, hugging people, smiling. He had tired hazel eyes. They hid in dark hollows. *Sad and exhausted*, Parente thought. *But full of kindness, an almost embarrassing honesty.*

"Professor Zolkin," Parente shouted. "This is the first time you've joined the Jewish protest. Why?"

"Because I did not have the courage to come sooner."

"Lay off, Tony," Levitch laughed. His English was American-accented. "Don't get the professor to say things that'll get him in trouble."

A weedy woman from the BBC, in a black fur parka and designer boots, thrust a microphone at Zolkin. Her name was Agnes Wardle. "Does this represent a new policy in the dissident movements? A union of Jews and democrats?"

"It does," Zolkin said gently. He coughed. "My friend Abram Levitch and I have come to the conclusion that we must join forces."

Floyd Hanson nudged Parente. "Is that important?"

"It's the *lead*, Flerd. I only hope the morons on the foreign desk realize it."

Brian Cardwell, the man from the British newspaper, joined them. "Thought Zolkin was about to be rehabilitated, Anthony. Wasn't that the word? The Politburo was supposed to be anxious to make their peace with the great dissenter."

"Sounds like a KGB shithouse rumor." Parente did not care for Cardwell. He had suspicions about him. "Listen to what he's saying. You'll learn something."

"Dear friends of the foreign press," Zolkin said. His English was thickly accented, almost, Parente thought, like a radio comic's—Bert Gordon, or Parkyakarkus. "What I have to say today is simple and easily understandable."

"Even for us journalists, Professor?" Parente laughed.

"Yes, Tony, even for you."

"Abram Moiseivich Levitch and I met last week and came to a long-overdue conclusion. Our aims are the same. Our desires are the same. Freedom, liberty, the right to speak out, to disagree, to read and write and publish, to travel, the right to emigrate. If we, the democratic dissidents, are concerned with internal liberties in the Soviet Union, and our Jewish friends are concerned with emigration, we are nonetheless members of the same brotherhood. We have no arms. We have no power. We have no money. We are small in number. We ask only that the Soviet Union fulfill its destiny and renounce tyranny and the imprisonment of the human spirit."

He had a soft voice, but his words were clearly heard. A KGB man was recording everything with a directional microphone. Two others took photographs.

"Mr. Levitch, you are in accord?" Agnes Wardle asked.

"Me?" Levitch asked. He grinned. "Me? I should argue with Professor Zolkin? Sure, I'm in accord."

"Abram, baby," Tony Parente said. "Cut the innocent act. Who went to whom? Who got this thing going?"

"It had a life of its own, Tony."

"Yeah. I bet."

Parente scowled at Levitch, shook a gloved fist. He knew the refusenik well. Homeless, jobless, Levitch often slept on a sofa in Parente's living room.

"Abram Moiseivich does not take enough credit," Zolkin said. "He approached me. He is more courageous than I am. We have been too preoccupied with our individual goals. But the struggle to liberalize life in the USSR is *one* struggle. The non-Jewish democratic movement is in accord. We will support the efforts of Soviet Jews to emigrate. They will support us in our struggle for internal freedom."

"Good luck," Parente said softly. He nudged Hanson. "Nice idea, but who's listening?"

"We include also," Levitch said, "all minority peoples in the Soviet Union seeking freedom. Lithuanians, Latvians, Ukrainians, Uzbeks. And all religious groups—Baptists, Moslems, Catholics. We make common cause."

"Are you concerned about repression?" Brian Cardwell asked. "Really now, aren't you presenting them with a nasty challenge?"

"We are nonviolent," Levitch said. He smiled. "Who can we hurt? How many guns do we have? I don't even own a cigarette lighter. I can't fight. If somebody punched me, I'd fall down."

Parente, a veteran of six years of reporting in Vietnam and the Middle East, had a nose for danger. His peripheral vision warned him of the KGB men converging. Three galoots from the left, two from the right. The KGB cameramen stopped filming. They wanted no record of what was to happen. Parente could not imagine them attacking Zolkin. The Jews, as always, would be fair game.

As the pummeling and shoving began, some of the reporters shouted curses, protests. They had observed the handling of peaceful protests before. Bulky, hardfisted men with bland flat faces, wide mouths, smiling pale eyes were pushing people down, hitting them at random, grabbing others by collars and sleeves. In seconds the demonstrators scattered, ran for the columned portico, vanished down side streets.

An old woman lay in the gutter, holding a hand to her bleeding forehead. Her husband bent double over a car fender, vomiting from a blow to the abdomen.

It always amazed Parente that the hoodlums would do this—not too often, he realized—in full view of the press. Then he understood why. Zolkin's appearance and Levitch's cockiness had unnerved them. Any alliance between Jews and democrats would have to be snuffed out with a show of violence. It was as if the KGB were saying *we don't give a damn who sees this, or knows about it*.

Cameras were routinely smashed. Film was seized. A West German cameraman, Schultze, a friend of Parente's, tried to guard his Auricon, took a crack across the nose from Gorchakov, fell to the cobbled street. His camera was kicked, stomped.

"Watch it, Jack," Parente said to a slab-sided man in a brown fur hat. "You lay a hand on me, you'll answer to the Italian-American Mutual Aid Society."

The street was suddenly cleared except for Zolkin and Levitch. No one had touched them, threatened them, spoken to them.

Zolkin stood isolated—a tall tree on a windy plain. "These people have committed no offense, gentlemen. Let them speak. Let us tell our story. We threaten no one."

With professional expertise, two men suddenly grabbed Abram Levitch. He did not resist. *Smiling that childish smile*, Parente thought. The guy had too much guts for his own good. But he had Zolkin on his side now. It would make it harder for them to knock Levitch around.

The plainclothesmen swiftly dragged Levitch into a waiting Zhiguli. Only when the car took off from the icy curb was it evident that they were beating him. Methodically, dispassionately, they were punching him in the stomach, battering his chest.

"Brave bastard," Parente said. "Hang in there, Abram."

Zolkin shook his fist at the departing car and at the KGB men who remained to observe the demonstrators.

"You are Fascists!" Zolkin cried. "You are no better than Fascists! I will fight you!"

He turned and shouted his defiance at the remaining

policemen. They made no move to arrest him. One turned his back and laughed. The other lit a cigarette.

"They won't mess with M. I. Zolkin," Parente said. "Flerd, we got us a first-class dustup. Jews, they can handle. Zolkin and his crowd, they can make sweat. But the combo may give them trouble."

Women were sobbing. People drifted into the synagogue. Zolkin put his arms around an elderly couple. Semonski, the pianist, and his wife, Parente told Hanson. Others gathered around Zolkin—Slesik, Leah Rostov, Nadya Burik.

The KGB men moved in, spouting insults, tearing up the yellow sheets. None of them looked at Zolkin or gave him an order.

"Mikhail Ivanovich. You do us honor by being here today," old Semonski shouted.

"I am with you. We will make these Red Fascists listen to us."

Parente and the journalists gathered around Zolkin.

From the opposite side of the street, Malik watched them for about thirty seconds, then called two of his thick-faced aides.

They trooped across the Bolshoi Spasoglinishchevsky Pereulok, three porcine men in ill-fitting clothing.

Parente saw them. "Malik. Holy horror."

"Who's he?" Hanson asked.

"Deputy boss of the Jewish Department. He'd make a spitting cobra back off."

"Zolkin isn't Jewish."

"He might as well be now."

Malik took off his hat as he spoke to Zolkin. "Please, Professor. You are creating a disturbance talking to foreign journalists. Who knows which one is a spy?"

"Tell him you *are*, Hanson," Parente whispered. "New spy in town."

Agnes Wardle said, "Professor Zolkin has done nothing."

"Be quiet, lady," Malik said. "Leave, Professor. Go home. Do not come to the synagogue anymore. You are an honored citizen of the USSR. It is beneath your dignity to associate with spies, Zionists, saboteurs, defamers of the Soviet Union."

Chaim Slesik shuffled on unsteady feet and stood next to Zolkin. Zolkin smiled at him and took his hand. Dramatically, he raised both their arms. "We are together, Captain Malik. From this day on, the movement for freedom is united."

"Big doings," Parente said to Hanson and Agnes Wardle. "This will be a front-pager, friends. Bet me it leads the AP budget."

"They dare not hurt Zolkin," Miss Wardle said.

"But they got no worries about Slesik," Parente said. "Don't take any bets on *him*, Agnes."

Malik's men dragged the cadaverous Slesik away from Zolkin. Like Levitch, he was pushed into a car. From the portico, people cried out angrily.

Zolkin tossed his scarf over his shoulder and walked away. He waved once to the Jews. *"Baruch ha-Shem,"* he said. "Blessed be the name."

Uniformed city police and KGB militiamen suddenly poured out of buses, double-timing with rifles at port arms down the main street. It took them less than a minute to disperse the people lingering around the synagogue, send the curious running for cover, order the reporters to leave.

A sergeant of militia methodically walked around the square, crushing the flimsy yellow papers, Levitch's weekly bulletin, into the gray slush with his black boots.

Colonel Sergei Dort, head of the Second Directorate of the KGB, had learned of Zolkin's appearance at the synagogue and had anticipated the roar of anger from his superior, Reshev.

Reshev blamed it on Levitch and the other Jewish refuseniks. Every good Russian knew that they were well-poisoners, carriers of infection. They had somehow—magically—induced Zolkin, hero of the Soviet Union, into this doomed alliance.

"We'll smash it," Dort gargled into the phone. His voice was clotted. On his desk, resting on brown paper, was a Hungarian salami and a sharp knife. A glutton with earthy tastes, Dort, a chunky squat man with a shaved head who affected incongruous gold pince-nez, had the salamis delivered in the KGB pouch from Budapest every week.

The paprika-laced sausage wafted tantalizing aromas into Dort's fleshy nostrils. The aroma helped neutralize Reshev's peevish, schoolmasterish voice.

"Détente, détente, Comrade Colonel," Reshev droned on. "Don't you know what the fuck détente is?" Up there in Politburo circles, Dort knew, they tended to be pedantic and overbearing, convinced no one else understood foreign policy, military strategy, world politics.

"I'm aware of it, Comrade Colonel," Dort said wearily. He munched salami, felt the oily garlic-rich beef caress his palate.

"The smashing of this partnership must be your first priority," Reshev said gloomily. "We can't tolerate Zolkin speaking out for Jews. He's too famous. Keep track of him, discourage him, keep him quiet."

"That will be hard to do."

"All right, work on the Jews. Shut Levitch up. Find out who his contacts in the West are. Threaten his people."

Dort swallowed, cut another slice. "May I ask why we just don't give that little bastard Levitch his visa and get him out of our hair? None of the other Jews give us that kind of trouble. None of them would have thought of enlisting Zolkin on their side. Why not let Levitch go?"

"It is being considered. You must realize that the Soviet Union cannot be in the position of being bullied by Zionist thugs."

Some thug, Dort thought as Reshev hung up. A soft, helpless, unarmed Yid with a big mouth. The colonel sighed, studied his salami with affection and dialed Karpov's number.

The throbbing moved from Karpov's left temple, fastened itself at a point behind his left eyeball, deep in his agonized skull. Before leaving his office he'd popped two ergotamine tablets and a tumbler of Narzan sparkling water. The pills would make him nauseous, but with luck they might reduce the cutting pain to a dull ache. The ergot didn't always work. He worried he had waited too long to take it. Later, he would sleep, and awaken dry-mouthed and dizzy.

Walking down the green corridors of KGB headquarters, he recalled his first seizures, years ago when he was a student, working too hard, fired with Komsomol ambition, courting his wife-to-be. Too many things to keep track of at the time. After graduation, after enrolling in the police academy, he'd improved, finding himself on track, discovering he was a born policeman. But the headaches seemed to recur whenever he was in crisis, challenged, worried, driven by ambition, a new goal. . . .

He could recall twelve years ago, when he was in his thirties—shortly after Marfa had shown the first signs of insanity and had had to be committed for treatment—how the headaches had become daily events, pain-laden ordeals that rendered him helpless, weak-kneed. And how he had gone to the eminent neurologist Dr. Irina Tashenko. The migraine had become an adversary, assailing him with fainting spells, loss of appetite, inability to focus. He appealed to her to rescue him.

Dr. Tashenko had put him on ergotamine, warning him not to overdose, to use it cautiously, to try to cleanse his mind of guilt, of any dread feelings about his hopelessly unbalanced wife. Later, the tall serene woman in the white smock had helped him in other, more personal, ways. Ah, the sweetness, the perfection . . .

Gone, gone, Karpov thought. In his pain, he wanted Irina Tashenko again. He had occasionally tried, been rebuffed. Now she was one of the USSR's most eminent neurosurgeons. He rarely saw her. When he did, he tried to remind her of their shared past. She looked at him with cool blue eyes, unrevealing, unresponding.

But I saved your husband's neck, Karpov had told her a year ago. *He's free and working because Major Andrei Borisovich Karpov fixed his dossier, got him off the hook. Otherwise he'd be in the gulag. . . .*

She had responded that she was grateful. Lev Tashenko was grateful. But there would be no stoking of old fires. She had left him with a warning that he looked pale and under strain, that perhaps he should find a hobby—painting, music, chess.

These recollections, honed by the headache, flitted through Karpov's mind as he walked to Malik's office. He did not want Levitch in his own office. Leave it to that Jew to start mocking stories about the Picasso serigraphs, the Japanese porcelains, the Mexican artifacts, the Pakistani rug. Whenever possible, Karpov avoided interrogations in his sanctuary. Better the dull green rooms of underlings.

Levitch rose when Karpov entered. He had no idea who the slender man was. Malik had told him nothing.

"Sit, sit, Levitch," Karpov said. He offered the prisoner a Marlboro, pushed matches toward him.

"I suppose we shouldn't," Levitch said.

"Capitalist products?"

"No, sir. Cancer."

Karpov waved smoke away from his chiseled face. "Nonsense. It relaxes one. I imagine you can use a bit of relaxation."

Levitch looked hesitantly at Malik, standing with arms folded at the door. No one else was in the office. The window was heavily barred. A bronze Lenin inside a Red Star frame furnished wall decoration.

Interesting, Levitch thought. He'd always regarded Lenin as a decent sort. Tough, shrewd, brilliant. Levitch's late father, Moishe, had been a party member, an organizer in a factory that made Red Army uniforms. He had raised his son to believe in the revolution.

"Yes, I need relaxation. And maybe medical help. I have to protest, sir, that Captain Malik's friends punched me on the way over here."

"Is that true, Captain?"

"The prisoner resisted, Major Karpov."

Levitch drew his breath in, sat up in the hardback armless chair. He fiddled with his unkempt collar, yanked up his threadbare corduroy pants, crossed his chubby legs. *Karpov.* The name was a cold draft.

"Are you uncomfortable, Levitch?" Karpov asked.

"No, sir. Just awed."

"You know who I am?"

"Who doesn't know about Major Andrei Karpov? You are a legend."

"Nonsense. I am a good citizen of the USSR. As is Captain Malik. As we expect you to be."

"I try, sir. My problem is I don't want to be a citizen of the Soviet Union. I respect the great motherland and I honor its glorious history. But my home is in Israel, with the people of my blood. I ask only to go there. To join my wife and my friends."

"That is all?"

"Yes, sir."

Karpov studied him a moment before opening the blood-red folder on the desk. The Levitch file. An average-looking Russian Jew of thirty-three, chunky, round-faced, with a shock of wavy red-brown hair and lively features. The brown eyes smiled a great deal; the mouth moved too much. The tufted red eyebrows had a habit of rising in tolerant response. Did they rise when Malik's thugs were punching his stomach?

"You came late to this Zionist commitment," Karpov said. "Levitch, Abram Moiseivich. Born in Kharkov, 1950, the son of Moishe Levitch and Lydia Gusev. Studied at local schools and the Kharkov Polytechnical, served three years as an ordnance specialist in the Red Army, since then employed as a teacher of mathematics in the Frunze Secondary School, Kharkov, until voluntary retirement ten months ago—"

"I was fired."

"As you should have been. Zionist agitation. Anti-Soviet propaganda. Defaming our leaders and the state. Somehow you wangled your way to Moscow and through bureaucratic bungling, have contrived to remain here, where you have become the spokesman for the so-called refuseniks. You are a disgrace and an annoyance, Levitch."

"Then expel me."

"That is not in my hands. While you are here, you will comport yourself as a decent citizen. You will stop circulating these."

Karpov held up a sheaf of yellow papers. Malik had dutifully collected a complete file—every list of protests, appeals, challenges to the potent state.

"Why do you do this?" Karpov asked. "Why all this treasonous pamphleteering?"

"Because in the Soviet Union, Comrade Major, it is illegal to use a photocopy machine without permission from the police. What the Americans call a Xerox. If you let me have access to one, I could dispense with those badly typewritten sheets. The foreign correspondents would be grateful to you. And your KGB men would get clearer copies."

Clever Yid, Karpov thought. He was by now well enough known in the Western press that it would be a tricky business to shut him up, to neutralize him. Karpov detested him. At the same time he had to give him high marks for courage.

"How do you live, Levitch? You have no job."

"You know how I manage. Captain Malik's associates watch me all the time. I sleep at friends'. I am taken in like an orphan. People feed me. They give me odd jobs tutoring their children."

Malik interrupted: "The pig gets money from his Jew friends on the outside. We'll catch him yet. He and his Zionist pals work a money racket. American dollars, West German marks. How do you think he buys food and keeps himself in boots and wool shirts?"

In a calm and reasonable voice, as if discussing a problem in algebra with a slow student, Levitch said, "I'd no longer be a bother to anyone if you'd let me leave."

Karpov smiled. "Really, Levitch?"

"Yes, sir. I have repeatedly applied to the Ministry of Internal Affairs for an emigration visa. I fulfilled all the requirements. I was invited to come to Israel by a close relative, namely my wife, as is required. Her letter to me was sealed in an envelope bearing Soviet Union postmarks, as stipulated."

"Is this so, Captain Malik?" Karpov asked.

"Yes and no. Like all kikes, he can twist the language. There were inconsistencies in his wife's letter. Her letter was not classified as sufficient motive to grant a visa."

All three were silent a moment. They understood that a discussion of motives was irrelevant—from the standpoint of the citizen, or the state. The state did what it wanted and offered no excuses, no explanations. If it did not choose to grant Levitch the postcard-sized notice of approval, it had no obligation to give reasons.

"Some question that he was legally married to her," Malik said, yawning. "If it wasn't a legal marriage, his wife has no right to invite him. She's no wife, just a girl friend."

"I was married, I assure you," Levitch said boldly. "By the rabbi—"

"Crap." Malik folded his arms, glowered at Levitch. "There's no official record in Moscow of the marriage."

Karpov studied Levitch's earnest, moist face. How could such a marginal, minor man be such a problem to them? "Levitch, you cannot be permitted to set a bad example. You can't be permitted to give other Soviet citizens the notion that by trafficking with the foreign press, indulging in currency speculation, defamation of the USSR, and undermining the processes of government, you can bend us to your will. Your wife, if indeed she is your wife, had the right idea. She kept her mouth shut and she was allowed to leave. Besides, she'd been raised as a Jew, and she had a claim. Levitch, when did you become so holy? You had no religious upbringing. Your father was an atheist. Your mother was a member of the Orthodox Church. You never went to a Hebrew school or attended synagogue, until you met Sonya Varvansky. Now, I'm told, you study Hebrew. You impress me as a hypocrite."

"I am sincere, Comrade Major. From what I have been told of you, I assumed you would be able to distinguish sincerity from fakery."

"Watch your tongue, Levitch," Malik said. "This isn't a meeting of your fellow Yids. You want to get hit?"

"That's all right, Malik, let him talk. Levitch, how did you float to the top as a leader of the Jews? The men who preceded you, Barbash, Matzkin, they were educated men of some stature. We let them leave eventually. But you? A third-rate teacher of long division?"

"Lucky, I guess."

"And how is your Hebrew coming? Are you fluent?"

"Not as good as my English."

Karpov sighed and leaned forward. The cursed headache again. Like pincers squeezing a nerve in back of his left eyeball.

"Your English. It's in the file. Absolutely fluent. Slang, jokes, technical terms. You read Hemingway, Steinbeck, Faulkner. Did you enjoy the last batch of books you borrowed from the journalist Anthony Parente? Let me see. It included a new history of the Romanovs, did it not? And a biography of Peter the Great?"

"Both were excellent, Comrade Major. With astonishing insights into the Russian character."

"Pre-Bolshevik character."

"Certain similarities persist. I'm no psychologist, but there is continuity of sorts among our people."

"*Our* people?" Karpov asked. He leaned back. "You see, Levitch. Your mother's Russian blood may be stronger than you realize. You are not much of a Jew. You know that in Israel you will not be regarded as a Jew. The line of descent among the Chosen People is always by way of the mother. To them, you will be a *goy*. Perhaps you will not even be allowed to enter the country."

"Some honor," Malik said. "To be hated, despised, shot, gassed, shit on. Is it any wonder everyone hates you people, Levitch? Who gives a damn about your blubbering and lamenting? You think you're the only ones who died in the war? What about all the Russian citizens who died for you assholes?"

Levitch said nothing. The sad smile left his face. He stared at Malik's oak-barrel figure in its lumpy gray suit. The lank blond hair combed straight back; the broad, sweating forehead; the wide face of the essential Slav; the head crammed full of old garbage, old hatreds. Levitch wondered, *Does this Karpov, this graceful, scented man feel the same way?*

"Your English is your worst enemy," Karpov said. "I speak it well also, but I see to it that it never compromises me."

"Compromises?"

"You've become a pet of the foreign journalists. Bad judgment, Levitch. All of them are spies. That hooligan Parente, whose home you are always visiting, is one of the worst. He's hand in glove with the American military attaché."

"Comrade Major, I have never once discussed anything of a security nature with Anthony Parente or any other journalist. What would I know anyway?"

"You have friends who know things." Karpov studied another blood-red folder on his desk. He began to read off the names of other refuseniks, men and women who allegedly had access to military and scientific information.

"I assure you, Comrade Major, these friends want to emigrate as earnestly as I do. Why would they endanger their chances by giving secrets away?"

"In your case, I would say it would be a tendency to talk too much," Karpov said. "You understand that this friendship with Mikhail Zolkin will not help you."

"Zolkin is our friend."

"You think so?"

"I hope so. He's an honored hero of the Soviet Union. People will appreciate our cause now that he has joined us. May I say, too, his cause will be strengthened. Forgive me, Comrade Major, but what we ask is so simple that I wonder you go to all this trouble over us. Ship us out. Give those who remain a chance to be free."

"Freedom," Malik sneered. "What do you know about freedom? You and your kind have never had any. You're lucky to be alive."

Karpov motioned Malik to be silent. "Levitch, you don't seem to understand that every day fewer people have any use

for you. Or for Zolkin for that matter. In spite of your kind
we continue to build Socialism. We are improving the supply
of consumer goods and services. The USSR has never been
more respected in the peace-loving world. Why should any
Soviet citizen give a damn about you or Slesik or Semonski or
those other whiners? Keep your mouth shut. Stop handing
out slanderous papers, stay away from Zolkin, and maybe
someday you can go to Israel. Can't you understand?"

Levitch said nothing. He shrugged and opened his damp
palms. He felt soggy and stifled in the office. Always cold, he
wore three sweaters, long drawers, two pair of heavy socks.
Then he would enter an overheated Moscow apartment and
begin to sweat. At age thirty-three he was short of breath,
paunchy, given to sudden raging hungers, bouts of nausea.
But he did not complain. Not even to Ivan Belus, the physician who was a part-time member of their group. Dr. Belus
looked after them, prescribed medicine, took pulses, administered injections, drove them to clinics in his rattling Volga.
Levitch decided he'd have to invite Belus to their next meeting.
Several of the refuseniks—himself included—needed medical
attention.

"Major," Levitch said. "Why does the USSR have to imi-
tate Fascists?"

"Fascism, you said?" Malik asked. He rubbed a fist, took
two steps from the door.

Karpov, battling the cruel bite of the headache, stopped
him. "You seemed to be about to make a comparison, an
invidious one," Karpov said.

"Did I?"

"Levitch, you are in serious trouble. You like to talk. Your
people are the biggest gabbers in the world. Please, talk
some more. Theorize. Speculate."

Levitch inhaled, crossed his legs, as if to say *What can I
lose?* "Forgive me for being candid, but it has always seemed
to me that Communism succeeds to the extent that it becomes Fascism."

"Major, he needs a half hour downstairs with me," Malik
said.

"Go on, Levitch."

"Look at the problems of the Soviet Union—hunger,
inefficiency, internal disorder, poor production. But ever since
we became an avowedly anti-Semitic state, full of nationalist

fervor, military parades, chauvinism, overseas adventures—everything seems fine. You yourself said the country has never been happier. I mean no insult, but when we were a purer variety of Communism, we seemed to be failing all the time. With a good dose of racism and militarism, flags, armies, oratory and Jew-hating, we—*you*, that is—stay in power and can watch your power grow."

"That son of a bitch is slandering us, Major."

"I suppose he is. But it's all recorded. As I'm sure he is aware, if we ever bring him to trial it will be useful. Levitch, I did not mean to entrap you. But should you break our laws and be tried, your words are here for us to turn over to a court."

"It doesn't matter. I'll say it *out* of doors, too, and so will Professor Zolkin."

"The old bastard shouted *Fascists* at us today," Malik said. "That's how this Hebe became so brave."

Karpov got up. He longed for a steam bath, a massage, anything to drain the gnawing pain from his skull. The bone felt as if it were being riven by a cleaver. "Malik, release him."

"I thank the Major," Levitch said.

"Don't be excessive in your gratitude. Now that you've enticed Zolkin into your circle, your surveillance will be increased. Everything you do and say will be known to us. You would do well to stop attending meetings, talking to Zolkin, handing out inflammatory literature and giving interviews to Parente."

Levitch brushed back his red-brown hair. Malik grabbed him by the arm and pulled him jerkily to the door.

They're worried, Levitch thought. *More worried than I've ever seen them.*

Jimmy Parente, aged eleven, answered the doorbell. He leveled a plastic ray gun at Levitch and said, in welcome, "Halt, Alien, and state your asteroid."

"Jimmy, this is your friend Abram Levitch. Where do you want me to be from? Mars? The moon?"

"*Zzzzzzzt. Zzzzzzzt.* You've been atomized. Space Rangers win again."

"Get lost, space ranger," Tony Parente said. In shirt sleeves and a yellow apron, Parente walked into the foyer, gave his son a swat on the rear and took Levitch's fur hat and short coat.

"Followed?" he asked.

"No more than usual. It is three days since Karpov warned me, and still there is only the one KGB guy at night, and one during the day."

"Wait till you distribute next Saturday's Freedom Committee statement. With M. I. Zolkin's name on it, as well as Arkangeli, Muraskin and a few other choice non-Jewish democrats. Karpov thinks he's scared you and your refuseniks off. He's giving you a week to smarten up."

"I haven't learned anything, Tony. Here I am with an American journalist again. You're a spy, according to Karpov."

"Plural. Journalists. Floyd Hanson's here."

Parente led Levitch through the ocher foyer, into a cavernous ocher living room. The walls were hung with vivid posters the Parentes had brought from Paris, where the journalist had been posted before coming to Moscow. *Vuillard, Bonnard, Braque, Rousseau* . . . Levitch always looked at them with wonder and longing. Free artists, doing precisely what they wanted to do, taking orders from no one, directed by nothing but their own mind, will, art, conscience.

Martha Parente waved at Levitch from the alcove leading to the kitchen. She, like Tony, wore an apron. Meals were always elaborate affairs at the Parentes. They augmented their larder with provisions from the Embassy, from Helsinki, gifts from visiting Western friends.

"Welcome, Abram," Martha said. "Leg of lamb tonight and a real green salad. My little old lady from Tashkent came through with greens and beets."

"It sounds beautiful. I am not worthy."

Parente said, "You're not. But you're always hungry."

Floyd Hanson and an angular blond woman in her early thirties got up to meet him. Hanson, the newest member of the American press colony, had seen Levitch for the first time on the Saturday past. A day later he had asked Parente, the correspondent closest to Levitch, to arrange a meeting.

"A pleasure, Mr. Levitch," Hanson said. He extended a hand.

"Mr. Hanson, I'm pleased also."

"This is Treva Siddons from our Embassy."

"Ah, you're not worried about meeting the dangerous Levitch?"

"Goodness, no. We admire you."

"I try harder."

Everyone laughed.

Parente said, "Abram gets his education from *Time* and *Newsweek*. He loves the ads. Right, Abram?"

"Thanks to you, Tony. And my other journalist friends. Imagine. Détente, grain deals, computer sales, friendship societies, the Helsinki Agreement, and you still can't read a copy of *Time* in Moscow."

Levitch wandered to the bookcases, in which the Parentes, in a style suggesting the household of an overworked journalist, had stacked magazines, newspapers, books, notebooks.

Jimmy Parente ambushed Levitch, blasted him with his death ray gun when the Russian was leafing through a *National Geographic. Zzzzzt. Zzzzzt.*

"He sure doesn't look like a hero," Treva Siddons said to Hanson.

"The genuine article. He and a few dozen others."

Parente passed around a tray of black bean soup in steaming mugs.

"Delicious," Treva Siddons said. "Real Cuban soup. I bet it's the same recipe as Victor's in New York."

"Campbell's," Martha Parente said.

"Don't knock it," Hanson said. "It beats all that borscht I've been drinking." He turned to his host. "Is it okay if I ask him, Tony?"

Levitch was out of earshot, leafing through Parente's library. "Sure."

"I thought it over. Levitch is usually interviewed on refuseniks, dissidents, that kind of thing. And now with his association with Zolkin, he's hot stuff. But all I want are some leads on modern surgery in the USSR. Don't ask me why, but the magazine wants a big takeout."

"Ask some official news guys. Novosti. Tass."

"I don't trust them. My editor says they'll steer me into propaganda. Levitch knows some doctors, you said. If he vouched for the guys I talked to, I'd believe them."

"Ask him."

"Dinner, such as it is, is served," Martha Parente said. She was a husky blond Iowa girl, a former school psychologist.

She was four months pregnant and was growing bored and uncomfortable in Moscow. But she knew the post was a boost to Tony's career.

They walked into the dining room—more ocher walls, chocolate-brown trim, double-glassed windows, ponderous brass chandeliers. It was an older apartment house, reserved for foreign press and diplomats.

Levitch found three books he wanted to borrow. One was a Graham Greene novel. The others were biographies: an autobiography of Moshe Dayan and a book entitled *Joseph Conrad: The Three Lives*.

"A slight charge for use of the library, Abram," Parente growled.

"Tony, you know I don't have three rubles."

"Just keep those onionskins coming, folks."

Martha darted a look of reprimand at her husband as they sat. A browned roast leg of lamb, surrounded by onions, carrots and potatoes, graced the center of the table.

"Tony, the *bug*," she said. "Shouldn't we watch our language?"

"So what?" He looked annoyed. His black eyes clouded. He waved away an imaginary gnat.

"What bug?" Floyd Hanson asked. "Oh, I get it. The place is wired, right?"

"Not until a few months ago. Then they stopped. Now I think it's back, but I'll be darned if I can find it. What good would it do anyway?" Parente rose and began to carve the roast.

Levitch's eyes widened: *Real good, good food.*

Treva Siddons was watching Levitch's moist eyes. His button nose was sniffing. She thought: *What an undistinguished man, in his ratty brown sweater, soiled maroon shirt, baggy brown trousers.* He had shaved poorly, his hair wanted cutting, and his left eye drooped. *A hero? Someone to rouse the wrath of a superpower police state?*

"Son of a bitch," Parente said. "I think I hear it."

He was in the act of dropping a slice of pink-brown lamb on Treva Siddons's plate. He held it deftly between knife and fork, turned his head. "They've moved it."

"You're hearing things, Tony," Martha said.

"Can't believe this," Hanson said. "I wonder if I'm wired also? Maybe my beard?"

"After tonight you will be, my friend," Levitch said. "You meet with me, you are on the list."

Parente dropped the carving tools and walked to his right, to the rough-surfaced plaster wall in back of Hanson. The young reporter turned.

Jimmy Parente jumped from his seat and ran to his father.

"The finks moved it." Parente bent an ear to the wall, motioned everyone else to be silent. He ran his fingers along the wall. "Ears like a jackrabbit, that's me. Eyes like an eagle. Just call me Horowitz."

"Gorovich?" Levitch asked.

"It's a joke, Abram," Martha said. "You know Tony. He can't be serious for a minute."

"It hums," Parente said. "*Hmmmmmmm.* For a while I thought I was off the list. Now they've got me wired for sound again. Ah, well, we got no secrets."

Jimmy Parente aimed his space gun at the wall. "*Zzzzzt. Zzzzzzzt. Zzzzzzt.* Got 'em all, Dad." He put his small face an inch from the wall. "Hey! You hear me? We know you're there! Leave my father alone!"

2

"SO WHO IS Gorovich?" Levitch asked.

They had finished dinner and were back in the living room. Hanson asked if he could do a brief interview—an evening with Abram Levitch, the man, his personality, his mission.

Levitch had no objection. Parente warned Hanson not to say anything that would compromise Abram. But there was no harm in a profile.

"Oh, Horowitz," Parente said. "Guy says his golf game is killing him. He hits the ball a mile but he can't see it. So a friend says, take Horowitz with you. He's ninety-two but he's got eyes like an eagle. You hit the ball, he'll see where it lands. So he takes Horowitz to the first tee and tees off. Turns to Horowitz and asks, 'Did you see it?' 'Yes,' Horowitz says. 'You see where it landed?' 'Yes.' 'Where?' *'I forgot.'* "

Everyone but Levitch and Jimmy laughed.

"My English is good, but with your jokes I have trouble. Why is it so funny? Jewish people in America all play golf?"

"Some," Parente said. "I'll explain it later, Abram. Maybe Karpov will figure it's a code. Next time he grills you, tell him Horowitz is the guy he really wants."

"Sometimes, Tony, I cannot make sense of you."

Martha poured coffee for the guests. "You're not alone, Abram."

"Be double careful," Parente said. "You know why I'm tapped and bugged again, friend?"

"Sure," Levitch said. "No mystery."

"I can guess," Hanson said.

"Go on, Flerd," Tony said. "See if you caught on."

"The Zolkin business. They know you're Abram's friend. His best friend in the foreign press. They know you've interviewed Zolkin. They want to know everything about this new alliance."

"Just think," Treva Siddons said. "In a little room somewhere, they're recording every word we say. I don't think we've ever said anything they'd consider important."

"It doesn't bother them," Parente said. "My old man was a New York City cop. He had to make his quota of arrests, fill his quota of parking tickets and summonses. Same with the KGB. They got a detail, they got to deliver. Abram is the best friend they ever had. Without him, they'd have to scratch for enemies of the state. Anyway, life is a lot easier in the motherland with some of Martha's chocolate espresso cheesecake."

"Delicious," Levitch said. He took a second helping. To his embarrassment, he was becoming fat. Floating from house to house, always being fed, never exercising. *Oh, to be in Israel with Sarah—the beach, the sun, the hot dry hills, where a man could hike, brown his skin, harden his muscles* . . .

"About these doctors," Hanson was asking.

"Which?" Levitch was lost, transported. His eyes were misted over. Staring at the Mediterranean sun.

"I mentioned it to Tony. I want to do a magazine article on surgical advances in the Soviet Union. Tony agrees I shouldn't trust the official people, that you and your group have good contacts. Could you ask?"

"Of course. You are a friend of Tony's. But you have little Russian."

"You could interpret for me."

Levitch shrugged. "I will be glad to help, Floyd. I can call you Floyd? But my time is given to the committee, to press conferences, to trying to avoid my guards. Maybe it's better I take some time to help you. It will confuse Karpov. I have medical friends. I will ask tomorrow."

Later, while Levitch played Monopoly with Jimmy Parente and Treva Siddons, Parente took Hanson aside. He led him into the corridor. Under a dim naked bulb, he warned the young reporter to be careful in reporting anything of a scientific nature.

"Why? Can't you trust Abram?"

"Him you can trust from here to Lodi, New Jersey. He's tamper-proof and he will never throw you a curve ball. But he's on the spot since he and Zolkin joined up."

"You mean I won't be able to trust the people he finds for me?"

"Maybe. Maybe not. Floyd, the KGB will use any excuse it can to lay into him. You have any doubts, call me. What's your angle on the medical story?"

Hanson shivered. He could not get over how bleak, dark and miserable the hallway was—compared to the warmth and intimacy of Parente's apartment. Hanson lived in the Ukraina Hotel, a stark skyscraper where he was checked in and checked out by a stout mustachioed woman who squatted at a desk next to the elevator. *What a country!* A prison. He wondered how long he would last—single, lonely, struggling to learn Russian.

"My editor wants to do this takeout on advances in surgery, worldwide. The West, the East, China. He says they're doing big things in brain surgery."

"Yeah," Parente said. "But they can't manufacture a decent electric bulb. Look at that. The whole hallway lit by one twenty-watt bulb. Lenin said Socialism plus electricity equals Communism. I figure they got another fifty years to go, the dumb bunnies."

A few days after the dinner at his apartment, Parente dropped by the American Embassy to pick up a batch of magazines that had been sent to Moscow via the diplomatic pouch. Treva Siddons invited him into her small office for coffee. She covered a sheaf of cables on her desk before speaking.

"I didn't want to phone you about this," she said, "because you're convinced your phones are tapped."

"Yours may be also."

"Well, I doubt they'd bug the office of a minor consular official. Anyway, one of our people, I can't tell you who, heard a rumor about your friend Levitch. Incidentally, I adore Levitch."

"Rumor . . . ?" Parente's mind leaped ahead. *A plant? A bit of disinformation to paint Abram as a mole, a KGB operative?* Nothing was beyond the twisted imagination of the guardians of the motherland.

"There was some heavy drinking at a party the other night, and a person with connections in the Ministry of Internal Affairs let out that Levitch was going to be kicked out. That they were fed up with him, and the best way of shutting him up would be to give him his visa."

"On the level?" Parente wondered how he could check the rumor. "It would be great. The poor guy is headed for trouble if he keeps doing what he's doing."

"Don't quote me. I got it thirdhand. But my source swears it came from someone who should know."

Parente thanked Miss Siddons. He would tell Abram at once, warn him not to be too daring, too defiant. Maybe silence would be advisable until they got a better reading on his status.

At the next meeting of the refuseniks, Levitch brought up Hanson's request for contacts with some eminent Soviet surgeons. It was a minor matter, and was not discussed until after the usual business of new applications for visas, acts of persecution and the content of the weekly bulletin.

Although Parente had warned Levitch that he might be in line for his visa, Abram did not bring the matter up. It seemed to him that if it were true, he did not want to hurt the feelings of others less fortunate. If it were not—why waste time on dreams, impossibilities?

To Parente, Levitch had said with a wry smile, "I really don't believe it. The Ministry doesn't leak rumors about people like me. I'm a number in a file. And why should they let this information out to an American diplomat?"

"I agree," the journalist responded. "It doesn't sound kosher. But maybe you should lay off. Skip a few meetings. Don't show up at the synagogue. Avoid Zolkin. Don't issue any bulletins. If you're in line for your visa, why screw it up?"

"Tony, I thought you were a friend."

"I am. I'm trying to get you the hell out of here."

"I will go when I will go. But while I am here, until I learn from them that I will be permitted to leave, via the official postcard, I must continue to work for the others, Jews and non-Jews."

This very issue—the broadened movement—was the subject of angry debate at the refuseniks' meeting. Chaim Slesik, for one, veteran of twelve years in Soviet jails, was not sure they had done the right thing in joining forces with the non-Jewish "democrats."

"It dilutes our Zionism," Slesik said. "Abram Moiseivich, when you made a speech for the rights of Ukrainians, I had to fight nausea."

An uproar ensued. The Semonskis threatened to leave. Nadya Burik, widow of the poet Kalman Burik, called Slesik a reactionary fool. Always calm, Dr. Ivan Belus shook his head and tried to restore order.

Slesik pursued his point. "Mikhail Zolkin is all right—don't misunderstand me. *But do we need him?* What do we care what happens in this hellhole once we leave? All that should concern us is getting out, getting others out. Listen, my contacts in Jerusalem tell me this is a bad idea. We have committees for Soviet Jewry working for us. Not committees to bring Democracy to the Soviet Union. Let them figure out how you get democracy for themselves. Should I worry about some Ukrainian who helped gas Jews at Treblinka? Or a Latvian whose father worked for the SS, and shot Jews in Riga?"

"Men change," Levitch said.

"Not fast enough," Chaim Slesik said. "And we can't change whole governments. It's not our job to save the world, like some of those writers on the Holocaust tell us. We have no right to be praying for Cambodians, Afghans, Poles. Our job is to save our necks. Sure, I sympathize with Zolkin, but . . ."

Levitch listened to the arguments with a tolerant smile, nodded his head, smoked. *Two Jews, three synagogues*. Oh, how they loved to eviscerate each other. They would argue through the night in Nadya Burik's choking apartment, drinking glasses of tea, studying the text of the report for the foreign press, examining the merits of Levitch's new alliance. And always, dispute, analysis, talk. He was glad he had not raised the rumor of his possible departure for Israel.

Abram Moiseivich studied their weary faces. Faces too

white from too many hours indoors, bad diets, irregular habits. Apart from Dr. Belus, none of them worked regularly. Belus had influential friends. It was no secret to the Maliks and the Karpovs, Levitch thought, that Belus was the group's physician, the only member with a car, and that he communicated freely with refuseniks. Indeed, some weeks ago, Mikhail Semonski had suggested to Levitch that perhaps Belus was an agent.

"Suppose he is?" Levitch asked. He smiled. "He can't tell them anything they don't know. We're tapped, followed, questioned. What do they gain? I'll accept a decent spy in our circle in exchange for a ride in his car and a prescription for sleeping pills or codeine."

As for Dr. Belus, he was always helpful and sensible, Levitch noted. Right now he was arguing in favor of a common front with the "democrats," praising Zolkin, and praising Levitch for including other nationalities and religious activists.

Crazy, Levitch thought. *Here we are, a dozen unarmed, impoverished people of middle age, trying to challenge the Soviet Union, the vastest force of policemen ever assembled, a giant prison of a country. They probably laugh hysterically at KGB headquarters when they listen to the tapes. That is why,* Levitch thought, *even when we are in pain, we must learn to laugh also. . . .*

Nadya Burik, a shapeless, gray-haired woman in her seventies, reread the statement for the Saturday gathering at the synagogue. "In honor of Kalman's memory," she said with schoolmarmish precision to Slesik, "please try to improve the figures of speech. It's badly written. Not forceful enough."

Olga Semonski asked Levitch if he had a place to sleep. They had a "job" to do the next morning and could use his help. She whispered behind the whistle of the steam kettle on Nadya's gas ring.

"Business?" Levitch asked.

Olga, pale and pretty, her face heavily lined, nodded. She and her husband had contacts with American Jews. "Business" meant a black market arrangement to raise funds to keep the activists alive. Usually it involved buying tape recorders, watches or radios in the Beryozka, the shop that accepted only Western currencies. The items could then be sold for fifteen times the purchase price in rubles.

"Perhaps I am too hot to go to the Beryozka," he said to Olga Semonski. "They've increased the surveillance team."

"Good. You can pull a few of them away from us. I'll do the buying and selling. We've reached the point where we have nothing to lose."

The press release was reviewed in detail. Levitch, as unofficial chairman, approved it. Cigarette smoke clouding his eyes, his throat scratchy, he read aloud the typewritten report.

> *Amram Manilovich, 32, and his wife Ganya, 26, Jewish residents of Kiev, discharged from their positions, he with the Central Kiev Technical School, she with the Municipal Health Services, for circulating a petition to allow free emigration. . .*
>
> *Josip Glazukov, 43, widower of Leningrad, arrested and held incommunicado for seven hours by KGB agents, for distributing leaflets asking freedom for his brother Yuri, 37, an organizer of last year's hunger strike . . .*

Levitch initialed the copy. *Ah*, he thought, *pebbles, grains of sand*. How painfully he wanted to be in Israel with Sarah, his bride of three months. His warm, loving Sarah. To hold her. Stroke her hair. Listen to music with her. And someday a child. Theirs. Born in sunlight. In freedom. Not in this ice desert.

Maybe Slesik was right. Maybe they did themselves no good by challenging the whole corrupt apparatus. He had been told that Zolkin was a saint, a man of infinite courage and goodness. *I am no saint*, Levitch thought as he knotted his wool scarf, clamped the ratty fur hat on his head, kissed Nadya Burik's coarse cheek. *Just a man trapped by history*.

In the snow-dusted street a quartet of men waited in a Volga sedan. Levitch shivered. No doubt about it, he was marked, a new member of Captain Malik's special list.

He, Dr. Belus and the Semonskis halted at the physician's rust-pocked car. Levitch motioned to the others to wait. He strolled over to the Volga. The driver looked at him through the frosted glass.

"All for me?" Levitch asked. "Four of you, just for me?"

"Go home, Yid."

"I have no home."

Ponderously the driver got out of the car and shoved Levitch. "Go on, go on."

Steamy clouds flavored with brandy issued from the man's mouth. *The ultimate citizen of the total state*, Levitch thought. *He bears me no malice. He merely does his job.*

Dr. Belus watched nervously. "Abram, come."

The Semonskis decided to walk home. Better to split up, to give the watchdogs more work. Besides, it was Levitch who was drawing the lightning.

Belus invited Levitch to spend the night with him. He could sleep on the sofa in the living room. Abram agreed happily. He recalled the physician's flat as snug and warm. Attractive American posters on the wall, a decent library.

They bid goodbye to the Semonskis—two aging figures huddled against the rising wind, the swirling dry snow. The Volga followed Dr. Belus's car from a distance, then vanished somewhere between the Byelorussian Rail Station and Dynamo Stadium.

Levitch was tired as he had never been before, a deep wasting in his inner organs. A bleeding fatigue, as if gears and pulleys were dragging at his stomach, his lungs. He groaned. How long could he keep doing this? Wandering, eternally under observation, abused, distributing his pitiful yellow sheets to the foreign press. And now Zolkin as his ally. A whole new dimension, a new corridor of danger.

Belus stopped his car at the curb outside his apartment building. It rose in a monolithic gray block. Exterior drainpipes, a cracked pediment, the sidewalk crumbling.

A policeman in a sentry box, an AK-47 slung on his shoulder, made a note of Belus's license and nodded at the doctor. He ignored Levitch.

The two men walked to the prisonlike outer gate of the building. "This matter of the surgeon the American writer would like to see . . . what is the young fellow's name?"

"Hudson. No, Hanson."

"I have someone in mind. I'll have to contact her and let her get the clearance. But she'll supply him with an excellent story. She's quite a brilliant woman."

Levitch stumbled across the threshold, followed Dr. Belus to the inner door. A woman concierge studied them as they entered.

"Who is your guest?" she asked the doctor.

"Levitch, Abram. Spending the night."

She shuffled in felt boots to her cubicle, made an entry in a ledger. If she knew who Levitch was, she did not seem to care. In the morning her contact at the KGB district office would get a report.

The men were in the clanking elevator, an antiquated iron cage. "Ivan, we don't want to get this young man Hanson in trouble. All he is, is a reporter. His Russian is terrible. Whoever the lady is . . . you know, no funny business, nothing the big shots might find objectionable."

"Why should I endanger myself? Or you? Or Parente? Irina Tashenko will be perfect. You know who she is?"

Levitch nodded. He dumbly followed Belus out of the cage. "The brain surgeon. She operates on monkeys and dogs. Right?"

"Another headache, Karpov?"

"Some discomfort. The pain isn't severe."

Karpov sat opposite Colonel Dort, trying to focus his eyes on a point a meter above Dort's gleaming pate and below the yellow metal plaque of Lenin, enshrined within a hammer and sickle. Whatever one could say about Communism, Karpov thought, it produced no worthwhile ikons. Any obscure Byzantine madonna in any Italian church would put the holy art of the USSR to shame.

"Your trouble is, Comrade Major, you spent too much time in the West." Dort's eyes were invisible behind rimless lenses. Cigarette smoke drifted into his nose and the shielded eyes, but it did not impede his vision or speech.

"Please, Colonel, the correct term is *decadent* West."

"Good old Andrei Borisovich. A talent for precision. That's also a Western trait. Not like our sloppy Slav habits, eh, Major? Come on, we're old friends. So you showed me up in Mexico. What can one say? You had been there longer, had all the contacts. You spoke perfect Spanish—and French, Italian, English and German."

"We worked together on the Mexican matter, Colonel."

"Of course. Made me look like an idiot, but that's the past."

Why this review of an old rivalry? Karpov wondered. The headache bit into his upper left temple, as insistent as a metal clamp, a reptile's teeth. It dug deep, stretched the nerve receptors in the arterial walls, taunted him with the promise of worse to come.

Dort droned on. Levitch. Zolkin. The whole shabby bunch of liars, spies, defamers . . . The top men wanted action, swift Draconian action that would shut the troublesome bastards up for a long time.

He has come to the right man, Karpov thought. In Mexico he had taught Dort a lesson. Revolutionary zeal, an appetite for disruption and violence did not come from the listless peasants, the dull workers and their corrupt union officials. The poor of Mexico had been co-opted, gulled into believing they were part of some grand continuing revolution. Karpov understood that it was a revolution of rhetoric, empty promises and deceit, preached by bankers, industrialists and crooked politicians. Where to turn? Students, Karpov advised Dort, after the latter's attempts to infiltrate unions and farm syndicates had come to a bloody, pointless end. *Students, middle-class kids.* The whole Mexican program had been reappraised and revised. Credit for Karpov, demerits for the bumbling Dort. Dort had not forgotten.

"With your languages and your contacts in the West, Andrei Borisovich, you're the right man for this. You're the one to shut Levitch up, smash their organization, and make it clear to the West that we're doing the proper thing to these Jew traitors."

"Zolkin is not a Jew. He is a hero to the West."

"Zolkin's turn will come."

Karpov's mouth was a taut scar. The pain of the migraine, intensifying with each word from Dort; the shame of having to act against Zolkin and Zolkin's friends. In a sense this was Dort's revenge for Mexico. The colonel knew that Karpov would secretly (perhaps not so secretly) admire Zolkin, and perhaps even retain a bit of admiration for cosmopolitan grubs like Levitch.

"You've had a good career," Dort said. "A good life. Don't spoil it. I don't detect much enthusiasm on your part."

"I'll do as told."

Karpov reflected: *He's right.* A good life. A good career. Father a supervising clerk in the Moscow city bureaucracy. Karpov senior—a party member, a Great Russian, a hard-working, brooding man who had lost his revolutionary ardor and realized there was nothing left to replace it. Karpov's mother was a more exotic bloom—a handsome Baltic German, never fully trusted in the Moscow party hierarchy, a woman who read French and English novels and taught foreign languages. She had neutralized her husband's sourness, raised her only child with an overview of the world. *Yes, Andrusha, there are cities other than Moscow, great cities of beauty, art, music. . . . And someday you shall see them.*

A sharp mind, a retentive memory, a domineering, angular face and manner, a willingness to act ruthlessly, to follow orders with precision and speed—all these had propelled Karpov into a rapid rise in the KGB. Overseas, he had made his mark—London, Stockholm, Mexico City, San Francisco. He had been, variously, a "commercial attaché," "cultural adviser," "scientific aide"—a series of fake titles and nonexistent jobs that gave him access to trusting Westerners. He was the agreeable Dr. Karpov, who spoke English so well, played excellent tennis, ordered wine like a Parisian.

And there were the women. Scented, draped in silk, brittle and beautiful, intrigued by his chiseled profile, the faint scars around the mouth left by an errant grenade during his cadet days, the charm, solicitude, excellent manners. Hardly one's notion of a Russian police thug. Rumors that Karpov was indeed a KGB operative, a high-level one, surfaced regularly, and just as regularly were dismissed by his foreign hosts and acquaintances as ridiculous.

And here I am, Karpov thought. *Dort senses I am ill. These damned headaches. But he may sense more. That I am weary with Moscow? With this endless life of entrapment, persecution, hate?*

Karpov tried to let part of his mind concentrate on Dort's blatherings about Levitch, about Zionist traitors and bastards like Zolkin, while another part of his mind was spending a cool afternoon in the Jeu de Paume, or ordering oysters and champagne at Prunier. . . .

"Have they been involved in any serious provocation?"

"Ah, who . . . ?"

"Karpov, am I boring you? The Jews, the Jews. Levitch, the others." He leafed through Malik's report on the Saturday meeting at the synagogue.

"No real provocations, Sergei Fyodorovich. Levitch performed for the foreign press. Jokes, sloganeering, all in perfect English. He and Zolkin said they would hold joint briefings for the press from time to time. What were the words Levitch used? Ah, yes. *Common cause."*

"We need a provocation," Dort said. "A serious one. A crime against the state."

"What would you like? A hijacking? A bombing? An act of terrorism by those miserable Jews? They are so law-abiding they won't cross against a red light."

"Do we have someone with them?"

"For some time."

"I assume he keeps us informed. Irregularities, violations. Like selling jeans."

"Yes, Comrade Colonel. The Jews deal in jeans. You recall last summer? I got you three pairs for your daughter from Semonski, the pianist. His grandson had smuggled them in. In exchange for letting Semonski stay in his apartment, I relieved him of the jeans, so your daughter could have an enjoyable vacation at Lake Balaton."

"I remember. Karpov, why is it Jews have no trouble getting things like mini-computers and jeans, and our own people clamor for them?"

"Trade is a way of life with them. It's a wonder they win so many Nobel prizes. You'd think all they do is trade, buy, sell and lend."

"Yes, one would think so. Karpov, you look like a bleached dog turd."

"A migraine. I didn't sleep last night."

"This Zolkin-Levitch business is no help, I take it?"

"You assigned me against my will to the Jewish Department to rouse that cretin Malik, and I'm not sure what's expected of me. Do you want a serious provocation? Not just black marketeering or currency dealing? A state crime?"

"Zolkin is not to be involved. Levitch is. He's not going to be allowed to organize his Yids into a mob of counter-revolutionaries. He's not going to get his job back. Or his flat. He's going to get in terrible trouble."

Karpov held his breath. *Four . . . five . . . six . . .* It seemed to help. Years ago Irina Tashenko had shown him an article by an American physician on relaxing oneself, reducing headache in seconds, through deep breathing and mental imagery.

"You're in pain."

"A little discomfort."

They were silent a moment. Karpov studied his superior—a bespectacled shark. Dort's hairless head and jaw were raptorial, predatory. Karpov often wondered about his intelligence. Was he really the cunning spymaster he was said to be—or a dull functionary, ready to take on the worst jobs, act in the most brutal way when necessary? He knew that Dort had no affection for him. *No room for court favorites or ballerinas in the service,* Dort used to say in his coarse voice. The shark teeth would be bared in a greenish smile. Dort knew all about Karpov's cleverness, his skill with languages, his dandyism. These qualities disgusted him, but he tolerated them; they not only made a better agent of Karpov, they assured that he would rise no higher.

"Sergei Fyodorovich," Karpov said, "I may have something that is ideal for Levitch."

"So quickly? I knew you were bright, Andrei Borisovich, but just like that? Faster than a hawk on a one-legged hen."

Dort's ruralisms rendered Karpov queasy. The egg-bald monster was forever recalling his boyhood on collectives. The sturdy performer of homely chores, risen to be subhead of a directorate. But at heart always a farmer. Yet why were there no plants in his office?

"Malik's man relayed a request to us yesterday. It sounds routine but it might be what we were looking for."

"Act on it. Tell me after it's done."

"I prefer, Colonel, that you know in advance." Karpov would not let Dort trap him. Dort would profess ignorance if the scheme fell apart. It was a reptile's world and one had to be wary of snatching jaws, tearing teeth.

"Levitch, on behalf of an American journalist, has asked for the name of an eminent Soviet surgeon he might interview."

"You have someone in mind?"

"Irina Tashenko."

"Ah, the lady who slices brains. An old friend of yours—isn't that right, Karpov? We usually frown on these ties."

"The idea was not mine. Malik's man suggested Dr. Tashenko. Malik concurred. But she seems to make sense to me. Of course she would not be compromised."

"And the journalist?"

"I would think he would have to be included. It would make a better case."

"Stealing scientific information? Trafficking in secret data? That sort of thing?"

"Yes, espionage. Dr. Tashenko will be an unwitting pawn. Only Levitch and the American will be targeted."

Dort took off his glasses and tugged at his shirt collar. "What control do we have over Dr. Tashenko? She's been in trouble, has she not? I don't mean her affair with you. Some other business . . . What?"

Karpov flushed. Dort knew. Dort had always known. He was taunting him. "She was never in political difficulty. Her husband was. Before you headed the directorate, I handled the case. Lev Tashenko got too close to Zolkin. He's a failed poet, a bad critic. I called him in a few times and advised him that not only his job but his wife's career would be endangered by his association with enemies of the Soviet Union."

"He has behaved?"

"Not a squeal out of him for three years."

Dort's mouth cut his face laterally. "I'm troubled by her relationship with you. It's in your file, Karpov. I don't like these romantic relationships. Agents don't play around. By the way, where did you screw her first? London? Or Stockholm? It must be infinitely more fun in a foreign hotel room than in Moscow. Flowers. Fine wine. Gourmet food. And all those marvelous lace and satin things, the enchanting shoes one can buy for a lover. I've never had your touch, Andrei Borisovich."

"You know that the matter ended years ago. I hoped you wouldn't hold it against me. We are policemen but we are human. I don't intend to use this programming of Levitch to resume my relationship with her."

Dort got up, signifying that the meeting was over, and that for the time being he was approving the plan to crucify Levitch. "Why should she go along? Why does she owe you any favor?"

"Her husband keeps his editorship of the *Modern Literary Review* thanks to me. After he signed one of Zolkin's petitions, there was sentiment to render him unemployable. I gave the clearance to let him work again."

"You are a resourceful fellow. Saved his neck, got to kiss hers. And that is how you got her to meet you in hotels in London and Stockholm. And in Paris, Karpov? The Ritz or the Plaza Athénée?"

"Is our meeting over, Colonel?"

"Yes."

Dort paused at the door, smiling broadly at Karpov. "How's your wife?"

"The same."

"Pity. I sort of liked her. How long is it now?"

"Four—no, five years." The headache blinded him for a moment, sent a wave of nausea through his bowels, stomach.

"Shame. Good peasant stock, your wife, like me. A healthy woman like that, locked up in a nuthouse for the rest of her life. Ah, that's the way life is. You get to screw around with high-class beauties like Tashenko and God knows how many others. And poor . . . what was her name?"

"Marfa Galina." Karpov could have strangled him with his hands, enjoyed listening to the last hiss of breath from his lungs.

"Yes, poor Marfa Galina, locked up forever. And we know how they're treated in our state mental hospitals, don't we, Andrei Borisovich?"

Karpov flushed, ducked his head as if evading a blow, walked past Dort brimming with anger and sorrow. He would do as told, deliver Levitch trussed and plucked.

In his office, Karpov put in a call to the State Scientific and Technical Committee. It was heavily staffed with KGB officers. He did not want anything to go wrong with the Tashenko-Levitch plan. The committee would have to pass on the granting of the interview to Floyd Hanson, but they would be kept in the dark as to the ultimate purpose of the operation.

Karpov anticipated opposition from the committee. Dr. Irina Tashenko ranked high among Soviet scientists—precisely the reason they would want her protected from foreign reporters. Moreover, her husband had a spotty record.

"Tashenko?" Karpov's underling at the committee asked. "She won't give any interviews. Major, how long is it since you talked to her?"

"Some time. What is wrong?"

"She's in line for a Lenin prize. Original work in brain surgery. She's too busy, too important, and she is not as politically aware as we would like. Really, you should have asked us first. We're not so sure she's reliable or cooperative, or that we want her to talk to a journalist."

"She will cooperate. Colonel Dort and I want clearance issued for an interview with an American named Hanson."

"What if she says no?"

"I assure you she won't."

On a bench in the little park outside the Ukraina Hotel, Levitch, wind stirring his curling hair, read again the letter from Sarah and blinked away tears.

It had been delivered to him by an American clothing manufacturer named Sheldon Blum, a tanned and handsome man in his forties, as fit and muscled and well-dressed as a movie actor. Blum and his wife had also left a bundle of jeans with Levitch when they had delivered the letter, fifteen minutes ago. Then they had gone for a stroll.

Across the park, two of Malik's hoodlums watched. They had made no effort to halt the daylight transaction. *Why do they hesitate?* Levitch wondered. Maybe it was because Blum and his wife—was her name Nancy?—seemed so young, so vital, so American. Nothing apologetic or submissive about them. Mrs. Blum had a mane of sleek blond hair, a slender figure, a determined stride. *Jews!* Levitch thought. *Oh, what a varied people we are*. He would tell Sarah all about the Blums, their daring, their generosity, how much they had enjoyed their visit with her in Jerusalem. He could hardly wait to respond.

One of the underworld loafers who flocked outside the Ukraina on the lookout for foreigners sidled up to Levitch.

"What do you have in the bundle? Stuff from America?"

"Books. Not worth anything."

"I saw those Americans give it to you. Don't I know you? One of those Yids who sells watches and computers?"

Ah, Levitch thought, *the bracing, leveling effects of anti-Semitism*. This black marketeer was as free to abuse him as a colonel of the KGB or an editorial writer in *Pravda*.

"Wrong person. I'm an Azerbaijani. Just visiting."

The galoot sneered, looked greedily at the package. Levitch kept a hand on it. Theft had become endemic in the Proletarian Paradise. There were textile factories that closed down because of stolen machinery parts, offices that were idled when typewriters vanished. From each according to his worth; to each according to his needs?

The Blums had given him fifteen pair of jeans. He'd sell them at the university in a classroom that had been set aside by enterprising students for black market dealings. He'd get $150, in rubles, for each pair. The money would keep the movement alive a few more weeks—food, stationery, transportation, rents, telephone calls.

It dawned on Levitch: *I have no right to be snooty about these hustlers outside the hotel. I've become one of them.* But how else survive? He was vaguely shocked by his awareness— Abram Levitch, the politest boy in his class, an obedient, good-natured lad, surviving in his manhood by illegal trade.

He would joke about it in his next letter to Sarah. She tended to be a bit solemn, literal-minded. The natural consequence of being raised in a family of dedicated party members. He could recall his father-in-law, a former watchmaker, one-armed after an encounter with a Wehrmacht 88 at Kharkov, cocking his head and saying, "We have to give Stalin credit, give him high marks. The man stood up to them. We needed a tough man, a cruel man, and Josef Vissarionovich supplied that need."

What self-deception! When Sonya Varvansky applied to emigrate, her father promptly lost his job (a party sinecure) as "morale officer" in an explosives factory. No reason given. It was his daughter's decision, of course, that had destroyed him. And still old Varvansky remained loyal to the hard-liners, the defenders of the bloody past. Soon he and his wife (equally loyal to the Great Vision) became cool and distant to their daughter, now Levitch's fiancée. Levitch did not see them. They lived in sour retirement on Varvansky's Red Army pension and some translating work. Of Judaism they knew little and cared less. Or so they told Abram.

But we shall start a new family in Zion, Levitch thought. His mother would come to Israel with him, bringing his late father's books, papers and photographs. Like Varvansky, Moishe Levitch had been a Communist, a partisan of the faith, abandoning Judaism in the flush of the new dawn. Old Levitch had died of pneumonia. An erudite Stalinist. With the taste of ashes in his mouth. Principal of a secondary school in Kiev, he arrived one day to be informed he had been fired, and would be called up on charges of "cosmopolitanism," whatever that was.

Abram read Sarah's letter once more, finding in the tidy slanted script, the loving words, an antidote to the poisons around him. Contraband jeans, a day free of curses and punches, and a letter from his beloved. *Not bad,* he thought without bitterness.

> *Dearest Abram—*
> *The sun is high over the sea and the soft wind from the south makes the pine trees bend. I am here for a rest in the Galilee at Kibbutz Agam, with our good friends. How you would love it here! Life is simple, a routine of work, friends at one's side, a sense of all of us being one. One of the young Americans staying here had a new record, of that silly disco music, a Negro woman singing a song called "We Are Family." How we all laughed and applauded, and played it over and over. Yes, we are family here, truly a big family. If only you were with me, dearest Abram . . .*

He read the rest hurriedly and got up, picking up his package. He would head for the university and transact business. His watchdogs studied him from across the park but did not board the bus with him. He could not tell whether they were following him in their car. Wedged between bulky housewives redolent of sweat, craning his neck to see if he was being pursued, Levitch wondered if the eternal game was worth it. Perhaps he could abandon his activism, disassociate from his friends, let Zolkin find another emissary from the refuseniks. But would it help at this late stage? He had the dread feeling that he was isolated and doomed.

"Ground rules," Parente said roughly. "How it works before we buy it."

"Ground . . . ?" Dr. Ivan Belus's brow crinkled and his tufted golden eyebrows rose. He looked to Parente like Allie Cooperstein, his old handball partner from the Bronx, forty years older.

"I don't want Floyd, or Abram, or you for that matter, getting into trouble."

Parente, Hanson, Dr. Belus and Levitch were in Parente's

blue Peugeot. It was parked on the Mira Prospekt. Parente was at the wheel. Levitch sat in front. Hanson, excited but letting Parente do the talking, sat in back with the physician.

"It works simply," Dr. Belus said. "Request was made by me for Dr. Irina Tashenko for interview. The indication from the State Scientific and Technical Committee is that she will agree to talk with Mr. Hanson, and allow a tour of her laboratory. You know how these things work, Tony. Someone besides Tashenko will go along, but that will present no problem. Once they decide the story can be done, she will make certain that no sensitive matters are discussed. In a sense, the presence of a third person is a safeguard for Mr. Hanson."

"Sounds good to me," Hanson said. "I'll play along. New York shipped me literature on brain surgery. Right-hemisphere left-hemisphere stuff. I'll have questions in advance. What's Irina Tashenko like?"

"Lovely woman," Dr. Belus said. "Tall, dark hair, pretty enough to be an actress. In her early forties but looks ten years younger."

"Yeah, she's quite a doll," Parente said. "I saw her at the Bolshoi last month. Great cheekbones and a high forehead. Not your usual babushka shoving a broom. What's with her husband, Abram? Wasn't he rendered an un-person?"

Levitch nodded. "I knew him slightly. A critic, a poet. He was with Zolkin's group. The police put a scare into him. He keeps his job at the magazine because he's promised to keep his mouth shut."

Belus laughed. "And because he is the husband of the Soviet Union's most eminent neurosurgeon."

"Sounds like a nifty marriage," Parente said. He looked at Hanson. "Floyd, I don't know why I'm so nice to you. I guess I don't regard magazines as competition. Tip number one: Don't ask about Mr. Tashenko or try to interview him. Your article is on brain surgery in the USSR. Tip number two: Don't accept any documents or papers, or photos, from anyone but Dr. Tashenko."

"Why?"

"Listen to your Uncle Tony. Scientific data assumes strange forms in this place. You and your donor may regard it as innocent stuff, but some cop may get other ideas."

"I don't get it. If they've cleared Dr. Tashenko to speak to me—"

"I said it was okay to accept papers from her. No one else."

Dr. Belus and Levitch listened, impressed with Parente's shrewdness and his solicitousness for the young reporter.

"How soon can I call her?" Hanson asked.

"It works the other way," Parente said. "Don't call us; we'll call you. Someone from Tashenko's department will get in touch with you, assuming this goes through the way Dr. Belus thinks it will. The guy who calls will probably be a KGB informer."

"You're kidding."

"Abram, educate our friend Hanson."

Levitch sighed. "It is true, Floyd. For any scientific data, any interviews with Soviet scientists, there is always a KGB person controlling."

"Even for someone as important as Dr. Tashenko?"

Parente frowned. He seemed to be chewing on gravel as he started the car, swung it around, and drove toward Dzerzhinsky Ulitsa. "Remember, to the KGB, anyone from the outer world who asks questions is under suspicion. Good luck on your interview."

They passed a grocer's. In midmorning a long line had already formed—stolid women, a few older men. They stood silently, their breath forming white puffs. A city policeman watched them from the curb.

"Sad country," Levitch said. "Police are the basis of life. Without police and army, everything collapses."

Hanson said the city seemed peaceful—no violence, little crime except for street drunks.

"They had the mickey taken out of them," Parente said. He turned left at the Hotel Metropol, drove on to Solyaner. Levitch and Dr. Belus asked to be dropped off at the corner. They would walk to the synagogue. Levitch wanted to plan a Passover seder with the refuseniks.

"It's more complex than that," Levitch said. "You see the lines outside stores? People waiting in the cold to buy shoes, meat, a knife? That is *part* of the system. Soviet leaders say they will get more goods into stores, make a better life. But they really do not want that. The lines give them *control*. So they like shortages. A shortage means a line, people standing, waiting, hoping. As soon as you have a line, you need something else."

Parente parked the car.

"What's that?" Hanson asked.

"A policeman. Shortage means lines. Lines mean police. It is part of the system. From the housewives on the street to the Presidium, the system needs police. Many of them. One policeman for every ten Russians! Our answer to the problem of full employment. Also useful for finding jobs for misfits, psychotics, sadists or stupid people. We need all these police, not only to control the people but to keep the Socialist motherland from falling apart. Without them, we have unemployment, riots, social disintegration."

The Russians got out of the car. Dr. Belus told Hanson he would be contacted soon on the Tashenko matter.

"By you?"

"Oh, no, Mr. Hanson. Someone else. If a week goes by and you do not hear, let me know."

Levitch shook hands with the Americans. He told Parente not to miss next Saturday's rally at the synagogue. They were being joined by Ukrainian dissidents protesting the suppression of their language.

"Good luck, Abram," Parente said.

When they were out of earshot, Parente said, "Belus is a little slippery for my taste."

"I was wondering myself. How come he can transmit my request? Shouldn't I have gone to the State Scientific Committee, or whatever it's called?"

Parente shrugged. He stopped for a red light on the Ulyanovskaya Ulitsa. "They do things ass-backwards here. You could have, but I figured if we went through Belus—he's a shifty type with connections—they might respond sooner."

"Why?"

"They'll figure if you know Belus, you also know Levitch and his crowd, and they might get something from *you*. Or on you. Don't ask me to analyze it, and don't look shocked. Anyway, if I were Levitch, or Nadya Burik, or the Semonskis, I'd think twice about accepting so many free rides from Belus, or even taking vitamin B injections from him. He smiles too much and he uses lousy cologne."

"I don't follow you, Tony."

"I'm not sure I follow myself. You see, if the guy's a KGB plant, he's so obvious it's laughable. Only trouble is, nobody laughs much around here anymore."

3

"MURICIDE?" KARPOV ASKED. "The word is new to me."

"It means mouse-killing," Irina Tashenko said.

"Muricide, muricide. A nice sound for a terrible act. Who does the killing?"

"Rats."

"Ah, one of your laboratory experiments."

"A minor one. It's part of our long-range work in brain laterality in animals."

Unannounced, Karpov had come to Dr. Irina Tashenko's laboratory. Karpov rarely made field appearances. Of late, he had become an office man rather than a line operative. Colonel Dort preferred to have him nearby—to keep an eye on him and to make use of his keen mind. The burdens thrust upon the organization were becoming intolerable. Andrei Karpov, Dort realized, for all his snooty personal habits and his disabling headaches, was an important asset to the Second Directorate.

Flashing credentials and making contact with the KGB man assigned to the All-Soviet Research Institute, a fortresslike building across from the Lenin Stadium on Komsomolsky

Prospekt, Karpov demanded to see Dr. Tashenko at once. One did not deny entrance to a subdirector of the Second Directorate. He was taken to the animal laboratory.

Karpov's nose flinched at the stench, a pungent mixture of excrement, urine, rotting grains, chemicals. The laboratory was in the basement—the walls a dark green, the ceilings a maze of exposed and flaking pipes. On tables and in wall racks, mice, rats, rabbits and dogs lolled in cages. They barked, chattered and squealed. Many had metal sockets set in their heads, wore transmitters lashed to their backs. The room was overheated. For a moment Karpov wished he had waited for Irina in her office. But he had a sense of the dramatic. He was pleasantly surprised that she did not react angrily.

The sight of her, studying a clipboard, her lustrous brown hair piled high, American-style eyeglasses balanced on her straight nose, made him shudder slightly. He had not seen her in eight months.

Astonishing, Karpov thought. In a white smock and low-heeled shoes, without cosmetics or perfume, she was the most desirable woman he had ever seen. *And what a waste!* Obsessed by her work. Married to a cipher, a literary wanderer and coward. He told himself that for all her protesting, her attempts to turn him away, she had savored and valued their affair.

A woman technician, a round-faced Asiatic girl, perhaps a Buryat or a Yakut, lowered a trembling white mouse into a cage with a white rat four times its size. The mouse skittered to a distant corner, rose, squealed, looked for an escape. Its tiny pink paws clutched the wire mesh. The rat viewed the mouse indifferently.

"I wish you had waited for me upstairs," Irina said.

"I've always wanted to see some of your experimental work. Forgive me."

Dr. Tashenko's luminous eyes stared at him. They were not welcoming or warm. "What do you wish to see?" She turned to the girl. "Mirka, you may go. Finish the computation on laboratory-handled rats."

A young man walked by, carrying a yellow mongrel dog in his arms. What looked like a socket had been screwed into the dog's brow. The dog did not seem impaired. It licked the young man's face, wagged its tail.

"Muricide. So that's what you're studying?" Karpov asked.

"Are you really interested, Major Karpov?"

"The formality isn't necessary. You know I have the highest regard for you. On every level of human relationship. I do have something official to discuss with you. But it can wait till later. Meanwhile, I would like to know about your work here."

Irina studied his lean face. It was the mask of authority, the visage of power. Handsome, cruel, hard. She detested herself for having given in to him. Yet she had had no choice. *Lev Tashenko, you have signed your name to this scurrilous letter attacking the internal policies of the Soviet Union.* They always knew who were the weak ones, the ones who would bend, whimper, surrender. Karpov had been unsubtle. In London he had tracked Irina to an international conference on neurophysiology. Editor Lev Tashenko had been arrested. Things would not go easily for him, unless . . .

"I'm involved in research part-time," Irina said. "I operate three days a week."

"A complete woman. The ideal Soviet woman."

"That party-line nonsense is less becoming from your lips than it would be from mine. No one in a Savile Row suit should spout such cant."

"I was teasing. You look splendid, if a bit tired. Maybe you need a vacation. London, Stockholm. Surely your international colleagues have some conference in the offing?"

"And with my KGB watchdog along?"

"You would never have a more considerate one. A shepherd dog, perhaps, a loyal one."

In the cage the white rat approached the mouse, sniffed it, pawed at it. The mouse shivered and chattered. The rat appeared bored. It turned away and went to the rear of the cage, where it pressed a lever and was rewarded with a pellet of grain.

She should be mine, Karpov thought. Not just a lover. A wife. A companion. One with whom one shares love, intellect, cares. She was light-years removed from the hysterical peasant he had married, the unbalanced country girl (lightly varnished with a university education) who had lost her mind after two stillborn children, a Slav rustic, pretty in a heavy-limbed way, with a mind cluttered with witchcraft and prejudice.

He could see an inch or two of Irina's strong white neck below the thick dark hair. In bed he would rest his lips on her neck, peck gently at the vertebrae, tell her, as she laughed, that she reminded him of Ingres's "Grande Odalisque" in the Louvre. She would nestle closer to him. He had to believe that for all his guile and cruelty in forcing her into his bed, she had come to love their relationship.

"I'm here because I want information," Karpov said. "And also because I deeply miss you. Why are you so distant, so unfriendly? I wrote to you. No response. I tried leaving messages. Silence. Why?"

"Andrei, stop. I don't want to see you again. I am married, content."

"You remain married out of pity for a wretched man. I want you to reconsider, to think about me differently."

"I won't talk about it. If you are here to gather scientific information, ask your questions. You are embarrassing me."

He scrutinized her high forehead, fine nose, arched dark eyebrows, wide lips. Passion camouflaged, desire hidden. He knew the truth—the violent release of emotion, the lie given to the severe smock and low shoes.

"Tell me about your work."

"We do many things. In the animal laboratory we're concerned with laterality in the brains of animals."

"Laterality. That right-hemisphere–left-hemisphere business."

"You seem to know something about it," Irina said.

"Only what I read in popular journals."

"There are two schools of thought about hemispheric laterality in animals, that is, a differentiation of function in the right and left hemispheres of the brain. We call one the ontogenetic view—that organisms have functionally symmetrical brains at birth, both hemispheres controlling similar actions, but that random events in the environment act to bias individuals one way or the other."

"A behaviorist approach?"

"That is more or less correct. We call it the asymmetry lottery."

The mouse would not leave its corner of the cage. The rat came halfway across the cage, studied it with soulless eyes, turned away again.

Irina Tashenko went on. "There is also the phylogenetic position, which states that an asymmetry, a basic differentiation in the hemispheres, creates behavioral differences. It is an initial condition, a genetic condition, equally distributed in any given animal population."

"And what are you trying to prove?"

"Many things. Can early experience induce laterality, a different functioning of either hemisphere? Or can early experience, the effect of environment, modify inherited laterality? We know for example that in rats, right hemispheres are activated when spatial performance is required. In chickens, an emotion-provoking situation will also activate the right hemisphere. It gets a bit complicated, since the two hemispheres can inhibit each other, or couple in certain situations."

"Such as?"

"There is evidence of interhemispheric activation and inhibition in attack, killing and copulation."

"Ah. An internal struggle for the soul of the rat or the fate of the chicken."

"In a sense. Are you truly interested in this?"

"Fascinated. I assume all your studies, your abstracts and reports go to the proper authority."

"Major—"

"I wish you would call me Andrei."

"Major, you know damned well your agents infest every scientific establishment in the Soviet Union. Even if we wanted to keep things secret, your policemen would prevent it. I'm certain that the louts you've sneaked into the Institute haven't the faintest idea what our research is about. If you get garbled reports, blame them, not me."

Karpov stared at her. The dramatic cheekbones, the liquid brown eyes, the mass of dark hair. Her hands gave her away. The long hands of a sensual woman. Hating him, she had responded. Choking back her passion, trying to stifle the ringing climaxes with tears. Finally unloosing herself to the thrusts of a man she could not love. *Ecstasy*, Karpov thought, *is the conjoined passion not of lovers, but of haters*.

"And what about this—what did you call it?—mouse-killing?"

"Muricide."

"What a marvelous word. Why is this rat indifferent to the mouse?"

"That's what our experiments deal with. Are you sure you

have the time to stay here? You are not here for a lecture on differing functions of the hemispheres of the brain."

"I'm not, but I'm intrigued. I regret that in our previous meetings I didn't query you more thoroughly on your work. I knew you were one of our great surgeons, but all this is a revelation to me."

"I'm tired. I have two operations tomorrow. May we go to my office?"

"Tell me about muricide."

"Very well."

Karpov was peering into the cage, staring at the cowering mouse and the waddling rat. The rat knew he was omnipotent, a despot of the wire prison. He could take his time and enforce his will. A supreme ruler. Karpov knew the feeling. It was not unpleasant. But did the rat possess any capacity for savoring his power?

"When a mouse is put in a cage with a rat," Irina said, "several things can occur. The rat may kill the mouse—at once, or at some later time. It may ignore the mouse, as this one seems to be doing. Or it may interact with the mouse."

"Inter—?"

"Play, joint feeding, sleeping together. The killing is a spontaneous act, in the nature of the species, and it is not dependent on the need for food. Our rats are well fed. Our experimental rats are raised in different fashions. Some are handled by technicians. Some are untouched. Some have either the right or left hemispheres of their brains removed. Do not look shocked. A rat functions quite ably with half a brain. Some were placed in an enriched environment. Others were isolated in laboratory cages. Later, we tested them all for mouse-killing."

"And which of your rats was the most consistent killer?"

"Those rats that had been handled and then raised in a cage showed significant differences between right- and left-brain dominance. Rats with intact right brains, but lacking a left hemisphere, had a markedly higher killing rate than rats with an intact left hemisphere."

"The right brain is the villain?"

Irina shrugged. "I would not put it so simply. It is true that rats in an enriched environment—adequate food, space, sexual stimulation—did not show significant differences in mouse-killing as between left-brain and right-brain subjects. It was also significant that in intact animals—"

"With whole brains?"

"Yes. In these rats, there were lower killing percentages as compared to right-brain rats. We concluded that the left hemisphere acts to inhibit the killing mechanism in the right hemisphere."

"And you intend to extrapolate these findings to men?"

"By no means. Rats are rats, and men are men. We know a great deal about hemispheric laterality in men already. Domination, interaction, inhibition. The left side can inhibit the right, or the right can dominate."

"The right side seems to be the Nazi in the brain?"

She stared at him coldly. "Perhaps the KGB policeman."

"Touché, Irina."

Suddenly the rat skittered across the cage and pounced on the mouse. It broke the victim's neck with a deft bite, shook the squealing ball of fur, tossed it aside.

Muricide, Karpov thought.

"Not to eat, you will notice," Irina said. "A spontaneous species-specific reaction."

"Species-specific?"

"Rats are genetically programmed to kill."

Karpov stroked his nose. "Unlike humans, who must be conditioned to do so?"

Irina pushed back a strand of hair. Watching her, Karpov had an impulse to do it for her, touch her neck, kiss her ear. "You're a policeman. Not a geneticist or an anthropologist. I can't see any value in discussing with you whether the impulse to kill is biologically based, or the result of environment."

"You're right. It isn't my discipline."

Irina gave orders to a laboratory assistant. She gathered up her clipboards and notebooks and started to leave. Karpov allowed himself a moment to admire her figure. He was pleased that his thoughts were not entirely, or even predominantly, sensual. To his eyes she was aesthetically and intellectually desirable—a dear friend, someone with whom to share a love of art, music, good wine.

"Have you reached any dramatic conclusions?" he asked, as they exited the animal laboratory into a dark corridor. "About this brain laterality?"

"Some. In animals it is likely that certain species—as a

population and not as individuals—have lateralized brains.
Each hemisphere specializes, although one may interact with
the other or inhibit the other."

"And in people?"

"A great deal of evidence to that effect. I've published
material on it, which you can read if you are really interested.
It's hardly the reason you came to see me."

"Of course not. I ask your forgiveness in using my preroga-
tives as a KGB functionary to barge in on you. The truth is,
Irina, I admire you enormously. For what you are, and what
you've meant to me. It's a tragic pity, perhaps the great
sorrow of my life, that my sentiments were never reciprocated."

He tried to sound sincere, affectionate, wondered if he was
succeeding. Karpov, a master dissembler and liar, now questioned his ability to express valid and profound emotions. Nor
had he had any premonition that he would react so strongly
to her beauty, her intellect, her very presence.

She halted at a landing. "I don't want to see you. If you're
here on business, I can guess what it is. Lev is in trouble
again? I beg of you, don't persecute my husband. He's
harmless. Foolish, quixotic, but harmless."

"It doesn't involve Lev. I gave you my word that he'd be
safe in that job I arranged for him. What I have to discuss
does not relate to him."

She nodded, not quite believing him.

"May I say, I admire your loyalty to him."

"Do you?" Irina bit her lip. "Or is it that his running afoul
of the law made it possible for you to use me?"

"No. Believe me or not, I loved you, and I still love you."

In her small office, Karpov offered her a Marlboro. She
accepted readily, inhaled the rich American tobacco and ordered tea for them.

Karpov got to the point. An American magazine writer,
Floyd Hanson, had requested an interview with her for an
article on advances in Soviet surgery. She was to cooperate.
Of course, nothing of a security nature was to be revealed.
During the interviews she would have at her side either a
KGB agent assigned to the State Scientific and Technical
Committee, or Karpov himself.

"I have no choice?"

"None."

"Why was I selected? There are other surgeons doing work just as interesting."

"Because I know you and trust you."

Irina did not smile. "Perhaps because you saw a way of approaching me again? Or compromising me?"

"By no means. You are a luminary, an important person. In the overall scheme of things, a more important person than I am. You attend international conferences, exchange data with American scientists, contribute to their journals. I see them on your desk. I am impressed. So are my superiors. So was this young man Hanson."

Karpov pointed to a brown-covered journal with the title *The Behavioral and Brain Sciences*. He turned it toward him and saw her name, as author of an article entitled "Split Brain Phenomena in Post-operative Patients under Controlled Conditions."

"I have my own feeling as to why I was selected," she said icily. "You are convinced I'm safe. I'll obey orders. I'll know that if I step out of line, you'll hold the whip hand. There is always a chance that charges against my husband can be reopened."

"Dear Irina. That is not so."

Karpov said it lightly, knowing that her accusation was partially true. They knew each other well—as lovers, bedmates, he adoring her, she hating him. Nothing was ever the same between two people who had known each other's bodies. Yet she had responded to their sexual encounters; she could never deny that she had.

"When do I meet with this Hanson?"

"Within a week. You must have heard something about it. Inquiries were made to the committee."

"Yes, but I had no idea I would be selected. Ivan Belus's name was discussed at lunch one day. An inquiry had come from him. I thought it odd. A general practitioner of no particular prominence. Why is he involved?"

"I don't know," Karpov lied.

"This Belus. Isn't he involved with the Jews? With Levitch and others?"

"He's of no importance. I suspect I know what happened. Hanson, like the rest of the foreign press, is intrigued with these refuseniks. He met Belus at one of those gatherings. The question came up and Belus made an inquiry."

Irina turned in the chair, looking away from Karpov, trying to analyze his offhand comments. He lied the way other men breathed and ate. A species-specific mode of behavior, she thought. Deceit, brutality, connivance, an absence of mercy. She barely knew Belus. A yellow-haired clownish man, one foot in the refusenik camp, another in the medical establishment.

. "Well, then. I am busy. Let's get it over with. I suppose I shall have to talk to the committee concerning what I can tell Hanson and what I cannot."

"That would be advisable. Anything you've published or talked about publicly, in or out of the Soviet Union, is all right. Anything that is a work in progress, experimental, unfinished, should be considered off limits. Hanson will submit his notes and the finished article to the state censor, and then you and I shall review it. You'll have to be my guide and mentor, since I know very little about the human brain."

"But a great deal about the mind?"

"Enough to make me proficient at my work."

"Indeed? How much intellectual capacity does one need in your work, Andrei Borisovich?"

He got up, smoothing his dark-blue suit, adjusting the English silk tie. "Irina, do you still harbor hostile feelings about me?"

"I always will. But what does someone in your position have to know? That men feel pain? Can be made to scream and weep? Can be bent, manipulated, and forced to do whatever you want them to?"

Karpov smiled thinly, as if chastised. "You're right. My work is almost as culturally elevated as—an act of muricide. But please be fair with me, Irina. I maintain order. People must be hurt from time to time. These are the imperatives of an orderly community. Of growth, stability, the welfare of society. The Levitches and the Zolkins have to be educated, made to understand there's a greater good than their selfish needs."

"God in heaven, Andrei. What a tiresome, windy and pointless speech. I thought better of you. You can't really believe such drivel."

She walked him to the door. He kissed her hand and she shuddered. He smelled of a musky lotion, surely not a Soviet product. His skin was smooth, tanned, his hands muscular. The nails were glistening, trimmed.

"How is your wife?" Irina asked.

"Not well. She's still in the hospital. I'm afraid the drug treatment did not help her appreciably."

Irina felt a tremor in her chest, an arrhythmia in her heart. When Karpov had gone, she had to sit quietly at her desk for a few minutes, test her pulse, breathe deeply. His scent had lodged in her nostrils. Yet it was not entirely unpleasant—intriguing, foreign, erotic.

Hanson's New York office was delighted with the prospect of an interview with Dr. Tashenko.

Both the managing editor and the science editor got on the phone with Hanson. The writer was in his cluttered suite in the Ukraina Hotel. They complimented him on his coup. The science editor had checked neurosurgeons at New York hospitals. All confirmed that Dr. Tashenko was "a heavy hitter." Moreover, she had never been interviewed by the American press.

"We're interested in split-brain patients," the science editor said. "Did you get the literature I sent you?"

Hanson had. He said he'd scanned it. The fact was, he had not even looked at it. Hanson tended to be lazy. He spent much of his day taking Russian language lessons and discovering (to his distress) that he was a slow learner. He had always had this problem with foreign tongues. After two years as Rome bureau chief, Hanson could barely manage a *buon giorno.*

"Ah, split brain, yeah," Hanson said. "Different functions of the right hemisphere and the left hemisphere?"

"More specific than that, Floyd. Didn't you look at the article on split-brain operations?"

"Ah, not really. I'm digesting the stuff slowly."

"Do me a favor, Floyd. Don't walk in like a dummy. I know you aren't a trained scientist, but the material I sent you is written for the layman. Learn it. Get the lingo straight. By the way, how's her English?"

"Fluent."

"That'll help. Soft-soap her, play up to her, but get her talking about split-brain surgery."

"What if she won't talk about it?"

"Then I'm not sure it's a story. Read the articles, and call me if you have questions. I'll put you on the phone with Dr. Ellerman, who does the same kind of operation at Lutheran Memorial, and he'll explain it. He's met Tashenko."

The science editor was beginning to have second thoughts. Hanson, all of thirty-one, had come to the magazine as a whiz kid, a talented photo journalist, author of two successful travel books. But he was getting the feeling that Hanson was not terribly cerebral.

"The fascinating thing about split-brain operations, Floyd," the editor went on, "is not so much the surgery itself as the aftereffect. They cut through the nerve-fiber bundles that join the hemispheres of the brain and—"

"Oh, yes. I recall something about it. To treat epilepsy."

"Intractable epilepsy. Most patients show dramatic results. A lessening or termination of *grand mal* seizures. But there are curious side effects. In perception, language and so on. There is apparently less communication between the two hemispheres. Each begins to act independently. What we're interested in is how far Tashenko has gone, not only in performing operations but in observing patients afterward."

"What makes you think she'll talk about it?"

"It's no secret she's done these operations. They're called commissurotomies. *Callosal* commissurotomies. Cutting the *corpus callosum*, the band of nerve fibers that joins the two hemispheres. If she's published her work, then she'll probably talk."

The science editor asked him to wait a moment while he found notes. "Floyd, listen carefully. The stuff on the operation itself and the postoperative changes—right eye, left eye, right hemisphere, left hemisphere—that's not new. Americans have done that. But Tashenko may have some new twists. What deeply interests us is the concept of mental duality."

"Dua—?"

Hanson was certain he heard a clicking, a buzzing, as if someone had picked up an extension, or a recording mechanism was being amplified.

"Mental *duality*," the editor said. "There's a theory that split-brain people, whether as a result of a commissurotomy, or whether the division of the two halves of the brain is congenital, develop *different* personalities. It's almost as if the individual develops two brains. The left brain knows what the right is doing, and vice versa, but they can't do much about it. Double consciousness."

"Two people in one?"

"That's a simplification, Floyd, but it's the general idea. It's a sore point in neurophysiology and the experts are choosing up sides already. My information is that Tashenko has done dramatic work in this field and I want to know what it is. The general idea is—is this a modern Jekyll and Hyde deal? Can two brains exist in one person? One good, one bad? One dumb, one smart?"

"It sounds important. I'll work on it."

Hanson listened after the editor hung up. Again there was a dull buzz, a click.

"Who is the stocky man sitting with the Georgian dancers?"

Irina and her husband were dining in the Aragvi on Gorky Ulitsa. An orchestra of flutes and stringed instruments played in minor keys, summoning up visions of the sunny Caucasus, fields of melons, flowering orchards.

Lev Tashenko looked over his wife's shoulder. "Malik. From the Jewish Department of the Fifth Directorate. A thug."

"Why did he stop and stare at me? And why did he wave to you?"

"He was one of my interrogators," Tashenko said. "A lout, a drunk. He sits with the Georgians under the assumption he's an amusing fellow."

"Malik. I don't know the name," Irina said.

"He's a hooligan. Spends his time dispatching drunken policemen to spy on Jews. At the synagogue, at their meetings. Abram Levitch is never without a convoy of Malik's agents."

Irina sighed and pecked at her plate of Georgian appetizers. The pickled Georgian beans had the fizzy taste of food gone slightly bad.

"They are said to be good for fertility," Tashenko said. He was a lantern-jawed man with lank black hair and white smooth skin. He smoked continually. Wisps of smoke drifted into his mournful eyes.

"I hardly need them. And they've turned."

"Try the turkey in walnut sauce."

"I have no appetite, Lev."

"Do you have any appetite for me?"

"You are dear to me." She took his hand.

The Georgian musicians rattled tambourines, picked at their strings with rapid motions, thundered into a foot-stamping chorus. A song of sunny meadows and purple mountains. Wild mustachioed brigands in belted clothes, bandoliers. And bean salad gone sour.

"I'm grateful I have you," Tashenko said. "I am nothing without you. Today I requested that we interview a delegation of Holocaust survivors. Mostly American Jews, some French and Israelis. I was turned down. They'd been to Babi Yar, the Crimea, Leningrad. The editor advised me that the Soviet Union does not believe in a 'particularity' of victims. Those killed by the Nazis were Soviet citizens, no more, no less. To treat the Jews as a special case was an insult to millions of other Russians who were murdered."

"But that is not so. They *were* a special case. They were the first victims, the prime victims. And how many of our Russian citizens—Ukrainians, Lithuanians—helped the SS with their dirty work?"

"That is one reason they didn't want me to interview the Jews. There will not be a word on it in the gazette. The editor said, these Jews do themselves no good endlessly blubbering and lamenting, beating their breasts. The world does not respect them for this."

"It is obvious that the rulers of the motherland don't respect them."

Tashenko's hands shook as he tried to cut his pressed chicken. Irina watched him sympathetically. Wretched, timorous man. And yet she loved him. She had saved him from Karpov's cruel justice. Having written some of Zolkin's protests, circulated them to the foreign press and allowed himself to be recorded by a French TV journalist, he had given Karpov and Dort more excuses than they needed to arrest and threaten him. The final act of incrimination came when Radio Liberty had gotten a copy of the French interview and broadcast it. It was broadcast anonymously—"a leading Soviet critic and editor" —but it enraged the KGB.

Ten years? Fifteen years? She and Lev had often wondered what sentence could have been imposed had not Irina pleaded for him, used her influence in party circles, and ultimately accepted a temporary role as Karpov's mistress. Bitterly, she knew there had been an element of hypocrisy in this act of self-sacrifice, of donating her body to her husband's security. That was the worst of it.

In grim, unsparing moments she understood that she had enjoyed the luxurious hotel suites, the dinners at three-star Paris restaurants, the designer clothing. Indeed, she had, in some self-wounding fashion, savored the company of the lean, well-dressed, multilingual Karpov as escort, confidante, lover. He was the power who held the ultimate weapon over soiled, sorrowing Lev. For Irina to bed down with him, reduce him to whimpers and gasps, was some kind of twisted revenge.

Looking at Lev pushing aside his dinner, sipping Georgian wine, smiling at her with puppyish gratitude, she recalled Karpov, at their parting, discussing her husband. She had not argued. She was grateful that Karpov had gotten Dort to agree to hide Lev Tashenko at the literary magazine, provided he kept his mouth shut and avoided contact with refuseniks, dissidents, democrats.

Karpov had told her, "Dort knows about us, Irina. He knows everything. It doesn't bother him, except that the swine is jealous. You're too important; I'm too valuable. So he's accepting my proposal. Your husband will be safe. Let him live out his years criticizing other intellectuals, reviewing obscure books, coining clever phrases. That's all intellectuals are good for. They mean nothing. They don't affect history. They spend too much time talking, attacking one another, full of jealousies. No wonder he enjoyed hanging around Jews. They wrote the book on interminable gab, tiresome arguments. How you tolerated him all these years, and why you still love him, is a puzzle to me."

She could not recall how she had responded to Karpov. They were at the Ritz in Lisbon. Naked as herrings, drained of love's juice, she sullen and remorseful, he bursting with neurotic energy, his muscled body, the body of a thirty-year-old athlete (Karpov was forty-four at the time) pacing the elaborate room. She'd defended Tashenko—a decent, compassionate man. Once he had been talked of as Zolkin's heir. Courageous enough to circulate a petition for the refuseniks (there were tens of thousands at the time), not just the familiar names that made the newspapers—Semonski, Slesik, Burik, Levitch—but all the faceless, poor, unknown appellants . . .

She was thinking of them, those persecuted people she barely knew (except for the enigmatic Belus), and suddenly Lev was mentioning Abram Levitch. He was in the news again. Arrested and detained, after emerging from a meeting with his group. No question, Tashenko said, Levitch was now as important as Zolkin, emerging as a world-famous symbol of resistance. It astonished Tashenko.

"What do they want from the miserable man?" Irina asked.

"They hate and fear him because he's so innocent."

"But they all are. To ask to leave the country?"

"It isn't that. I met Levitch once. Hard to describe. A shabby, round-faced, smiling Jew. Yet there is some strange quality in him. A kind of dumb honesty, a saintliness, like a child's. No side, no trickery. His courage is innate, as much a part of him as his heart or his arms. He jokes. He accepts the world. And he will not quit. A much braver man than I am."

"What will happen to him?"

Tashenko shrugged. "We don't talk about them at the magazine. No one does. If the Politburo wants détente badly, if the military need computers, if the stores need bread, they may let him leave. There was even a rumor—God knows how it started—that he was about to get his visa. The refuseniks never know when it will be issued. They're kept guessing, on edge, fretful."

"Why was he arrested this time?"

"Black marketeering. Don't ask me how they do it, but the Jews manage to stay alive. Most of them have no work and are barred from earning money. Currency, watches, jeans. There are always American Jews coming in who bring gifts and get their stories out."

Tashenko indicated Anatoli Malik with a movement of his eyes, as if fearful of rousing the attention of the KGB man. "It drives people like Malik wild. They are under orders not to bother Americans. So they can't keep them from talking to Levitch and his crowd. But when Levitch trades dollars for rubles, or buys watches in the Beryozka, they know about it."

"I would think they can jail Levitch for a long time for such dealings."

"They're after something more important. Something that will tar Zolkin, discredit the movement, shatter the alliance Levitch has made with the non-Jews. The KGB knows what they're doing. They always do."

Malik left the Georgian dancers, who were about to take the floor. Tashenko told Irina that Malik's directorate was concerned not only with Jewish dissidents but also with other "nationalities." It did no harm for him to keep lines open to Georgians, Armenians. Lithuanians, any who might disturb the peace with nationalistic rumblings. The dancers appeared relieved when he left. There were no hearty exchanges.

Malik walked across the floor. Once he belched, hitched his trousers, paused when he saw the Tashenkos. He smiled at Lev and bowed to Irina.

"To remind me," Tashenko said.

Coward that Lev was, Irina still needed him, was obliged to protect him. She held his hand. It was wet, cold. Malik passed by, a gray shadow. He seemed to leave a stale reek of shame in his path.

"That Levitch, that obscure Jewish teacher," Tashenko said. "He is ten times the man I am. Ten times the man Karpov is. Someday they will come for him and he'll be brave. Not like me, who needed a woman to save him. Not like Karpov, who has the guns on his side."

"You are man enough for me," Irina said softly. "Look on it as genetic. Something in the central nervous system, perhaps. Some act; some think."

"Beloved wife. You're too good for me. Why do you tolerate me?"

"I love you. That also may be programmed in us. I accept it."

Couples rose to dance. A party of young Americans began to indulge in gyrations, jerking arms and legs in motions suggesting *grand mal*. Some native Georgians formed a circle, kicked, shouted. Other Russians held one another sedately and danced the two-step.

"We will dance our way into oblivion," Tashenko said gloomily. "The only society in history sustained by policemen and ruled by jailers. I'll tell you what truly upsets me, Irina."

"I suspect I know."

"Our people *accept*. They think this life is normal. God help us if the state ever gives them enough automobiles, TV sets, clothing and food. They'll never question the absence of freedom, or demand liberty, or ask to be allowed to speak and write and think as individuals."

"Don't despair, Lev."

"It is in my nature." He laughed. It was a self-mocking sound. "I suppose I am right-hemisphere dominated. Did you not tell me that right-hemisphere people tend to be gloomy?"

"A thesis, nothing more. We have each other. Things will change."

"For you, yes. For me, never. Karpov's shadow will haunt me forever. I'm sorry, my love. It is the truth."

Dr. Ivan Belus, bouncy and full of good news, met Hanson and Parente at the foreign press club a few days later. There was nothing in writing, he told them, and he was only an unofficial bearer of the news. But the State Scientific and Technical Committee had given its approval for Hanson's interview with Dr. Irina Tashenko. Further, Hanson would be permitted to see some of the neurosurgeon's research. It was a coup.

"Nice work, Doc," Parente said. "That's worth another Scotch."

Hanson was ecstatic. For a week he had been boning up on new developments in neurosurgery. Twice he had talked to the science editor in New York, taking notes on a variety of new studies: mental duality, split-brain phenomena, self-stimulation. He was eager to meet the Russian surgeon.

"How'd you manage it?" Hanson asked.

Belus held his palms up, a self-mocking gesture. "I was only a go-between, a marriage broker. I made a request for you. It was honored."

Parente sipped his Urquell Pilsener. It was one of the few advantages of living in the Soviet Union—Czech beer. The best in the world, the zestiest, mellowest, tastiest. The label amused him: *Special Purveyors of Beer to the Red Army.* Talk about armies marching on their stomach. Czech suds were too good for those peasant louts, he thought. It was like those fancy English toiletries and biscuits. *By Appointment to Her Majesty the Queen.*

"You look cynical, Tony," Belus said.

"I'm always cynical. You didn't meet Dr. Tashenko yourself?"

"Me? A family physician? To meet with one of the greatest figures in medicine? I made a request. Oh, I met her years ago at a conference. Now, of course, with my association with

Levitch and Slesik, I am not exactly a part of the medical establishment."

Hanson asked, "When can I call her? I'm really gingered up about this."

"Whenever you want," Belus said. "Once the word comes down, you are free to talk to her."

Emboldened, Hanson began to quiz Belus about reports that the KGB was running psychiatric hospitals that were full of dissidents who had become troublesome. Nothing psychologically wrong with them, but "hospitalized" nonetheless for their opposition to state policies.

"You ask *me?*" Dr. Belus asked. "How would I know? No, Floyd, these reports are propaganda."

My fat Italian ass, Parente thought. He did not trust Dr. Belus. Trusted him less each time he saw him. How did he flit so airily from Levitch's group, to Zolkin's, to the medical biggies, without so much as getting threatened? He practiced, he had a car, he was well dressed. The obvious conclusion was that he was working for the KGB. Yet the refuseniks continued to trust him. He was helpful and likable, and so far as Parente knew, he had never betrayed anyone.

Still, Parente had suspicions. He could recall a multilingual, charming, well-heeled Soviet "trade representative," one Gorchik, who had access to international meetings and Western industrial data, was wined and dined by commercial attachés and businessmen in Western Europe, a dapper womanizer, much trusted by reporters, who turned out to be a high KGB informant. But no one seemed to condemn him. Even after his cover had been blown, Westerners spoke enthusiastically of Gorchik. Was Dr. Belus in the same category?

Belus excused himself. He had calls to make. Olga Semonski was ill again—probably a recurrence of her ulcer. Could Tony possibly get him some of those excellent American medications, Maalox or Mylanta? There was nothing like them available in Moscow. Parente agreed that he would. The embassy had a well-stocked pharmacy.

A sparrowlike bronze-colored man, with a gleaming mop of black hair and a black handlebar mustache, approached Parente outside the foreign press club.

"Tony, Tony, old friend," the man said. His starched white

collar was so stiff, Parente noticed, that it restricted movement of his head, exaggerated the length of his eagle beak.

"Hrant, baby," Parente said. "Hrant Deroulian, the Armenian Richard Harding Davis. Still hacking away, Hrant? Feature stories for Novosti on all those Siberians meeting their norms in the gold fields? Or how the USSR has perfected the first nonproductive wheat field, the one that defies fertilizers and cultivation, and withers at a glance from the local commissar?"

"Oh, you are the same funny man, Tony."

The words matched themselves in Parente's mind: Deroulian—spy. The Levantine squirt was KGB up to his hairline.

"I don't get many laughs these days," Parente said.

They walked to Parente's car. Shaven-headed schoolboys in quasi-military uniforms walked by, grabbing and goosing each other. Parente was pleased; the less discipline the better.

"Perhaps I can give you some information that will make you smile," Deroulian said.

The American studied the hawkish bronze face. A tolerant man. Parente had long ago decided he had never known a dumb Armenian, or an Armenian he could not like. Was Deroulian the exception?

"Sure, I need good news," Tony said.

"Your friend Levitch. The word has been around. He may be allowed to leave. I can't tell you anything else."

"Why do I deserve this choice morsel? You know I won't print it. I won't do anything to jeopardize Levitch's safety."

Deroulian hunched his shoulders, revealed gold incisors in a wide smile. "Maybe he should stop trying to challenge the state, be quiet for a while."

"I get it. Shut him up with fake promises?"

"I am not in the Ministry of Internal Affairs, Tony. I don't know their rules or motives. I'm only a feature writer for Novosti News Agency."

Yeah, Parente thought, *and a KGB snooper*. Deroulian left him at the curb. Parente decided he would have to talk to Abram again. Maybe discretion and silence were in order on Levitch's part. Who ever knew the truth in the Big Prison?

From his office, Parente called Nadya Burik's apartment to learn of Levitch's whereabouts.

The mother hen was breathless with indignation. "Foolish

boy, foolish child," Nadya sputtered. "Tony, we all tried to stop him, but he left five minutes ago. *Baptists!* Demonstrating for Baptists! All of us—Slesik, Semonski, the Bakofskys—we told him, enough with this dissident business! Why must you stand up for Baptists? His heart is too good, but his brain is soft. We couldn't convince him."

"Where, Nadya?"

"On the steps of the Pushkin Museum."

Good Christ, Parente thought, *walking into the lion's den.* If they were considering giving him his visa—and who really knew?—this act of defiance, this quixotic support of people no one else seemed to give a damn about, would kill his chances, maybe forever. Parente raced out of the office, ran the seven flights to his car, sped off to the museum.

I'm in luck, Parente thought. He saw Levitch emerging from the Metro station, plodding along, the familiar happy, harmless look on his round face.

Shading his eyes, Parente saw a clutch of dark-suited Russians, six or seven adults and the same number of children, sitting together on the steps of the Pushkin. Levitch halted at a stoplight across from the museum. He had a manila envelope under his arm.

Parente parked illegally, yelled at a cop that he was press and that he'd be right back. Then he crossed the street with Levitch and halted him at the sidewalk fronting the museum.

"Abram, listen to me. Go home."

"Why? I have to help my friends."

"Listen, that rumor surfaced again. You're supposed to be in line for a visa. I got it from a good source, a guy who works for the KGB. Never mind who. He must have had a reason to tell me."

"So?" Levitch smiled at the mild sunlight. A forgettable, vulnerable man.

"So lay off. Let the Baptists handle their own protest meeting." Parente squinted at the steps. The members of the religious group had risen, lumpy, ill-clad people. Behind them and to their right, leaning on the stone balustrade, Parente could identify a half dozen of Malik's thugs.

"But I promised them. I promised Zolkin."

"Let Zolkin protest. He's the big wheel in the Helsinki Committee. Besides, you have a chance to get out. Abram—

think of it. Sarah. Israel. The sun. The sea. The goddam orange trees or melon fields or whatever it is you crave. You can pick grapefruit all day and get shot in the ass by Arabs. You want to miss all that fun? You've been bawling and hollering for two years—*let me out!* Now you got the chance. Don't screw up."

"Tony, how can I believe them? Why have they not told me? Why these rumors to people I don't know? It's their old cat-and-mouse game, my friend. In the past there have never been rumors. The release just happened. One day, a postcard in the mail, and you are free. I am convinced this is a scheme to make me stop my work for freedom."

"You've been hero enough. Others can take over. Slesik. Semonski."

"They are good friends and good men, but they can't do what I am doing. Slesik is opposed to my working with other religions, other nationalities. He calls me the new Saint John of the Cross. A missionary to the Gentiles."

Parente grabbed Levitch's forearm. He gripped the leather sleeve. "Beat it, Abram. Stuff those yellow sheets in a waste-paper basket. Lay low. At least till I try to find out more. Malik's gang is waiting for you. The guys who rule them—Karpov, Dort, all those other killers—they'll have reports on their desks this afternoon about new provocations against the state by A. M. Levitch. What happens to the visa now?"

For the first time, doubt shadowed Levitch's face. His red eyebrows arched; a thin furrow indented his forehead. He seemed to Parente lost and puzzled. "Ah, Tony, I am not sure what to do. They have this terrible power, this way of making you bend."

The Baptists were beckoning to him. A tall man, evidently their leader, called Levitch's name softly. They seemed pitiful, isolated. A group of roughly dressed hoodlums were shouting curses at the Baptists. A stone was thrown, another. A woman picked up the stones, studied them sorrowfully, set them down beside her.

Parente started to pull Levitch away. "Forget it, Abram. They can't win. You have a chance."

The scene blurred in Levitch's mind. His eyes were moist. The poor and defenseless, the victims of the metal state. Why was he here? Who had anointed him? Dutifully, he followed

Parente to the curb. His hand clutching the envelope was coated with sweat.

"Come on, Abram. We'll take a ride."

Levitch gently removed Parente's hand. "No, Tony. I have no choice. I can't betray Zolkin or those troubled people up there, or anyone who believes as I do."

Again the tall man was gesturing at Levitch, welcoming him to their ranks. Puffing, Levitch trudged up the stairs. He reached the Baptists and hugged them.

Parente watched, troubled, uncertain. From the corner of his eye he saw a stocky man who looked like Malik inside an official car. A lot of firepower for seven Baptists and one Jew.

A small group of foreign reporters had arrived. God knows how they had learned of the protest. Parente could see among them Agnes Wardle, and Dieter Schultze, the West German cameraman.

Seconds after Levitch opened his envelope and produced his sheaf of yellow onionskins, the KGB detail was upon the protesters, pummeling men, kicking women, seizing the papers.

"Oh, Christ," Parente said.

Agnes Wardle was sent sprawling. Schultze's camera was seized.

The tall man in the black suit was dragged down the steps. A river of blood ran from his forehead, down his nose, dripped from his chin.

Two men pushed Levitch down, hit him in the back of the head.

Sickened, Parente shouted curses at the hoodlums, heard his voice turn to an angry, sorrowing sob. What good would it do? And was Abram right or wrong in making his feeble protest?

Around the battered protesters, militiamen and local galoots formed a ring, shouting obscenities, egging the KGB agents on.

"*Hit the bastards again!*"

"*Fascist shit-heads!*"

"*Stick them all in jail!*"

Unable to contain himself, Parente dogtrotted to the car in which Levitch was being shoved by two of Malik's men.

"Let him alone, goddammit," Parente said. "Take your hands off him."

Malik waddled over. He ordered two agents to push Parente away.

"Hands off, scum-bags. I'm an American reporter. Abram! *Abram!* Get in touch with us!" He turned to Malik. "Lay off him, huh? This story is going to be in our papers tomorrow. You think you can get away with this forever?"

Studying Malik's flat, bland face, Parente suddenly worried: *What if they can get away with it? Now and forever?*

He saw Abram smile feebly and lift a hand in salute.

Uniformed militiamen cleared the curious from the steps. A few rumpled sheets of paper were gathered up, stuffed in pockets. A child who tried to retrieve one from the paving was halted by a militiaman and the torn sheet was confiscated.

That evening Parente attended a meeting of the refuseniks at Nadya's apartment. They knew of Levitch's most recent encounter with the police. Parente thought it was wise not to tell them of the random reports that Levitch was on the verge of getting his visa. What did it matter now? Parente was convinced that Levitch's most recent act of defiance would ensure a long sojourn in the Soviet Union. And perhaps worse.

In his hoarse cancer-ridden voice, Chaim Slesik clucked his disapproval. "Our Abram. His heart overflows and drowns him. I've been in the gulag, served my fifteen years, taken my beatings, eaten rats . . . . Abram doesn't understand. He would not seek martyrdom so enthusiastically if he had been through what I have been through. Poor man. This role he has sought, this birth as apostle of freedom for every persecuted soul in the USSR, it's too much for an unemployed mathematics teacher, a short Jew with soft hands. Let Zolkin do it. He is something of an untouchable, a member of the nontorturable class, as the writer Greene says."

Parente agreed. He would do his best to make Levitch a world issue. The Soviets were sensitive to criticism in the foreign press. They worried about their image. Parente would see to it that with the aid of the Western journalists in Moscow, Levitch's face would be known worldwide. His name would become a synonym for freedom.

"Pray God it helps," Slesik said. He coughed as if being torn to shreds internally.

Soon Nadya Burik's apartment was packed. Smoke blurred vision; hot tea burned lips and tongues. Parente hated himself for not being able to help them. He decided that the publicizing of Levitch would be his first priority. Abram would no longer be an obscure member of the refusenik group; he would become the symbol of the struggle for freedom in the Soviet Union. It would make it more difficult to persecute him.

Brooding, mulling possibilities, the American thought of Dr. Ivan Belus. Belus, who was alleged to have shadowy connections. Belus, who treated the refusenik ill, gave them rides, and who was now abetting Floyd Hanson in the Tashenko matter. Why was Belus not present that evening?

He asked Slesik about the absent physician. Slesik had no idea where he was. Belus was an occasional visitor to their meetings. One of their circle, not one of their circle.

Slesik and Semonski took turns for ten minutes trying to reach Belus on the phone. It was fruitless. Busy signals, wrong numbers, no responses.

Floyd Hanson arrived, flushed and eager to file a feature story on Levitch. He agreed with Tony: They had to hit the Levitch affair hard, let the KGB know that the world cared about him. Hanson would manage to squeeze the profile in, between his researches on the brain surgery feature.

The cigarette fumes became choking, the arguments more agitated. Parente felt ill, defeated, without visible function or validity. The damned system was getting to him, and he suspected he was not the man Levitch, or Slesik, or any of them were. He didn't have to be. He was an American, blessedly free, a man permitted to blow his top, insult the police, criticize the state. When Parente's grandfather landed at Ellis Island from Naples eighty years ago, he had kissed the earth. Parente made a note to do the same when next he returned. He didn't give a damn if Martha and the kids laughed at him, or the customs officers figured him for nuts.

"Let's beat it," he said to Hanson. "We'll hang around outside KGB College at Dzerzhinsky. The cops may get bored with Levitch's lousy jokes and spring him."

4

COLONEL DORT HALTED Karpov outside the office of the Chief of the Second Directorate. It was late afternoon of the day on which Levitch had been arrested outside the Pushkin Museum of Fine Arts.

"The Levitch business," Dort said. "Proceeding?"

"It's on schedule, Colonel. It has to be carefully constructed so he can't claim he was framed."

Dort was studying Karpov's shoes—the high gloss, the bloody hue of fine English leather. "London?" he asked.

"No. Stockmann's in Helsinki. I order them by courier."

"Ah, yes. I like the tie also. Small figures. What? Riding crops. And from where is it?"

"New York, Colonel Dort. One of our people at the United Nations sent it. From a store called Brooks Brothers. A present to mark the anniversary of the October Revolution."

"How thoughtful. Why is it none of our people send me gifts, Karpov?"

Karpov was tempted to say: *because you are a fat scheming pig*. But what would be the point? Dort knew he was hated and feared.

"The next time I'm in New York, Colonel, I'll buy you a similar tie. They have charming designs: wild ducks, pheasants. I know you are an avid hunter."

"Thank you, Karpov. But the nicest gift you can get for me is that Yid Levitch jailed, tried, convicted and put away for a long time. I assigned you to the case because Malik is a fool. I know Levitch was arrested today, but we can't hold him for demonstrating for Baptists. And we don't want him in a psychiatric hospital. We want him on ice for a long time."

"We're getting there. The ingredients are laid out on the kitchen table."

"Start cooking. Comrade."

Karpov noted a vague fear, a darting of the eyes. Someone was on Dort's back, no question. It came to all of them sooner or later. If you failed, if you proved soft and ineffectual, out you went. An end to Hungarian salamis, black limousines, Italian shirts. Ah, but then in the old days it would have been a bullet in the neck. So does the glorious revolution change its face. Karpov knew old-timers who poignantly hungered for Stalin's bloody times. The blunt Georgian. Murdering millions. Killing first and asking questions later. Cramming thousands and tens of thousands into ice-locked wilderness camps. Neater, cleaner, faster.

"Has any consideration been given to granting him a visa?" Karpov asked.

"Briefly. We floated the rumor, let Levitch worry about it. But he's stubborn. Showed up with the Baptists, even after he was told there was a possibility he might be let out."

"Which means—he'll have to go to trial."

Dort nodded. "Yes. If you do your job properly."

"I've read up on some of the material," Hanson said. He tried to sound confident, professional. "It's fascinating."

In accented but grammatically perfect English, Irina Tashenko said, "I'm not sure I can tell you anything new. Please ask specific questions. I am very busy."

Hanson stroked his wispy yellow beard. Quite a dish, Dr. Tashenko. Tall, slender waist, pleasantly rounded hips, long thighs, curving calves. Without a hint of cosmetics, dark brown hair piled high, peering at him over modish cheaters (surely not products of the Soviet Union), she was one of the best-looking women in Moscow. But edged with ice and disdain, almost hostile.

Maybe the official watchdog made her nervous, he thought.

Seated at Tashenko's right in her small office was Karpov. The KGB functionary wore a starched white coat and held several medical journals in his lap. He had been introduced to Hanson as "Dr. Lermontov," assistant director of the State Scientific and Technical Committee. Hanson had never seen Karpov before, nor had he seen a photograph of him. But he remembered from Parente's warning that the handsome man in the white coat was nothing more than a cop.

"Dr. Lermontov, are you a neurosurgeon also?" Hanson asked.

"No. My specialty is forensic medicine."

"I see. May I take notes?"

Irina looked at Karpov, clearly deferring to him. The interplay was not lost on Hanson.

"Of course." Karpov, in his role as Dr. Lermontov, was the essence of charm. "Naturally, the State Scientific and Technical Committee will have to pass on your story. But that should present no problem. Dr. Tashenko's work is well known. We are pleased to have it presented to our American friends. I don't know why Americans always assume we want to hide something."

"I wasn't assuming anything, Dr. Lermontov." Hanson poised his ball-point pen over his steno pad. "If I were to ask you, Dr. Tashenko, what you regard as your most important, most dramatic surgical work, what would you tell me?"

She exchanged a few casual words with "Lermontov." Hanson got the idea that both of them knew his Russian was weak. He caught a few words—*brain, laboratory*.

"It is not easy for one to make judgments about one's own work," Irina said. "Perhaps if I give you some articles, you could read them and then come back and ask questions when you are better prepared."

"I could do that. But I would like to get pointed in the right direction today."

"Then you must ask, and I will try to answer."

Karpov crossed his legs and lit a Marlboro. Where did he get American butts? the reporter wondered. Embassy connections probably. Medical friends in the States. He made note of the watchdog's black lisle hose, the burnished mahogany shoes with their winking lights. A dapper sawbones, this Lermontov, looking more like a British Foreign Office type than a Soviet physician with a minor in surveillance.

"Fair enough," Hanson said. "I'll be direct. Do you perform split-brain surgery? Commissurotomies? Did I pronounce it correctly?"

Tashenko smiled. She was very beautiful, the journalist decided. Odd, he thought, to find two such physically attractive citizens of the USSR in one room.

"Not frequently. But I perform them."

"Similar work to Bogen and Vogel in the States?"

"Similar."

"My understanding is that the operation is hardly ever performed anymore. Only in cases of intractable epilepsy. The kind that won't respond to drugs."

Tashenko nodded. "That is substantially correct. Success in relieving seizures varies. But we have found it to be generally effective."

"How many a year do you perform?" asked Hanson.

"No more than four or five."

"That few? Why?"

"It is an extreme measure. Only when all else has failed in cases of disabling epilepsy. You understand, Mr. Hanson, what is involved? It is no minor procedure. The *corpus callosum* consists of two hundred million nerve fibers. It connects the two hemispheres of the brain. We cut through them, separating the right and the left hemispheres of the brain."

"I've read that the patient rarely suffers trauma or severe aftereffects. That they come out of the surgery with a decrease in seizures, if not elimination. Are there personality changes, changes in behavior?"

"No noticeable change."

"Intelligence?"

"The same answer."

Karpov, in his role as Dr. Lermontov, yawned and looked at an abstract in his lap. *Left-Hemisphere Control of the Articulatory Mechanisms* . . .

"But there are peculiarities in perception, aren't there? Didn't American surgeons discover that in people who'd undergone split-brain operations, the left hand sometimes didn't know what the right hand was doing? That if the left eye saw

something, let's say a pencil, the information could not get to
the left hemisphere and the person would know what he saw,
but couldn't say *pencil?*"

"I can see you have read the literature," Tashenko said. "It
is far more complex than that. But basically you are correct.
A split-brain person will be able to report verbally on anything in the right visual field since the object will be projected to the left—the *verbal*—hemisphere. An image in the
left visual field will be projected to the nonverbal right
hemisphere. However, the left hemisphere, due to the cutting of the *corpus callosum*, will not be able to say what the
right hemisphere is seeing. The failing is verbal, not perceptual.
What often happens with split-brain patients is that the left
will try to guess, or formulate a verbal solution to the right's
nonverbal reactions. It is not always on the mark."

"Behaviorally, they're normal?"

"In every way. They eventually learn to handle their disa-
bilities through a method called cross-cueing. The brain is an
ingenious mechanism. It will take all varieties of information
and process it."

"Could you give me an example of this—what do you call
it?—cross-cueing?"

"An experiment I use is to give the patient a comb or
brush. It is hidden under a table. He is asked to feel it with
his left hand."

"So no information goes to the left hemisphere. The verbal
part of the brain."

"But the patient then is asked to run his nail over the teeth
of the comb, or ruffle the bristles on the brush. The *sounds*
are transmitted to both ears. The right ear will send a message to the left hemisphere, and the patient can then identify
the object verbally. Using sound cues, he'll guess *brush* or
comb. Since direct channels of information via the nerve
fibers are impossible, the hemispheres find new ways of
communicating. The brain makes use of every piece of information available."

Hanson looked at his notes. He wondered how much of
this was original, different from experiments in the States.
He needed something vivid, exciting.

"If I may say so, Dr. Tashenko, those all seem to me pretty
simple examples of—what? Perception? Cognition?"

"You might say so."

Karpov scratched a sideburn, stared at the ceiling. He had decided that Hanson was the ideal accessory. It would be easier than he had imagined. With a Parente, or any other of the Moscow-wise journalists, the risk would have been great. They'd have smelled the rat (apt metaphor in Irina Tashenko's hospital) and been extremely careful. But Hanson was new and spoke little Russian. He had no idea who Karpov was. Moreover, he was ambitious and talkative.

"I was wondering about more profound personality changes," the American went on. "Some of the articles I've read in American scientific journals talk about the difference in the *character* of the two halves of the brain."

"Character? Of course. Differentiation of function. We know the left hemisphere is linear and deals with temporal matters, sequences and rhythms at both the sensory and motor level."

"And also language, verbal skills? Mathematics?"

"Yes."

"And the right hemisphere?"

Dr. Tashenko crossed her legs and tossed her hair back. She accepted a cigarette from Karpov, who lit it for her. Hanson caught the gesture. It was one of intimacy. Why not? Two good-looking people, in a land of potato noses, thick ankles and paunches, would be drawn to one another.

"I don't know, Mr. Hanson, what is gained by giving you a lesson in brain function. This is material you should have read before coming to me."

To Hanson's surprise, the dapper specialist in forensic medicine intervened. "Dr. Tashenko, our American friend seems to know a great deal. Perhaps he's just trying to ascertain if your views are analogous to those of American neurophysiologists."

Cold, cold lady, Hanson thought. She inhaled and exhaled cigarette smoke like a steam engine, making it an oddly provocative act. She was upset, he guessed.

"There is nothing new about these theories," Dr. Tashenko said in a monotone. "Work in both the USSR and the West demonstrates the same modes of hemispheric specialization. The right hemisphere is characterized by control of spatial aspects, the mapping of body space, positioning of fingers, limbs and articulators. The left hemisphere is analytic. The right is holistic, perceiving things as a whole, as a *gestalt*. The left hemisphere matches things by name, the right by physical identity. And so on."

Hanson held a finger up. "I'm looking for evidence you've found of hemispheric specialization of a more emotional, well, value-oriented nature. Like good behavior and bad behavior. Gloom and joy. Feeling happy and feeling rotten."

"Most of it is theorizing," Dr. Tashenko said. "We don't put much faith in it. Some Americans have typified the right hemisphere as a criminal, a killer, an aggressor. The left, with its verbal capacities, is said to be kind, ameliorative and understanding. Some of your American scientists claim that the right hemisphere is gloomy. It doesn't understand jokes. It is filled with guilt, despair and anger. The left, on the other hand, is reputed to be cheerful, elated. It laughs at jokes. It is innocent of evil. It denies the existence of crime and wickedness."

"What do you think of that theory?" asked Hanson.

"It is speculation. Moreover, the limited evidence they have shows that for these conditions to be observed in either hemisphere, the opposite hemisphere has to be *seized*."

"Seized?"

"Subjected to convulsion and malfunction by epilepsy, surgery or drugs. To create a happy, innocent, left-hemisphere-dominated person, the right half of the brain must usually be excluded. Conversely, to achieve this allegedly gloomy right-hemisphere person, the left must be rendered inoperative. Which tells us that there is far more interplay between the hemispheres than has been imagined. There is no rigid dichotomy. There are differences, but they are quantitative rather than qualitative."

"So a split-brain patient would lose this factor of interplay. The dichotomy, the specialization, would be more pronounced?"

"Perhaps."

She spoke quickly and in a low voice, in Russian, to Karpov. He nodded and got up.

"Mr. Hanson, Dr. Tashenko will take you on a tour of her laboratory. No photographs will be allowed. Later, you may request official pictures through Novosti, our feature news agency."

Run by KGB operatives, Hanson thought.

"We like our own photos," the American said. "Could I

request that my own cameraman be allowed to photograph some of Dr. Tashenko's work? With proper clearances?"

"Perhaps later. When you know exactly what you want."

Again Karpov muttered something in Russian to Irina. She looked preoccupied, distant.

Hanson was tantalized by her. All that beauty, that long, well-formed body, hidden by the antiseptic smock. Parente had told him that her husband was a chastened dissident, an editor who'd once been a disciple of the great Zolkin. But the KGB had held Lev Tashenko's feet to the fire. Made a believer out of him. *Hell of a thing,* Hanson thought, *being a coward and turncoat, and married to a dynamo like Irina Tashenko.*

"Come along, Mr. Hanson," she said. "I can spare fifteen minutes in the laboratory. I will not have time to explain it all. My assistant speaks no English, so you will have to leave."

"May I request another appointment?"

He caught a faint nod of Dr. Lermontov's head, a movement of the eyes. The elegant gent was calling the shots. He'd have to ask Parente about him.

"Tomorrow afternoon call my secretary. I will be able to see you later in the week."

Lermontov shook Hanson's hand. It was a steely grip. *Not only fluent and well dressed but in great shape,* the newsman thought.

"Thank you, Dr. Lermontov. I'm grateful." He felt the need to babble on. "I assure you, this will give the magazine a chance to do a real upbeat story on Soviet science. . . ."

Karpov's iron hand was navigating him through the door.

"You're not joining us?" Hanson asked.

"No, no. I was just here to make certain, Mr. Hanson, that you are sincere and qualified. You are both. You see, we're not that fictional police state created by your journalists. You are free to ask Dr. Tashenko anything, study whatever literature she gives you, observe her experiments. How do you say it? You are on your own."

Elated, Hanson thanked him and followed Irina Tashenko to the foul-smelling lab. White rats with sockets and electrodes planted in their furry heads sniffed and squealed, hit levers, killed mice.

*   *   *

"Why didn't they keep me this time?" Abram Levitch moaned plaintively. "Enough with the beatings. Jail me—make me a celebrity."

He lay on the couch in Nadya Burik's apartment. Dr. Belus was inspecting his bare chest and abdomen. Cleverly, Malik's gangsters had not injured Abram's face or hands, so that there was no immediate evidence of the assault. But they had beaten him thoroughly nonetheless, ambushing him a block from the American Embassy, where he had hoped to stage a demonstration in behalf of a jailed Roman Catholic priest.

"Maybe they'll get around to it next time," Nadya Burik said. She dabbed at her nose, waddled in felt slippers to the couch, studied Levitch's cream-white body. Dr. Belus daubed the soft flesh with absorbent cotton soaked in witch hazel. "They'll make you the martyr you want to be, Abram Moiseivich."

"Ah, that feels good, Vanya. Better than Malik's galoots. Ah, ah. One of them, that big animal Rodenko. He used to be an Olympic weight lifter, but he was too drunk to compete. So he makes a living beating up people."

"How did they know you were going to the Americans?" Nadya asked. "You were stopped a block away."

"It was a good guess. They took the letter from me before they beat me." He began to cry softly. "Ah, Sarah, Sarah. I want you."

"Cry, Abram, it's good for you," Nadya said. "I get tired of your laughter, your courage. You make bad jokes when you're in torment. I never hesitate to weep. It's part of being a Slav."

"I'm no Slav. I am a Jew. Hebrew. Israelite. Ai, Vanya, it hurts."

"But as far as I know," Dr. Belus said with a gentle smile, "you aren't a Roman Catholic."

"No. But they have rights also."

Nadya, clucking, shaking her head, shuffled to the alcove-kitchen to brew tea for Levitch. He was becoming a burden; his daily martyrdom was making it difficult for them all.

"How well do you know Floyd Hanson?" Dr. Belus asked Levitch.

"Slightly. Nice fellow."

"Can he be trusted?"

"Of course. You think the Americans are like our journalists?

A bunch of drunken bums on the KGB payroll? Cowards like Lev Tashenko, kissing the KGB's behind? Or out-and-out agents like Deroulian? Hanson is a decent man. Why do you ask?"

"Nothing, nothing. I'm glad you trust him. I may have to get him some scientific data. Not secret. But important scientific information he needs. Suppose I asked you to deliver it to him?"

"Why not?" Levitch rubbed the purplish lump on his left breast. A hematoma, Dr. Belus had said: blood gathering where the weight lifter had smashed his fist into him. "But why don't you give it to him?"

Belus shrugged. "You know him. You see him all the time. At Parente's, in the park. I might be suspect."

"Sure. So long as it isn't information our friend Malik regards as a state secret."

"No, nothing like that. Here, sip the tea, and take two aspirin. If you can't sleep tonight, I'll leave some codeine with Nadya."

"Me, sleep? In the best of condition I don't sleep. And I can't tolerate codeine. It gives me a three-day hangover."

Old Nadya, the widow who had watched her husband marched off to a KGB van, removed forever from her life and officially listed as "dead of pneumonia" in Kolyma, watched them from the alcove. Why did they persist? Was there any longer anyplace to turn, any hope for salvation? Suddenly she felt a rush of warmth and love for Levitch. In his childlike bravery, his open-eyed acceptance of the world, his innocent humor, he might do more to change the horrid tyranny, to arouse the West, than all of them with their intellectualizing, argument, analysis, reliving of history, rivalries, microscopic examinations of the hair and the skin particles and the body fluids of Bolshevism. She regretted her mean thoughts about him.

He's no mystic, and he never was a true believer, and he wants only his wife, the sun, and his Jewishness, Nadya thought. *God help him; maybe he'll change things.*

"The hypo—?"

Hanson was taking notes, trying to keep up with Irina Tashenko's offhand explanations of her laboratory work. Karpov had left them in the lab with the Uzbek girl. He had warned

Irina: Show him only elemental work. *Keep him interested.*
Karpov was of the opinion that Hanson was not terribly
bright. That was all to the good; he could be easily deceived.

"Hypothalamus," Dr. Tashenko said. "And the septal area.
They are believed to contain rewarding sites."

"What kind of reward?"

"Feelings of pleasure, warmth, goodness."

Hanson scratched his chin. "I'll be damned."

Dr. Tashenko led him to a cage in which a large white rat
was nibbling at bits of grain. There was a metal plug in its
head, an odd socketlike apparatus affixed to the center of the
furry brow.

"This is rather elemental work," she said. "I don't think
your magazine will be interested."

Hanson peered through the wire mesh. At one end was a
feeding trough, from which the rat greedily ate grain. At the
other end of the cage was a plastic container of water. In the
midst of the cage was a metal pedal. The flooring of the cage
was divided under the pedal. Hanson could see a wire snak-
ing out.

"What's the pedal, doctor?"

"A stimulation switch."

"Stimulation?"

"Yes. When it's activated, it transmits a small electrical
charge into the rat's brain. The socket in its head is connected to a filamentlike electrode that reaches into the septal
region. When the rat touches the pedal, the brain is stimulated,
with resultant feelings of pleasure."

"Why isn't he hitting the lever now? Oh, I get it. He's
hungry. He'd rather eat."

"You really are uninformed, aren't you?"

"It was just a guess." *Rude dame,* he thought.

She looked disgusted with him, annoyed that she had to
waste time on an ignoramus. "The pedal is not connected.
There is no transmission of radio waves to the filament in the
brain. If there were, the rat would rather stimulate itself than
eat. Or drink. Or copulate. Or if it were a female, look after
its young."

"That's hard to believe."

The rat sniffed the air, raised a pink snout, skittered over
to the pedal, sniffed it, touched it once. He touched it again,
sniffed, pawed it, licked it.

"He is receiving nothing. But he knows that the pedal often functions when humans approach."

Satisfied that he was getting no happy fix, the rat walked to the water trough and drank daintily.

Irina Tashenko pressed a button under the cage. It made the faintest of sounds, but the rat raised his head immediately. The pink eyes were alert, and the nose worked busily. Then the rat ran to the pedal and struck it with his right front foot, struck it again. And again. And again. Then, in what seemed a frenzy, he began to hit the pedal with incessant rhythmic movements.

"Holy smoke," Hanson said. "He's getting his high."

"I beg your pardon?"

"A high, like from drugs. A rush."

"Yes, one might compare it to that. The sensation is very pleasant."

"Like sex?"

"The rat is a sophisticated animal, but it cannot communicate these matters to us. We do know rats often prefer this form of self-stimulation to copulation. Or in some cases, it will motivate them to mount another rat, male or female. Or, for that matter, try to copulate with a rubber ball, a toy mouse or a block of wood."

"Oh, boy."

"Rats have been known to so crave the pleasure that the shock creates in their brain, that they will work themselves into a state of collapse from pressing the pedal and refusing food and water. Most rats will pause to eat, drink, groom and sleep. In others, the feeling of pleasure is so exquisite that they cannot stop. One rat we observed operated the lever nine hundred thousand times in twenty-one days, an average of thirty responses per minute. It eventually died of exhaustion."

"Has this been tried on people?"

"Oh, yes. In the United States. Norway, Britain. There is considerable literature on self-stimulation."

The rat was tapping at the lever as if its survival depended on it.

"Look at him go at it," Hanson said. "It must feel super. An all-time high. Like what? An orgasm? A drug high? The top of a TM trance?"

"We have descriptions from humans who have had the experience," she said. "Their feelings differ. But all are pleasurable and complex. In many cases, sheer curiosity keeps the subject stimulating himself. To find out more about the sensation. Just what is it? Why do I feel so good?"

Hanson watched as she turned off the control. The rat tapped the metal lever a few times, realized he was no longer receiving good news. *Tap, tap, tap.* Nothing. No happy juice jolting his brain. He raised himself on his hind legs and began to groom, licking forefeet and forelegs. Once more he tapped the pedal, satisfied himself that it transmitted no stimulation, and went back to the grain.

"All that fun from a little wire in his brain?"

Dr. Tashenko turned away, indicating that the visit was over. She spoke in Russian to the Uzbek girl, who was injecting dark liquids into a white mouse.

"The experiments on humans," Hanson asked. "Are they much different?"

"In principle, no. But the human brain is so complex that the results of self-stimulation are quite varied."

" Such as?"

"The subject will sometimes form an attachment to the experimenter, associate him with the stimulation effect. The mere sight of the scientist will excite him. Or the subject may keep tapping the lever—not a few times the way the rat did—but a hundred times, two hundred, convinced he is getting the pleasurable sensation long after the current has been turned off."

"Rats have more sense than we do. Is that it?"

"No, just a simpler neurological system. We have also noted—"

"*We?*" the reporter asked. "Experiments you've done here?"

She did not answer. "It has been noted that the most intense pleasurable responses occur in patients stimulated while they are suffering intense pain, or anguish, rage, or fear. When implanted and taught to use the lever, they get profound relief. Patients who are well adjusted, or feel well at the time of stimulation, experience only slight pleasure."

Hanson followed her back to her office, convinced that her comments were surely about experiments she had conducted. That was the stuff he wanted. Nuts to that split-brain business. The notion of people—human beings, living men and women—giving themselves jolts of super-good feeling, a pleasure as sweet as an orgasm, higher than heroin, better than winning the Pulitzer Prize!

Outside her office she offered him a firm hand and a bland face. "I have no more time for you."

"But we've just started. We didn't even get into surgery. What I'd really like is to witness one of those split-brain operations. Or observe a subject undergoing self-stimulation."

"Submit your request in writing."

"To whom?"

"Dr. Lermontov. Good day."

"The business of implanted electrodes and that wonderful feeling it gives people," he said, trying to hold her attention. She had a hand on the knob of her door. "It's incredible."

"Not at all."

"But I was thinking. Those refuseniks, dissidents, all the people who give you trouble. Malcontents. People who want to leave—"

"What has that to do with me?"

"You could stick a filament in their brains, into the happy part, and let them stimulate themselves a few hours a day. People with anguish, fear, despair. They'd feel great. Solve a lot of problems. Guys like Levitch. Or Slesik. Or even Zolkin. They'd feed themselves funny shocks, and you wouldn't have to worry about them bad-mouthing the government, or giving interviews to foreign reporters."

Hanson realized he'd been talking too much.

"An idiotic notion," she snapped. "If people would consent to the procedure, they would already be under one's control. What makes you think a population would permit this?"

He could not resist the counterpunch. Hanson needed the story, but he was offended by her disdainful manner. "Who said a *whole* population? How many dissidents do you have? A thousand? Five thousand? You could take care of the Jewish activists in Moscow in one afternoon—"

"We are not barbarians. If you persist in these imbecilic comments, we can forget about the interview. Good day."

Alone in her office, she trembled, misread her operating schedule for the week, had to smoke two cigarettes. *Damn Hanson! With his fair skin, wispy beard and innocent eyes, that American simplemindedness!* She knew what was eating at her. Karpov and the KGB had neutered her husband, her love, the weakling editor, her dear Lev. They had needed no surgery, no electrodes, no self-stimulation, no induced pleasures, to destroy him as a man.

Levitch. Slesik. The Semonskis. Names she saw in the foreign journals from time to time. And the great Zolkin, whom she had once known—courageous and unsilenced. And now she was becoming part of the soulless apparatus that destroyed such people. She decided to go to the synagogue some Saturday when the Jews held their weekly outdoor meeting and look at Abram Levitch, at the face of bravery. From a distance, of course.

"A light supper at my apartment at eight," Karpov commanded. His voice seemed brittle and distant on the phone.

"Impossible," Irina said.

"It is purely in the nature of business. I want a report on Hanson. I want to move to the next phase."

"It will have to wait until the day after tomorrow. I have two operations scheduled."

"This is an urgent matter. I appeal to you not only as an old friend, but as a Soviet citizen who has a task to perform for the motherland."

"You can meet me Thursday afternoon at the hospital. I'll have a white coat for you if you're still playing the part of Dr. Lermontov."

There was a pause. Irina glanced at Lev. He sat huddled next to a small stove—the apartment building, though only three years old, had an inefficient heating system—reading a journal on Soviet-American relations.

Karpov spoke again. "I want you at my apartment within an hour. You will be interested to know that your husband has been seen in the company of certain French visitors. They call themselves Euro-Communists but they're a gang of neo-Fascist traitors. I am afraid their conversations were taped, and we have some distressing material on file."

Teeth bared, Karpov had revealed his truest self: the merciless policeman. During his recent visits, she had noted a cynical weariness in him, a kind of boredom. Now she decided it was nothing more than fatigue. He was still the conniving, heartless monster who had threatened Lev, then neutered him. And he was still adept at the game. It mattered not that her husband had spent ten minutes with the Frenchmen, and exchanged no information of importance, or that his magazine would print not a word of the encounter. The meeting was in Karpov's files, and it could be used, if not now, whenever convenient. For a moment she marveled at the dumb courage of a drifting soul like Levitch.

"I will be there," she said. She hung up.

"Hospital?" Tashenko asked. He put the journal down.

"Yes.

"The woman with brain damage? The young woman?"

Irina lowered her eyes. "I can't lie to you. It was Karpov."

"I understand. We're still his pawns. I wonder how it would be to live somewhere where the police did not dictate our lives, follow us, know all there is to know about us."

She knelt at his feet. He caressed her dark hair. "Lev, there will be no contact between us. He won't touch me. This is a complicated political matter he's involved in. He needs some help from me."

"You? Why involve you? You aren't political. You've never signed a petition for the Jews or the democrats." His voice quavered. "It's me he's after. Or else . . . he wants you again. God help us, it's my nightmare."

"No, Lev. I'm not sure what he wants. But you're safe. He won't take advantage of me."

"If only he would die. Or vanish. Irina, I love you so deeply, so utterly, that there isn't much left of me beyond my love."

"Don't say that, Lev. You are good. You are kind. And I love you with a passion equal to yours."

They kissed gently, drily, giving the lie to her words. His pale hands did not leave the journal in his lap.

Karpov was wearing an Irish tweed jacket so nubby that it seemed to have twigs woven into the warp and woof, clay-colored cavalry twill trousers, and Italian loafers with gleaming brass buckles. He looked tired, but he was freshly shaven and smelled of some arcane cologne suggesting wild grass.

"I can't stay long," Irina said.

"I have champagne already iced. Perhaps something to eat?"

"Nothing. I'll report to you, you can give me my orders, and I'll leave."

He took her coat, kissed the nape of her neck as he did so, and tried to embrace her. She moved away.

The living room was unlike any Russian living room Irina had ever seen. The furniture had come from Milan: devices of leather, chrome, burnished wood. The rugs were multicolored Swedish abstracts. On the walls were framed affiches from Paris, Mexico City, New York, San Francisco. Over the couch was Karpov's treasure, a large Miró full of whimsical egg-shaped objects, curving lines, droplets and streaks.

Irina sat underneath it, accepted a glass of Mumm's, refused a Marlboro cigarette.

"You used to love this room," he said.

"It is attractive. For a policeman, you have exceptional taste. But that's not why I am here."

"Of course. Tell me about Hanson."

She did so. The American had been intrigued with self-stimulation in human subjects. In fact it had gotten him sidetracked, off the question of surgery, the operations he had originally asked about. She did not mention Hanson's sly comment about implanting dissidents with electrodes.

"He didn't seem suspicious?"

"Of what?" asked Irina.

"Our plans for him."

She shook her head, let her eyes wander. The bedroom door was open. A dim light within. She knew the vast bed, the soft music from the Japanese stereo, the discreet drapes and heavy carpets. A shudder of remembered ecstasy, of illicit sensual joy with a man she hated and feared, washed over her.

Karpov did not notice it. He told her to grant no further interviews to the American. The journalist was to be referred to "Lermontov" if he became a pest. Meanwhile, Karpov would need from her a packet of papers—scientific data, reports as yet unpublished. She was to deliver these papers to Karpov in two days, keeping a detailed list of every document.

"What will be done with them?"

"That doesn't concern you. It won't compromise you and it won't compromise your husband. How is Lev?"

"Well." She got up. "I must go. You could have given me these orders on the phone."

He looked at her figure. A hurdler? In her youth, an eager Komsomol, she had won medals in track events. Suddenly he thought of her naked back. The straight, smooth spine.

"Like Ingres's 'Odalisque,' " he said. "Your back is so long and perfectly formed. Did you know Ingres painted an extra vertebra on her to give her that marvelous look? That's who you always reminded me of."

"That has ended," she said solemnly. "You used me once for your pleasure, threatened my husband. I told you when we parted I would never betray him again."

"I loved you. I love you now."

"No, no. It's greed, appetite. And now you're using me to betray someone else, to destroy someone. I am leaving."

Karpov seized her waist, drew her close, kissed her neck, her ear, her cheek. She kept averting her lips, moving away from him, pushing at his iron chest.

"Andrei, stop. I will not sleep with you. I am leaving."

Breathing noisily, he put a hand on her left breast. "Let me adore you again, Irina. It will be more pleasurable than the electrical shocks you send into people's brains. I need you."

She tried to move away.

Karpov did not let go of her waist. When she tried to disengage his hands, he grasped her wrists and did not let her pull free.

"A surgeon's hands," he said. "Long, strong. You are perfection."

"Good breeding stock, you once told me."

"A heavy-handed compliment. I want to love you. I need you. I haven't been in good health. Migraine. It's recurrent. Almost daily."

"You don't want a sexual adventure. You want a neurological examination. They do marvelous things with an American process called biofeedback. I'll enroll you for a course."

He would not be deterred. "The organization doesn't like us getting involved in these mind-altering fads. None of that nonsense . . . meditation, biofeedback, trances. It's all garbage anyway. The will triumphs. The mind can do anything it wants if it is sufficiently disciplined."

"Good God, do you still believe that Fascist idiocy? Someone who admires Miró and Giacometti? A Soviet policeman who has read Joyce and Eliot? Minds should be free, not fettered. When you start babbling your party lunacies, you are at your least attractive. Let go of me."

He laughed. He could be charming, boyish. Something of

a West European aristocrat about him, Irina had always thought—the mocking smile, the stylish clothes, the lean body.

"The Miró," he said. "I bought it in London some years ago. There was a companion piece that a lady from Texas bought at the same *vernissage*. She installed it in her mansion in Dallas and decided the colors clashed with the furniture. So she hired a local artist to paint out all the red and substitute green."

He told the story wittily, with a light touch: Karpov at his most engaging, joking with English horse-owners, trading stories with American journalists.

"Your Texas lady would have made an excellent KGB agent," Irina said. "Desecrating Miró for the convenience of the owner?"

"Careful, the room may be wired."

"It wouldn't frighten me," Irina said. "I'm a shining light of the system. I'm not a Jew, or a dissident, or a democrat. An accomplished surgeon who brings credit to the great Soviet society." She got up. "I'm busy tomorrow. I must go."

"A last taste of the wine," Karpov said. To Irina's amusement, he had picked up the habit of calling champagne *wine*. He also spoke of Bordeaux as *claret*, and pronounced *vitamin* as if the *i* were short, as in *vigor*.

Ill at ease, she nonetheless accepted a second glass of champagne. She took a few sips, set it down. He approached her and embraced her. "Don't go."

"I will not let myself give in. You gave me your word when we parted. Lev would not be harmed. You would not approach me again. Your word must be worth something."

"I beg of you, Irina, listen to me." His voice was muffled, breathy. "Never in my life have I enjoyed sharing love as I did with you. My marriage was a failure. Other women palled. Only you roused me from torpor, made me understand what love was."

"Lust, Andrei, lust. It was not love."

"Don't deny it. In passion, locked together with me, you shouted your love for me. Shouted it! In Stockholm. In London. You were part of me. There has been no passion in my life like that—before or after. I am weary of my work and my life. It's I who need you. I know you will find satisfaction and fulfillment in our bodies. Don't deny yourself this pleasure."

"Andrei, let go of me." She was vaguely disoriented by his hard masculine odor, the pervasive cologne.

"Come."

He drew her to the bedroom. The familiar setting made her giddy, weak-kneed. Japanese *sumi* paintings, a Japanese screen decorated with flying cranes. From the stereo issued a Mozart air, an overture she could not identify.

Karpov was on his knees, resting his head against her, placing his hands under her skirt, stroking, caressing.

"You must," he said. "You will. There'll be no threats by me. No harm to Lev. Help me, Irina. I adore you. I must have you."

Shivering, she recalled their trysts in a half dozen hotels— elegant surroundings, muted light, the prospect of an opera or the theater, fine wine, excellent dining. The two of them— free of the gray prison—infusing each other with their passion, exploring limbs and features, clinging to each other in the snowy Stockholm night, while outside the hotel, trams clanged, buses honked. In the morning the city came alive and they stirred, satisfied, pleasantly aching, full of each other's taste, smell, texture. She would be a liar to deny it. Hating him, she had come to love their sexual encounters, to anticipate them, at times to hunger for him.

"To bed," Karpov said. "Take off your clothing."

She undid her belt, unhooked the placket at the back of her dress. The sight of her in a satiny slip, her figure suddenly appearing longer, fuller, shining with a pink glow, almost caused him to faint. Half dressed, he came to her, embraced her, and gently lowered her to the bed.

"Slowly, Andrei, slowly."

He was kissing her with the hurried wetness of a starved schoolboy—lips and tongue searching her eyes, nose, mouth, ears, neck.

It occurred to her: *It is this passionate slavishness that attracted me to him*. The cold controlled KGB man, never contested, never defeated—was abruptly a slobbering youth, reduced to gasps and moans, someone who need not be feared.

"Andrei."

He was shivering, rising from her. His body trembled violently. One hand touched his forehead as if seeking a seat of pain. He half-rose, fell alongside her, rolled from the bed.

"Andrei!"

Irina jumped from the bed and bent over him.

He said nothing. His arms stiffened and hugged his sides. The fingers were frozen. His eyes were locked. The long body was as hard as a railroad tie, unmoving, insensate.

Irina ran to him. She raised his head and placed it on an eiderdown pillow. Then she unloosened his belt and removed his shoes. He was unconscious, breathing unevenly, stertorously. A dark stain bloomed on the clay-colored whipcord trousers. He had urinated.

"My God," Irina said. "A seizure."

There was something grimly humorous about it. He had forced her to come to his apartment, intent on seduction. Now, fallen into what surely appeared a *grand mal* convulsion, he was lucky to have her there—not for sex, but for succor.

She felt his brow: cold sweat. His eyes remained shut. He heard nothing, saw nothing.

After a minute of tonic rigidity, his limbs began to jerk. Head, trunk, arms, legs, began an irregular uncontrolled dance, jerking in spasms, reaching a crescendo of involuntary kicks and thrusts. Then the seizure appeared to run its course. Karpov's breathing became more regular and less noisy. His body grew limp. He appeared comatose.

Watching him from the sofa, aware that he had exhibited all the traits of *grand mal* epilepsy, she found it useful to regard him as a patient, a subject for analysis. Knowing that he was vulnerable, ailing, made him less of a menace, less an object of fear and hatred. He was human; he might die.

She put a wet cloth to his head, moistened his lips, removed his shoes. He began to mutter: masked phrases, mangled words. Once he opened his cold green eyes and stared at her—pleading, grateful.

The phone screamed, filling her with dread. In Russia one always weighed dire possibilities, painful eventualities. Better not to respond. As potent as Karpov was, there were people above him—the piggish Dort and others—who detested him. She would surely be arrested, investigated, kept under surveillance if she were found beside the comatose body of a KGB subdirector. A shadow would fall on her career. Lev would come under suspicion again. In their unreasoning rage, she imagined, it was not unlikely that Editor

Tashenko, that intellectual hairsplitter, would end up as the available enemy of the state.

It rang once, twice, three times, four. Then it stopped. She did not pick it up, praying that some frustrated functionary would not come to the apartment.

He stirred. His mutterings became louder.

"My head hurts," he said thickly. "Pain all around."

She tried to suppress a smile. Karpov, the ultimate policeman, the man who condemned people to prison, torture, drug therapy that made mush of their minds, to death in some icebound hell, whimpered that he was in pain.

"Irina, are you here?"

"I am."

"What did you do to me?"

A policeman, a schemer in his heart of hearts, she thought. One could not merely be ill, afflicted by some malfunction of body and brain. It had to be *done to him*.

"I did nothing to you. You fainted. Then you went into convulsion."

"Impossible."

"But it happened, Andrei."

His eyes roved aimlessly, veering from one side to the other. There was no question now in Dr. Tashenko's mind: He had had a *grand mal* seizure.

"I'm weak, awfully weak. Some bastard got to the champagne."

"You are hallucinating. You had a sip. So did I. Am I in convulsion? I never knew you had a history of this. Why did you never mention it?"

"Never . . . never in my life. Help me up."

She raised him to a sitting position. He crawled to the bed and she helped him lie back on the pillows.

"No history of epilepsy? A trauma some years ago?"

Wincing, he shook his head.

"You've had these periodic spells of severe headaches, haven't you?" she asked.

Karpov nodded, clenched his jaw.

She recalled once in Paris, his becoming violently ill with a tension headache, complaining of clamplike pain in the left temple, over the left eye. In the midst of dinner at the Tour d'Argent he had turned pale and sweaty, his left eye reddening, half-closing. She had had to escort him from the restaurant to their hotel, dose him with codeine (it had only a temporary effect) and press ice against his forehead. Yes, Karpov had said, he had these damned seizures, these assaults of intractable pain, from time to time. *Perhaps it's punishment*, Irina had thought. *Retribution for a life of cruelty*. She had mused: *Why am I not also punished for surrendering to him, affording him joy and fulfillment, while my miserable husband wastes away in a cold Moscow flat?*

Irina wondered: Could his periodic bouts of migraine, and the pain—as she recalled, Karpov's suffering had been devastating—be connected with this odd, out-of-nowhere convulsion?

Karpov's trembling hand went to his crotch. "I've wet myself. Like a baby. Irina, get my robe. Pajamas."

"I will. Then I'm going."

"You can't fear me now. Please stay. What happened to me?"

"You will need a neurological examination. If you come to the Institute, I'll assign one of our physicians to give you a work-up. Be thankful you didn't injure yourself when you fell. People can suffer fractures of the vertebrae when they go rigid as you did. You seem unharmed. You'll be drowsy for a few hours, and you'll have a long sleep tonight. Probably a severe headache tomorrow. There's an all-night pharmacy at the Institute. I'll phone and have them send over pheno-barbital."

"Don't leave me."

"No. Lev knows I'm here."

He managed a hard smile. "That cipher. He'll be grateful that you attended to the medical needs of someone who can restore his career. Or have him sent to a psychiatric hospital for the rest of his life."

She put her hand over her eyes. "Don't make me hate you unnecessarily. You know how terribly confused I am about us."

"Look at me as a patient. Compassion. Clinical interest. I'm weak, dry. How long will I feel this way? And why did it happen?"

"You're only forty-eight. I would guess you need not fear a lesion or a pathological condition." She dialed the Institute.

"Lesion?"

"A brain tumor." She awakened a sleeping pharmacist,

identified herself and told him to send an orderly to Karpov's apartment with the medications.

"God in heaven. A tumor. I don't believe it."

"I said it was unlikely. You'll have to have tests."

"What else could it be? I'm healthy, vigorous. I keep my weight down. I smoke too much. Drink very little. A tumor . . ."

Irina looked at his lean body, his sharply molded face. She suspected there was Scandinavian blood in him. He lacked the round pudginess, the flatness of feature of the true Slav. But his elegance seemed to have deserted him. No one could pee in his pants and maintain that air of rocklike hauteur that endowed Karpov with his talent for evoking fear.

"Idiopathic epilepsy," she said. "That means we don't know the cause. It just happens. Perhaps caused by electrical currents passing between the hemispheres. A malfunction we don't understand. Idiopathic is a convenient medical term. It means the ailment is simply there. No focus of abnormality, no trauma. It's rather the way you label people enemies of the state."

"And the treatment?"

"Rest. Medication. I can't stay any longer. As soon as the messenger comes with the tablets, I'm leaving. How do you feel?"

"Weak. Angry. I hate losing control of myself. I was in an earthquake once in Yugoslavia, near Sarajevo. Lifted from my bed as if by a giant's hand and shaken like a rat. I hated it. Because I had lost control. Can you promise me this won't happen again?"

She shook her head. Unwilling to press her advantage, knowing that he was frightened and debilitated, she dutifully found clean pajamas and a quilted crimson robe in the closet.

Reluctantly she helped him change, bathed his soiled abdomen and groin, and then sat apart from him, rejecting his appeal that she stay in his arms. But she held his hand and, for a while, stroked it.

Two days later, Karpov had a second seizure in Colonel Sergei Dort's office.

He had come there to brief Dort on the final plans for the Levitch-Hanson affair. There was growing pressure on Dort to get Levitch out of circulation. His superiors were willing to take their chances on a worldwide outcry over the refusenik leader.

"Move, *move,* Comrade Major," Dort growled. "Nobody is worried about the effect on détente or what the Hebes say. What can anyone do to us? So *The New York Times* raises a stink. Who cares? Can anyone be serious? Those shit-heads at the United Nations, all those cannibals and witch doctors and camel fuckers who are on our side, they'll thank us for arresting Levitch. It means one less Yid. So get going."

Karpov assured Dort that final steps were being taken. A selection of research papers from Dr. Tashenko's files were to be handed over to one Belus, a physician. He in turn . . .

"Oh, yes. That Jew doctor we have on payroll."

"Well, we gave him a car and other favors."

"Such as? Why wasn't I informed?"

Karpov ignored the second question. He felt giddy, dry-mouthed. "Access to dollar stores. Gasoline coupons. He's got an older brother we can send to prison anytime we want. He's been heard making offensive remarks about the party. That's how we keep Belus in line."

Dort was running his pink hand, like a pig's trotter, over his pate, mulling the plan. He was blustering a bit too much, Karpov felt.

It was evident that at higher levels, the matter of arresting Levitch had been debated. Perhaps some thought had been given to letting him leave—silencing him by sending him to Israel. But one never understood the motivations of the ultimate powers in the apparatus. Maybe they *wanted* to raise a fuss, anger the West, show them that they didn't give a damn about Levitch or refuseniks or dissidents.

Riffling through his papers, looking for the timetable he and Malik had drawn up for grabbing Levitch, Karpov went rigid. The papers slithered from his manicured hands. His back stiffened. His arms and legs became sticklike, unbending. Sliding from the chair, he hit the floor with a loud *clunk* and lay there in tonic rigidity. A board of a man.

"What in hell is wrong with him?" Dort shouted. "Comrade Major, what is this, a joke?"

Dort knew that Karpov was not a jokester. Sarcastic, a schemer—but pranks, no. As Dort shouted for help, yelling over the intercom for his secretary and the guards, Karpov went into his convulsive dance. Arms, legs and head jerked in a frenzy. The eyes rolled about, crossed, wandered blindly.

Dort smelled something acid, sour. Karpov was wetting his pants. Maybe crapping them.

"Karpov!" he shouted. "What in the hell are you doing?"

The subdirector heard nothing. A flailing left arm struck Dort's chest. The director could not help but notice the sapphire ring, the Piaget watch, the polished fingernails. *Whatever it is that's turning Karpov into a jerking puppet may be doing me a favor*, the colonel thought. *Once and for all I'll be rid of this elegant bastard. . . .*

Hours later, Karpov, head aching, feeling wasted and irritable, awakened in the KGB infirmary. A thin gray blanket covered his body. His shoes, tie, belt and trousers had been removed. He stank of dried urine.

An elderly gray nurse stood at his bedside. She looked terrified.

"What time is it?" he asked.

"Two in the morning, Comrade Major. You have been in a deep sleep."

"I want to go home. Help me get dressed."

She called outside the door. A lieutenant and a sergeant, KGB militiamen, appeared.

"You will escort me home," Karpov said. He tried to make it an order. But it sounded like a query, almost a plea.

"I'm sorry, Comrade Major, but Colonel Dort wants you taken to the Neurological Institute. He has been in touch with the physicians there."

"I can manage that by myself."

"We have orders from the colonel, sir."

"And you will stay with me while I'm there?" The dread began to germinate in Karpov's groin. A feeling of in-the-bone fear, like the incessant cold that drills its way through a flimsy wooden house on the steppe, permeates everything, freezes sensations. *So this is the way it begins*.

"No, Comrade Major," the lieutenant said. He had a round white face. "Only to make certain you get there safely."

Karpov sensed organs relaxing, muscles loosening. For the moment he was secure. So long as the Levitch matter hung fire, he was safe. When he was finished with Levitch he'd apply for overseas duty. Perhaps somewhere in the West.

Decent food, civilized cities, slender and accepting women
who bathed every day . . .

Dressing, he felt giddy, light on his feet. He took time to
wash his crotch and thighs with green soap, dried himself,
managed to revive some of his dapper manner. It must have
worked. The militiamen saluted him as they left.

Secretly pleased, Malik was informed by Colonel Dort that
in Karpov's absence, he was to take over the Levitch matter.
Dr. Irina Tashenko had been contacted. She was to supply a
packet of unpublished documents, research papers, experimental data, in an envelope. Malik was to give them to Dr.
Ivan Belus.

"And then?" asked Malik. He shivered. He was convinced
that Karpov had had no epileptic seizure. Oh, that cake-
eater, that dandy. They were after him. Fed up with his
fancy London suits and his French cologne. He'd strayed
somewhere, screwed up, gotten the big boys at Dzerzhinsky
angry.

"You'll get further orders," Dort said. "Don't mess this one
up. Fewer beatings and more planning. You'll be told what to
tell this Belus."

"How is the major?" Malik hesitated, trying to stifle a
smile.

"What about him?"

"I heard he was ill. Had a fit. Right here on the floor."

"They think he has epilepsy. Maybe a brain tumor. He'll
be out of commission for a while."

Dort appeared to be smiling. A mechanical grin. Steel
teeth winking in the lamplight.

5

PARENTE, HANSON AND Agnes Wardle were invited to a refusenik meeting at Dr. Belus's place. He was a bachelor, he worked, and so he managed to live a bit better than most of the others. Besides, he was not technically a refusenik but a sort of adjunct to the movement. Once, five years ago, he had applied for emigration, then quickly withdrawn his application when told he was ineligible. So the yellow-haired, good-natured physician went back to his marginal practice, attending to dissident Jews, working daily at a mouse-poor clinic in the Outer Ring not far from the Chaika swimming pool.

Around the packed apartment, groups chatted, smoked, discussed a Passover seder they were planning. A young rabbi from Detroit was coming to help them celebrate the feast of deliverance. He was bringing matzo, kosher wine, other delicacies. Nadya Burik said she would not attend. Medieval, primitive humbug, she told the Semonskis. They were offended.

Chaim Slesik and Levitch took up the argument.

"Wrong, Nadya," Levitch said amiably. "You cling to some old Bolshevik nonsense. Because your father was a Trotskyite?

Look what they did to him. Lev Davidovitch Bronstein,
founder of the Red Army. It earned him an ax in the head.
Even Trotsky, toward the end, started getting the idea. He
was a Jew. The Communists had no use for him. The Russians hated him."

"I'll skip the seder," Nadya said. "Last time that rabbi
made me eat a chunk of lettuce between two pieces of stitched
cardboard. I almost choked. And he spilled wine all over my
tablecloth."

"It's part of the ceremony," Levitch explained. "The wine
cups must be filled to the brim. And the lettuce was a Hillel
sandwich, as prescribed in the Talmud. Look, I'm no expert.
But all the traditions are important for us."

"Traditions, yes," Slesik said hoarsely. The cancer was
killing him. He would never see Zion. "Better traditions than
theirs. Nadya, I was a party member years ago."

"Right, so was I," Levitch said. "What is it? Lenin pre-
served like a fly in amber. A lot of babble. Words that mean
nothing. Judaism has been around longer. Talk about traditions.
We invented them. Maybe we invented God."

The arguments intensified. It seemed to Parente that the
participants covered the entire range of culture, civilization,
religion, politics, art, the meaning of life. Only Jews could
compress so many ideas, so many opposing viewpoints into
one small smoky apartment.

He watched Hanson offer to help Dr. Belus with the
sandwiches. Both vanished into the minuscule kitchen. He
wondered what Hanson was up to. Something on the surgical
story he was researching? Parente was about to follow him
when Mikhail Semonski buttonholed him, asking his opinions
on American pianists. Was he familiar with a man named
Lowenthal?

In the kitchen, Hanson helped Belus arrange bread on a
tray. The newsman noticed that the refrigerator was new.
There were attractive tiles on the wall. Evidently the doctor
had made his peace with the authorities.

"I need some of Tashenko's papers on self-stimulation,"
Hanson said. "Nothing secret or confidential."

"They're in Russian."

"So what? You could translate them for me. I'd pay you.
She won't let me see them."

Belus nibbled at a crust of black bread. "Why ask me to

help? I hardly know her. Bring her American stockings, jeans, music tapes."

"Come on, Doc. She's a class act. She's a big brain. All I want is the same stuff she showed me in the lab. You know— the rat who keeps hitting a pedal, to get a happy jolt in his brain. He'd rather hit that lever than have sex, Tashenko says. Is that a story?"

"Ask her again."

Hanson shook his head. "It won't work. There's something fishy going on. I think she'd like to help me, but she's being watched. Who is Dr. Lermontov?"

Belus looked blank. The name meant nothing to him. "I have never heard of such a man. Why?"

"He was at the first interview I had with her. Tall, thin guy. Cool. He didn't go to the lab with us. He was a supervisor of some kind."

Belus shook his head. Ah, they were arranging it perfectly. Poor Hanson. Belus was glad Hanson was a young bachelor. It would go easier for him.

"What makes you think I can pry research papers from her?"

"Come on, Doc." Hanson's eyes were sly. "You're the connection. You're the one who got me to see Tashenko."

"I carried a message." Belus nodded. "All right, I'll try. I promise nothing, but I'll try." He picked up the tray.

Hanson did not say what was truly on his mind. Belus was with them—the spies, the cops, the enforcers. Nothing got done without their okay. He had no idea how high Belus's connections were, but it was worth a try.

Belus left the kitchen, bearing the tray of sandwiches. Hanson lingered to fill his teacup. Parente's bulky figure lumbered out of the corridor. He let Belus pass, watched Hanson sip the hot tea.

"What was that all about, Flerd?"

"Tony, why do you call me Flerd?"

"Brooklynese. Floyd is Flerd. As in Greenpernt. What'd you and Belus cook up in here?"

"Nothing."

"Speak, farmboy."

"Oh, hell, why hide it? I asked Belus to get me some of Tashenko's research. Not secret stuff, or confidential, or anything like that. Just some interesting data in Russian she hasn't published yet."

"Yeah. I get the picture. Brilliant investigating reporter revealing brain experiments of devious Rooshians."

"Cut it out, Tony. You said that's how reporters always got stories here. Connections, back-dooring. What's wrong? I won't get in trouble. And Belus sure doesn't want to."

"I'm not sure what's wrong. Tashenko says to you *no papers*, but Belus, a small fish, says yes, he might try to filch some, sneak them to you. Why?"

"He's a good friend."

"Sure. A great man with a hypodermic needle. As Jack E. Leonard used to say, Flerd, watch yourself at all times. This is between you and Belus, you dig?"

"I understand, Tony. I'm willing to take the chance. Trust me, hey, pal?"

Something was askew.

The packet was waiting for Dr. Belus two days later. It was given to him not by Dr. Tashenko but by Anatoli Malik of the Jewish Department.

They met on Kalinin Prospekt, lost in the mass of midday shoppers, traffic, high-rises. It was cold and sunny. Dr. Belus saw Malik's Zhiguli stop. Malik flashed his ID card at the policeman.

Belus, carrying his scuffed leather bag, hurried from the doorway of a men's clothing shop. The suits looked worse than ever, shapeless, in shitlike colors. If he performed well for Malik, and if word got back to someone like Karpov, perhaps they'd let him visit his relatives in Chicago. Suits, toiletries, watches, tape recorders, even some medical equipment.

Malik slapped a thick yellow envelope into Belus's hands.

"Guard it with your life, Belus." He never called him by his title.

"I will."

"Simple transaction. On Saturday, when Levitch is outside the synagogue, give it to him. Have you talked to Levitch?"

"I will."

"Invent a story. You're being watched. You're in trouble. You can't be seen with American journalists anymore."

"What about Levitch? He's always watched also."

"Tell him he has to figure how to handle it. If any of this
gets fucked up, Belus, you'll be the sorriest doctor in Moscow.
We'll make you eat your stethoscope. Not here, but in the
gold fields of Siberia."

The car sped away, scattering pedestrians. Dr. Belus stood
with the thick packet in his hands, his fingers cold despite the
sun.

In a gray hospital robe, a threadbare garment that offended
his personal code, Karpov sat on the edge of a hard bed in
one of the few private rooms in the Neurological Institute.
He felt dazed, lightheaded. How long had he been here? A
day? Two?

He could recall needles being jammed into his veins and
his behind, being moved in and out of X-ray rooms. Electrodes had been attached to his head. An EEG, surely, an
electroencephalogram. He had answered a lot of questions
from Dr. Lydia Skiba, one of Irina Tashenko's underlings.
She was a sullen Latvian, silent, unresponsive. He had taken
tests to determine his perception, vision, balance, eye-hand
coordination. Dr. Skiba had even asked about histories of
epilepsy, or seizures of any kind in his family.

Sliding his feet into gray paper scuffs, he walked to the
window, looked through barred windows at an iron-gray sky.
He could see the hideous towers of Moscow University.
When would they learn to build something graceful and
beautiful? And why was so little of the past left standing?
Where was their Notre Dame, their Uffizi? No visual sense,
the Slavs. It's all mystical poetry, fake religious sensations,
endless drunken babbling.

When Dr. Skiba had asked him who should be informed in
the event of emergency, Karpov had no answer. His wife was
mentally incompetent, hospitalized. He had no children. An
only child, Karpov had cousins in Alma-Ata, others in Irkutsk.
People he barely knew. He was embarrassed by the question.
Finally, with a touch of grim humor, he had given the name
of his superior, Colonel Sergei Dort. Let Dort rejoice in
Karpov's misery.

He paced the room, sipped mineral water, felt a chill. He
would have to send his orderly to his apartment for a decent
robe, velvet slippers, clean clothing. This was ridiculous,
keeping him here. Someone, somewhere, had decided he

could not leave. He was unsteady on his feet, short of breath. Anxiety. Tension. That was all. The seizures were freakish, atypical. A man so sharply in control of himself could not become the victim of these chaotic fits. Were not the headaches enough of a burden?

He noticed that the telephone had been removed from the room. Dort? Keeping him incommunicado? Karpov wondered how the Levitch matter was proceeding. He did not want a bumbler like Malik to upset his plans. Leave it to that idiot to insult Irina, give Belus the wrong orders, screw up on Hanson. . . .

His head began to ache. His throat went dry. He sipped warmish water from a glass pitcher, struggled against nausea, forced himself to walk around the room four times on unsteady feet to get his circulation going. Craving a cigarette, he searched the flaking closet, the broken chest of drawers, and found nothing, not even his clothing.

Irina Tashenko entered briskly, a clipboard under one arm. She looked severe, unpitying.

"The eminent neurosurgeon. I thought I was to be left forever in the care of your Latvian assistant. She has sour breath and doesn't answer questions."

"She is an able neurologist. I have the report on you."

"Good. Then I can be discharged."

"Perhaps. Sit down, Andrei."

Ashamed of his meager robe, his bare protruding shanks, the poorhouse scuffs, he sat on the edge of the iron bed.

"I've reviewed the tests. We have ruled out focal epilepsy—a specific area of the brain impaired by trauma or lesion. You have what is known as primary *grand mal* epilepsy."

"Curable?"

"Quite possibly. As I explained to you, it is in all likelihood idiopathic, which means we do not know the cause. There is a remote possibility that you have a focal epilepsy that has spread, but I see nothing in the EEG or X rays to make me believe that is the case. The prognosis is therefore good."

"Treatment?"

"Drugs. But I should warn you that patients with idiopathic *grand mal* seizures may experience an exacerbation of their seizures if they undergo metabolic stresses, drug withdrawal, fever, hypoglycemia or emotional trauma."

"Do I impress you as that kind of patient?"

Dr. Tashenko pushed her American glasses up her nose and stared at him coldly. "I've sensed a tension in you, an unwillingness to confront your true self, a need to cover up the past and to fictionalize the present. Perhaps you're overworked. Or perhaps your work is not agreeable to you."

He was silent.

She showed him his EEG. It had been taken immediately upon his admission. She explained it was slow but otherwise normal.

Should he convulse again, she would want an EEG taken during seizure.

"You sound as if you expect these to continue. Irina, is it possible you are indulging in a kind of medical revenge?"

"I am trying to be dispassionate about you. I'm a physician and I want you to be cured."

"The drug treatment—how soon?"

"We've begun it already. You will be kept on a course of phenytoin. It can be given orally at first. You may have some side effects."

"Such as?"

"Gastric upset, in which case we will administer it intravenously. Perhaps ataxia—lack of coordination in voluntary movements. We'll reduce the dosage if that becomes evident."

"I don't like this," Karpov said. "I can cure myself. The seizures were freaks, out-of-the-blue events."

"The convulsions will recur and must be treated."

Her professional manner was disturbing him. He smiled at her, reached for her arm. "You seem to be enjoying this. Afflicting me with a sick stomach, bad coordination. I'm Major Andrei Karpov. Not an ounce of fat on me, no shortness of breath, all my hair and teeth."

"They may be affected also."

He frowned. "What?"

"I did not mention all the side effects. You may experience an increase in the growth of hair on your face and limbs. It can become unsightly and bothersome. A condition known as gingival hypertrophy may also occur, an abnormal swelling of the gums, affecting the appearance of the face."

"You're teasing me."

"You will have to shave a great deal more. As for the enlargement of your gums, I can make no suggestion. Should you find these cosmetic complications more than you can bear, we can switch to another anticonvulsant such as phenobarbital. But of course, only time will tell. Phenobarbital, in the dosage necessary to reduce seizures, may render you sleepy, mentally uncoordinated, dizzy, and subject to an allergic rash."

"My thanks to you, Comrade Surgeon," he said bitterly.

Irina did not smile. "You are ill, Andrei, quite ill. Dr. Skiba will be back to start you on an increased course of phenytoin. Stay in bed, eat lightly, do not smoke. Good day."

"No words of kindness for an old friend?"

"I wish you a speedy recovery."

When he took her hand again she returned the pressure, very faintly, and offered him a prim smile.

Two hours later Karpov underwent a third seizure, more violent and prolonged than the first two.

Rising from his bed to urinate, he turned rigid and struck the side of the bed as he fell. A bleeding gash opened on his forehead. He thrashed about the cold floor for a few minutes before the nurse and Dr. Skiba came. At once he was given an EEG, which indicated generalized "spiking," further evidence that he was experiencing *grand mal* convulsions. There was no evidence of a focus of abnormality, nor a lateralizing abnormality to suggest that only one side of the brain was affected.

He slept deeply, covered by a black suffocating cloud. He was full of drugs, sweating, breathing heavily. In the morning, Irina Tashenko increased his dosage of phenytoin to one thousand milligrams, administered intravenously at fifty milligrams per minute.

Outside the room, as Karpov lay in a dazed, irritable state, Irina told Dr. Skiba: "Monitor his pulse, blood pressure and respiration carefully. Watch his clinical signs. It is possible he will continue to convulse."

Plaintively, Karpov called for her to come back. Weakened by drugs, he felt dislocated, impotent. Would she please call Colonel Dort at once and inform him that he was recovering and would be back at his desk in a matter of days?

"I shall call him, but you will not be at your desk so soon."

"What will happen to me?"

"You will recover."

"Come here, Irina. Hold my hand. I have no one."

"Andrei, any of our past relationships are irrelevant. My interest in you is clinical."

"Only that? No memories of a more intimate nature?"

"All right. Some fragments. I don't deny them."

"Good. If I know that you don't hate me or fear me, I can confront my illness."

She said nothing.

On Saturday the Jews assembled outside the synagogue. They circulated in the thin April sunlight, pouring out of the temple, forming slow-moving gray-brown huddled groups in front of the chipped columns. Passover was a few days away. The house of worship had been packed.

Parente, Hanson, Miss Wardle, Brian Cardwell, and a few other members of the foreign press corps watched.

"Who's the tall dude next to Abram?" Hanson asked.

"Goldman. Rabbi from Detroit. He came out to run the seder. We're all invited. Good guy. Played basketball at Yeshiva University under the immortal Red Sarachek."

"Whah?"

"Forget it, Flerd."

Zolkin did not appear, but one of his fellow "democrats," Colonel Grigor Arkangeli, court-martialed, disgraced, thrice jailed, moved among the Jews, shaking hands, expressing solidarity with them, taking copies of Levitch's onionskin handout. It was a log of violations of the Helsinki accords, including the jailing of a group of Moslem mullahs in Samarkand.

Levitch looked chalky and sweaty.

Parente nudged Hanson. "Lessons in photojournalism, Flerd. Observe the ice cream cart."

From behind a wagon selling vanilla ice cream—a queue had formed in minutes—Gorchakov, the KGB photographer, was clicking away. Alongside him another KGB man worked a hand-held motion picture camera.

"Why?" Hanson asked. "You'd think they got enough stuff on Levitch and the others."

"Keeps them busy."

"Yes, I guess they have a big payroll."

Parente tried to count heads. He decided the turnout was about the same. A few faces were missing. Chaim Slesik wasn't there. Sick again, the cancer eating his guts. Nadya

Burik seemed to have lost interest. She no longer came to the Saturday gatherings. Old survivor, old believer, old confidante of Trotsky's. Nowhere to go, nothing to believe in. Parente pitied the old hen, raddled, waddling, full of bloody memories. Her husband, a feverish poet, starved to death, taunted by drunken galoots in Vorkuta . . .

"Belus," Parente said. "He usually hangs back. A foot in each camp."

Dr. Ivan Belus, buttoning a trench coat, smoothing back his curly yellow hair, was crossing the street. He glanced at a black car and nodded at someone.

Miss Wardle commented that Dr. Belus was such a good-natured man. He treated the refuseniks for very little, often didn't get paid at all. "He isn't really one of them, is he?" she asked Parente.

"Who knows? A free-floating type."

Belus walked into the crowd of Jews. He shook hands with the Semonskis, kissed Olga on the cheek, waved to the young American rabbi and walked toward Levitch. Abram was chatting with Colonel Arkangeli.

Missionary to the goyim, Parente thought of Levitch. Tired, innocent, beat-up Levitch. A hell of a burden for one small Jew.

Belus walked up and grasped the colonel's hand. The dissident was a gaunt, hollow-eyed stork, six and one half feet of outrage.

Parente and Hanson crossed the street. As they did, both got a glimpse of Dr. Belus giving an envelope to Levitch. Levitch nodded and tucked it under his arm.

Behind the newsmen, the KGB photographers, using long lenses, took photos—Belus's arrival, the meeting with Levitch, the presentation of the envelope.

"What's new, Abram?" Parente called. "Anything good?"

Levitch waved his free hand. "Not too dismal. The Bakofskys are getting their visas. Not bad, hey, Tony?"

"Are they here?" Hanson asked.

Levitch laughed. "No, no, they can't agitate anymore. It would only make trouble. Listen, in a week they should be on the plane to Vienna. Who knows, maybe I'd be on my way to Vienna if I'd listened to you and stopped handing out bulletins. You think they really were going to give me a visa?"

"No point in worrying now, Abram," Parente said. He hoped the Russians would get sick of him, ship him out. The issuing of visas followed no pattern, made no sense. Long-time activists suddenly found themselves free to leave; anonymous people who never raised their voices would be kept waiting for months, years. There was still hope.

"He looks punk," Parente said to Hanson as they walked away.

"Who?" asked Hanson.

"Levitch. Sometimes I think we take advantage of the guy. All the space we give him, the way we run his stories. It can't be doing him any good."

"In Gorky Hospital, in psychiatric ward," Colonel Arkangeli was saying, in accented English, "in whole ward are twenty dissidents, my comrades from patriotic war, officers, heroes, honest men, all in hospital for what KGB calls mental problems. A lie. All sane, healthy. Drugs, injections, tied to beds. Please, you gentlemen from foreign press, tell world about us. Tell United Nations."

A big help they would be, Parente thought. The last time the UN debated the Afghanistan mess, not a single "Third World" spokesman dared mention the Soviet Union by name. *The other nation; the neighboring state.* A hell of a lot the UN cared about old Arkangeli, with his brains scrambled by too many beatings, jailings, drugs shot into his veins by the fraternal doctors of the USSR.

"Party tonight," Levitch said to the newsmen. "At the Bakofskys. To celebrate their departure. Please come."

Hanson stared at the envelope under Levitch's arm. The data he'd requested from Belus. He did not tell Parente. Nor did he waste time musing as to why Levitch hadn't given the papers to him right away. Probably the setting—too open, too public.

When Parente and Hanson, at eight-thirty that evening, reached the apartment building where the Bakofsky party was taking place, the older newsman stopped. The street was frost-covered, glistening.

"Volga sedan," Parente said. "Three, no four, of the fuzz."

"That's not unusual."

"And two more standing at the entrance to the apartment house."

"Six?"

Parente stopped. "Bad vibes." He halted Hanson. "Maybe we shouldn't go up. Or maybe we *should*. Screw them. If they're planning something heavy, it might help if you and I are around, Floyd."

"They don't scare me."

"You aren't Levitch."

They walked by two men in dark-gray overcoats. Parente recognized one of them: Blatnik, a "regular" assigned to Levitch, a drunken bum who followed Abram in and out of elevators, stores, public buildings. The other was the mammoth Rodenko, the former weight lifter.

"Whaddya say, pal?" Parente asked the cop. "How're they hanging?"

Blatnik smiled. He was not a bad sort, Levitch had told Tony. He didn't hit as hard as the others.

"You know what George Washington said to the Indian when he crossed the Delaware?" Parente asked Hanson as they entered the dim lobby. It was refrigerator-cold.

"I give up."

" *'Facc' una còzza de fredda.'* "

"What does that mean?"

" 'It's fucking cold.' You know what the Indian said to Washington? He said, *'Eppure tu Italiano!'* Never mind, you wouldn't get it. He said, 'Hey, you're a wop also!' "

In the elevator, Parente, peering back at one of the KGB men who was staring into the rising cage, gave the hoodlum the crook of his arm, slapping his left hand into it.

"Don't provoke them, Tony," Hanson said. "What if they get insulted?"

"They can't be insulted."

At the landing on the fourth floor, another KGB man was sitting on the steps reading *Red Star*.

"How'd the Mets do, buddy?" Parente asked him.

The man did not smile. He had a broad pockmarked face, lank black hair. He looked new to Parente, someone recruited to beef up the Jewish detail.

Parente rang the buzzer. He felt uneasy. Too many KGB men around the building. Unsubtle bastards. All-powerful, they didn't have to work scams or cons or ambushes. Who were they after? He was glad he and Hanson had come. The

American rabbi was also at the gathering. It might make it less likely that anyone would get roughed up or arrested.

Marfa Bakofsky came to the door. She was a small woman in her late thirties, her black hair piled high in a braided bun. She welcomed both newsmen warmly.

The room burst with people, was thick with cigarette smoke and loud voices. Through the good offices of Rabbi Goldman a table had been laden with sturgeon, smoked salmon, fresh vegetables.

Parente shook hands with the rabbi and introduced Hanson. "Father Goldman, tell this farmer Hanson who Red Sarachek is," Parente said.

"One of the greatest. My basketball coach."

Hanson looked bewildered.

In a corner, Levitch and Mikhail Semonski were going over the list of refuseniks, trying to guess why the Bakofskys had gotten their visas. They had no answer; it was caprice, the luck of the draw. Marfa was a midwife. Her husband, Fyodor, was a medical technician. They had a four-year-old son who would be allowed to leave with them. Neither had police records, but they had attended meetings.

"Maybe because they kept quiet," Semonski said. "We shout and complain and make trouble, so we stay."

"Someone has to shout," Levitch said.

Olga Semonski looked sadly at him, sipped tea from a cracked cup. Levitch knew what she was thinking—*maybe you, Abram Levitch, with your English language and your jokes, the fact that you are young and a little crazy. But why Mikhail and me? How did we get dragged into this? We should have kept our mouths shut, taken orders, obeyed the rulers.* . . .

Rabbi Goldman was discussing the formation of a new committee for Soviet Jewry in the United States with Parente, Agnes Wardle and Chaim Slesik. The last, gray-faced and unhealthily thin, like a man who has been drained by vampires, slouched on a low chair. His papery hands were clenched. He seemed defeated, resigned to a painful death in the Soviet Union.

Hanson watched, pityingly, as Levitch came over and patted Slesik's frail head, talked to him in a low voice. He seemed to be reassuring him that things would improve, that perhaps the issuance of the visa to the Bakofskys was a harbinger of better days to come. Once Slesik even smiled, grasped Levitch's hand, kissed him.

Hanson joined them and spoke a few vague encouraging words. They appreciated Hanson's blundering attempts at Russian, teased him about his enlistment in the cause of the refuseniks. It happened to most Western journalists, Levitch said, proof that decency and honor were not dead.

Levitch touched the inner pocket of his rust-colored pea coat. "Oh, Floyd, I almost forgot. I have something for you."

"Right. I saw Belus—"

Levitch held a finger to his lips. He gestured to Hanson to follow him into the dark foyer and gave him the tan envelope.

"For you," Levitch said. "But please, tell no one where you got it."

"Thanks, Abram. It's not the kind of stuff that can get anyone in trouble, I assure you."

"Medical information?"

"Yes. Material on brain experiments. It's out-of-channels, but no secret, not classified. For the article I'm doing on advances in surgery in the USSR."

Laughing softly, Levitch said, "Maybe they have a new operation for making people disappear and then turn up in Israel."

Stuffing the envelope into the inner pocket of his whiskey-colored suede blazer, Hanson saw Parente peering at them. Tell Tony or not? Hanson decided not to. Tony was a friend, but he didn't have to know everything. Besides, hadn't Parente himself said that foreign journalists in Russia had to scramble, connive, cheat and dig deep for information? The trick was to know in advance what would get the authorities' backs up, and what didn't bother them. Had not Dr. Tashenko assured him that her work was not secret and had in fact been duplicated in other countries?

"What are you guys doing?" Parente asked. "Trading baseball cards?"

"Information, Tony, just collecting information."

"I bet."

Something bothered Parente. He had a policeman's sense of imminent danger, infused in him by his late father, Sergeant Angelo Parente, 42nd Precinct, the Bronx, whose motto was *Ya gotta watch out*. He was tempted to convey his father's warning to Hanson, but Floyd had lost himself amid the party, and was earnestly asking the rabbi to explain the meaning of a seder.

Bleary-eyed, rasp-tongued after too many hours of cigarette smoke and intense talk, Parente and Hanson left the party as Rabbi Goldman distributed Haggadahs, leaflets that described the order of service for Passover. The Bakofskys were kissed, hugged and congratulated for the last time by the two newsmen.

"We'll expect you for the seder," Rabbi Goldman said. "Both of you."

"Couple of *goyim* like us?" Parente asked.

"The door is always open to the Gentile."

"Easy for me, Father Goldman. I used to be the *shabbes goy* of Tremont Avenue. Floyd here, he isn't much on asking the four questions. In Nebraska they think the four questions are a 4-H Club quiz."

They laughed. Parente liked the rabbi. A no-nonsense, gutsy man with a sense of public relations. He had actually gotten into the offices of some of the high Soviet officials in the Ministry of Internal Affairs to plead for the refuseniks.

"Nice party," Hanson said, as they stepped into the hallway. The pockmarked man sitting on the steps got up, tossed a smoldering butt onto the cracked floor.

"Hiyah, fellah," Parente said.

The caged elevator came clanking and banging upward. It halted with a shudder. To Parente's surprise, the KGB man got in with them, sighed, did not return Parente's grin.

"Not much eye contact here," Parente said.

They hit the lobby with an echoing metallic clank. The policeman stayed at the rear of the cage. Parente walked out first. Hanson followed him, hunched up in his sheepskin coat. He could feel the tan envelope forming a lump in the breast pocket of his jacket.

They were waiting for the Americans in the lobby. Four men abreast. Behind them—like a rook hiding behind pawns—stood Malik, bulging his gray coat, sucking on his steel-capped teeth.

"*Facc' una còzza de fredda,*" Parente said. "Baby, it's fucking cold."

He held Hanson's arm for a moment. "Let's try to hang

around. I have the feeling they're going to make a bust. This may be the last party our pal Levitch attends for a long time."

But it was not Levitch they sought. Malik muttered something to one of the four men. As he did, the pockmarked man grabbed Hanson's arms and yanked them back. Two other KGB men walked up, tore open the reporter's coat, frisked him, pulled the tan envelope from his jacket.

"What the hell is going on here?" Parente shouted. "Haven't you people heard of the Bill of Rights?"

Malik came forward. Parente recognized the flat face, the pale eyes. "You, Mr. Parente, go home. Mr. Hanson is under our care for a few hours. He is all right. He is safe."

"I'm going to the American Embassy and raise hell."

"Do as you wish."

"Hey, let go of my arms," Hanson pleaded. "Give me my notes back. Tony, what do I do now?"

"I dunno," Parente said. He turned to Malik. "You can't do this to an American. You can't haul him off in the middle of the night. Where he goes, I go."

Two of the KGB men grabbed Parente and gave him the bum's rush to the door. The journalist, burly and fit, struggled briefly, then realized it was pointless. They carried saps, guns, and there were far too many of them. He was escorted to his car.

"*Va fa in cuolo,*" Parente said.

He watched as they hustled Hanson across the icy street to a black sedan. Four of them got in with him, two in back, Malik and the driver up front.

Parente cursed, gunned the engine, cursed again when he flooded it, and took off for the American Embassy. His premonition had been right. His father's advice taunted him. *Ya gotta watch out.*

Hanson was taken to Lefortovo Prison, an ordinary white brick building on Eneryiske Ulitsa. He had never seen the neighborhood, but it seemed peaceful and pleasant—streetcar tracks, a few trees and a playground.

"What's this all about?" Hanson protested. "Mr. Malik, you know me. I'm a reporter. What can you possibly want?"

"Mr. Hanson, all will be explained."

"I want to call the American Embassy. You have no right to pull me off the street like this."

Malik roughly shoved him toward the door, across a paved driveway where the sedan had halted. A cold mist was falling, not quite rain, not quite snow. Hanson shuddered.

"This, this, Mr. Hanson," Malik said. He waved the thick envelope under the journalist's nose. "This is why you are here."

"Give them back to me. They're nothing. No secrets. Ordinary scientific papers. You have no right to do this."

"Please go in," Malik said.

Hanson was ushered past two glass booths in which KGB militiamen were on duty, then into a green-walled reception room. Malik ordered him to sit in a straight-backed chair.

"I protest this whole thing," Hanson said. He was dreadfully tired but oddly optimistic. And not frightened. They could do him no harm. And his arrest and detention (if indeed they intended to hold him) would make a front-page story, a lead for his magazine, possibly a series.

He watched Malik go into one of the glass booths and pick up a phone.

Karpov had left orders to be awakened. A nurse shook him gently. He was heavily sedated. Dr. Tashenko had switched him to phenobarbital after he complained that the phenytoin made him nauseous. He put on his quilted red satin robe and velvet slippers—an orderly had brought them from his flat—and walked to the nurse's station. He was furious that someone, apparently Colonel Dort, had ordered the phone removed from his room.

He heard Malik's coarse voice. "We got the American reporter, Comrade Major."

"With the papers?"

"In his coat."

"Hold him there an hour, then release him, but advise him he will be expected to be available tomorrow for further questioning."

"Ah, yes. Who shall handle this?"

"I will."

"You? I'm glad you're feeling better, Andrei Borisovich."

"I'm fully cured. Tell Hanson to report back to Lefortovo at three P.M. tomorrow. Advise Colonel Dort of everything that has happened."

"Take care of yourself, Comrade Major."

Karpov hung up. His head began to throb. He breathed
deeply, then asked the nurse for another phenobarbital. On
cautious feet he walked back to his bed. *Work, work.* That
would cure him. That would end the seizures.

He would dress in the morning and, with or without Irina
Tashenko's permission, go to Colonel Dort, pick up the loose
ends of the Levitch matter, and personally undertake the
interrogation of the fool Hanson, who—just as Karpov had
planned—had blundered into the trap.

Released after an hour, Hanson, enjoying his importance
and his freedom, found Parente waiting for him in his blue
Ford.

"Get in, farm boy. What happened?"

They drove through silent ill-lit streets. A drunken brawl
spilled off the sidewalk into the gutter—a groaning mass of
three or four dark bodies, flailing padded arms, rough shoes
kicking. Parente skidded around them.

"I have to come back tomorrow at three."

"Why?"

Hanson ducked his head. "Some notes I had with me.
They took them."

"What kind of notes?"

"Oh, medical information for my article."

Parente's eyes were bleak, yet full of pity. "Who gave them
to you?"

"Levitch."

Groaning, Parente accelerated. "Jesus. So that's it."

"What's it?"

"They don't care doodly squat about you. They're after
Abram. Didn't I tell you to be careful of accepting information like that? Levitch'll be in the clink, maybe worse."

"I'm sorry. But it doesn't reflect on Abram. I asked Dr.
Belus to get me some material—legitimate stuff, nothing
secret. You see . . ." He paused, aware of Parente's scowl.
"That Tashenko dame was giving me a hard time. Didn't
want to see me again, not willing to talk. I figured if I read up
on her experiments, I'd be better equipped to con her into
another session. Also, it would help me sell the story to New
York."

"So Belus got you the papers?"

"No problem. How secret can they be? I mean, how harmful to anyone, if a drip like Belus, a refusenik—"

"He's no refusenik. Go on."

"Anyway, he got them for me, and I guess he handed them over to Levitch, and Abram gave them to me at the Bakofskys. That's it, Tony. Believe me, there isn't a thing in those papers that hasn't been published somewhere. I stressed that to Belus. Rats stimulating their brains with electric jolts."

Parente sighed. *Where to? What now?* Informing the embassy was no help. They'd have plenty of time in the morning. He would tell Floyd to insist that an embassy officer go with him to Lefortovo in the afternoon. Once home he would contact Levitch and warn him to be on guard. Then he would file a story on Hanson's detention. Or would he? Going public with it might make it tougher for Levitch. Then again, Parente thought, he might be Kelly-sledding, anticipating the worst. Maybe all they were after was Hanson and the papers. Maybe Levitch was incidental.

"Wonder what they'll ask me tomorrow," Hanson said.

Icy yellow streetlights hovered over them, charged the sky with an amber mist. They halted at a red light near the foreign compounds.

"Maybe they want the NCAA basketball results," Parente muttered.

He dropped Hanson outside his apartment building. There was a KGB plainclothesman on duty with the uniformed militiaman. They were making sure Hanson kept his appointment.

"Leave Levitch out of it," Parente said.

"Of course I will. He had nothing to do with this. He happened to be the guy Belus gave the papers to. Belus knew Abram sees American reporters all the time and—"

"Yeah. Get a night's sleep. I'll bring as many foreign newsmen as I can hustle up to Lefortovo. We go to the mattresses, Flerd. Stand up, I got a bet on you."

"Thanks, Tony."

The plainclothesman asked for Hanson's ID before letting him enter the compound.

"Dr. Tashenko says you are quite ill, that you shouldn't be here."

Colonel Dort, like a mushroom or a nocturnal mammal,

favored dark rooms. The curtains were drawn in his square green office. Lenin, immortalized in yellow metal inside a metal star, deprived of natural light, looked vaguely African.

"I'm much better, Comrade Colonel."

Dort opened a folder on his desk. Karpov understood: a medical report on him.

"Since it was I who initiated the plan to use the American, I have a right to see it to its conclusion," Karpov said. He was giddy, a persistent pain in his left temple—not the hard-throbbing headache, but a low-grade pressure.

" 'Patient suffers from *grand mal* seizures of unknown origin. The severity of the seizures may intensify, since thus far there is little evidence the patient has responded to drug treatment.' " Dort blinked.

"Nonsense. Dr. Tashenko is being overly cautious. Do I look ill?"

"Pale, Karpov. Almost milky."

"It's your lamp. Tashenko is a great neurologist, but she obviously is trying to restrict my work. For reasons known to both of us."

As oblivious as a stone mountain, Dort read on. " 'More severe epileptic seizures may result in life-threatening acidosis or hypoxia.' Whatever that means. Oh, I understand life-threatening. We can't put you in such a vulnerable position, Andrei Borisovich."

"I am in good health. The tests were normal. The EEG was normal."

"Not according to this report. During your last seizure it showed 'abnormal spiking.' I can interpret that. Brain waves. Zigzag up and down, correct? You are one of my best men, Karpov, but how can I endanger you like this? Worse, how can I endanger our work, if you are subject to these fits, losses of consciousness? Who knows what you may start blabbing when you're in this condition or when you're full of drugs?"

"She has not even given the medication a chance to work," Karpov said irritably. "Let me handle Hanson this afternoon. I'll wring everything you want out of him. Then we can proceed with the rest of the operation."

"I was going to let Malik do it."

"That idiot. He can't speak six words of English. We've known each other for a long time, Comrade Colonel. You don't approve of the way I live, my tastes, my needs. I'm aware of that. But when have I failed you? When have I failed the Second Directorate?"

"I want no first occasion, Karpov." He locked his fat pink hands. "Go on. Handle the Hanson matter."

Parente took Hanson to the American Embassy on Tchaikovsky Street at ten in the morning. Treva Siddons, the political officer, was terribly upset. New in the post, she spent an hour phoning for instructions, talked to Washington, got the ambassador out of a meeting with a Jaycee touring group, and finally agreed to accompany Hanson to his afternoon meeting.

"What does it mean, Tony?" she asked.

"It isn't Hanson they're after. It's Levitch."

"Poor man."

Hanson tugged at his blond beard. "I'm sorry. But Levitch has nothing to do with this. I can prove that. Oh, he's told me about refuseniks, dissidents, those kinds of things. But this business with the neurological research—he wasn't party to that. If anyone should be in hot water it's Dr. Belus."

"Yeah," Parente said. "But you asked Belus for the papers, didn't you?"

"So what? It's done all the time. You told me yourself. Reporters here get lots of unofficial information. As distinguished from illegal information."

Treva Siddons listened attentively. She dialed a contact in the Soviet Foreign Ministry and talked to him at length. He knew nothing of Hanson's detention and the interrogation set for the afternoon.

"It's out of his hands, he says," she told the journalists.

"It always is when the KGB runs the show," Parente said. New fears, new terrors germinated in him. He felt helpless, unarmed.

Leaving the Embassy, Parente told Hanson he'd assemble the foreign press outside Lefortovo. Let the KGB know the story was out and that it was going to be a worldwide scandal.

"What can happen to me, Tony?" the younger man asked. He did not seem frightened.

"You'll probably be booted out."

"But I've only been here two months. My big chance. My career."

"Forget it. You can write a book. I'm not worried about you, kid. It's Levitch. That little guy may have a load dropped on him."

"I wish I could help."

"Tell the bastards the truth. Levitch had nothing to do with those papers. He was set up. I'd like to get Belus alone in a hotel room and pry something out of him. Good luck, kid."

It took all morning for Parente to track Abram Levitch down. Apparently he had spent the night sleeping on a sofa at Chaim Slesik's place, made some phone calls at Nadya Burik's, and then tried his luck trading dollars for rubles at the university. The usual cadre of KGB men had followed him, letting him engage in less-than-rewarding currency dealings.

"Building the case, Abram," Parente said sorrowfully. He had located Abram back at Slesik's cramped flat, and had told both of them about Hanson's arrest.

"They can arrest me anytime they want. Why all this fuss with Floyd?"

Parente shrugged. He did not want his gloom to be contagious, to spread to the refuseniks. He invited them to lunch. Slesik was too ill to go. He was heavily dosed with pain-killers, settling into a twilight state. Less pain, less awareness, he told Tony. Not a bad way to be when one had so little hope, Chaim said.

"If they want to make an example of someone," Slesik whispered, "let them take me. I'm burned out. Abram's young. Young wife. A future."

"Getting older every day," Levitch laughed. "Who's afraid? What can they do to me? Chaim, we'll bring you something. Some liver dumplings maybe? A lamb sandwich?"

"Nothing. Another advantage of cancer. Loss of appetite. Thirsty all the time. I could use two bottles of mineral water."

In the street Parente struggled to keep from weeping. *Sentimental wop,* he told himself. Slesik. Levitch. The Semonskis. All of them braver than he was, braver than he could ever be. Fat, happy, prosperous Americans. Did they know how lucky they were? Slesik, that honorable man, wanting only two bottles of mineral water. Anger replaced sorrow. Parente was seized with a hard hatred for the policemen, the jailers, the brutes and Fascists who ran the goddamned country.

Over dumpling soup and black bread in a messy neighborhood café, a place filled with husky workmen and pale office types, Parente told Levitch he was fearful Abram would be taken into custody.

"You are probably right, Tony. What is there to do?"

"Find Belus. It's your only chance."

"So he'll back me up? He got some medical papers for Hanson? And I had nothing to do with it?"

"That's the idea. How much do you know about Belus?"

"Not much. From Kiev. Lost most of his family to the Germans. Divorced. He was once with us, but no more. No interest in emigrating or Israel. He skipped the Passover seder last year. But always sympathetic."

"What do they have on him?"

Levitch shoved his soup away. He had no appetite. "Something, I guess. His ex-wife was a Komsomol officer. A big party member, turned against him. He's got a brother who got into trouble. He was fencing hospital drugs on the black market."

"Why should he be any different? Without the black market the Soviet economy would collapse."

"Well, he was a good addition to our group. A doctor, a car."

Parente paid the check. "Find him."

At Slesik's apartment—Chaim was in sedated sleep—they tried without success to locate Dr. Belus. He was not at his office, nor at either of the two clinics, nor at home.

Parente, after much inquiring, was able to get the director of one of the clinics. The physician was a woman with a harsh voice.

"Dr. Belus is no longer with us."

"Resigned?" Parente asked. "Since when?"

"He was called to Magnitogorsk. His mother is ill. He may be gone a long time."

They tried the Semonskis, Nadya, Mikhail Zolkin. None had any information on Belus. The earth (or at least Magnitogorsk) had swallowed him.

"So?" Levitch asked.

"I don't know. If they grab you, Abram, get word to me as fast as possible."

They listened to Chaim Slesik's labored breathing. Poor sucker, Parente thought. He's out of it. And Levitch may soon be out of it, too.

Treva Siddons was not allowed to accompany Hanson to the inner office. She was seated in the green anteroom, where she protested the incident.

"Representations will be made on the highest level," she told a minor functionary. He was not impressed.

Hanson was led through gray metal doors that opened when a combination was tapped into a set of buzzers. He was accompanied by a uniformed guard and the man he now knew as Captain Malik of the Jewish Department. The hallways were dark, floored with stained linoleum. The few windows—high and gray—were heavily barred.

A third door brought them into a larger room than the one in which Malik had spoken to him. Green walls, the usual Soviet artwork—Lenin, the Red Star, a hammer and sickle, a faded reproduction of a painting of the cruiser *Aurora*.

Two men awaited him. One was stout and bald. His neck at its base was as wide as the broadest part of the man's bleached face. It was a physical conformation Hanson had often noticed on interior linemen in his home state of Iowa.

To Hanson's surprise, the other man was Dr. Lermontov, the physician who was present when Hanson interviewed Irina Tashenko. Hanson blinked at the graceful figure. Dark-blue suit. Black shoes with the look of English leather. A dapper man, with a lean, faintly eroded face. What was he doing here?

"Oh, hi, Dr. Lermontov," Hanson said. "What a relief to see you. You were there when I interviewed Dr. Tashenko. You can explain it all, I'm sure."

There was a moment of ticking silence—Dort looking at Karpov, the two of them amused by the young man's innocence. It would be hard painting such a guileless man as an enemy of the Soviet Union. Still, there was a job to be done.

"Mr. Hanson," the stout man said, in an accent suggesting spoiled borscht, "you are mistaken. This gentleman is my associate, Major Karpov. He is not Dr. Lermontov. I am Colonel Dort."

I'm losing my marbles, Hanson thought. *Lermontov. It had to be him. The cool dude in the white coat. Sitting next to Dr. Tashenko.* He wished they had let Treva Siddons come with him. She would know the ropes. What they could ask him, what they couldn't. What he should do, say, plead. Better yet, Parente, that street-smart New York Italian. He felt air-headed.

"No, no. You're the doctor who—"

"Enough, Mr. Hanson. You are disturbed, upset." Dort said something in Russian to Karpov. Karpov closed his eyes and nodded.

"Mr. Hanson," Karpov said. "I shall read to you a statement delivered to your embassy by our Ministry of Foreign Affairs an hour ago. It reads, in part, as follows: 'The American journalist Floyd Elliot Hanson, citizen of the United States, born in 1951, has engaged in activities incompatible with his status as foreign journalist accredited to the USSR, specifically, the collection of secret information of a political and military character.

" 'Mr. Hanson was apprehended on the thirteenth of March of this year, carrying in his possession scientific documents of a secret, classified nature, which he secured illegally, under suspicious circumstances. In doing so, Mr. Hanson violated several laws of the USSR. He was observed to have these papers in his possession after leaving a meeting of so-called dissident citizens, criminals and parasites who themselves have been in violation of the laws of the Soviet Union.

" 'The Ministry of Foreign Affairs takes this opportunity to advise all American journalists now in the USSR that they must not follow Mr. Hanson's example, and that they must conform to the laws of the country in which they are guests.

" 'Further, Mr. Hanson will be required to attend interrogations, and until such interrogations are concluded to the satisfaction of the authorities, he is not to leave Moscow.' "

Hanson managed a weak smile. "I guess that says it all." He took out a notebook and started to jot down some of what Dort had read to him.

"You are not here as a journalist," Karpov said. "Put the pen and the pad away."

"Self-protection." Hanson was pleased with his courage. "Why can't I?"

"It will not be necessary," Karpov said. "You'll receive a

complete report on all that occurs in these interviews. In fact, you will be asked to sign it and verify its accuracy."

"What if I won't?"

Again Dort whispered to Karpov. Then the colonel got up, looked past Hanson and left. Karpov and the American were alone.

"We'll cross that bridge later," Karpov said.

"I don't get it. Who are you? A doctor? A cop? Both? I know I saw you."

"Someone who resembled me, perhaps?"

"You, *you*. The voice. The perfect English. What the heck, you're in charge. I have nothing to hide. I'll tell you what you want to know."

"Good. How long have you known Abram Levitch?"

"Abram? A few weeks. Mr. Parente introduced me. Not that Levitch is hard to know. Every foreign journalist in Moscow knows him. Better than they know anyone in the KGB, for sure."

"What kind of discussions have you had with Levitch?"

"Mostly about refuseniks. Problems with visas. Persecutions. The usual Jewish problems. Anti-Semitism. Violations of the Helsinki agreements."

"Have you discussed scientific matters with him?"

"No. He's a math teacher. Or he was. Look, if you mean those medical papers, he had nothing to do with them. He was just a sort of courier—"

"Courier?"

"I mean, he got them from . . . someone . . . got them from . . ."

"Yes?"

Hanson was hesitant about mentioning Dr. Belus. The KGB surely knew the routing of the neurological papers. But Hanson was reluctant to mention anyone's name. He crossed his legs. "Suppose I don't want to answer any of your questions. I've done nothing wrong. None of my contacts has. Suppose I say to heck with it, and clam up?"

"Clam?"

"Dummy up. Just stop talking."

Karpov leaned forward. He clasped his long corded hands and lowered his head. Lights winked on his aristocratic forehead. He suggested to Hanson a Russified Giscard d'Estaing, or that Danish count who had been tried in Rhode

Island for zonking his rich wife. A kind of fatless grace. But cold; ice-cube cold.

"Mr. Hanson, you are under Soviet law. You are without diplomatic immunity under Soviet law. You have no choice but to answer."

"I repeat, what if I refuse?"

Hanson waited for a response, got none. Instead, Karpov was bending his head and pressing his hands against his temple. His eyes were locked and his mouth taut. He remained in this position a few seconds, uttered an audible gasp, as if battling excruciating pain, then forced himself to look up.

"Is anything wrong, Major Karpov? Are you okay?"

The lunacy of the situation was not lost on Hanson. Here he sat, in the grip of a KGB officer who had killed, tortured, jailed and otherwise maltreated God knows how many Russian citizens and foreigners. And he found himself feeling sorry because the bastard had a headache. *A headache!*

"I am all right. Your question . . . ?"

"What if I refuse to answer?"

"You will be held here until you do."

"You can't do that to me. I'm an American."

"Without immunity. A violator of our laws. Now tell me everything, Mr. Hanson. Who got those papers for you? Levitch? Slesik? Dr. Belus?"

"I get it. It's a television game. Name That Jew. Sorry, I won't play."

Karpov sighed. "You must realize we know everything you've been doing, all the people you have talked to. Perhaps you would rather discuss your work for the CIA. You are, of course, a member of the CIA. We have evidence to prove you are."

"*Hah? Whah?*" Hanson's mouth widened. His beard fluttered and his cornflower-blue eyes were the size of bar coasters. "I've never heard such bullshit in my life. Listen up, Karpov or Lermontov, or whoever you are. You got the wrong number. I've never run errands for the CIA or anyone else. You must have looked at those medical papers. Some brain experiments with rats. Hey, man, I want to go."

"Tell us about your connections with Dr. Belus."

"What about him?"

"How and where you met him, how he worked with you."

"I met him at one of the refusenik meetings. He volunteered to help me get the appointment with Dr. Tashenko.
You were there when I spoke to her! Then I asked him to
help me get the papers, the ones your guys stole from me.
That's it."

"Is it?"

"Yes. And leave Levitch out of it. He had nothing to do
with it. Not him, not Slesik, none of them."

Karpov opened a drawer in the desk and took out the tan
envelope. "You had time to look these over?"

"Hell, no." As soon as he said it, Hanson wondered if it
were the right answer.

A smile distorted Karpov's lips.

"I mean, they're in Russian anyway. I was going to have
them translated."

"They contain, Mr. Hanson, a great deal more than routine
reports on brain research. They are full of classified information.
Secret military information which proves that you and certain
Soviet citizens are engaged in espionage."

Gray-coated militiamen armed with Kalashnikov rifles kept
Parente and his fellow journalists a block away from Lefortovo
prison. Miss Wardle had turned out, as well as two West
Germans and Brian Cardwell.

Parente checked his watch. It was five. The sky was
darkening. A cold northerly wind was rising. Bare branches
fluttered. Dark birds circled, went into an aerial fandango,
settled on cracked cornices, barren trees.

"Bad news, bad news," Parente said. "He's in there too
long."

"This is appalling," Miss Wardle said.

"Tony, what good are we doing him here?" Dieter Schultze,
the West German photographer, asked.

"Show of strength. Let the bastards know we know, and we
aren't happy."

Fifteen minutes later, in the misty darkness, Hanson came
out of the prison. He was accompanied by Treva Siddons.

The militiamen kept the foreign reporters well back. Hanson and the woman from the embassy were allowed to join
the others under the leafless trees. Bundled kids shouted in
the playground. An old man selling *kvass* wheeled his cart
past them.

"How did it go, Floyd?"

"You were right, Tony. It had to do with Levitch."

Miss Wardle was scrawling notes. "What did they say?" she asked.

"They claim Levitch gave me secret military information. That's nonsense. All I wanted was stuff on brain experiments with rats. I hadn't even looked at it."

"What else?" Parente asked.

"I had to sign something called a protocol."

"You signed it?"

"What else could I do? I'd be there forever. It wasn't a confession or anything like that, and I didn't implicate anyone. Just what went on at the interrogation. That I knew Levitch, and Slesik and Dr. Belus, and that I got some papers from Levitch. That's all."

"Doesn't seem much harm in that," Agnes Wardle said.

"Who talked to you?" Parente asked.

"Well, at first a big guy, Colonel Dort."

"Top cop," Parente said. "KGB heavy hitter. Who else?"

"This was crazy. I'd swear he was a doctor, a Dr. Lermontov who was with Tashenko when I interviewed her. But they insisted it was a mistake. His name was Karpov. Major Karpov."

Parente swallowed. "Yeah, the brain. The only KGB officer who wears Turnbull and Asser shirts. Skinny guy, high forehead, perfect English?"

"That's him. He was using a phony name and keeping his eye on Dr. Tashenko the first time I saw him."

"What else, Floyd?" Cardwell asked.

"Nothing much. I have the feeling they may boot me out. Unless they want to keep hammering at me about Levitch. I told them all I knew. Which wasn't much. Holy smoke, all this fuss over some papers? I don't get it."

"A very suspicious people," Parente said. "Come on. Let's visit our friends." He could not find it in his heart to fault Hanson, to criticize him. Again the cold fears made him shiver, forced him to think of Levitch. His mind raced ahead: What could he do to stop them? How could he save Levitch, protect him?

6

APPROACHING NADYA BURIK'S building, where, Parente had learned, Levitch was due to spend the night after a meeting with Rabbi Goldman, the two American newsmen halted, astonished by what they saw.

Levitch was walking toward them, past a row of ramshackle stores. He was not alone. Instead of the two or three KGB men who usually tailed him, he was enclosed by *eight* policemen in civilian dress—bulky dark coats, ill-fitting hats. They surrounded him. Three on each side, a point man, a rear guard.

"A new one on me," Parente said. "Eight guys."

"Ah, Tony, Floyd." Levitch grinned from inside the human wall. "Look—my cage. Yuri, Ivan, Nikita, Boris, Alyosha, Karel, Pavel, and one fellow who won't give me his name. What have I done to deserve such attention?"

The party halted. Parente blinked. Eight men, surrounding one small, short-of-breath, unarmed Jew. Parente had a momentary vision of photos from the Warsaw ghetto: a line of Nazi soldiers leveling rifles at women and children. Helpless people, shabbily dressed, arms raised.

Parente spoke in Russian to the point man. "What's this all about, comrade? You guys going to encircle Levitch everywhere he goes?"

"Go away."

"Come on, talk. What is this, a new Olympic sport? Eight cops and a Jew?"

"I said move away or you'll be sorry."

In English, Parente said, "Up yours too, Jack. Abram, they don't follow you inside, do they?"

"No, just in the halls, outside the door, the elevators. They're not a bad group. They haven't hit me once."

Entering the doors of Nadya Burik's building was a mob scene. The eight guards jostled one another, squeezed against Levitch's stubby body, reassembled themselves in the lobby. Four stayed below. Four followed him up the steps.

"Like protozoa," Parente said to Hanson. "Tropisms. They respond to light stimuli, with no understanding of what they're doing." He shouted at Levitch: "Hang in there, Abram. Help is on the way."

Inside the apartment Hanson reported on his session with the KGB. Levitch seemed unperturbed. Parente was not. He was certain the increased guard was related to the interrogation. They were getting ready to pounce.

"I'm not afraid," Levitch said airily. "Now that the Bakofskys have their visas, why not me? They'll be glad to get rid of me."

Disturbed, Rabbi Goldman was on the phone, trying to call some sympathetic senators in Washington.

Oddly buoyant, Levitch displayed photographs of his wife, Sarah, pictures that had arrived in the morning mail. She looked pretty and tanned, standing in front of a cinder-block house bordered with flowery shrubs at a kibbutz in the Galilee.

"See, see, Tony," Levitch cried. "All is for the best. How can I not be hopeful when Sarah sends me pictures, when she is so beautiful?"

For a mathematician, Parente thought, he is not much on logic.

They could hear the rabbi in the next room. "Senator? Senator? Dave Goldman in Moscow. We need your help. It's going to get sticky here."

Nadya Burik shook her leonine head. "They hear every word. What good can it do us? They know, they know."

"You'll see," Levitch said. "I'll be in Jerusalem in three months."

"What do I do now?" Colonel Dort shouted into the phone. "You're his doctor. Why in the devil's name did you let him out? What good is he to me?"

On the toxic-green carpet of the office in which Hanson had been interrogated and made to sign the protocol a half hour earlier, Karpov jerked and kicked in the grip of a *grand mal* seizure.

Dort's frightened secretary had called for an ambulance. As usual there were problems, false starts, the vehicle going to Lubianka instead of Lefortovo. A grim joke, Dort thought; probably the driver was thinking about some miserable bastard who'd taken a bit more questioning than was good for him.

"Put him in a prone position," Irina Tashenko said. Her voice was cold. "Head down to prevent aspiration. Loosen his tie and belt and take off his shoes."

"Jerking like a perch on a line," Dort bellowed. "His eyes are rolling around; he's pissed his pants. He's out, out."

"He should recover in a matter of minutes. Make sure a passageway is kept open for air. When the doctor arrives he'll know what to do. If he has trouble breathing, he will have to be intubated."

"I want him back in your hospital, goddammit. I want him there until he's recovered. Understood?"

"Yes, Comrade Colonel."

Dort thought: *You slept with him, licked him, kissed him, did whatever the fancy bastard wanted. Now get him better.* Dort was in the midst of the Levitch business. Karpov was his architect, his grand conniver. Karpov had written the script. Now he lay flopping and twitching on the floor, his crotch a dark wet stain, his eyes darting about, his jaw clenched.

They had been going over Dr. Belus's statement, the key to the Levitch business. The Belus letter, awaiting only the physician's signature, lay on the desk. In mid-sentence—*since 1975 I have worked as an agent of the American CIA and have recruited members from among the so-called dissidents—*

Karpov let out a shriek, turned into a wooden board, flopped across the desk and crashed his nose against the glass top. Blood gushed from the nostrils. He had rolled over, hit the floor with a noise suggesting he was made of oak or limestone, and lay there, unconscious, immobile, all but dead. Then the convulsions had begun.

Two medical orderlies in soiled white suits were ushered in by Dort's secretary.

"Get him out of here. To the Neurological Institute. He's Dr. Tashenko's patient."

Karpov's tortured eyes opened, wandered aimlessly, saw nothing.

"He's got to calm down before we can move him," one of the orderlies said.

"As soon as possible," Dort snapped.

Slowly, Karpov's body began to return to normal. Astonishingly, he tried to raise himself on one elbow. The orderly pushed him back into the prone position, rolled up his sleeve, and began to prepare a syringe.

An Italian journalist, Guido Arbetta, from the Communist daily *L'Unità*, arranged to interview Levitch. They met on the steps of the Pushkin Museum. The eight-man team, Levitch's "cage," stood a few yards away, joking, smoking, reading sports magazines. Two of them lounged several yards behind Levitch and the reporter. The other six sat on the steps.

"This is crazy, *pazzo*," Arbetta said. "Eight men just for you?" He spoke good, if accented, English. Levitch's English was crisper, more colloquial.

"I am a person of importance in the USSR. A menace to the state."

The Italian shook his head. He was reed-thin and gray-haired, with a cross-notched face, a veteran of the Partisans, an old friend of Togliatti, Longo and others who had shaped the party in Italy. He chain-smoked and fluttered his hands.

"It is hard for me to believe," the journalist said. "Anti-Semitism in Russia? The anti-Fascist motherland? Your people—the Russians—died by the millions to save us from the Nazis, all sorts of Fascist swine. Why this?"

Ah, the burdens of history, Levitch thought. Collections of collective memory. And Babi Yar, with not a word that the victims were Jews. He sniffed the mild air. Passover was coming. Renewal, spring, life again. He craved Sarah.

"My friend, we know all that," Levitch said patiently. "It is all the more reason for the leaders of the Soviet Union to behave decently. But why argue? I'm sorry for the millions of Soviet citizens who perished, the starvation, the shootings. But why not learn from it? Answer: They are in a grand European tradition, a great Christian tradition, and now a Communist tradition. When the system fails, when people are angry, when ideologies clash, beat up Jews. If necessary, kill them."

"But no one is killing Russian Jews."

"No, not in great numbers and not methodically. But they are trying to destroy our souls. We want to leave. We are unwanted here, shamed, forced out of jobs, made to practice petty crimes to survive. Why? Why all this fuss over a few Jews? Lunacy. Here, enjoy some official reading from the state printing house."

Levitch reached in his jacket and got out two dog-eared pamphlets. He gave them to the Italian.

"I'm sorry, Levitch, but my Russian is virtually nonexistent."

"So look at the pictures."

Arbetta did, and was revolted. Jews with huge noses, greedy eyes, hands like claws, fat, ugly, hideous monsters, escapees from Julius Streicher's vile Nazi magazine, gutter caricatures. The anti-Semitism of thugs, street hoodlums, the scum of *lumpen* Europe.

Levitch saw the horror on the Italian's face. "Standard stuff in the schools, Arbetta. Here is a new edition of *The Protocols of the Elders of Zion*. Every time the grain harvest falls below its norm, or there are rumblings of discontent among steel workers, you can count on a new edition of this classic."

Arbetta turned pages. More horror pictures. Jews as rats, snakes and loathsome toads. Encircling the world, stealing bread from Soviet children, murdering Arabs, chaining Africans.

"I shall write about this in my paper."

"We will be grateful. I assume you will clear it with your editor. You see, Arbetta, I was once a party member, and I know how it works. God forbid one of you should be allowed an independent thought. I often wonder. How did all those American and European intellectuals—writers, critics, scientists—how did they stay so long with Marxism, knowing what it had become?"

"They were anti-Fascist, Levitch."

"Not good enough. Take a look at the other book."

Unfortunately, there were no illustrations. Levitch translated the title for him: *The Creeping Counter-Revolution*.

"On a more elevated level. The worldwide Zionist conspiracy to take over the Middle East, then the oil fields, then everything else. It could have been written by Himmler."

Chaim Slesik, bent with pain, waved to Levitch. He walked up the steps of the museum, dragging his spare, ravaged body. He clutched a newspaper.

"Abram, Abram," Slesik called. He waved the paper. It was the latest edition of *Pravda*.

"What is it, Chaim?"

Tourists and Muscovites strolled by them on the wide steps. A group of East Germans in shorts, nylon socks and open-toed sandals (in defiance of the brisk weather and in acknowledgment of the pale sun) trooped past. They gave off an odor of potatoes and menace.

"Belus."

Levitch blinked. "What about him?"

The Italian journalist cocked his head and tried to pick up a word of Russian. As a party member for many years, he had once tried to learn the language but had given up when he could never recall whether there were seven or nine cases.

"His confession," Slesik said. "A whole page of it."

"What is he confessing? That he meets with us? Everyone knows that."

"Belus, dear Vanya. He has stabbed us, delivered a death blow. He says he worked for the CIA. That we all worked for him. That every one of us is a spy and traitor, and we have violated the laws of the Soviet Union. Read it."

In English, Arbetta asked, "What is happening?"

"I don't know yet, *amico*," Levitch said.

Slesik gave the paper to Levitch, then rested his tortured body against the balustrade. It was odd; faced with the horror of Belus's lying indictment, Slesik felt calm, soothed. His abdominal pains had diminished. Could they have been in his mind? Impossible. But he did know of cases where mental torment reduced physical pain. The body could take only so much. It quit after a while. It accepted the inevitable. As he should have years ago.

Levitch read aloud. " 'I, Dr. Ivan Belus, Candidate of Medical Sciences, of Moscow, USSR, do with this letter declare that I have been in the pay, and at the command, of the Central Intelligence Agency since April of last year, and that in my role as a CIA agent, I did enlist the services and cooperation of the Jewish dissident movement in the Soviet Union.' "

The Italian pleaded for translation. Levitch obliged him. Then he said, "Some distribution list. He sends this statement not only to *Pravda* but to the United States Congress, the Presidium, and the UN. Everyone but B'Nai B'Rith. Ah, Vanya, Vanya, our yellow-headed doctor with the easy smile and the pacifying injections."

"He has signed our death warrants," Slesik said. The voice was hollow. Pigeons wheeled and dipped overhead. Slesik's weary eyes sought the sky, stared at the contrail of a jet. Escape. Freedom.

" 'In my capacity as CIA informer, I was recruited by Mr. Harrison Eaves of the United States Embassy, now returned to his CIA activities in Washington. I also was advised to aid the CIA by correspondents Anthony Parente and Brian Cardwell. The former is an American. The latter holds dual citizenship in Britain and the United States, and has been connected with the Israeli intelligence organization Mossad.' "

"Cardwell?" asked Levitch. "That string bean with the fishy eyes? A spy? This is garbage, Chaim Yankelovich."

"A man can be suffocated in garbage."

Levitch read on. " 'On orders from Eaves and Cardwell, I have spied on the Soviet scientific community for the past year and recruited others to assist me in these treasonous endeavors.' "

Agitated, the Italian requested a translation. Levitch obliged him. Arbetta rolled his eyes. Cardwell? Everyone knew he was a party member. How could he be working for the CIA? Then it dawned on him. "Of course. That is exactly how. Because he is working for the KGB."

Levitch laughed softly. "Vanya really goes on. 'At meetings in the flats of Chaim Slesik, Mikhail Semonski and others of the Zionist clique, I learned that these so-called dissidents were concerned with distorting the aims and views of the peace-loving Soviet Union under the guise of requesting emigration. A great fuss and hullabaloo was raised about their alleged persecution, all of it a screen for treasonous activities designed to poison the international atmosphere.

" 'Their aim is to slander the Soviet system and create tension between fraternal Socialist nations and the West. In this regard, they have been abetted by M. Zolkin, the scientist, who has been enticed into their group and adds his voice to the blackguarding of the USSR, in the name of so-called "human rights." I am happy now to expose them, to admit my past association as a CIA informer, to confess all my crimes, and to reveal to the world the hoaxes and crimes of this group.

" 'Particularly, I wish to denounce the activities of Abram Moiseivich Levitch—' "

Levitch halted and held the newspaper away. He arched his eyebrows and smiled.

"Why do you smile, Abram?" asked Slesik.

"What else can I do?"

"We all suspected him and we all went along."

"He had a car and he gave us pills."

The eight members of Levitch's "cage" had gotten wind of what he was reading. They smiled, nudged one another, lit cigarettes. Slesik heard Gorchakov, the photographer, say, "The little Yid's caught it. He won't be needing us for long. . . ."

"But who would believe he would do this?" asked Levitch. "Really, who?"

Slesik coughed. It was the sound of death. "He was threatened, Abram. You believe that trash about the CIA? He was *told* to approach them by the KGB, by your friend Karpov. Belus was perfect. Charming, spoke English, a sort of dissident. Meanwhile, they've got a file on him as thick as the Talmud. If he steps out of line, he's finished."

"Parente never hinted at it."

"Tony? He probably didn't know. I doubt he ever used Belus as a source. Tony is too smart. But think of the way Belus was helpful to Hanson. The Tashenko matter. Why Belus?"

"He's a physician. He knew her. And he also knew Hanson. And he knew I see American reporters all the time. It's logical." Levitch rubbed his nose. "That's what Karpov must have thought. It worked."

Levitch read on. " 'To increase tensions between the USSR and the West, Levitch and others of his cabal plotted with Western journalists, among them Floyd Hanson, to steal secret data from Soviet scientists and make it available to the CIA. Many such incidents will be brought to light, but the most recent, and the most serious, concerns the theft of data about defense-related experiments in neurology, stolen by the aforementioned Levitch and illegally passed to Hanson.

" 'All of this was conducted by CIA agents in the American Embassy, including one Treva Siddons, who poses as a political officer, and by several American journalists, among them the aforementioned Hanson and Parente.

" 'All this should make clear how these alleged dissidents are actually Zionist imperialists and neo-Fascists, and are deliberately exploiting the so-called question of human rights in the interests of imperialism and world reaction.

" 'As for my own role as a CIA agent, I profoundly apologize to my fellow citizens of the USSR, and I am honored to enter the battle against the renegades, traitors and spies who are seeking to destroy the Soviet Union. I could not live with my conscience if I did not expose deceivers like Levitch, Slesik and others who prattle on about their Zionist homeland, but seek only to defame the USSR.

" 'I call on the Congress of the United States, as well as the United Nations, to investigate immediately these nefarious deeds by the CIA and its agents, these traitors and criminals who work against world peace and harmony.' "

Arbetta took more notes. Abram gave him a digest of Belus's letter.

Levitch smiled at Slesik. "An achievement by our friend. He'll be in the history books."

Slesik breathed deeply. "So will we, Abram, so will we."

What has happened? the Italian journalist wondered. *How did our glorious Red banners become smeared with slime and shit? Who did this to our noble revolution?*

"I hope I have fulfilled my part," Dr. Belus said.

"Thus far." Karpov, sitting up in bed, his back propped by three eiderdown pillows, scanned the letter in *Pravda*. On the table next to him was a thick file on the Levitch case. He had been reviewing Belus's work for the KGB.

"And I hope Comrade Major is feeling better. These persistent headaches can be bothersome." He did not know that Karpov had been in the grip of convulsions. After the seizure in Dort's office, Karpov had returned to the hospital. A day later he had a more violent attack. The drugs did not appear to relieve the terrible seizures. Something was awry in his brain. Karpov had come to hate the sound of the word *idiopathic*—something of the idiot in it, something of pathology. Maddeningly, Irina kept repeating it; *no focus of illness, no lesion, no damage. Idiopathic. Unknown origin.*

"I will be at my desk in a day or two. We must start preparing your testimony for the trial."

"Trial?" Belus started. He looked through the thick double windows, saw dark birds wheel.

"Levitch will be tried for espionage."

"Oh, yes. Naturally. After this. How can we—you—avoid it? He is a marked man now."

"You will be our key witness, Doctor."

"Me? I? I thought part of the arrangement was that I was to be transferred to Sochi. Under a different name, and with new papers. And that my brother was to be released from house arrest. Isn't that so, Comrade Major?"

"After the trial."

"How soon will that be?"

"A matter of weeks."

"Levitch hasn't been arrested yet?"

"Avoid him."

Dr. Belus found his right hand trembling, tried to still the fluttery motion with his left hand, failed. They both shook. *Damn Karpov. Fuck him. May the gods destroy him.* Belus gazed at the man who lay there in bed looking bleached, drained of blood. Scheming, plotting, heartless as an amoeba, as powerful as an African buffalo. They owned the world; they had it all; they could not be brought down. No wonder the clods in the street, the drunken, sullen, brutish people accepted them. They were all they had ever known. Maybe Slesik and Levitch and the Semonskis and the others had the correct idea after all—get out, or die trying.

"Would it not have been expedient, if I may suggest it," Belus said cautiously, "to let Levitch leave? Before he becomes even more of an international figure? I am told he is now quoted in *The New York Times* and *Time* magazine. He will be a *cause célèbre*."

"That is not your concern. He'll be dealt with under Soviet justice."

"I see. And I shall testify."

"You and others."

"And, of course, I must sever my connections with my former friends."

"You must. And obviously you will not attend the Passover dinner that American rabbi will be conducting." Karpov's bloodless mouth turned wider in a bleak smile. "I doubt you'll be invited now."

"I doubt it also, Comrade Major. Of course, we have a tradition of Elijah the Prophet coming through an opened door to a prepared table setting. I might play the role."

"*We* have a tradition?"

"A slip of the tongue. I mean the community of law-abiding Soviet citizens of Jewish ancestry. I have not dissociated from *them*. Just the traitors and spies."

"You can go. Use the hotel room Malik has rented for you. Stay away from patients, the hospital, and your former friends. You'll be summoned to the trial."

"But my practice. I have patients who need me."

"Make some arrangement, Doctor. You have committed yourself to the preservation of the motherland. Sacrifices must be made. After Levitch is convicted, we will look into another post and new identity for you."

Bowing, wishing Karpov a speedy recovery, the physician left. He bent his head and stroked his cheek, as if he had been whipped across the face and the welts lingered, burning reminders of shame.

Dr. Tashenko read Belus's lengthy confession. She visited Karpov on her morning rounds, first with her assistants, for a medical checkup—heart, lungs, perception, reflexes—and an hour later, alone.

Karpov, in red quilted robe and black velvet slippers, was sitting on the edge of the bed, leafing through a heavy brown folder. She saw the tab on it: LEVITCH.

"You should rest as much as possible," she said. "You must be weak."

"I am. And that low-grade throbbing in my head doesn't stop. Maybe I've taken too much phenobarbital."

"I'm stopping it. It doesn't seem to have much effect." She

held a curled paper in her hand. "Your last electrocardiogram was not normal. You're showing PVCs—premature ventricular contractions. Drug reaction, perhaps. Maybe the violence of your last seizure. You were unconscious more than fifteen minutes."

He reached for her wrist when she came to take his pulse. His touch was cold, damp. He stroked her hand.

"No, Andrei. Just a doctor-patient relationship." She pointed to *Pravda*. "I read Belus's letter."

"And?"

"Your style was in evidence. You wrote it for him, didn't you?"

"Of course I did."

"And it's a collection of lies, isn't it?"

Karpov shook his head and leaned back on the pillows. He was exhausted, as if a draining wound had opened in his chest. A minatory dread infused him. He feared the next convulsion, the rigidity, the insensate flailing, the intractable pain of the headache that followed, the dried-out, debilitated sensations.

"More truth than lies. But what does it matter? Levitch is a nobody. A worm. We can't let that kind of filth destroy our work for international peace and brotherhood."

She shook her head and stared at him. "Oh, dear God. A few years ago you at least had the virtue of cynicism. You could secretly laugh at your plots and deceptions and cruelties. Now you spout party nonsense. For shame."

"Be careful." Karpov shook a finger at her. "I'm an important fellow. You utter anti-Soviet statements, and who knows? Men have gone to the gulag for less poisonous remarks. We had a fellow, an engineer, who did three years at hard labor for calling Kosygin a prune-faced old woman."

She felt disgust rising in her. "Am I to be involved in the Levitch matter?"

"Perhaps."

"I don't want to be. I had no idea this would come of my interview with that stupid American. You were present. Nothing happened. Then you asked me to give Belus papers for Hanson. And now I see it was a trap to catch that miserable Jew."

"I gave you no such order."

"You did."

"Oh, I did. But in testimony—if it comes to that—you will say that Belus tricked you into surrendering the papers. You will be protected. We will say you were not aware of their importance."

"Who'll believe that? *Secret papers?* Belus keeps blabbing, in this piece of tripe, that all kinds of state secrets were in them. That is nonsense. There was nothing in them that American neurologists have not known about brain stimulation for five years."

"Don't concern yourself, Irina. Belus will have a sound story. In addition to what you gave him, he stole papers from you. It's Levitch who concerns us, no one else."

Irina stared at his lean aristocratic face. His features were carved and hard-edged. Even his movements—now less coordinated than normal because of his ailments—were delicate and refined. He held a cigarette the way she imagined a ballet master would, fingers extended, full of languor and grace.

"I resent your involving me in this."

"Ah, the small voice of conscience."

"I detest myself for having given my body to you, and worse, for letting you control my husband, for letting you turn him into a groveling coward. I despise all of you. Controllers, brutes, jailers. How can you live like this?"

"A neurologist should know about survival." Karpov lit a Marlboro, blew smoke at the cracked ceiling. "What did you call it? Muricide? Mouse-killing. Something that the rat, willy-nilly, can't avoid. Oh, he has options. He can kill because he's hungry, he can play with the mouse, ignore it, or simply kill it because he is a rat."

"Your analogy is most apt."

"But we do not attack our mice without reason. Our muricide has a purpose. The state must survive. Of course we don't seek to kill the mouse Levitch. But he must be rendered silent and useless."

"To teach a lesson to other mice?"

"Exactly. Enough of this purposeless sympathy. Irina, since when have you been a partisan of Zionists? Pests, parasites, locusts. Our good Jews give us no trouble. It's these mystics, these latter-day prophets who have to be silenced."

She studied his tense face. It was icily handsome. The power of command had left deep incisions around the jaw, on the high brow. Fearing him and hating him, she had nevertheless been drawn to his body. In spite of assuring herself that she had been in his arms only because of his hold over Lev, she knew in the recesses of her heart that she had been profoundly, achingly attracted to him. Hard and muscled, agile and tender. The encounters with him had been more than pleasurable. They had been soaring, erotic adventures— edged with danger. *Do we seek a certain strange death in sex?* she often wondered. Had Karpov, dispenser of pain and destruction, offered her some occult unearthly fulfillment?

She thought of lavish hotel suites, ormolu mirrors, baroque fireplaces. The champagne chilling in a silver bucket. Black lace underclothing he had bought for her on the Champs Elysées, on Regent Street. Warm with winy unsteadiness, they would progress from gentle caresses and probings to lubricious acrobatics on the wide welcoming bed. She could not deny that she had lost herself utterly in passion, surrendered to him somewhat less than willingly, but surrendered nonetheless. No man had ever gratified her more on the purely sensual level. In the very sinfulness of their cohabitation, swooning in the palpable sense of power he exuded—almost an essence, an aroma—she had abandoned her body, her soul, and her moral view of the world.

"What is to be done for me?" he asked.

"I'm not certain. You're seriously ill. You aren't improving."

Karpov coughed, snuffed out his cigarette. "I'm in your hands. I trust you. I know you have mixed emotions, but I reject these moral judgments you make about me. I'm a policeman. A brilliant one. I will make no apologies for my life and my work. Try to understand me a bit better, Irina. The Levitches of the world have to be educated, as did your husband. What I'm saying is, I want some tolerance from you. If you are to be the agent of my recovery, I'm grateful. I only ask that you smile at me from time to time, respond when I take your hand, and think in terms of—what shall I say?—some happy future for us."

"I have always kept my professional work separate from my personal life. I intend to continue to do so."

"No argument. Now I should like to know what can be done for me."

She sat on the edge of his bed. He moved his leg close to her thigh and pressed against her. She did not move away.

"Surgery may be your best hope. A rare operation, but one that has good results. Meanwhile, I'll change your medication. The names of the drugs will mean nothing to you."

"I'll be a good patient."

She felt the pressure of his lean hard leg against her hip. It was not unpleasant. She shivered, left the bed for a wooden chair.

"I'm puzzled by your illness," she said. "No trauma, no evident lesion in the brain. What then? The brain is full of secrets, Andrei Borisovich. There's an American neurologist who claims that the brain is really three different organs—a primal mind derived from reptiles, an emotional mind which we have received from early mammals, and a rational human mind. All three function in humans. In some people one dominates, in others another, but in most people there is a balance among the three."

"And what brain dominates me?"

"The reptile."

"I can't believe that you truly hate me. What kind of reptile, Irina? A snake? A lizard?"

"Perhaps one of those Komodo dragons. Giant lizards that stalk their prey for days, corner it, charge, devour it. A creature controlled by the R-complex, massive ganglia that include collections of gray matter, the olfactory *striatum,* the *corpus striatum,* the *globus pallidus.*"

Karpov smiled. "You make me sound more Roman than Russian."

"Andrei, for all your intellect, I've concluded that your brain is affected by its R-complex. The unthinking, ritualistic and aggressive traits of the hunting reptile."

"Irina, old love, your analogies are strained. I don't hunt to eat. I track down snakes and toads. I'm a specialist—"

"Snakes and toads like Levitch? Or Zolkin, who is a hundred times the man you can ever be? Or my husband?"

"These are police matters. People who break laws of the Soviet Union must pay the price. Whether they're clowns like Levitch, or intellectuals like Zolkin. I have a job to do. I do it."

"That was Eichmann's defense."

"So I'm in his category?" He smiled. "You're upset. Irina, you're not a political person. You never have been. You're a scientist. A great one. This chatter about my reptilian brain doesn't offend me. It amuses me. Now tell me, how will you cure me? I can't tolerate any more of these seizures."

"We'll make one more effort with medication. The matter of surgery remains open."

"What's involved? Please tell me."

"Later. I'll arrange for a sedative and a new regimen. You are not to leave the hospital again. If you do, I can't be responsible for what happens."

Four days later, while Karpov remained in the Institute—he had suffered two more seizures—Flying Squads from the KGB's Jewish Department raided the apartments of Chaim Slesik, Nadya Burik, and the Semonskis. Karpov gave the orders to Malik on the phone. Despite his illness he was orchestrating the affair.

In Nadya Burik's flat, sofas and chairs were ripped apart, drawers dumped open, beds dismantled, papers, books and letters confiscated. Slesik, who lived like an ascetic, suffered less damage. So meager were his possessions that the raiders found little to destroy. Mikhail Semonski's Bechstein, on which he had once performed and given lessons, was smashed, the strings left ruined on the floor, the keyboard torn apart. The old couple wept and sat shivering in a corner as Malik's agents seized yellowing sheets of music as "evidence."

"Comrade," Semonski said to a young thug, "what crime can you find in Borodin? What is reactionary in Moussorgsky?"

Malik phoned the results of the raids to Karpov.

"Good," Karpov said. "Did you find anything?"

"The usual Jew garbage. Hebrew books, prayer books. That American rabbi brought them a lot of stuff. Special books for their holiday."

"Any resistance?"

"From Yids? Are you joking, Comrade Major? They whimpered like drowning puppies."

A vise tightened over Karpov's head. New pains, new dread sensations. Irina would have to save him. Speaking to Malik, listening to the drone of his spongy voice, he had a memory of struggling from the cold floor after his last attack, helped to his feet by the nurse and an orderly. It was just before dawn. A steely-gray darkness outside the windows. On his feet now. But with a strange gait. Stiff-backed, his arms dangling. Like a beast on the prowl. Was it he? Did he dream it? No, no. He could recall the nurse saying, "Comrade Major, why do you walk like that? What pains you?"

A hazed memory: He was threatening the hospital people, grunting at them, sensing a need to get on his knees and knuckles, to pursue someone, to escape a predator. . . .A dream, of course. Doused with drugs. The effect of Irina's blather about a reptilian brain . . .

Malik was chuckling on the phone. They'd found a store of that thin Jewish bread, a kind of wafer, in boxes at the Semonskis' place. They'd taken it into custody. Gorchakov and some others on the raiding party were munching the crackers right now, laughing over it.

"The bread of affliction," Karpov said. "Malik, don't eat the evidence. Illegally smuggling foodstuffs into the USSR. That's something else we can charge them with."

"Sure, sure, just sampling it. It isn't bad." Malik sounded as if he had a mouthful of matzo. *I survive among toads and snakes, it's quite true*, Karpov thought. *But I'm better than all of them*. Once the nasty business of Levitch was concluded, he'd ask for a transfer. A foreign post. Bring her there— Washington, London. Among civilized people, away from these crude louts.

"What about the American rabbi?" Karpov asked.

"We won't touch him, as you ordered. He's been at the American Embassy all day screaming his lungs dry. The Voice of America will be full of his lies tonight. Senators, congressmen, journalists. Why do Americans care so much about Jews? Why can't they behave like everyone else and hate the bastards?"

"Make sure the rabbi isn't bothered. If he's a problem, I'll talk to the Foreign Ministry and they'll expel him. What is he like? Beard, black cloak? Some doddering old man?"

"No, Comrade Major. A young man. Tall, big shoulders, clean-shaven. He is not afraid, either. When we came out of Slesik's place, he confronted us on the street and demanded his religious books, with all that Hebrew shit in them."

Karpov mulled the notion. A bit of courage. Maybe the fellow—Goldberg? Goldman?—would have to be expelled. Instead of a Passover celebration, they'd award him an Exodus.

"Malik, you seem to be doing well." Karpov looked at his Piaget wristwatch. Six in the afternoon. In one day of raids and threats, they'd put the devil's fear into the heart of the dissident movement. There remained Levitch.

"Pick up Levitch tonight."

"Tonight?"

"Yes. Contact the detail that follows him. When he's finished with his nocturnal visits, wherever he is, arrest him. I'll speak to Colonel Dort on issuing a statement tomorrow. Put Levitch in solitary."

"To Lefortovo?"

"Yes. In solitary, after the charges are read."

"Rough him up?"

"Only if he resists."

Resting, letting the soothing drugs work their way into his bloodstream, into his agonized nervous system, Karpov dreamed again. He was in that curious stance, back stiff, arms dangling, as if his knuckles were reaching for the ground. On all fours. Scampering after a rabbit, pursuing a wounded bird. Trap them. Tear their flesh apart. His dreams were thin, papery, close to his consciousness, images and actions perceived in a semi-awakened state.

Save me, Irina.

7

RABBI GOLDMAN AND Levitch came to Parente's for dinner. In the hallway outside, three of Malik's men waited. Below, five more paced the cold lobby of the building in the foreign compound.

"Spend the night here, Abram," Parente said. "You, too, Rabbi."

"Me? Are you kidding? They can't touch me. I'm an American."

"They stole your Haggadahs," Parente said gloomily. "There goes the seder."

"That's what *they* think. I can run a seder from memory." Goldman rubbed his eyes. He'd been on the phone for three hours. The State Department. Senators. The *Times*. Committees for the Jews of the USSR. "Tony, we'll have our seder and to hell with them. Don't ever show them you're frightened."

Levitch, playing Monopoly with Jimmy Parente, smiled, shook the dice, made his move. He picked a card.

" 'Bank error in your favor,' " Levitch read. " 'Collect two hundred dollars.' "

Jimmy, whining that he was never lucky, landed on Levitch's Tennessee Avenue. It had a red hotel. He shoveled paper money to the Russian.

"When I go to Israel," Levitch said, "maybe I'll build hotels. Jimmy, you can stay free with me. Swimming pool, tennis, all for you, my Monopoly opponent."

"Nuts," the boy said. He moved his marker, landed on Ventnor, paid Levitch for rental on two houses. "Abram's got all the luck, Pop."

Parente, his wife, and the rabbi watched them—silent, troubled.

Two of Malik's men crammed themselves into the elevator cage with Abram and Rabbi Goldman. The third hurried down the stairs.

"You had a pleasant evening, Yuri?" Levitch asked one of them. "Maybe next time I'll ask Mr. Parente to invite all of you in for a glass of tea, an American beer?"

"Shut your hole, Levitch."

The rabbi smelled their unwashed bodies, felt the overcoated bulk of the bigger man pushing against him. He pushed back. A strong, athletic man, Goldman did not take abuse lightly. In Brooklyn, as a boy, he had organized flying squads of young Jews to battle anti-Semitic hoodlums.

Levitch smiled dopily. He continued to babble. "Yuri, how is your family? Your older boy took the examinations for the university?"

"Go to hell."

"Don't get them angry," Rabbi Goldman cautioned. "Abram, they don't appreciate your kidding around."

"Who is kidding? I see them every day. We might as well have conversation. Listen, if the kid needs coaching on mathematics, I'll be glad to oblige. I was a good teacher a few years ago."

The elevator clanked to a halt. The rabbi and the bigger man engaged in a pushing contest, silent thrusts and surges, heavy shoulders and muscled arms. Goldman eased up and let the agent barrel past him. He thought of tripping him and apologizing, then refrained. They had all the numbers, all the guns, all the jails. Watching Levitch walk out of the elevator, he experienced a rush of love and pity for him. Courage that had to be seen firsthand to be believed. Compounded of what? Stubbornness, faith, outrage, love. And a childlike acceptance of the world. He had never seen Levitch weep. Always the faint smile, the trusting light in his brown eyes.

In the lobby two other agents were waiting for Levitch.

"Ah, gentlemen," Levitch said. "I'm sorry it was a long evening. I had to play an extra game of Monopoly with Mr. Parente's little boy. I won."

"Move, Levitch," Rodenko said.

"I was not aware that the speed of my locomotion was an issue. I'm tired. You mind if I take my time?"

"For God's sake," Goldman protested, "why don't you leave him alone? Eight of you for one harmless man?"

They walked into the cement courtyard. It was deserted except for the armed militiaman in the sentry box. Then they proceeded through the iron gate.

The rabbi saw the black Zhiguli with its street-side doors open. He had a premonition of bottomless tragedy.

Rodenko grabbed Levitch's arm. Yuri took his left arm. They lifted him roughly from the pavement. A second black Zhiguli was parked behind the car with opened doors. Both motors were being gunned.

"In, Yid," Blatnik said.

"Get your hands off him," Goldman shouted. "You've no right to do this. I'm witnessing the whole thing. It will be in the newspapers tomorrow."

The biggest member of the team, the man Goldman had engaged in a shoving contest, barred the rabbi's passage. "Stay away, you. You are a guest in our country. Go away."

Levitch was flung into the first car. Two agents flanked him. Two others sat in front. The other four got into the following car.

"Rabbi," Abram called. "Tell Slesik, Zolkin, the others. Go back and tell Tony. Please telephone Sarah and tell her I am all right, she must not worry about—"

Rodenko cracked the back of a huge hand against Levitch's mouth, cutting him off in mid-sentence. Blood trickled from Levitch's lips.

The automobiles sped off.

Goldman, his fear diluted by anger, turned and went back to Parente's building.

*   *   *

"He couldn't hide and he couldn't run, and he wouldn't stop being the kind of gutsy guy he is," Parente said.

"Is Abram in jail, Pop?" The boy was in pajamas and bathrobe. He was stacking the Monopoly money, putting the pieces back in the long box.

"He will be, Jimbo. Go to bed."

"I hate those guys. Cops are supposed to be good, right, Pop?"

Parente sighed. "It's how they run things, kid. Go on. Rabbi Goldman and I have to talk."

Martha Parente joined them and cried softly.

"It was a matter of time," Parente said. "Once Belus's letter was printed, I knew they'd pull Abram in. Miserable, rotten bastards." He rose. "I got to file a story. The sooner we break this, the better for him."

"Shouldn't we wait?" the rabbi asked. "Suppose he's just held for questioning and released? That's happened before. Maybe we'll make it worse by going public."

"No way, Dave. He's in for good. The whole business was a KGB special. Hanson, Belus, Levitch. The first two didn't matter. It was Abram they wanted and they got him. I have a gut feeling we won't see him till they put him on trial."

Martha gasped. "Oh, dear. That poor man."

Goldman got up. "I'll start calling the others. I'll do it from my hotel room."

"It won't help," Parente said. "But you might as well. Don't wake Slesik up. The guy's dying. Make sure Zolkin knows. Good luck, Dave."

When Goldman had gone, Parente scribbled notes, then dialed the home of the newspaper's Paris correspondent. His voice hoarse and weary, he relayed the basic facts for immediate transmission. By morning, the story would be carried by the Associated Press and UPI. The world would know.

" 'Abram Levitch,' " Parente read from his pad, " 'a leader of the Jewish dissident movement in the Soviet Union, and a member of the Helsinki Committee which monitors violations of human rights in the USSR, was arrested tonight by Soviet authorities. . . . ' "

" 'Abram Moiseivich Levitch,' " Anatoli Malik read, " 'you are charged with treason, under Article 64-A of the Criminal Code, and with anti-Soviet agitation and propaganda under

Article 70.1. Specifically under the latter, you are charged with violations of the law through illegal contacts with American journalists and diplomats, the spreading of slander against the Soviet Union through false charges of anti-Semitism, and by conducting Zionist meetings and discussing and disseminating Zionist propaganda designed to slander the Soviet Union. . . .' "

Malik droned on. He read badly, hesitating, mispronouncing anything of three syllables or more.

Levitch yawned and shifted in his seat. He felt in need of a bath, a change of clothing. Fatigue ate at his muscles, invaded his brain. How tired could a man get? Could someone die of exhaustion?

"Are you listening, Levitch?" Malik asked.

"Have I any choice?"

The voice of the policeman-bureaucrat was like an oily liquid flooding Levitch's ears, making him want to cover them, protect them from the endless assault of false charges and nonsense.

" 'Further, assembling other criminal persons, and encouraging them in the dissemination of calumnies about the Soviet Union through the so-called Helsinki Committee, a collection of traitors and—' "

"Like Mikhail Zolkin?"

"Be silent until I have finished reading the charges. You have no rights here. You are a prisoner charged with serious crimes."

"In civilized countries even the accused have rights."

"Do you want to get hit? Talk will be your death, Levitch. All those words, all that crap, those meetings, those bulletins, more talk. We'll see to it that you remain silent for a long time."

He started reading again. There was more about Levitch's acts of treason. Secret medical research, related to defense matters, stolen by Levitch. Conniving with Ivan Belus, the CIA agent turned patriotic, to steal certain papers from the files of one Dr. Tashenko, destination the American Embassy via the spy Floyd Hanson . . .

Levitch said no more. His eyes wandered around the dark-green room. Lenin. The Red Star. Odd, how he had always admired Lenin when he was a schoolboy. The bald head, the fatherly smile, the simple clothes. Would it have been different if Lenin had lived? Or if someone other than the madman Stalin, the ogre lusting for blood and mounds of corpses, had succeeded him?

Probably not. The system was inherently corrupt and corrupting. As Zolkin had often said, and as Levitch had reasoned long ago, it had become a form of Fascism. Things had to be packaged, tied up, finished, no matter the justice of the case, or the cost in human suffering, the moral issues. Arrest, confession, trial, imprisonment. No loose ends, no doubts, no room for nonbelievers.

"You will be held in custody pending the disposition of your case," Malik said.

"Am I entitled to counsel?"

"Eventually. At the moment and until our investigation is completed, you will not be allowed to speak to anyone."

"My friends? Relatives?"

"No one."

"Can I go to the bathroom?"

Malik shook his head, in mocking bemusement. *Ah, that funny kike; jokes, jokes, jokes.*

"You'll have a chance in your hotel room."

"Hotel?"

"The Lefortovo palace. You'll have the royal suite. Lots of famous people have stayed here. Beria, Solzhenitsyn, a lot of your agitator friends. Cheer up, Levitch. It isn't as bad as you've heard."

"How long, if I may ask?"

Malik shrugged, lifted his hands, raised his brows. His silence was more terrifying than anything he had said.

Two uniformed prison guards accompanied Abram down semi-dark stairways. The floor and walls exuded cold moisture. There was a pervasive odor of urine. He was surprised that he was given no prison garb, had not been registered or fingerprinted.

He was shoved through a stone archway into a dimly lit corridor. On either side, widely spaced, as if the intervening walls were extremely thick, were the metal doors of the cells.

The guards halted him at a door halfway down the row of cells. One of them jammed a key into a hole.

A voice called from a nearby cell. A man's voice, falsely cheery, speaking in what sounded like a Ukrainian accent.

"Welcome, brother. What are you? A Ukrainian? Balt? Maybe a wild Uzbek or a Buryat? Don't tell me. I can guess. You're a Yid. You Yids make it worse for the rest of us. The only thing worse than a Yid is a political."

"Shut up, jerk-off," one of the guards said. "You know the rules. No talking. Not even for halfwits."

"Duly noted, Comrade Guard."

Duly noted. An educated man? wondered Levitch. A teacher, a scientist, a writer who got in trouble? Still an anti-Semite. The great universal solvent of Europe. Doomed, they still gave voice to the old hatreds.

"Get in," the guard said.

"I have no toilet articles. No soap. Nothing."

"You'll get them. Get in."

Levitch walked through the rusted metal door. It had a small peephole, a barred aperture that could be opened only from the outside, probably for meals.

The door rang behind him. The clanging noise echoed in the underground chambers like a roll of summer thunder. Key turned in lock; metal clicked against metal.

"I'd like to send a letter out," Levitch said.

The prisoner laughed loudly. "Letter. Jesus, this idiot thinks he's on vacation. *Letter.*"

"You can write to the prison administrator once every two weeks," the guard said. "Tell him who you want to write to. No direct communication."

In the murk and stench Levitch felt his feet grow cold and wet. He looked down. There were six centimeters of scummy water on the cement floor. A stuffy drain perhaps, a leak from an underground water main. The entire cell was flooded.

His eyes looked about. A bed? A chair? Something to get him out of the cold muck? But there was nothing in the room. Water, bare stone walls, a bucket for waste. One small canted stool.

"Now is when I need a good joke," Levitch said softly. He reasoned to himself: *They can't keep me here long. I will die of cold and exposure.* Enervated, disoriented, he sought a dry spot on the floor, a place to sit. The water covered every inch of space. He leaned against a wall and tried not to weep.

He heard the Ukrainian. "*Pssst.* Comrade. After you confess, they'll give you a dry cell and a bed. So you have to think if it's worth it. The water is full of crap and piss. They block the drains, the fuckers."

A guard's voice boomed down the row of cells. "Hey! You Ukrainian shit-head. Shut up, or you'll be back in the swimming pool."

"Keep standing as long as you can," the Ukrainian whispered. "My best advice."

"I said shut up."

There were footsteps, boots hitting a stone floor, the clank and bang of a door opening. Then soft blows, muffled thuds, gasps from the prisoner. Now he was crooning to his jailers, pleading. Then more blows. He was being hit so hard, Levitch sensed, that the guards were grunting with the effort. Then silence.

Levitch waded around the room. He hadn't sought torture and martyrdom. All he had wanted was to leave, to join his wife. How had he come to this? Why had he chosen to play the hero, the leader of a helpless army? He thought of Sarah, leaned against the door, sobbed.

He heard a spaced knocking coming through the wall. A signal. A code of some kind. But he could not listen, found no solace in this pitiful attempt of a fellow sufferer to reach him. The water soaked through his shoes, his socks, froze his feet, sent a chill through his fatigued body.

"Confess, confess," the voice whispered.

And the guard shouting, *"You want the club again?"*

Levitch's arrest did not make front-page news in the West. Parente, the first journalist to file the story, was furious with his foreign editor. They'd played the arrest on page 7, a small item with a one-column headline.

Parente raged. The editor explained: Another dissident jugged. The Russkies do it all the time. So what else is new? Parente tried to explain: Levitch was more than just another refusenik. He was the bridge to Zolkin, the leader of the politicals. This little guy, this round, smiling man, had thrown the KGB for a loss. If the West jumped on the story now, the Russians would be very uncomfortable. . . .

In a few days the protests mounted. Wire services picked up the story of the arrest. There were interviews with the refuseniks—Chaim Slesik, the Semonskis, Nadya Burik. Zolkin, under KGB surveillance, gave an exclusive to *Time* magazine, protesting Levitch's jailing.

A week after Levitch's arrest, Floyd Hanson was expelled from the Soviet Union for "acts of hostility and other criminal behavior, against the Soviet Union."

Parente, his wife and Agnes Wardle saw the young reporter off. Treva Siddons, accused by *Pravda* as a CIA agent (although no further word had been heard on that score, nor had she been threatened), also came to see Hanson leave.

"I'm sorry about Abram," Hanson said. "If only I could help the guy. Tony, I told them fifty times Levitch had nothing to do with it."

"Forget it, kid. If not you, someone else. Maybe me. These bastards make their primitive minds up to frame someone, and that's it. They could have tricked Agnes, or Dieter Schultze, or any of us."

Treva Siddons said that the Embassy was preparing a lengthy statement on the Hanson-Levitch affair. Several senators had been on the phone demanding more information. The President would discuss the Levitch matter at his next news conference.

"Will he talk about Belus?" Parente asked slyly.

Miss Siddons's eyes widened. "Why?"

"Because my guess is Belus really did work for the CIA. The old U.S. of A. was suckered. Sure, he was planted by the KGB, but the CIA swallowed him, made him one of their own, without even knowing he was a mole. Belus wasn't lying about that part. Just about the way he suckered Floyd and Abram into this mess."

"You have no proof of that," Treva Siddons said.

"Educated guess."

"Look who's coming," Martha Parente said.

Approaching them was a dapper straw-thin man, dark as burnished walnut.

"Hrant Deroulian. Our friendly Novosti feature writer," Parente growled. "Buddy-buddy with the foreign press. Probably a last shot at getting you to confess, Floyd."

"Fat chance."

The Armenian journalist grinned at the reporters. "Tony, Martha, Agnes. Ah, dear Floyd."

"The name is pronounced Flerd," Parente said. "Get lost, Hrant. Where were you when we needed you?"

Deroulian whipped out a pad and a pen. Parente's eyes goggled. He was after an interview with Hanson! Last words of the departed.

"So, Floyd," the Russian journalist asked, "you carry with you good feelings about USSR? Would you wish one day to come back for visit?"

"This is outrageous," Miss Siddons said. "You arrest this man, charge him with crimes, all lies, force him to sign a worthless paper and throw him out, and now you ask if he wants to return?"

Deroulian grinned. "Why not? You were treated fair, no?"

"No." Hanson frowned. His sunny nature was offended. "No. And what you people are doing to Levitch is worse."

"Not to worry about him," Deroulian said airily.

Parente's eyes glinted. Most Soviet journalists, but notably smoothies like Deroulian who were in contact with the foreign press, were KGB.

"What's the plot, Hrant?" he asked. "What happens to Levitch?"

"Oh, a few days interrogation, a confession, and perhaps he will be expelled."

"Yeah, yeah. Once you confess, it's the gulag. Come on, Hrant, level with us."

"Or get away," Miss Siddons said.

The Armenian put his pad away, bid them goodbye and minced off.

Hanson's Aeroflot flight to Paris was called. They all embraced him and wished him well.

"Tony," Hanson said, "try getting to Dr. Tashenko. She might want to help Levitch."

"Why?"

"I don't know. I got the feeling she's honest. I can't imagine a woman like that being part of this cruddy thing. And there was the funny business of that so-called doctor sitting next to her. I'm not crazy. That was Karpov. The KGB biggy."

Parente said, "They'll throw a scare into her. She'll be compromised, told to dummy up. Look at Zolkin. The most famous nonpolitical Russian since Pavlov. And he's on ice. These are goddamn beasts."

"I know. But when I think of Levitch . . . At least call her, Tony."

"I will. But I know what the answer will be. So long, kid."
They shook hands for the last time.

Martha Parente watched Hanson's loose figure depart. A
free soul in a sheepskin jacket and drainpipe jeans. It hadn't
been his fault, she thought. He'd been used. And now Levitch
was under the gun. He might die; he might succumb slowly
in the snowy hell of the North. And he would never be the
same.

"Nice guy," Martha said to her husband. She sniffled. "But
innocent. He's hurting."

"Don't cry for him. He's free."

"Not for him. For Abram and the others. Slesik's dying."

A meeting of refuseniks was held in Nadya Burik's apartment.
Slesik, defying medical opinion, would not die. Levitch's
arrest seemed to endow the frail bachelor with new strength.
He spoke more, announced he was ready to take over the job
of distributing weekly bulletins.

There was no news of Abram. For weeks now, he had
remained in prison—obliterated, erased. But the world press
was taking cognizance of his case. There had been protests
from Israel, the United States, the West, but silence from the
Soviet bloc and the Third World.

An attempt to bring his case before the United Nations was
dismissed by an overwhelming vote of Third Worlders. A key
speech had been made by a West African delegate who in his
youth had been convicted of cannibalism by French authorities,
and had indeed admitted that he had eaten his uncle's left
buttock. He denounced Levitch as "an enemy of mankind."

"Zalman Sokolov will write the bulletin from now on,"
Nadya said irritably. "Chaim, you can't run any risks. Mischa
will give it to the reporters."

Sokolov was a young electronics engineer, a new member
of the group. He was a ruddy-cheeked, rugged man, with a
cap of curling black hair, a full beard and merry black eyes.
He wore a yarmulke and fringes, corresponded with American Jews in the Lubavitcher movement. His wife, Chana, was
a plump dark woman, four months pregnant. Both were
Hassidic and cheerful.

"Zalman is so new," Chana Sokolov said. "Maybe someone
who knows more."

"We all write it," Semonski said. "Bits, notes, pieces of

information. But someone should talk to the press. Your husband's English is the best."

Sokolov agreed, as if to say *what choice do I have?* Slesik looked admiringly at the recruit. Broad shoulders, strong limbs. Sokolov had done himself no good, applying and reapplying for visas for himself and his wife. His hope was to join a Lubavitcher community near Tel Aviv. *Electronics and Torah? Micro-circuits and Hasidism?* Slesik wondered. Judaism could encompass all.

"They say Abram Moiseivich is ill," Olga Semonski said.

"How do we know?" Slesik asked. He had collapsed on the sagging sofa. Nadya Burik spooned hot soup into his mouth.

"Word gets out," Mikhail Semonski said. "The prisoners have ways of getting information to us. He gets three hundred grams of bread a day. A cup of water twice a day."

"Starvation," Nadya said. "My husband died that way. The eyes go first. Then the kidneys."

Chana Sokolov shifted her abdomen, lowered her skirt. "This can happen to my Zalman?"

"It can happen to any of us," Slesik said. "But if you want to go to Israel and find your Lubavitcher brothers there, you'll work with us."

"Maybe it'll only make it worse," the young woman said. She wore a round reddish wig; like all Lubavitcher women, her head was shaved.

"No one forces you to stay with us," Slesik said gently. "This must be your own decision."

There was knocking at the door. The people in the room froze. No one spoke. *So,* thought Slesik, *this is how it ends. A knock at the door at four in the afternoon. A mild April day. Passover has gone and the earth renews itself. But not for us. For us, spring is the tread of the KGB thug, the clank of the gate.*

Nadya hefted her old body across the living room to the scarred door. "Who is it?" she asked.

"Please. Open up."

The voice was soft, cultured, familiar.

Nadya opened the door. Mikhail Zolkin was standing there— tall, gray, elegant despite his threadbare brown jacket, his ragged muffler.

"Mikhail Ivanovich," she said. "Welcome."

The scientist entered. People rose in homage to him. Slesik

struggled from the couch and embraced him. "Bless you,
Professor Zolkin. You're here because of Abram. Please sit.
Tell us what you know."

Introductions were made. Young Sokolov and his wife were
properly awed, but a bit distant. They'd made their choice:
separation, isolation, seeking their God, their destiny. Still,
their Rebbe preached kindness, tolerance, acceptance of the
help of Gentiles, an awareness of the good in all people—not
just Lubavitchers.

"I have a word from Abram Moiseivich," Zolkin said. His
voice was resonant, soft yet echoing. He lived with his wife in
a dingy two-room apartment. Karpov's goons never left his
side, yet they dared not harm him.

"Is he all right?" Slesik asked. "A trial?"

"Within the next two months That's why I am here. We
need to start preparing his defense."

Slesik doubled over in a fit of coughing. "What about a
lawyer?" he gasped.

"He's refused the court-appointed lawyer. I doubt there's
any lawyer who will volunteer to defend him," Zolkin said.

Nadya shifted her body and groaned. "How do you know
all this, Mikhail Ivanovich?"

"We get information from Lefortovo. Abram is in solitary.
He sleeps sitting up on a stool, with his feet in dirty water.
He's fed dry bread, cabbage soup and tea twice a day. He
suffers from diarrhea and respiratory ailments."

"They'll fatten him up for the trial," Slesik said. "They
always do. Dope him with drugs to stop his cold, feed him
beef and fruit."

"But what about the lawyer?" Zalman Sokolov asked.
"Someone has to defend him."

"The court will appoint a lawyer," Zolkin replied, "whether
he wants one or not."

"Tell us what we must do," Slesik said.

The scientist cleared his throat. "We must have a complete
file of all statements issued by the Helsinki Committee. All
records of meetings of the refusenik groups. Clippings from
Western newspapers and magazines. Affidavits from the Western journalists who spoke with Abram. Parente, Wardle,
Hanson, all of them. We must demonstrate to the court that
he is innocent, did nothing of a criminal nature, and wanted
only to leave the Soviet Union."

"Will it save him?" Slesik asked.

"It will not save him from conviction."

"Then why bother?" Sokolov asked. "Why doesn't he just refuse to recognize the authority of the court, refuse to cooperate and let them do their worst?"

Zolkin sighed. "We must tell the world he's innocent. That what is being done to him is a crime against not only Abram Levitch, or the refuseniks, or the dissidents, but against humanity. Let the Fascists be exposed and brought to the judgment of civilized men."

"It won't stop them," Nadya said.

"We would not be true to our consciences if we were silent. Those who advocate silence, withdrawal, an intellectual boycott in the face of evil, do the work of the jailer and the torturer."

They talked far into the waning light, gathered papers, made notes, drew up lists of people to be called. Chaim Slesik, scrawling names and dates on a pad, often thought of Zolkin's advice. *Silence*. The worst of all responses. It did the work of the criminal.

Slesik, dozing, soothed by pain-killers, could hear young Sokolov's voice.

"Professor Zolkin," the Lubavitcher was saying, "I do believe in miracles. I must believe in them."

"Why is that, young man?"

"To be a realist, I must believe in miracles."

It made sense of a sort, Slesik thought.

Shadows and voice sounds. They were near yet distant, unformed yet suggestive. Who? Saying what?

Deeply sedated, Karpov slept. People were standing at the foot of his bed. A man. A woman. He knew them, did not know them. . . .

In his veiled mind, memories of his wife were surprisingly clear and distinct, images in cartoon outlines and primary colors. Marfa at their university graduation, a rosy-cheeked, wide-eyed girl. A true Slavic beauty with a broad face, sturdy limbs. Full breasts, narrow waist, generous buttocks. He had seduced her, made her pregnant, gone to an illegal abortionist and brought her, bleeding and weeping, back to the drab dormitories at the University of Kiev. . . .

Then marriage. *Why?* he wondered. She was uncomplicated,

shy. Two years into marriage, Karpov, now enlisted in an
advanced KGB language program, outdoing his classmates
and impressing his superiors, found her boring, given to long
silences and weepy remonstrances over her lost child. Some
trauma, some slip of an instrument had rendered her sterile.
Karpov mocked her. Children were an impediment, an
annoyance. Swallowing her agony, Marfa worked as a kinder-
garten teacher, adored the little ones, tried her hand at
writing a children's book and failed to have it published.

Meanwhile Karpov was promoted, recruited by the First
Chief Directorate, and assigned to the First Department,
which covered the United States and Canada. Fluent in
English and French, he rose quickly as an agent of the feared
Executive Action Department. With his dapper clothing, ex-
cellent English and knowledge of vineyards and French
cheeses, Karpov was admirably suited for a diplomatic cover.
An elegant fellow, well spoken, graceful, not your typical
Russian, his fellow diplomats said.

Not so Marfa. She was never comfortable overseas. With
Slavic slovenliness she put on weight, was careless in her
dress, mooned and wept about their childless marriage. Within
five years Karpov wearied of their frenzied sexual encounters.
Within ten years he was actively pursuing affairs.

In Mexico City, posing as a commercial attaché while he
organized Communist cells among university students, Karpov
began the first of several long-run, intense love affairs. His
partner was an elegant raven-haired Mexican aristocrat, six
years older than Karpov, who traced her lineage back to
Cortes and several Aztec princes. Marfa learned of the affair
and descended into a dank depression. Soon she had to be
repatriated. In Moscow she did not respond to therapy or her
mother's peasant affection or the sights and sounds of her
homeland. On leave from Mexico—Karpov had since scored
his triumph over Dort—he decided to have Marfa committed
for "tests" and "rehabilitation."

That was sixteen years ago. She had never, except for brief
periods, left the "psychiatric hospital." Flabby, whey-faced, a
shapeless woman in a stained robe, she saw him twice a year.
They said little, showed no affection. Many of the other
patients were politicals, dissidents, alleged enemies of the
state who had run afoul of Karpov and other KGB functionaries.

It was not that their minds were askew; it was their view of the all-powerful state that had to be "corrected."

Softly, as through a wall, he heard a woman's voice. Marfa? That whining voice he had come to hate and to resent? No, someone else. Who? Irina?

Colonel Dort's pudgy hands gripped the railing of Karpov's hospital bed. His wrestler's body was bent forward. The round bald head drooped slightly. The Tatar eyes were merciless.

"Sleep. Is that all he does?"

Irina brushed back a strand of hair. "He's sedated."

"Why? Every time I ask to talk to him, he's under drugs. Is this some kind of game you're playing, Dr. Tashenko? I know about some of the games you've played with Andrei Borisovich. But they weren't like this, with him snoring all the time."

"It is no game."

"What then?" Dort's baleful eyes took her in. The long line of back, hip, buttock and leg. Too good for that natty bastard Karpov, that sniffer of brandy, client of London tailors.

"The seizures are daily occurrences. We hope that by putting him on concentrated dosages we may break the cycle."

"But no luck so far?"

"No."

Dort circled the bed, squinting in the half-light at Karpov's slender form. *Jesus and Mary,* he thought, *even under dope, half-dead, Karpov looks haughty.* The face was waxen, the nose a blade, the lips a bloodless crack. Arched in sleep, the eyebrows seemed to sneer.

"Cure him," Dort said.

"He may be incurable."

"Nonsense. The motherland needs him. Some crazy fits? What did you call it—idiopathic epilepsy? Get him on his feet. I need him."

She saw his distress. He not only needed Andrei, he needed her. "For what? The Levitch trial?" she asked.

"So. He talks to you, is that it?"

"You need him to convict Levitch. Why? The case against Levitch will be faked, no matter who prepares it. Major Karpov needs complete rest." She marveled at her own courage in baiting Dort.

"Crap. I want him to prepare the case."

Laziness, she understood. Sloth, indolence. She sometimes wondered if the KGB was as efficient as its adversaries believed it to be. Dort was a sloven, a brute. The case against Levitch was a formality. Papers, documents, forgeries, lies. Dr. Belus's rigged testimony, the prepotency of the all-powerful state against one miserable victim.

"I advise you to keep Major Karpov here," she said. "I can send him back to his office and he'll be falling to the floor, in convulsions that may kill him. What good is he to you?"

"I want him. I also want to make sure he doesn't start blabbing to the wrong people. If he's out of control, who can promise what he'll do next?"

"I should have guessed. I wouldn't fear on that score, Colonel. Karpov's control of himself is total. He would die of cardiac arrest before revealing anything about the way you—" She paused.

"Yes? Say it."

"Very well. The way he trapped Levitch."

Dort sat on the window ledge and smiled. "Oh, what a brave one. Not at all worried I'll arrest you? You were part of the trap, Doctor."

"I have friends also." She did not sound convincing.

"Of course. You're a future Nobel Prize winner. Let's get back to Karpov. You said something about an operation. Tell me."

"A callosal commissurotomy."

"Dangerous? Life-threatening?"

"No. It's a simple procedure."

"Does it cure them of fits?"

"Usually. But it is rarely performed."

Dort rubbed his hands, circled Karpov's bed. The major breathed evenly and deeply. *Leave it to that slick bastard,* Dort mused, *to be awake all the time, taking in everything.*

"Why is it rare?"

Irina paused. "In cases of unexplained epilepsy, the medications are usually effective. I can't tell you why they haven't worked with him. If anything, the convulsions are getting worse."

"Tell me what is done."

"A flap of bone is removed from the skull. The two hemispheres of the brain are pulled apart. We cut the nerve bundles connecting them—the *corpus callosum* and several smaller commissures or connectors—the anterior and hippo-campal."

"Sounds bloody. What does it do?"

Irina shrugged. "We aren't certain. In epilepsy, there may be transference of impulses through the connecting tissues. When they are cut, the seizures end."

"The patient is not affected?"

She got up. "We give no guarantees. In almost all instances a cure is affected. There is no noticeable change in temperament, personality, or intelligence. There are some changes in perception of objects, speech, and so on."

"Such as?"

"They involve the differentiation between left and right hemispheric capacities. For a while, a person recovering from such surgery will favor the right side of his body, which is controlled by the left hemisphere of the brain. The left half is the dominant hemisphere. After surgery, the left side of the body—controlled by the less important right hemisphere—will rarely show spontaneous activity. The patient may not respond to stimuli to the right brain."

"You said right *brain*. What does that mean? He comes out of it with two brains?"

"Not exactly. Although some neurologists regard the split-brain person as having a dual brain. In time he must condition himself to function with two partially disconnected brains. But the organ is extremely adaptable. One side learns from the other."

"But he's cured?"

"Yes. There is an elimination of attacks."

"And the side effects?"

"They disappear with training."

"How soon before Karpov is back in action?"

"A few weeks. He'll need cosmetic care—a wig, makeup. But his mind should be functional. People recover swiftly from brain surgery if the organic condition is relieved. I had a member of the Ukraine Agricultural Commission a few months ago who underwent surgery for the removal of a nonmalignant brain tumor. In ten days he was back at his desk."

Dort laughed. "Ready to bungle grain production again."

"Karpov's efficiency will not be impaired."

Dort was frowning. "Am I imagining something? Are you

saying he comes out of the operation two different people? One Karpov is enough."

"At times he will behave like two separate people in one body. But these are rare instances. In time he becomes an integrated personality."

Dort nodded. He looked at the insensate figure of his troublesome underling. "Operate on him."

"When?"

"Tomorrow."

"Do we need clearances? Permission from him?"

"I just made the decision for him. Karpov has no family. His wife is incompetent. If I say operate, you do so."

"All right."

"And keep me advised of the outcome and his recovery. I want to make sure he's functional before I turn him loose on Levitch."

He no longer heard the woman's voice. Silence. A dull hum?

The kind of humming silence he remembered in the psychiatric hospital, seated in a vast, cold gray room, facing Marfa. And she, wringing her hands, looking at him with pained eyes.

But I am not sick, she was saying. *Andrei Borisovich, I should not be here. I can be your wife, cook and sew for you, go to the theater, walk in the park, share things with you. . . .*

And he, silent, stone-faced, trying to stroke her hand, repelled by the white flesh, disgusted by the bland pale face, the reddened moist eyes. He craved Mexico. Sun and dark flesh.

I am not sick. Why did you send me here?

I'm dying, Levitch thought. *No one will believe me. Death due to isolation, fear and wet feet.* He slept curled on the stool, trying to keep his feet out of the shit-colored stinking water. Twice a day they shoved bread and thin soup at him. Slamming of metal on metal, boots in the stone corridor. *How long?* He tried to keep count of the days, failed, decided he was not much of a mathematician. Pain, cold, exhaustion drained his mind. Mentally, he did his Hebrew lessons, his English lessons, tried to recall pages from the grammar books. *Complete the following sentences using forms of the verb. . .*

Every other day he was taken out of the cell to interrogation. He was not beaten. What would it avail? He was so terrified, weak and hungry that beatings would only underscore what already existed: the wreckage of his body, the terror that devoured him.

Usually it was Anatoli Malik sitting behind the desk, furrowing his brow, licking his thumb as he turned pages in the dossier. Once a week Colonel Dort appeared, informing Levitch that Chaim Slesik had confessed, that Nadya Burik was talking, that Floyd Hanson, in an interview in New York, had admitted his role as a spy and that Levitch was part of his network of agents.

"And Dr. Belus?" Abram asked.

"Chattering like a housewife in a fish store, Levitch," Dort said.

"I'm not surprised about Belus. But could you find me a newspaper clipping about Hanson, a story in the Western press? I find it hard to believe."

They never produced anything. Nor did they show him evidence that Slesik or Nadya had confessed. *The idiocy of it,* Levitch thought. *They can say anything they want, do anything they want, yet they persist, demanding that I lie, convict myself, implicate others. Why?*

He refused to confess. Yes, he met with Hanson and with Parente. Yes, he gave out bulletins in behalf of the Helsinki group. Yes, he agitated for emigration, for the rights of Ukrainians, Baptists, Pentecostals, Tatars, as well as Jews. But he did not conspire. He did not steal secrets. He merely gave papers to Hanson at the request of Ivan Belus.

Over and over they droned on. The same questions, the same insistence that he confess. And at every session Levitch told them the same thing: *I'm no spy. I have nothing to confess. I have no idea what was in the envelope.* Yes, Belus was a friend. So was Hanson. And Parente. And all the refuseniks: Slesik, the Semonskis, Nadya Burik, many others. But what had they to do with espionage?

He asked to call his friends. A lawyer. His wife in Israel.

Impossible, Malik said. Someone as deeply involved in crimes against the state had to be prevented from making contact with the outside.

"But that is inhuman," Abram said. "That goes against all kinds of civilized behavior. The worst criminals are allowed legal help. They are permitted to write to their loved ones. What are you proving, doing this to me, Comrade Captain?"

Malik barely heard him. When Levitch asked him something, he often waited for thirty seconds, mulling the reports on his desk, before responding with a flat distant *What? What did you say?* The absence of communication frightened Levitch. At times he would have preferred a snarl, an angry shout, even a blow to the face. The icy indifference was worse than overt hostility. It denied his existence, made him subhuman, a smear.

"Confess, Levitch, and you can come out of that hole," Malik would say. "You'll be in prison, but you'll have a bed, a toilet, a sink, better meals. You might even be allowed to see a lawyer and write letters. But if you insist on being stubborn, you stay there where it's wet."

"But I can't confess. I didn't do anything wrong."

And so he went back to the cold cell, his feet recoiling from the first contact with the fetid water, his heart turning to stone.

The Ukrainian had vanished from the adjoining cell some time ago. When? Ten days? Two weeks? He did not know. Now there was a new prisoner, one who appeared to be in terror of the guards. He never spoke, never cried out, appeared to stay huddled in a corner of the stone cage like a nocturnal animal in a zoo. In a few days Levitch realized that the prisoner was tapping messages to him in the left-hand corner of the cell. He was using a stick or a piece of metal, perhaps the edge of the waste bucket. An old-timer, a veteran of Red prisons, no doubt.

Ah, a human connection, if only this hollow tapping. It took Levitch the better part of two days to figure out the code. The initial tap was always in a sequence of one, two, three or four. There would be a long pause, then a second tapping, this time of anywhere from one to eight taps.

Our alphabet, Levitch understood, in a burst of *gestalt* cognition. *The Cyrillic alphabet—thirty-two characters.* Arrange them in four rows, one atop the other, each row eight characters long. The first tap indicated the row. The second tap was the position of the letter on the row. Two taps at the start, second row down; then five taps, counting across the line to the letter *em.* Four taps at first meant the fourth or bottom row, followed by a single tap, indicating the first letter: *shah*.

He was grateful to the prisoner. In a long day of tapping and deciphering, four rows down, eight characters across, he learned that the man was a currency speculator. *You will get it bad*, the tapping informed Abram. *Why?* Abram tapped back, muffling the noise with his turned body, fearful the guards would discover him. *You're a Yid*, the answer came back.

Even here, Levitch thought grimly, *even here*.

He sighed, walked the perimeter of his cell, trying to ignore the icy water caressing his feet, wondered how long they would keep him here. Trial, conviction and imprisonment somewhere in the East would come as a relief. To see the sky, sun, a tree . . .

Only when the guard presented him with a single sheet of paper and a pencil did Levitch realize he had been in prison for two weeks. He recalled that every two weeks he could address a letter to the administrator.

His hand shook when he tried to write. What to say? How appeal to these iron men? *Esteemed warden? Honorable jailer?* He settled on *Comrade*. Would they please send word to his wife, to Chaim Slesik and Mikhail Zolkin that he was in good health? For a moment Levitch was tempted to tell the truth—*I'm cold, sick, hungry, frightened, wet*. But they'd change it, and he did not want to worry Sarah. In his heart, he was convinced he would see her again.

The operation took somewhat less than two hours.

It was a relatively simple procedure, not life-threatening. Deep in anesthesia, Karpov, his head shaven, the bald skull fixed in the stereotaxic instrument, felt nothing, saw nothing, swam in a misty green sea of soft images, scenes of his childhood, visions that sometimes defied description. Once he saw Marfa naked on a stone bed. No, an altar. An Aztec sacrificial stone?

Working swiftly with her neurosurgical team, Dr. Tashenko removed a flap of bone from the midline of the skull, peeled back skin and split bone, cut deep into the *corpus callosum*, severing the 200 million bundles of nerve cells connecting the hemispheres.

On the monitors all was normal. Karpov was healthy and

vigorous, his blood pressure properly low, his brain waves
only faintly affected by the shock of surgery. Blood gases,
breathing, heartbeat, lungs, all performed with encouraging
normality under the insult to the tissues. Toward the end,
when Irina replaced the flap of bone, secured it with acrylic
cement, and ordered her assistants to intubate him, maintain
nourishment with an IV line, and check his production of
urine, he opened his green eyes and stared at hers.

Admonition? Fear? Appeal? She could not tell. In all likelihood he saw nothing. The eyes opened as a reflex. His brain
was cloudy. He had not protested the decision to operate.
Indeed he had welcomed it. He could not live out his life
flopping on hard floors like a beached perch. He could not
tolerate one more session of convulsions, drooling, wetting
himself, awakening sick, exhausted, in the vise of a savage
headache.

"I trust you," he had said thickly before the operation.

She said nothing, cautioned him to be silent.

"Your hands," Karpov said. "I knew them so well. Long,
gentle. I know what pleasure they gave me. They'll inflict
pain. But in the end I'll be a better man. At the mercy of
your hands. Almost medieval, isn't it, Irina? A laying on of
hands."

She was candid with him. She told him Colonel Dort had
visited her and had ordered the operation.

"He wanted me back at work? This isn't a ruse to turn me
into a cabbage or a carrot?"

"He needs you. He's lazy and incompetent, and he wants
you to wind up the Levitch matter. I told him you could be
back at work in two weeks, and there is every chance you'll
be cured."

"Or changed?"

"There will be no change in your personality, Andrei
Borisovich. The operation has one purpose. To relieve you of
seizures. It is not a mind-altering process. You will be your
old self, as resourceful as ever, full of guile, intelligence and
tenacity. But you will be free of epilepsy."

"I believe you." He took her hand. "I might *will* a change
of character after this. Is that not possible? Perhaps it's time
we rearranged our lives."

"No. Don't talk about it."

During the operation, keeping one eye on monitors and

dials, manipulating sawing and cutting instruments, handling
the cauterizer, snapping orders to her team, she wondered if
she were now a full accessory to Levitch's doom—beyond the
matter of the research papers. It did not matter. If not
Karpov, someone else would have destroyed Levitch. It was
not a question of a lone KGB agent against a defenseless Jew.
It was the huge, unfeeling machine of the state—inexorable,
dispassionate, grinding down its victims with relentless
efficiency.

In the recovery room Karpov slept. His head was bound
with white bandages. Beneath the elastic head-wrappings the
bone would mend, tissues heal, blood vessels seal themselves.
The mysterious communication between hemispheres, sparked
across connecting nerves, had ended. Irina studied his handsome face, phthisic and strong at the same time—knife of a
nose, high forehead, flattened ears, lipless mouth. He had
the cruel beauty of a snake, a predatory bird.

She studied his sleeping head. Beneath the bound and
divided skull, billions of neurons were activated. In parts of
the divided brain, a center that controlled aggression, violence,
obsessive-compulsive neuroses, mass hysteria and deception
remained intact. She thought somberly: *I have cured him,
making him whole and functional, so that he may again
indulge his rituals of deceit, ambush, entrapment and
destruction.*

"I'm cold," Levitch said.

"Still?"

"Yes. I know the room is heated, but I'm cold all the time.
My feet are soaked, Comrade Attorney. The chill works its
way into my bones. Forgive me if I shiver. I assure you it
isn't fear. It's just that there's a Siberian permafrost in my
guts."

The lawyer, one Ovsenko, moved his head from side to
side in disbelief. He was a ruddy man of middle age with a
high crown of waved gray hair. He wore thick eyeglasses, and
an Order of Merit on his lapel. He had a blunt manner but
was not unkind to Levitch.

"You can spare yourself all of this, Levitch. Confess."

"People keep telling me that. Listen, you can do me a
favor. Make sure they got word to my wife. Can you?"

"Levitch, you have worse worries than a letter to your

wife. You're going to be tried in four weeks. If you talk, it'll go easy. If not—"

"You're some lawyer. No offense, Comrade Ovsenko, but I didn't ask for you. The prosecutor assigned you to me, correct?"

"That is so."

"I don't want you."

"You have no choice."

"I'll defend myself. I tried to get word to my friends to ask that I be represented by a foreign lawyer, an American or an Englishman, but I can't even communicate with anyone—"

"That's impossible. A foreign lawyer in a Soviet court? Are you crazy, Levitch?"

"Realistic. I have nothing to say to you, and I can tell by the look in your eyes you have no use for me, but let's keep chatting as long as possible. It's warm and dry in here, and I need warmth. Fair enough?"

Ovsenko moved as if to return his papers to his briefcase, then stopped. Levitch knew why. Even if he had rejected the attorney, the man would want to talk to him, draw information out of him. It would, of course, all be given to the KGB and the prosecutor.

"What shall we chat about?" Levitch asked.

"Your involvement with Hanson and Parente."

"Friends, no more, no less."

"Contacts for espionage, weren't they? The papers you gave Hanson—you knew they were secret documents on brain research, didn't you? He asked you for them, didn't he?"

"No, no. Belus had the whole idea. Belus asked me to give them to Hanson, that's all."

Ovsenko shuffled papers. "Dr. Belus has given the prosecutor a sworn statement that you and he conspired to steal papers for Hanson."

"Garbage. Lies. My old friend Belus. He's one of *them*, comrade. Isn't that obvious?"

"Originally he was a CIA agent. He then saw that he was engaged in criminal acts and, with admirable patriotic motivation, turned his evidence over to the proper state agencies."

"I think I'd rather be cold and wet than listen to any more of this. Belus betrayed me. He has to live with what he did. I'll live with what I've done—nothing criminal, nothing rotten, only my desire to leave the Soviet Union and be with my wife."

Levitch got up. "Will you please try to reach my wife and tell her I'm all right? And don't bother coming back here. I'll defend myself. What good will a lawyer do anyway?"

Ovsenko stuffed documents into his case. *Crazy little fellow,* he thought. *Courage, but no sense.* Not that a confession would have helped him. He'd be guilty from the day he walked into the courtroom. But a confession might lighten the sentence.

"Anything else?" the lawyer asked.

"Yes. Have you heard about the new Trans-Siberian railroad?"

"Rail—?"

"We're building it in two directions, East-West and West-East. A peasant asks Andropov: 'Comrade Chairman, is this going to be a one-track or a two-track railroad?' Andropov thinks a minute. Then he says, 'Well, if the two lines meet, it's a one-track, but if they miss each other, it's two-track.'"

Ovsenko smiled.

"Hey, you didn't bring me the newspaper articles about Hanson's confession. He never did, did he? And how's Slesik doing? Maybe we can work out a deal. I'll make believe I want to engage you, and we can sit and talk, and you'll bring me news—"

But the lawyer had put on his coat, shaken his head and was walking to the door and out of the Levitch case.

"It's Zolkin," Lev Tashenko said. "He wants to speak to you." The editor, looking frail in a shaggy green sweater, handed the phone to Irina.

They had finished their evening meal, which had included a decent bottle of Georgian wine Irina had purchased from a black-marketeering farmer who showed up at the hospital once a month with a few crates of private stock. Tashenko had cooked, cleared the table and washed the dishes. His wife worked longer, more arduous hours. Often Lev wondered if he served any function beyond his housewifely chores. He was beginning to pride himself on his breaded veal cutlets, the clever things he did with leftover vegetables.

"Yes, Mikhail Ivanovich, I understand," Irina said. "I know it's a serious matter."

Lev watched his wife. No agitation on her face, no movement of her beautiful head. Even though drained by a long day at the Institute, she was serene. Two major operations, including one performed on his old nemesis Andrei Karpov.

"I am afraid I can't participate," Irina said. "Whatever my sympathies, I can't help you." She hung up.

"What did the great dissident want?"

"A petition to free Levitch. Justice for Levitch, that sort of thing. He wanted my signature."

"Zolkin should know better. You can't be compromised. Not with me in your household. I carry the taint with me."

She lit a cigarette, reclined on the sofa, tossed off her shoes. "With or without you, I would not sign it. Zolkin has his honors, his career is over, and he is already marked. So are all the people who are signing it. The democrats, the dissidents, the unstable, the courageous, the foolish."

"Many names?"

"Not too many. Zolkin was decent about it. He understood my career is all I have. I'm not a ballet dancer who can defect. We live well. You're an eminent editor and critic—"

"A hollow reed. No courage, no character. I can't even be a braggart about my selling out. I hide behind obscure essays, pointless ratiocinations, all the intellectual muck, the convoluted lies that pass for cerebration in the motherland."

"Don't judge yourself." She shut her eyes. "Zolkin is a very brave man."

"Yes, it would be more decent and gratifying if we could sign a petition someday. But over Levitch? Oh, I'm sympathetic. But let's be honest. An obscure Jew? Who told him to get involved?"

Irina said nothing. The papers she had given Dr. Belus had helped doom Levitch. Asking no questions, she had let Karpov use her to inflict suffering on an innocent man. How good it would have been to join Zolkin!

"Second thoughts?" Tashenko asked. He dusted bread crumbs from the tablecloth, collected them in his palm. Then he lifted the cloth and went to the window to shake it out.

"I suppose not. How many sacrifices is one expected to make? Levitch will be imprisoned and his life ruined. Another Russian tragedy. My name on a petition would not save him."

"I agree. It's unfair of him to make these demands on you."

Lev drained the last of the red wine, shook the bottle to release a few bits of sediment. Bitter at the end, like his life. "But think, Irina. Wouldn't it be soul-nourishing to sign the petition and make our stand with Zolkin?"

"For what purpose?"

"Yes, you have a right to ask me that. I made my brief stand once, and was punished for it. Emasculated, shamed in front of my wife."

"I don't blame you for it."

Tashenko got up, came to her and knelt at her feet. He buried his head in her lap, lost his guilt in the sweaty perfume of her thighs, the scent of a hard-working body, laminations of blood, the aromas of disinfectant, laboratory, a musky soap.

"How I love you," he said. "I think of this man Levitch and how he loves his wife. How does he do it? How does he live from day to day? He'll be found guilty and put away for a long time. He cannot imagine what imprisonment is like, the torture of solitary. I lack his courage. His honor."

"Don't talk about it." She stroked his thinning black hair, felt no passion, wondered what the rest of their lives would be like.

8

"SHALL WE TRY some short-term memory tests?"

Irina, in white smock, holding Karpov's chart in one hand, sat opposite the KGB man in a shaded green room at the Institute. He was in a wheelchair. His head was swathed in bandages. In his quilted red robe and black velvet slippers he was much too grand for the hospital. His eyes were preternaturally bright, a glinting green.

"My memory seems to me excellent, short-term or long."

"Who is Mikhail Semonski?"

"Jewish musician. Piano teacher. A refusenik."

"Ivan Belus?"

"Doctor. Another of that crowd."

"Did you ask him to do something for you a few weeks ago?"

"To get some papers from you. Research papers."

"Very good." Irina turned a page in the folder marked KARPOV. "What did the research consist of?"

"Oh, brain data. Rats, mice. What was that fancy word you used? Mur—Music—?"

"Muricide. The fact that you don't recall doesn't mean your

memory's impaired. Muricide is an odd word. Actually the papers I gave Belus had to do with another experiment."

"Was I aware of it?"

"That's for you to remember."

"I don't believe I read them. Belus was ordered to give them to Levitch, that was all. It doesn't matter what's in them. If we call them state secrets, they're state secrets. But I am interested. What did they concern?"

"Conditioning rats to respond to the odor of explosive— gelignite, TNT, plastic bombs. The rat is implanted with a fiberlike electrode in one of the brain's pleasure centers, the lateral hypothalamus. He's taught that whenever he smells the explosives, he gets a jolt of almost unendurable pleasure. We can't describe it, since we're not rats, but the pleasure transcends orgasm, food, drink, the maternal instinct. Naturally he reacts—accelerated heartbeat, spiking brain waves, and so on. In time, he need not receive the electrical shock. The scent of TNT alone will excite him."

"And the application of this?"

"I thought you might guess. The rats can be used to sniff out hidden explosives. A simple monitoring system tells us when the rats become aroused, anticipating the stimulation of their brains, or indeed actually experiencing it by smelling a cache of explosive."

"Marvelous. We can hang Levitch with that."

"Or anything else you decide to hang him with."

Karpov stretched. "I suppose so. Irina, am I making progress? You said Dort wants me in good condition so I can make final arrangements for the trial. Do I pass muster?"

She studied the medical file. "You had four days of severe headaches after surgery. You had a brief period during which you lost your short-term memory or had it severely impaired. That condition seems to be correcting itself. Periods of drowsiness, which were probably due to sedation as much as the aftereffects of the commissurotomy. A tendency to favor the right side of your body in performing chores. Your left side shows a reluctance to initiate spontaneous activity, as if it's waiting for a cue. All that should disappear in a matter of weeks. Your speech is normal. I had one patient who lost the power to speak for twenty-seven days. How do you feel in general?"

"A little disoriented, but strong."

"We are going to conduct some simple tests. The results may indicate a lapse in perception. Don't be upset. These are normal results for the kind of operation you underwent."

Irina got up and wheeled him toward a white screen, stopping the chair four feet from the blank surface. She darkened the room and turned on a small projector. A tiny white dot appeared in the geometric center of the flat white plane.

Karpov asked, "Have I become one of your white rats?" He sounded amused, not wary.

"In a sense."

"I'm flattered."

"I have to determine the extent to which the surgery altered your ability to recognize objects. Look at the screen, fixing your gaze on the illuminated dot. Ready?"

Karpov nodded.

Irina pressed the switch on the projector. For a tenth of a second, a row of white spots of light were flashed across the screen.

"What do you see?"

"Flashes of light. White spots."

"Where? On what side of the screen?"

"The right side."

Once more she pressed the switch. This time the white dots appeared only in the left half of the field.

"What did you see this time?"

"Nothing. I don't . . . nothing."

"We'll try again. But this time, don't tell me what you saw or did not see. Wheel yourself to the screen and point to the area where images appeared."

Once more she pressed the switch. Again the white dots appeared in the left half of the field for one-tenth of a second.

Karpov frowned and squinted. He wheeled himself forward and pointed to the left side of the screen. "I saw . . . something. Here."

"Why did you deny it the previous time?"

"I . . . didn't . . . I'm not sure."

"But you did deny it. You couldn't describe what appeared. In fact you said you saw nothing."

"I said . . . damn . . . what did I say?"

She turned the lights on and turned off the projector. "Your problem is a linguistic one, not one of perception. The right side of the screen was projected to your left hemisphere, which controls speech, so it verbally identified the dots. From your first negative response to the lights in the *left* visual field, one might assume you were partially blind. But you aren't. It was simply that the image was flashed to your right hemisphere and it could not respond. When you were asked to indicate *manually* where the dots were, you un-hesitantly showed me the left side of the visual field."

"What does this mean? That every time I see something with my left eye alone I won't be able to identify it?"

"Only for a while. Your right brain harbors some rudimentary powers of speech. In time it will learn from the left, or become skilled at taking hints, finding clues to words."

She directed him to a small table with a shelf under the writing surface. "Place your right hand inside and feel the object in the right-hand corner."

Karpov did so.

"Tell me what it is."

"This is ludicrous. Of course I know what it is. It's a pencil."

"Now remove your right hand. Touch the object in the left corner with your left hand."

Karpov reached in and found a wooden ruler. He fingered it a moment.

"What is it?" she asked.

"Ah . . . ah . . . I don't know."

"Never seen one before?"

"I think so. But I can't tell you what it is."

"Cover your right eye, then come to my desk."

Karpov obeyed, rolling lightly in his chair.

"Find the object on my desk that matches the object you just touched under the table."

He scanned the desk, pointed quickly to a mate of the hidden ruler. "That's it."

"What is it called?"

"I don't know."

"All right, uncover your right eye."

"It's a ruler, damn it," he said.

"Don't be upset. Your right hand touched a pencil and sent information to your left hemisphere, which spoke the word pencil. But your left hand, fingering the ruler, sent the data to your *right* brain, and it failed to make a verbal response because surgery has disconnected the halves of your brain."

"Is my right brain an imbecile?"

"By no means." She wheeled him back to the screen. "Let's try a few more. Cover your right eye again."

Karpov did so. Irina flashed a drawing of a cigarette lighter on the screen.

"What is that object?" she asked.

"Ah . . . a can opener. No. Ball-point pen. Damn, what is it?"

"Describe what it does."

"Ah, smoking . . . tobacco . . . fire?"

"Very good."

"Look at it with your right eye."

Karpov obeyed. "Cigarette lighter. I see. The left hemisphere speaks."

She tested him for the better part of an hour. His performance was what she expected: a failure of speech when the left eye or the left hand tried to identify objects. But with auditory cues, Karpov's left hand was able to select the proper objects from a canvas sack by touch. She would command him: "Find the thing that cuts cloth," and his left hand would locate a scissors. Five minutes later, holding the scissors in his left hand, his eyes closed, he could not identify the scissors by name.

Toward the end of the session she was forced to smile when Karpov's hemispheres began to contest one another. It was a simple test. With his right eye closed, Karpov fixed his left eye on a screen on which red or green lights flashed, and was asked to identify the color. For a while his guesses were a bit better than chance. After a minute or so, his guesses improved. Irina watched him carefully, realizing that the two halves of his bisected brain were struggling for dominance.

The light flashed red.

"Green," Karpov said. His mute right hemisphere could not find the correct word.

"Is it?" she asked. "Are you sure?"

Karpov frowned and shook his head. "No, no, I meant red."

"Which is it?"

"I'm not sure. Ah, gr . . . Red. Yes, red." He looked at her almost appealingly. His lean face was strangely vulnerable.

"Don't be upset," she said. "Your right hemisphere saw the red light, but there was no communication to the left. So the left made a guess. The wrong one. The right hemisphere, which is no fool, became annoyed with its partner. Hence your frown, the shake of your head. These gestures were directing the left hemisphere to the fact that its response was wrong and that it had better correct itself."

"Remarkable. A bit frightening."

"Almost like the way you interrogate people, don't you think?"

"That's a fair comparison. Considerate one moment, angry the next. How long do I remain in this condition? I can't go through life waiting for my left brain to identify things, and to supply answers."

"Under normal conditions your right eye and your right side will transmit information to your left hemisphere. You don't normally walk around with your right eye covered, or your right hand inoperative. Since the left hemisphere can function, your speech and your power to associate speech with objects, with people, with your environment, will not be affected. In time you'll start using the left side of your body with more ease. Moreover, your left hand will develop heightened skills—in such things as spatial matters, visual tasks, so on."

"And the seizures?"

"We can hope we've cured them. I'm continuing you on a mild course of drugs for ten days. After that, we'll be able to take you off them altogether."

Karpov rubbed his forehead, patted the white bandages on his split skull. "I still have some deep pain."

"Understandable. Your brain and your skull have been severely insulted. It takes time."

She went to the corridor and summoned a nurse.

"A moment," Karpov said. "I realize that my skull will grow together, that the nerve endings will heal, that all the physical changes will be corrected. But what about my mind?"

She thought: *yes, your mind. That cunning instrument, that stalking apparatus that motivates you, gives you your skill in tracking down the defenseless, tormenting your victims, trapping and jailing them.*

"It's hard to predict," Irina said.

"Don't spare me anything. What can I anticipate?"

"People who have undergone this operation recover."

"I don't mean being able to identify a bottle opener or a pen. You've explained how I'll master such chores. But about my powers of concentration? My memory? My reasoning?"

"They'll improve. Indeed, Andrei Borisovich, you may emerge in a month or so more gifted than you are now."

"Really?"

"Some split-brain patients double their attention span. They can handle twice as much information. Or carry out two tasks as fast as a normal person does one. I'm hesitant to say it, but in cases such as yours we may be dealing with two brains."

"Two brains . . ."

"Each learns some of the other's function. The right hemisphere develops the power of speech, while the left picks up some of the right's talent for spatial skills. Each becomes capable of functions of a higher order. I would think two gifted brains would be of use to an important police functionary."

"You mustn't tease a convalescent. Especially one who has experienced—what did you call it?—insult to his brain."

"I'm not teasing. There's a growing feeling that separation of the hemispheres creates two independent areas of consciousness within a single cranium. It's been postulated that if a human brain were divided in a very young person, both hemispheres would develop, separately and independently, mental functions at a level attained only in the left hemisphere of normal people."

"What a pleasing prospect."

"I hope so. It won't affect your character, however. There may be two of you, but both will be as efficient and as dedicated as the single Karpov."

In ten days Karpov was strong enough to return to his office and the Levitch matter. He wore a finely crafted light-brown wig to cover his shaved skull. The surgical scar on his forehead was already turning pale. He spent several minutes each morning under an ultraviolet lamp to hide the white stitch marks.

Tired at first, he slowly regained his strength, stopped smoking, slept soundly, ate sparingly, and was delighted to find himself free of convulsions. The headaches ceased, although the healing process in his skull touched off disconcerting pains. Withal, he was satisfied with his recovery, grateful to Irina and ready to resume his labors for the KGB.

Dort gave him his marching orders: Get Levitch to trial, wind it up, crack down on the others. Zolkin too? Yes, Dort said, Zolkin too. Once Levitch was convicted, Zolkin would be shooting his mouth off. They would have to nail him with something, find him guilty, banish him. They could not send a man like Zolkin to prison or work camp, but isolation and house arrest in the East might be in order. The men at the top were getting fed up with Zolkin's slanderous outbursts, his attacks on the USSR. Ever since he'd joined forces with the refuseniks, he was getting to be as nasty as they were.

"You realize, Karpov," Dort lectured him on his first day back at work, "the Western governments and their press are going to raise hell over this Levitch business. The little bastard does something to them. All that innocent charm. I don't know what all the fuss is over one more Jew. They let millions of them die when Hitler was roughing them up and no one made a squawk. But we move against one Jew and the newspapers in America start screaming. The Americans carry on as if Levitch matters. If I had my way, it'd be like the old days. Take him down to the cellar and finish him off with one clean shot in the neck. Trial, my fat ass."

Karpov said, "You want the case against him airtight. No loose ends. No doubts. Nothing he can point to, nothing he can contest. Is it true he's defending himself?"

Dort nodded. "Yes. And it's a shame, but we'll have to have a public trial. Oh, we have nothing to lose. In fact, the big boys want it that way. Let the world see him for the scum he is."

"How long a trial?"

"Four days. Get to work. How do you feel, by the way?"

"A little shaky."

"Head all right?"

"Fine. No more seizures."

Karpov, aware of the way the right side of his body was dominating, got up. He held his left arm stiffly at his side. He sensed a rigidity, a reluctance in his left leg.

"I like your wig," Dort said. "Nice shade. A sort of shithouse brown. Makes you look younger. Who knows? You clean up Levitch and the rest of that crowd, you might get that foreign post you want."

"I'd be grateful."

"Don't count on anything. But once Levitch is on ice, and we go to work on some of the others, maybe you can get back to overseas duty."

"I think I can still be of great help to the motherland, now that I'm cured."

"Right." Dort smothered a thick laugh. "We can all thank Dr, Tashenko, eh, Andrei Borisovich? The lady and her scalpel did you a great favor."

"She is a talented surgeon."

"Talk to Levitch. Get the confession. We don't want the runt standing up in court making heroic speeches."

Irina gathered literature on self-stimulation of the brain and sat alone in her office late one afternoon, after an exhausting four hours on her feet. She had removed a tumor of the pituitary gland from a teenaged boy. The operation had gone smoothly, but she found that during the last hour or so her strength flooded out of her, as if her veins had been opened. Her energies seemed awash on the floor, like excess blood. Her team finished closing the boy's skull.

Something about Karpov bothered her, gnawed at her. Something wrong about his quick recovery. Not anything organic or physical. Rather she was disturbed by some kind of moral equation, an imbalance. His good health, his intact personality, the way in which he had thrown off his seizures and reentered his grim profession. There would be more Levitch cases now, more falconlike swoops on harmless pigeons. It was unfair. The apparatus would always do what it wanted. Why did she have to contribute to more rapacious assaults on the innocent?

During her work on the self-stimulation of rats, the experiments designed to create explosive-detecting skills in the animals, conditioning them to grow hyperactive at the scent of TNT, she had accumulated a file of articles on the subject. (Ironic, she thought, how they would now hang Levitch with this information, claiming it was defense-related secret material. In a sense they were right—it was defense-related. But hardly secret. The Americans, notably a Professor Morris Weintraub in Stamford, Connecticut, had five years ago evolved an identical detective-rat, using a similar program of self-stimulation.)

She located a yellowing article in English on a curious early experiment by scientists in the United States Army. Electrodes had been implanted in the hypothalamus of a mule, a pleasure center. A brain stimulator was placed in a pack on the animal's back. When the stimulator was activated it charged the electrode. The mule experienced a rush of intense pleasure, whatever a mule felt when in ecstasy.

Then came the ingenious part. Also on the mule's back were a prism and mirror. When the animal was oriented toward the sun, the mirror operated a photo cell, which then programmed the stimulator to deliver bursts of electric current to the electrode in the mule's brain.

Turned loose in a sunny field, the animal stayed "on beam," always walking in a direction that enabled the sun to strike the prism and mirror—and thus activate the pleasure-giving rod. If the mule deviated, the stimulation ceased. In time the animal learned to "follow the sun." When the mirror was reversed, away from the sun, the mule quickly learned to alter its path so that the sun could strike it, and again fill the mule's consciousness with bursts of pleasure.

An older article—it was still classified—had to do with the training of dogs by Soviet scientists during World War II. The experiments were crude but they appeared to have produced interesting results. Like the mule, the dogs had their skulls pierced and electrodes plunged into the lateral hypothalamus, a "pleasure center." Whenever the dogs approached a captured German tank, they were stimulated with a jolt of good feeling. Turned loose on the battlefield with explosives strapped to their bodies, the dogs unerringly raced to the armored vehicles, convinced they'd receive the pleasurable sensation.

After that early experimentation, Irina noted, Soviet science had tended to reject the technique. It went hand in hand with new scientific prejudices in the USSR—a deemphasis on the roles of punishment and reward in learning experiments. Her own work with implanted rats, and the emergence of patterns of self-stimulation as a reward, had marked something of a departure from the official line. But as yet no one had criticized or impeded her work.

She located another article by a Norwegian neurologist and reread it, marking comments in the margin. Dr. Sem-Jacobsen had pioneered self-stimulation experiments in humans, nota-

bly with epileptics, depressed patients, criminals. She read
the words carefully.

> The reasons given by patients for continuing self-
> stimulation seem as complex as man himself. In man,
> curiosity is probably the most dominant causative fac-
> tor in initiating self-stimulation. If a patient feels
> something, he might wonder, precisely what is the na-
> ture of this sensation? What am I feeling? Let me try it
> once more. Once more. Is it tickling? Is it real pleasure?
> Other patients speak of a need to obey the stimulus, to
> cooperate with the examiner. Some patients are known
> to continue to operate the stimulation switch long after
> the current has been turned off. . . .

An American neurosurgeon reported more startling results
with self-stimulation. A patient who had just attempted suicide started to smile when an electrode in his septal areas was
stimulated. He did not know why; he simply felt good, as if
he had a date with a beautiful woman arranged for that
evening. In several instances, the American researcher
suspected, patients achieved *orgasm* with self-stimulation of
the brain. If not actual orgasm, they reported an encompass-
ing sexual gratification. In any event, the feeling was deeply
pleasurable and satisfying.

Finally Irina located the most recent work in the Soviet
Union. Colleagues of hers, some years ago, had employed
self-stimulation with people suffering Parkinson's disease and
other brain disorders that affected bodily movements. Stimulation of the septal regions of the brain evoked erotic sensations.
One woman reported orgasm. So pleased was the subject that
she kept returning to the hospital, haunting corridors, asking
when the next session would take place, manifesting affection
for the technicians and doctors—male or female—who conducted the experiments.

And yet there were odd irregularities and inconsistencies
in reaction to self-stimulation. In patients being treated for
anxiety, high voltages to the ventrolateral and dorsolateral
thalamus produced feelings of anxiety and terror. Nonetheless the patients agreed to return for further stimulation, in
the hope that they would produce information of therapeutic
value.

She checked the file again, tried to recall other experi-

ments of self-stimulation of the pleasure centers of the brain.
As far as she could determine, no split-brain patient had ever
been implanted with electrodes and subjected to controlled
tests. The combination in one human being—a split brain and
electrical stimulation—might produce singular results.

"You're convinced you don't want counsel?" Karpov asked.

"Only of my own choosing. I can't think of anyone in the
Soviet Union I want to represent me." Levitch rubbed his
nose. It was cold all the time, even on those blessed occasions when he was out of his damp cell.

"That is strange, Levitch. Thousands of lawyers in Moscow
and not one pleases you?"

"Excuse me, Comrade Major, but your lawyers are either
part of your police force or terrified of it. No thanks. I'll do
my own talking."

"What makes you think the judge will permit you to prattle
on?"

"Well, it's a public trial. I won't prattle. But I'm allowed to
explain what I did, and why I did it. That will be defense
enough for me. When does the trial start?"

"Monday. You have four days in which to confess. I have
all the papers here for you to sign. It will spare all of us a
great deal of trouble. The trial can be wound up in one day if
you do the intelligent thing and confess.

"I thank you, Comrade Major, but I can't."

"Confess. Maybe you will be allowed to leave."

"I don't think so. In your eyes I've committed serious
crimes. No one gets off easy."

"More stubborn than I thought."

Karpov's left hand tapped the desk. He lifted a pen and
pointed it at Levitch while he discussed the nature of the
evidence accumulated against him.

Levitch thought: *That pen in his left hand is like a weapon,
a knife at my heart.* An odd-looking bird, this Karpov. He'd
heard about the handsome KGB operative, an international
dandy and linguist. But the man looked artificial. It dawned
on Levitch: He was wearing a wig. His face had been
cosmeticized. It appeared to be coated with wax or paint.
There were faint stitch marks on his forehead. Surgery? It
would explain the wig.

"I'll have to stand by my principles and my friends," Levitch said. "Besides, I'd prefer a long trial to a short one."

"Why?"

"More time in a warm courtroom. Comrade Major, do I really have to spend so much time in a cold cell, with my feet soaked? How about a bed or a blanket? I need a bath. I stink. You don't want the world to think that the Soviet Union maltreats prisoners. You can't afford to make Solzhenitsyn look good."

Karpov smiled. "As a matter of fact, I am ordering your transfer to a different facility. Lubianka. Don't cringe. I promise you a better cell, a bed, decent food. You'll be allowed to bathe and shave. Your meals will improve."

"Thank you." Levitch, eager for the sight of another human, the sound of any human voice—even that of his captor— watched Karpov closely. Something strange, off-center, in his manner. As soon as Karpov began to talk about the new quarters and better food, offering hope to Levitch, his body shifted in his chair. Did Levitch imagine it? Or did he now move his right hand forward? Karpov dropped the pen in his left hand. His slender figure turned, offering the right side— face, arm, leg—to the prisoner. Levitch had no idea what it meant. It was a subtle spontaneous move, but it had happened, and it had been coordinated with the soothing words.

"Since you refuse to cooperate, and you refuse counsel, I won't talk to you again," Karpov said. He patted his wig, touched his left temple lightly, as if probing for pain. "If you decide to sign the papers, tell the guard. You'll be taken to Lubianka when you leave here. You will be afforded all the rights of a prisoner of the world's greatest democratic socialist state."

He has got to be joking, Levitch thought. Karpov did not offer his hand. But he again moved his right hand across the desk. It turned into a fist and came to rest on top of the flattened left hand.

"Let's get the troops together," Parente said. "Anyone get lucky and get a courtroom pass?"

Twenty-odd members of the foreign press had gathered under a rain-drenched linden tree outside the Moscow Central Palace of Justice. No one had been issued a pass. Parente counted heads. A good turnout: Americans, British, a Canadian, the West Germans, the French, a Belgian, a Dutchman, three Scandinavians. No one from the Eastern bloc, none of the Third World sycophants. There were five TV camera crews, a half-dozen photographers.

"It's outrageous," Agnes Wardle said. She glared at Brian Cardwell. "I suppose you have an excuse for all of this?"

"Dear Agnes, I don't make the rules here."

"No, but you approve of them."

Stammering, cheeks reddening, Cardwell offered a lame explanation of the issuing of passes for the Levitch trial. There was an official pass, a white card enabling the holder to come and go as he pleased. A green pass gave the possessor priority; a red pass meant you were allowed in if there was room.

"A papered house," Parente said. "Stooges, cops, locals."

"Beg pardon?" Cardwell asked.

"None of us got a pass," Tony said. "They even closed you out, Brian, and you're one of the boys."

A bus pulled up and a file of lumpy, undistinguished people stepped down and were marched into the courtroom building. Some had green tags tied to their lapels.

"Trucking them in from the suburbs," Parente said. "Party members, small-time bureaucrats, army reservists. They won't even give Levitch a cheering section."

Four uniformed militiamen walked down the steps of the building and moved metal barricades toward the knot of reporters, photographers and the curious.

"What gives?" Parente asked.

"Move, move," the sergeant of militia said. "More distance between you and the court."

"Creep," Parente said.

The reporters reassembled, stomped cold feet, complained. Agnes Wardle, in sensible hiking shoes and a sturdy British mack, observed wistfully that they could use hot coffee or tea, a place to rest while awaiting the results of the first day's hearing.

"Here come Levitch's people," a Canadian reporter said. "With Zolkin."

Cameras were unlimbered. The news-film teams began to shoot. The Zolkin presence would make headlines, front-page photos, a lead for the evening news on television.

Parente saw all his friends from the refusenik movement:

Mikhail and Olga Semonski, Nadya Burik, Slesik, dragging one leg after another in defiance of his illness, the bearded young Zalman Sokolov, who would succeed Levitch as spokesman. In the midst of the group was a short gray-haired woman with a timid face, fearful as a trapped mouse.

She was introduced by Sokolov as the mother of Abram Levitch. Parente remembered. She was not Jewish, a lapsed member of the Orthodox Church. He recalled Abram telling him how his KGB interrogators had mocked him—in Israel he was not even regarded as a Jew. Line of descent on the maternal side. Levitch had brushed the taunts aside; he would be formally converted.

"I am here to see my son," Levitch's mother said haltingly. "But please, don't ask me to say anything. I'm tired."

Zolkin said, "Mrs. Levitch will ask to be allowed into the courtroom. I'll plead in her behalf."

The reporters stood aside. Mikhail Zolkin led the birdlike woman around the steel barricades to the high double door of the courthouse. Astonishingly, the militiamen let them pass. Zolkin had authority, an aura of command.

At the steps an official in a blue suit came out and spoke with Zolkin. The reporters and the refuseniks could see the man shake his head and gesture toward the far side of the metal barriers. There would be no seat at the trial of her son.

The woman turned away. Zolkin did not. "You have no soul," the scientist shouted. "The world is watching this mockery. To deny a mother her wish to be at her son's side is inhuman, the work of Fascists. Damn you."

The man in the blue suit smiled—a flat, wide smile. Parente saw it. *Why do they smile so much? Are they embarrassed? Shamed?* It was the smile of the SS men rounding up Jews in the Warsaw Ghetto, the smile of Red Army soldiers cutting down Hungarian boys in Budapest in 1956, the smirk that hides fear, shame, disgust.

Zolkin came back to the reporters and spoke for the cameras. "I'm full of grief and indignation over this. We have no choice but to make our stand with Abram Levitch. This is not justice. It's sadism, a mockery, a perversion of law. They have the power and the guns, but they will be called to account someday. I'm sorry. I can say no more."

Two more busloads of civilians disgorged more gray-brown people into the square around the courthouse. These new arrivals did not enter the building. Instead they clogged the area, facing the refuseniks, jeering and hooting at them.

"Punks," Parente said to Agnes Wardle. "Party finks. Komsomols. To show the world the whole country hates Levitch and wants his scalp."

"Traitors, spies," the new arrivals shouted. "Capitalist scum."

"Kike Fascists."

"Zionist pigs, go home."

There was a momentary wave of fear in the party of journalists and the dissidents. Zolkin took a few steps toward the hecklers. His hair was ruffled by the wind; his eyes were angry and clear.

"You are a disgrace," he said. "You shame the Russian earth."

Zalman Sokolov took out his book and led the Jews in prayer. Most of them couldn't read Hebrew. A few knew the words by rote.

"They look so awfully defenseless," Agnes Wardle said. "One can't help but feel that the odds are against them."

"Pity," a Canadian said.

Cardwell looked away and said nothing.

"The meek don't inherit the earth," Parente growled. "They get to pay everyone else's bills. Look at that kid Sokolov. He could keep his mouth shut, stay home, live on charity, maybe make it to Israel in a year or so. He can pick lemons at four A.M. on a kibbutz or open a dry-goods store in the Mea Shearim. But he laid it on the line. There's a longer price on his getting to where he wants to go."

The Canadian watched the bearded young man, bobbing, bending, eyes lost in holy reverie. "Maybe he's there already, Tony."

" '. . . collecting a list of nine hundred so-called refuseniks who were actually Zionist agitators, engaging in other anti-state activities. Further, assembling and disseminating illegally statements of the so-called Helsinki Committee, which reports were used as the basis for hostile radio broadcasts by such anti-Soviet agencies as Radio Liberty and the Voice of America; engaging in contacts with Soviet scientists in order to steal secret data in various fields of knowledge. All of the above are classified as acts of treason against the state, under Article 64-A of the Constitution of the USSR. . . . ' "

Levitch yawned, blinked, enjoyed the warmth of the packed steamy room. *Not bad, not bad.* Karpov had been true to his word. Clean underwear, clean socks, a tepid bath, a shave with tepid water. He had been moved to a cell in Lubianka—a narrow metal bed, a dry floor, a toilet. When a man swam in cold filth, he welcomed anything.

Levitch looked around the courtroom from his front-row seat. He was flanked by two uniformed militiamen. On the high bench were the assessors—the lay judges. At a table to their left were the secretary of the court, the clerk, Ovsenko—the lawyer whom Abram had already rejected—and the prosecutor. This last was Natasha Kralik, a stout woman with frizzy auburn hair and a huge thrusting bosom. Comrade Prosecutor Kralik had a spongy voice and a cold gray eye. Tatar blood had narrowed the predatory eyes, endowed her with broad cheekbones. She planted herself to the left of the bench, hands on hips, and poured out the crimes of Abram Levitch as if reading from a timetable.

" '. . . further crimes of the accused include anti-Soviet agitation and propaganda, as defined in Article 70.1 of the Soviet Constitution. These include the exchange of telegrams and letters with American politicians and journalists attempting to influence foreign policy, and defaming the Soviet Union. Among the issues raised by the accused: repeated false charges of anti-Semitism in the USSR, and other false charges concerning the alleged persecution of national minorities.' "

Lulled into half-sleep by her voice, Levitch peered behind him. A full house. Every seat taken. Party faithful, cops, street galoots, the kind who could be assembled on short notice to beat up demonstrators, wreck an art exhibit, demolish a protest. Not one of his Jewish friends was on hand. Not Zolkin, not Colonel Arkangeli, none of the democrats. And of course no journalists. He tried to find a Soviet or Eastern bloc reporter, without success. Possibly a dark-mustached man in the fourth row. Deroulian? The Armenian working for Novosti? He looked familiar. Someone Tony may have introduced him to some months ago. Abram smiled at the hawkish face. The man smiled back. Ah, progress. Armenians, even when in the service of the motherland, tended to be civilized. Mikoyan was said to have been the most decent of the old Bolshevik leaders.

" '. . . through all these criminal endeavors, the accused

Levitch betrayed his motherland, and deliberately engaged in acts harmful to the state and the military strength of the USSR. His contacts with foreign journalists were occasions for the distribution of military data, information involving the security of the motherland. . . .' "

Oh, the dullness of it, Abram thought. *Did I do all this? Me. Levitch, a poor math teacher who wanted only to be with my wife?* He swiveled his head as Natasha Kralik drilled on, her voice harsh and invasive, like a piece of machinery running without enough oil, or on the verge of tearing a belt.

For a moment, he thought he saw Karpov seated at the rear of the room. He looked again. His hunter, his jailer. There was no mistaking the dark glasses, the hard-edged face. Few Russians wore smoked glasses indoors. Levitch could not see the scars, but he noted the curious brown wig, the erect bearing. Karpov sat alone, immobile, enigmatic.

I can't think too badly of him, Levitch thought. *He got me a better room.*

"What are the odds?" the Canadian asked Parente. "Guilty or not?"

"Graham, you got to be joking."

"I know. Just to relieve the boredom. Put it this way. What'll he get?"

"I don't want to think about it."

Agnes Wardle asked, "Is there a chance of a trade-off? Is there a Russian spy in custody in the United States whom the KGB wants back?"

Tony stretched. "Yeah, a dozen of them. But the way they're developing the script here, they want to punish Abram, hit him hard. Break the backs of the refuseniks, throw the fear of God into them." He paused and looked at Zolkin. The scientist had his arm around Levitch's mother, shielding her from the curses of the state-sponsored mob. "And maybe it's a warning to Zolkin."

"You mean they'd go after him?" asked the West German.

"Why not? He's got no guns. If they can land on Levitch, and they don't get hurt, why not finish off the democratic movement altogether? Miserable, suspicious bastards. Maybe we could get Kerensky back. At least he didn't go around jailing and killing everyone in sight."

*   *   *

The chairman of the court, or chief judge, a mop-headed man affecting pince-nez, made an announcement. His name was Moresha. Levitch suspected he was a KGB operative. There was some hint of the snoop, the brute, in his hard voice, his blunt manner.

"The court wishes to announce that the accused, A. M. Levitch, has been offered counsel in the person of Comrade Ovsenko, of the Faculty of Jurisprudence of Moscow University. Does the accused accept Comrade Ovsenko's services?"

Levitch got to his feet. "No, Comrade Chairman. I'll defend myself."

"Comrade Ovsenko is excused."

The lawyer got up, bowed to the court and walked out.

"Does the prosecutor have any objection to the accused defending himself?" the chairman asked.

Kralik shook her frizzy red hair. "None, Comrade Chairman."

Chairman Moresha studied papers on his desk. *An odd bird*, Levitch felt, moving his jaws as if chewing, but clearly there was nothing in his mouth. *Except me?*

"The accused can make an opening statement," the chairman said.

Levitch got up, gave a hitch to his belt. He'd lost weight on KGB fare. His jailers had spent the last four days nourishing him with meat and milk, apples and potatoes. But his gut rumbled in alarming new ways and his head was airy.

"Comrade Chairman," Levitch said. "I submitted thirty pages consisting of documents and other evidence, attesting to my innocence. Has the court considered them?"

"No."

"May I ask why?"

"There hasn't been sufficient time. The papers were scanned by the prosecutor and found to be worthless."

"No time? I'm told the case against me consists of one hundred and twenty volumes of evidence. Your court was able to peruse them. Why not my submissions?"

Kralik struggled to her feet. "Comrade Chairman, all this is irrelevant. The accused's submissions were a stew of rumor, hearsay, old newspaper clippings from the capitalist press, affidavits from criminals and other enemies of the state—"

"Like Mikhail Zolkin?" Levitch asked.

The room hummed, a susurration of annoyance, subdued anger. Packed with sympathizers, the crowd understood the power of Zolkin, the meaning of his association with Jews. No one could have been more Russian, more a part of the earth and sky and soul of Mother Russia, than the physicist. His name caused confusion, embarrassment.

"The accused will not attempt to draw in the names of other persons, unless those names are raised by the court," Moresha intoned. He chewed on invisible crackers.

"That's unfair, Comrade Chairman. This is like a basketball game in which the referee is playing for the other team."

There was nervous laughter.

"I assure you, Levitch, this is no game."

"I am aware of that. It was surely no game to keep me in jail three months without communication with my friends or family. I was not allowed to see a lawyer nor permitted to contact my wife. Why is my mother not in this courtroom? Why is the foreign press excluded? Why aren't my fellow Jews or members of the democratic movement present? This is no trial. This is a joke, a hoax. What do you fear? Suppose you let in the foreign press—"

Moresha banged his gavel. "The accused knows that the foreign press is full of spies and agents of the West, and that these people were among the accused's contacts. They should be allowed in here only as witnesses or as fellow defendants."

The mob howled and applauded.

Karpov sat stick-straight, faceless and emotionless behind his dark glasses. His hands were locked in his lap. They clenched one another, the right hand locked on the back of the left.

"Well, then, serve papers on them and try them with me. Yes, I have friends among the Western journalists. Why can't they be here to report my trial?"

"The accused will terminate these provocative remarks," the chairman said.

Kralik was up again. "Comrade Chairman, the reason the accused Levitch's mother is not present as a spectator is that she may be called as a witness. Under Soviet law she therefore cannot be present during the rest of the trial."

"My mother? A witness?"

"Silence."

The prosecutor was asked by the chairman to present documents relating to the case. These included a file of the yellow onionskins Levitch had distributed to journalists in the past year, other "secret" publications by the refusenik movement, and several dozen newspaper articles filed by Floyd E. Hanson, Anthony J. Parente, Agnes Wardle and other Western correspondents. Finally, there were a dozen books in Hebrew, the titles of which Kralik, to the amusement of the spectators, read off in rolling accents. It was clearly an anti-Semitic performance, the fat woman speaking in what she perceived to be a Yiddish whine, slurring vowels, grimacing and winking.

"If it please the Chairman," Levitch said. He was on his feet.

"Yes?"

"The last two books mentioned by Comrade Prosecutor are not of a subversive nature, and have nothing to do with espionage or treason or any of the other things I'm supposed to have done."

Kralik, the assessors, the clerk, all the officials of the court, stared at him. Disbelief, shock. No one spoke that way in a Soviet court. Stunned, Moresha allowed him to go on.

"One is the *Siddur Beth Tefilah*, the book of daily prayer in the Jewish religion. It's all in Hebrew, and if anyone bothers to read it, they'll see it's just that—prayers."

There were snickers, mutterings of *Yid, kike, Jew scum*.

"The other is a *Hummash*, the first five books of the Old Testament, our sacred text. Genesis, Exodus, Leviticus, Numbers and Deuteronomy. Why are they included in the documentary evidence against me?"

Kralik went to the prosecutor's table and picked up the prayer book. "It is not the book itself, but the uses to which it was put," she said to the chairman. "On the face of it, this is a jumble of primitive nonsense, incoherent incantations, of no consequence to the modern world, or the development of Socialist proletarian society. But the accused and his associates used this book and the others mentioned as wicked inspirations for an assault against the Soviet Union and the peace-loving Socialist democracies."

"No, no, it was just for prayer—"

Kralik's voice rose. "One might argue that *Mein Kampf* was merely the biography of Hitler, nothing more, nothing less. But if a group of latter-day Hitlerites came to exist in the USSR and used *Mein Kampf* as an inspirational text, a vade mecum, a guide to action, it would surely be considered evidence, relevant to any legal action against such a group."

Levitch shook his head. "I must object, Comrade Chairman. The prosecutor has compared the Holy Bible to the book that caused the murder of six million of my fellow Jews and many millions of Russian souls. How can this be permitted? How can the court let such statements go unchallenged? Well, I challenge it."

"That is not your privilege," the chairman said. "Sit."

Levitch hesitated. "Do I have the right to object to some of the evidence?"

"Yes, but your objections are out of order and cannot be accepted."

"Can I suggest additional evidence?"

The chairman, the prosecutor, and the other officials stared at Levitch as if he were a feebleminded child.

"What does the accused have in mind?" Prosecutor Kralik asked. She raised her ledgelike bosom, a great purple escarpment, as if intending to bludgeon the small Jew with it.

"Some additional books. Begun's *The Creeping Counter-Revolution*. The government-approved new edition of *The Protocols of the Elders of Zion*. *Judaism and Zionism*, by T. Kichko. *The White Book*, issued by the Juridical Literature Printing House, and edited by one of the Chairman's esteemed colleagues, the director of the Association of Soviet Jurists. All of these are explicitly anti-Semitic works, no better than the racist slanders published in Nazi Germany. They are condoned by the state and are aimed at stirring up hatred of my people and the crushing of Jewish identity."

Karpov listened, shifted his legs. Levitch was digging his own grave. Like one of those luckless Jews shot down by the SS in the Ukraine, in Lithuania.

"That is enough, Levitch," the chairman said.

"But all of this relates to my trial, Comrade Chairman. Is the court aware that anti-Jewish materials are regularly circulated to the Red Army? Or that in the last fifteen years, no less than one hundred and twelve anti-Jewish books and magazines have been published in the USSR, some of them reprinted in editions of as much as two hundred thousand copies? Why not add some of these books and magazines to your list? Surely, if I am a spy and a traitor, these publications will explain how I got to be the way I am. The answer is that those books are a collection of lies and trash, the leavings of the criminal scum of Fascist Europe, and this court will not introduce such writings because they will make a mockery of your case against me. I am innocent. I want to go to Israel. That is all."

There was silence. Then a hissing, a low rumble. Voices were raised, fists shaken.

"Shooting's too good for him."

"Hang him."

"Hitler didn't kill enough of them."

"Get it over with. Find him guilty and put him away."

Moresha struck the gavel twice, three times. As swiftly as the murmurings against Levitch had arisen, they halted.

"The prosecutor will proceed with the case against Abram Moiseivich Levitch, accused of spying under Article 64-A of the Criminal Code, and anti-Soviet activities under Article 70.1."

Karpov got up silently. He walked stiffly to the rear doors. His left side ached—arm, leg, face. The pain was different from the headaches or the malaise that preceded his seizures. He felt drained. In the moist cold air he paused, looked at the knot of dissidents and correspondents who were blocked by the metal barriers. In the center of the square, the sympathizers, rough-featured kids with a military look about them, lounged, spat sunflower seeds, drank *kvass* and jeered at the demonstrators. There were a few signs in evidence.

HANG ZIONIST TRAITORS
NO MERCY FOR ZIONIST SPIES

He stopped to talk to a captain of KGB militia he knew from Dzerzhinsky.

"Who arranged the turnout?" Karpov asked.

"Captain Malik, Comrade Major. Orders from Colonel Dort."

"It's the biggest I've ever seen. Very good organization, Captain." He pointed to the crowd with his left hand, turned his body so that the left side of his face, his left eye, studied them. Rude, coarse faces.

"Thank you, Comrade Major."

Karpov walked down the steps to his car. Passing the demonstrators, he stared at Mikhail Zolkin's spare figure. The scientist was brushing back his wispy hair, speaking softly to foreign reporters.

Karpov had never met him. But for reasons he did not fully comprehend, he waved to him, a curt gesture with his right hand.

Parente scrawled notes on a pad after dictating his story on the second day of the trial. He used a phone connection to Frankfurt. The story was getting a big play and he was gratified.

"The *Times* put it on page one," he told his wife. "Ditto *The Washington Post*, and our own esteemed journal."

"Is that good for Abram?"

"No, but he wouldn't want it any other way. Everyone knows he's going down for the count. So he might as well score points before he's put away."

Martha shuddered. "Points. Three or four years tacked onto his sentence? Isn't that what it will mean, all this defiance on his part? Maybe he shouldn't be so brave."

Parente looked at the notes he'd taken: *Need more interviews with L's friends. Get Zolkin exclusive.* Time *and* Newsweek *trying same, let's move.*

"It's got a life of its own," Parente said. "Little Levitch. He's going to make it bigger than he ever wanted."

"It was inevitable, wasn't it?"

"I guess so. For better or for worse, he's a star now. He's not some mumbling old Jew, some sad sack. He's gutsy, and he speaks English, and he can laugh at himself and everyone else. Give it a week, and he'll be as well known as Mother Teresa."

"But in more trouble," Martha said.

"I hope we didn't do it to him." Parente clenched his fists, pressed them against his head. He had promised to make spaghetti *aglio olio* for Martha and Jimmy. Now he had no appetite, didn't crave his nightly half-bottle of red wine. Levitch was frail, out of shape. He'd die in the work camp, or he'd get so sick he'd want to die. How long? Ten years? Fifteen? And the young wife wasting away, weeping for him in Israel.

"You didn't. He wanted the world to know about him and about his friends."

"It doesn't make it easier."

"Maybe he's glad."

"Glad? Come on, Marty."

"I don't mean overjoyed, dancing in his cell because he's going to prison for a long time. I mean . . . for what he's done. Maybe it will change things."

Parente scowled at his notes. Levitch was page 1, three-column headlines, a cover face, a magazine lead, like Jackie Kennedy, the Pope, Muhammad Ali. He lowered his head to the table. "I miss him. Nobody wanted it to go this far. We thought we'd help him get out."

"You still may. They switch signals sometimes. They let Ginzburg out. Amalrik, others. They may sentence him, let him serve a few months and ship him out as a nuisance, someone they don't want to be bothered with."

"I hope so. But I don't think so. It's not just policy. It's not just that he's broken their laws. It's *him*."

"Him?"

"That's right, Marty. He's a menace to their whole rotten system. He's too damned human. The smile, the jokes, the courage, the defiance, the forgiveness. They've got to sit on him, and sit on him hard."

Jimmy Parente came in and leaned against the doorframe. He had his workbook under one arm. "We won't see Abram anymore, Pop?"

"Not for a long time, Jimbo."

"Rats. He was a neat guy."

"He still is, Jimbo." Parente turned away. He didn't want his son to see his tears.

On the second day of the trial, Karpov slept past the opening session of the court. He was upset with himself. He rarely needed a wake-up call, never set an alarm. But without medication the night before—Irina had taken him off drugs—he had fallen into a profound, restless sleep, full of troubling muddled dreams. The dreams were vivid and explicit, but on awakening at noon, after eleven hours of slumber, he had to strain his mind to give them substance.

In one sequence, so real that he recalled colors, settings, even a date on a calendar, he had made sexual advances to, and then seduced, his niece. The girl wore pastels. A flouncy dress, petticoat and underpants, flowery pink and blue things, and Karpov, sweating and turning in bed, had dreams of tearing at her clothing, violating her, thrusting deeply. He half-expected to find his sheets wet with discharge. An insane dream. Why? He had not thought of his niece in years. He had had little contact with her. She had gone off to Kiev, to the university, married an army officer and had been stationed with him in Irkutsk for five years.

In the dream he had entered her brutally, tearing apart the Renoir-like garments, arousing not fear in the girl (she appeared to be in her teens, soft, round) but rather a tolerant smile, a giggle.

What does it mean? Karpov wondered. He washed and shaved. He felt ravenously hungry, but at the first sip of tea, the first bite of bread, he lost his appetite. Dressing, he stumbled while pulling on his trousers. He battled vertigo, prayed he would not convulse again, and by force of will got himself to the street, where his chauffeured car was waiting.

"I passed the courthouse on my way over, Comrade Major," the driver said.

"And?"

"A bigger crowd than yesterday. More Yids, more reporters. Colonel Dort doubled the police. Also there's more of our people. Letting them know how good citizens feel about them."

Hidden behind dark glasses, elusive in his dark tailored coat, Karpov passed unnoticed through the crowd of progovernment demonstrators. He looked at the "others" behind the steel barricades. There seemed to be two KGB militiamen for every protester. He could see Zolkin and some of the Jewish figures who had been part of Levitch's group, the American Parente, other Western journalists.

The stooped gray-headed woman was there, wearing an old brown coat. She had been identified by Malik as Levitch's mother, *A pain in the ass, Andrei Borisovich, an old hag who had no use for her son for years and suddenly shows up to support him,* Malik had said. She did not look like an enemy of the state to Karpov. Still, one had to be consistent. There was no room for sentiment or exceptions. Malik had informed him the woman was not Jewish. A lapsed Christian living on her late husband's pension. Malik suggested that if she kept pestering the court, kept granting interviews, the pension could be stopped.

Karpov found himself breathing heavily as he ascended the

twelve steps to the court. He steadied himself, inhaled, caught Malik's eye at the entrance.

"Are you all right, Andrei Borisovich? Maybe you shouldn't be running around like this with your head healing."

"I'm fine. Slept too much."

"I'll cover the trial for you today."

"I want to see Belus. I spent two days with him, giving him the right answers, putting cement in his spine. He'd better deliver a performance or he may have to be educated again."

"I could report to you . . ."

"Belus was my creation. I want to take responsibility if he fails us."

They took their reserved seats at the rear of the courtroom.

Dr. Belus was being questioned by Prosecutor Kralik. She paced in front of him, her hips suggesting the flanks of a Red Army tank, her bust as terrifying as a heavy mortar.

"Tell us what the accused said about the television news report on Zionist agitators," she commanded Belus.

The physician brushed his yellow hair back. He was sweating, but otherwise calm. "Yes, the film. It dealt with the illegal activities of the defendant and others in his group. It also showed me, although I was at that time working for the state, collecting information on Zionist agitation and espionage."

"What did the accused say?"

"He was worried that by showing the names and addresses of the members of the Zionist clique, mobs would be incited to attack them."

"Did that happen?"

"No."

Levitch squirmed in his seat. *Some film.* He recalled it as blatantly anti-Semitic. And some of those depicted, while not attacked by mobs, were now in jail. Two of his predecessors as leaders of the refuseniks—Matzkin and Fryd—were in prison, rotting away. A third, Kalmanson, had been driven to suicide. Levitch raised his arm.

"The defendant will await his turn to interrogate the witness," the chairman said.

"What about the request made to you by the defendant for secret scientific papers?" Kralik asked.

"I recall it. He was acting in behalf of the American Hanson. He told me that Hanson was on the payroll of the CIA. I knew this to be true, since I myself had CIA connections up until March of last year, when I severed my relationship with them. Levitch gave me a list of papers filed at the Neurological Institute. I was to get them, give them to him, and he in turn would get them to spy Hanson."

"Why did he ask you?"

"He trusted me. He thought I was one of their number, as I had been at one time. Also, I had access to the Institute in my capacity as physician."

"How did you get the papers?"

"I stole them from the office of—"

"That will do. There is no need to implicate others. You stole them."

"Yes."

"Was the person from whose files you stole them aware of this?"

"No."

Karpov, in the rear row, pursed his lips, tried to smile, found he had little to smile about. Belus was doing splendidly, adhering to the script Karpov had prepared. Dr. Irina Tashenko was not to be implicated in any way. Belus, as a double agent, could steal, lie, dissemble—provided it all was in the interest of the Soviet Union. Any lie about Levitch or about Hanson would do. Why should the court not believe him? Dr. Tashenko need not be involved.

"Was this the first time Levitch made such a request?"

"By no means. He frequently accosted professors at Moscow University about technical data. He had daily contacts with reporters besides Hanson, such as Anthony Parente, Agnes Wardle and Brian Cardwell. The first two were known to have connections of a suspect nature with the American and British embassies respectively."

"Do you wish to say anything to the accused?"

Dr. Belus nodded, raised his head. He looked at Abram. "Abram Moiseivich, how can you have done this to the Jews of the Soviet Union? How could you behave so abominably, so traitorously? How can so many of us continue to live here in peace, and be trusted, after all you have done to shame us?"

There was applause from the packed house. People were crying out *tell him, tell him, let him know.*

Levitch was invited to cross-examine his former friend

Belus. Baggy-trousered, shuffling in cracked shoes, Levitch
stood at his table and smiled at the physician.

"Ivan, old friend," he said, "admit that what you told the
court was a basketful of lies."

The chairman leveled a finger at Levitch. "Confine yourself
to questions."

"Comrade Chairman, I'll be glad to oblige. Ivan Belus, can
you deny that it is a lie that I ever asked you for anything
from the Neurological Institute? Or from any other medical
or scientific organization? Can you deny that you came to me
and asked me to give an envelope filled with papers to Floyd
Hanson? Can you deny that you assured me that while it may
have been unofficial, it was not an illegal act, since the papers
were not secret? Can you deny that you infiltrated our group,
posed as one of us, and betrayed me? Can you deny that you
have direct knowledge that I'm no spy, know nothing about
espionage, and was trapped and used by you and your
masters?"

"I deny it all, Abram Moiseivich. You are a spy."

"Oh, my old friend, how can you do this? How can you
face yourself?"

The low chorus of voices, as if activated by a buzzer or
switch, rose again. People were cursing Levitch, hurling
insults at him. Levitch threw up his hands and sat down.

Karpov looked icily ahead. Malik nudged him. "Well done,
Comrade Major. Belus was a good investment. He made the
case for us."

"See that he's taken care of. He wants to go to Sochi."

"I'll arrange it."

Another witness was called by the prosecution. He was the
Novosti feature writer Deroulian, who at tiresome length
described Levitch's "anti-Soviet activities"—his work for the
Helsinki group, his fraternizing with Western journalists, his
frequent interviews on alleged anti-Semitism, his repetition
of false and slanderous charges against the USSR.

Karpov got up. "Window dressing," he said to Malik. "He's
finished. Turn all the documents over to me. I'll write the
final report for Colonel Dort as soon as sentence is handed
down."

In the cafeteria of the Neurological Institute, Irina Tashenko,
having finished a difficult operation to relieve a hematoma of

the brain in a young construction worker who had fallen from scaffolding, opened *Pravda*. Dr. Skiba, her assistant, and the senior resident in neurology, Dr. Ovinov, sat with her, sipping hot tea, enjoying an early lunch.

"Here, on the back page," Irina said. "A short report."

"The Jewish trial?" Dr. Skiba asked. "Why do they make so much trouble?"

Irina adjusted her glasses. They were clouded with steam from the tea cup. She wiped them, read the item aloud.

" 'The state prosecutor today concluded the case against Abram Moiseivich Levitch, thirty-three, a leader of the Zionist clique in Moscow. Levitch stands accused of spying and anti-Soviet agitation. In today's court session, evidence of Levitch's involvement in the theft of secret medical research papers was revealed by Dr. Ivan Belus, a onetime associate of Levitch's, who is cooperating with the prosecution. Levitch attempted to deny the accusations but failed to shake Belus's account of espionage involving a leading medical institution.' "

"They should lock them all up," Dr. Skiba said. "They make it difficult for everyone."

"Why do you say that?" Irina asked.

"They are different from other Soviet citizens."

Irina stared at the blunted face, the lank black hair. Anti-Semitism, the glue that held society together. Poor Skiba, whose parents had been exiled for failing to meet production norms on their sheep station. It helped her forget, Irina imagined, if she could fix blame on Levitch, Zionists, all those mysterious enemies of the state.

A male orderly approached them. There was a call from her patient Major Karpov. He was waiting on the line. Irina went to the hallway outside the cafeteria and took the call.

"Yes?" she asked.

"I'm not right, Irina. Sleeping twelve and fourteen hours. Is this part of my hemispheric duality? I need help."

"I'll have to examine you again. It sounds like some postoperative effects. When can I see you?"

"I'm not sure. Perhaps you can come to my apartment."

"A medical appointment, nothing more. Can I see you today or tomorrow?"

"We're winding up the Levitch business. I want to make sure it goes well. Incidentally, you can thank me for keeping

your name out of the proceedings. You'll note there's no
mention of your involvement."

She sounded bitter: "Thank you. I see there's no mention
of yours either." She had a sudden inspiration, almost a
compulsion to be at the trial to see Levitch. Who was he?
How did he find the courage to defy the state, the platoons of
police, the bigots, the armed thousands, the mobs of hating
hoodlums?

"I'd like to come to the trial tomorrow."

"You? Why?"

"To satisfy my curiosity. Call it a medical visit. To see how
you're handling your convalescence. Can you get me a pass?"

"Of course. But . . ."

"I'll cancel my appointments. Don't worry. I won't compromise you. I'll sit by myself."

"It won't be very dramatic. The prosecutor will ask for the
sentence, and Levitch will be allowed his final summation. It
will all go according to plan." He coughed. "I'll send your
pass over by messenger this afternoon."

For reasons that were not entirely clear to her, Irina wore
dark glasses and a babushka to hide her face. She turned up
the fox collar of her coat, walked quickly from the taxi across
the esplanade in front of the courthouse.

Her husband, Lev, did not come with her. He had tried to
dissuade her from attending the trial. "What do you want to
see?" he whined. "I know what it's like. How many of my
friends have I seen forced to play a role in that kind of
Russian farce? There's nothing new about it. It's rigged,
fixed, scripted. Maybe that's the way it's destined to be in the
motherland. If we had freedom, what would we do with it?
And who are we to say our people want it? If not one
tyranny, another. Why did a million and a half Russians
desert to join an army for Hitler? And millions more not even
counted—manning Hitler's guns, his fortifications." He laughed.
"When the Americans landed in Normandy, the pillboxes and
trenches were full of yellow Mongolians, along with Kalmuks,
Buryats, Bashkirs, Uzbeks, all our Asians, happily dying for
the Third Reich. The Americans were totally confused by
them. They thought they'd landed in China by mistake."

"What are you trying to say?"

Embittered, frightened, Lev made less sense each day.

The endless piddling and nitpicking of intellectuals, she realized. Science was so much better, so much sounder. Philosophers and belle-lettrists, poets, mystics and other ethereal types muddied the waters, sought glory in exotic and shocking theories, spun their nonsense about moral silence, lofty disdain, notions too rarefied for the common mind—while the Karpovs and Dorts of the world pressed their boots on the collective neck.

Lev's words were like windblown chaff, dry leaves. She saw Zolkin's noble head, the group of Jews around him. A few seemed to be praying, jerking and bobbing as they read from small books. She recognized some foreign journalists, saw the camera crews, the photographers. How would it feel to toss career, luxuries, security aside, her right to travel and lecture and achieve, and join their ranks? Zolkin had. And Zolkin was a hero of the Soviet Union, a giant in the earth.

She stared at him and at the refuseniks around him. She recognized the bald, hot-eyed head of Colonel Arkangeli, three times detained in "psychiatric" hospitals, tortured, stripped of his war honors—and still protesting.

Her green pass afforded her ready entry and a seat near the rear. She looked across the stifling room and saw Karpov. He nodded at her. He looked pale and thin, but he sat erect, gloved hands folded in his lap. Alongside him was a loutish blond man she recognized as Malik, subchief of the Jewish Department. The room seemed packed with brutish young people spitting on the floor, belching, talking in loud voices. She had seen others like them outside, shouting insults across the street barricades.

The chairman of the court called the session to order, and the prosecutor, Mme. Kralik, dragged her heft out of her chair and faced the judges.

"Comrade Chairman, the state will begin by reviewing the crimes committed against the Soviet Union by the accused, A. M. Levitch. First, acts of treason under Article 64-A . . ."

As the prosecutor droned on, her angry words sounding like a tribal incantation, Irina looked across the room to the defendant. Levitch. What a small and inoffensive man he was! She had expected someone with the burning look of a prophet, or a slightly mad religious figure. But no. Levitch was round-faced, with a fringe of curly reddish hair. He had arched reddish brows, suggesting puzzlement over the sorry

affair. His eyes were dark-brown and wide open, and his face
was chubby and unsubtle. He looked like what he had been:
a teacher of mathematics in an obscure secondary school. He
sat with hands clasped on the table, listening to Kralik's
scathing speech as if she were discussing someone else. Once,
when she accused him of having conspired with the military
attachés "and other CIA agents" in the American Embassy,
he smiled gently, shook his head, held his hands palms up, as
if to say *why all these lies?*

"And so, Comrade Chairman, having reviewed for the
court what should now be obvious to all honest people, that
the accused is guilty of treason, espionage and anti-Soviet
agitation and propaganda, the prosecution requests a sentence of twenty years, to consist of five years in prison and
fifteen years in a special labor camp. Some may view this as
harsh, but it is best to nip these treasonable activities early,
and post a warning to others of the Zionist-Fascist clique, that
they will be dealt with swiftly. Thank you, Comrade Chairman."

Kralik labored back to her chair and sat down heavily, to a
burst of applause. Spectators were on their feet, shaking fists
at Levitch.

"Jew traitor."

"Zionist spy."

"Hang the bastard."

The chairman made no attempt to silence them. Irina
glanced across the rear rows to Karpov. His head was lowered and he was stroking his left temple. His skin seemed
chalky white, possessed of a powdery quality. Malik seemed
unconcerned. He leaned toward Karpov and whispered something to him.

"The court calls on the defendant to make his last statement before verdict and sentencing."

Levitch got to his feet. There were mutterings, muffled
shouts.

Irina saw that he was no more than five feet five inches in
height, fattish, unathletic. His hands were small and he kept
flexing the fingers nervously.

He began to speak, in a low, clear and, to the ear at any
rate, confident, voice. There was no tremor in it, not the
faintest hint of fear. Irina wondered: *Is it conditioning? Or a
sense that all is lost anyway, and he might as well behave
nobly?* She had seen this in terminal patients, modest people

doomed to a painful death from a brain tumor, cancer of the spine. They never cried. They rarely complained. They smiled, ate, talked, even joked. It was as if death gave them a chance to play the hero for the first time in their lives.

"Let me state that I rejected counsel and attempted to defend myself," Levitch began, "because I knew that I would be found guilty, no matter how ridiculous the charges, how flimsy the evidence, how idiotic the case against me. I have been tried and found guilty in the daily newspapers of the USSR many times, on the radio and television, and in public pronouncements.

"The absence in this room of my friends, colleagues and relatives, and the foreign press, is further proof of the corruption and illegality of this court, and I do not recognize its jurisdiction."

Someone shouted from a rear row: "Kill the spy! Shoot the Yid!"

"That is what I mean," Levitch went on, unshaken. "The room is packed with paid hoodlums, stooges of the army and police. If this is justice, it is a mockery. I am certain I'll be convicted and given the maximum sentence, but that is to be expected from a system that defies freedom, degrades man's soul, knows only its own preservation, its own lust for power and its hatred and fear of anyone different, anyone who speaks out.

"You can jail me forever, you can kill me, but you won't put an end to the Jewish people. You know it's true. What has been our sin? To want our own home? To want to practice our religion? Why are we a threat to the armed might, the hundreds of millions of people in the USSR? Only you can answer that. But by persecuting me, and all the Jews of the Soviet Union, you follow in traditional European ways, and I would think you'd be ashamed of yourselves. We make no apologies for who we are and what we've done. We owe you nothing and we owe the world nothing. We'll take our share of blame for historical errors, but we'll also accept some credit. Abraham, Moses, Jesus, Maimonides, Spinoza, Marx, Freud, Einstein, Nobel Prize winners, scientists, writers, artists in embarrassing numbers. And yes, many of our people who helped mold the Bolshevik Revolution, before the tyrants took over and began to murder and torture—"

"Shut the little Yid up."

"String him up!"

"Who cares about his goddam Jews?"

"Listen to them," Levitch said. "The children of Stalin. Comrade Chairman, have you see Goya's painting of Saturn devouring his children? That's what the Soviet Union has become. An ogre biting off the heads of its sons and daughters. Well, that is your worry.

"All I ask, and all I ever wanted, was to leave, to stop pestering you, and to have you stop bothering your Jews. I wanted to be with my wife in Israel. Is that so terrible? Is that treason, espionage, or an anti-Soviet act? I was asked over and over by your KGB agents, and by the prosecution, and by the man who was to be my lawyer, to confess. Tell all, Levitch, confess, admit you're a spy, inform on your fellow refuseniks, tell us about Mikhail Zolkin, and we'll go easy on you, a year or two in prison, and then you can go. I refused. I would be a coward and traitor to my conscience and my people if I did that."

He halted his speech, seemed to stagger, leaned on the table.

"Are you finished?" the chairman asked.

"Not yet. I never committed any crime. The papers I gave to Floyd Hanson—I had no idea what was in them. Ivan Belus asked me to do it as a favor. I called him a liar to his face, and I stand by it. He knows he's lying. He got those documents—I don't know how, but I can guess. The police gave them to him. He asked me to give them to Floyd. Neither of us had any idea what was in them, and I'm sure there's nothing that's secret. So I deny the charge of espionage.

"As for anti-Soviet acts, all I did was speak the truth to the journalists. When I gave interviews or handed out our bulletin, or supplied lists of names, I was doing things that are allowed in any free society. It is just that we are forced to live in an atmosphere of fear and repression, so these simple acts of information, of protest, these appeals for freedom, are considered anti-state acts. What nonsense!

"I'm proud to have worked with men like Chaim Slesik and Mikhail Semonski and Mikhail Zolkin and Grigor Arkangeli. If there's hope for Russia, it's in men like them, who are in the finest Russian tradition. You'd have thought something would have been learned from Czarist times, when freedom of thought and speech was suppressed, and the system decayed.

Well, the leaders don't seem to learn, and this system, too, will decay and pass into history.

"I say to my fellow refuseniks and dissidents, be brave and forthright, keep your heads up, and stand fast in the battle for freedom. To my own people, the People of the Book, I ask that you shed no tears for me. We have waited two thousand years for deliverance, and someday, the Almighty willing, we will pass over to dry land as did the Children of Israel when they were pursued by Pharaoh's armies. We will someday say 'Next year in Jerusalem'—and laugh and sing because at long last we have arrived."

Irina Tashenko lifted her dark glasses. She looked at the short, gesticulating figure of the defendant and wondered: *Where does the courage come from? How can he be so brave when he knows what he faces?* She had no answer. She thought of her husband, the weak man she loved, the lazy, word-shuffling literary man who had bent and confessed when the screws were applied. It was bred in the bones, she decided. A genetic code for courage, another for cowardice.

The chairman asked Levitch if he had anything to add.

"Only this, Comrade Chairman. I have not given up hope. My wife will not give up hope. My people will not give up hope. As we learn in Exodus, the Lord brought us out of slavery and He will do so again. To this court, which condemned me in advance, without evidence, with charges rigged and arranged by the police, I have nothing to say."

Levitch turned, faced the jeering mob and held his arms high. "God forgive all of you, and may peace come to all people."

For a second the paid hoodlums were silent. Then, like a rush of sewage, their curses were unloosed.

9

IRINA WATCHED KARPOV get up and walk stiffly to the door. Malik followed him. Karpov paused, one hand adjusting the blue silk scarf at his throat. He and Malik lingered, their eyes on the high bench.

"The decision of the court will now be handed down," the chairman said. "The defendant Levitch is found guilty on all counts and is sentenced to five years in prison and fifteen years at labor in a correctional camp. There will be no appeal. The trial is adjourned."

Levitch half-turned again, and with a shy smile looked at the mob. He shook his head sadly, then rose. His two guards each took an arm.

The obscene cheering sickened Irina. Loud, malicious noises that jammed her ears, made her giddy. *An act of muricide.* The rats kill mice because they are programmed to kill mice. . . .

Outside the courthouse, someone—an anonymous spectator, a guard willing to inform the protesters—had hurried across the plaza to the knot of dissenters. Irina, from the top step of the courthouse, could see people weeping and embracing one another. Zolkin and Colonel Arkangeli moved away, letting the Jews have their moment of communal sorrow.

Karpov dismissed Malik. He waited at the curb alongside his chauffeured Zhiguli. He seemed much too dapper and manicured for the setting.

"What are they singing, Comrade Major?" his chauffeur asked.

"A Hebrew hymn of some kind. It means *Hope.*"

"Not much hope for them. Twenty years. That Yid will be six feet in the Siberian mud, frozen like a dead perch. *Hope*—that's a good one."

The voices wafted across the square. Karpov understood none of it. *Hope?* Why did they persist? What was this idiotic compulsion to make trouble, stir up rivalries, assert their nonexistent claim to the Holy Land? Why could they not shut up and do their jobs?

"I'll give you a ride," Karpov called to Irina. "Please." He held the door of his limousine open for her.

"No, thank you."

"It will be my pleasure. My friend, my personal physician."

"All right."

She got into the car, Karpov, moving stiffly and favoring his left side, she noted, got in after her. At once he put his right hand on top of his left. His left leg rested limply, extended.

"You're interested in Soviet justice?" he asked. He looked out the window again. The police were dispersing protesters. Zolkin's figure, the gray head high above the Jews, was like a beacon. There was some shoving between an American reporter, possibly the hooligan Parente, and two plainclothesmen from Malik's squad. And still the Jews sang.

"I read about Levitch in *Pravda,*" she said. "The story was so vague that I decided to come. Especially since I was involved in the man's arrest and conviction. I did your bidding. And now an innocent man will spend twenty years in prison, and perhaps die, or go insane. Was it necessary to involve me?"

Karpov smiled. "I could have done it another way. But in my line of work, one seizes every opportunity. When Hanson surfaced, with his determination to get a story, I saw a chance to compromise Levitch. The fact that you were part of it made it easier. I trusted you."

"What do you know about trust?"

"Policemen know a great deal. Trust must always be on our terms. To betray someone like Levitch is not a breach of trust. A higher good motivates us. Levitch had to be silenced."

"What makes you think you've silenced him?"

"He'll have a hard time handing out yellow sheets from prison."

"God in heaven, Andrei, when does this wicked lunacy end? Can't you let people breathe, laugh, talk freely, argue with you? What was the man's crime? Wanting to be with his wife?"

"It was a complex issue. I obeyed orders."

"Like Eichmann. Like the commandants at Auschwitz and Treblinka. *Orders.* Let me out."

He grasped her wrist with his left hand. She noticed it was trembling. The agitation seemed to affect his entire left arm.

"If you don't like my profession, and can't bear to hear simple truths about the way we must live, at least stay as my physician."

"You're out of my care. I'll assign one of the staff neurologists to look after you."

Karpov's green eyes were moist with appeal. Was he ill? she wondered. Even someone with his steel will had to be affected by the trauma of the surgery. Yet he had seemed fit and energetic when he was discharged.

"I'm weak," he said. "Feet like water. Knees giving way. I'm asleep half the time. No pain, just weariness. You must help me."

"It takes time. You've had no seizures?"

"None. But the cure may be worse than the disease. Why am I weak?"

"You returned to work too soon." She studied his face. It was chalky, dotted with perspiration. He kept shutting and opening his left eye, as if it were irritated. The eye itself was red, as was the flesh around the eyelid.

"By early afternoon I'm exhausted," he said.

"Have you had any motor problems?"

"Just an unsteadiness when I'm on my feet too long. Irina, you must help me. Dort has mentioned a foreign post. It would mean a great deal to me to get out for a long spell.

Live like a civilized person. Breathe a different air. But if I'm unable to function . . ."

His appalling greed should have shocked her. But what else was she to expect? The rat killed, lived, ate, copulated. Until a bigger rat, or the lab technician, decided his life of endless gratification was over.

"Did you give any thought to Levitch's right to breathe a different air?"

He pressed his right hand against his forehead. "Why this latent philo-Semitism? What is Levitch to you?"

"I'm not sure. I can only think of him, that helpless man, alone, despised, isolated—for nothing more than wanting his wife, a place to live. It's horrid. It's the real betrayal. I wish I were braver than I am. I'd call Mikhail Zolkin and join forces with him."

"That would be foolish. Zolkin will be next."

"You would not dare."

"Dear Irina. How guileless you are."

She drew away from him. "Let me out at the corner. I can't be near you when you talk like that."

Halfway through the screening Karpov fell asleep.

Dort had arranged the showing—secret films of Zolkin. They had cameras on him virtually all the time. On the street, camera vans disguised as utility trucks followed him. In his apartment he was filmed from a nearby hotel, through two-way mirrors. His comings and goings, his meetings, his conversations. The cameras all but invaded his bedroom.

When the lights came on, Karpov started. His eyes opened quickly, as if turning a coin from obverse to reverse. He blinked as he heard Dort's voice.

"Boring, Major?"

"Sorry. I had a bad night."

Two weeks had passed since Levitch's conviction. The chief of the refuseniks would be taken to a maximum-security prison to start the first five years of his term. The world had responded with outrage. Not a day passed that the Levitch case did not make the newspapers, the magazines, television newscasts. In Italy the Communist Party denounced the Soviets and demanded Levitch's release. A serious split developed in the French Communist Party. In the Netherlands twenty leading figures in the Dutch Communist Party resigned.

"Major Zaitsev and I can report on the film if you wish," Dort said. Sarcasm was not his strong suit. "When the time comes to spring the trap on Zolkin, you'd better be prepared. Better than you were for Levitch."

Alyosha Petrovich Zaitsev was twenty-nine, a comer in the Second Directorate. He was sallow and saturnine, a lean, whippy man, one of Dort's pets.

"I'll be glad to brief Major Karpov," Zaitsev said. "The Zolkin matter has been of interest to me for a long time."

Dort dismissed him and told the projectionist to pack up. He wanted to be alone with Karpov.

In the darkness Dort lit a cigarette. He blew gray clouds against the blank screen. "Andrei Borisovich, you aren't well. You're sick as hell. I can't entrust Zolkin to you, after the way you fucked up on Levitch."

"I *what?*"

"You heard me. It's the truth. The people at the top are unhappy with your work."

"He's in jail, isn't he? We caught him with the evidence. The Jewish movement is smashed. We're making three more arrests this week. We're cleaning up the Zionists in Kiev, Leningrad and Minsk. Why are they dissatisfied?"

"You didn't get a confession."

"Since when do we need a confession to put people away? The man was a spy, a traitor, an anti-Soviet propagandist. Of course he wouldn't admit it."

Dort snuffed out the cigarette. "Sorry, old colleague. The chairman knows about your surgery, the fits, all that awful business you've endured. They feel you're not reliable. If you'd been free of those brain problems, whatever the hell it was that was afflicting you, you'd have gotten Levitch to admit everything. The way you straightened Belus out."

"It was a different situation. Belus had been on our payroll for three years."

"Then you should have gotten Levitch on your payroll."

"He isn't Belus. He can't be bought, or frightened."

Dort pushed off the padded arms of the viewing chair, yanked at his crotch, walked around the small theater. They were on his back every day, angry letters from the Central Committee to the chairman of the KGB, and into his office at the Second Directorate. There had been dark hints in the last messages, harsh criticism of the handling of the Levitch case, not-so-subtle threats that if the Zolkin matter was not expedited, someone would pay for it.

"Karpov, you need a rest," Dort said.

"I am a little weak. Dr. Tashenko thinks I went back to work too quickly."

"I mean a long vacation. The Black Sea. When you feel strong enough, when you stop these midday naps, maybe you can be reassigned."

"A foreign post?"

"I don't think so. The Technical Support Group needs an acting chief. It's been suggested you might be able to handle it."

Karpov's brow wrinkled. "Technical Support? What am I now, a burglar? Safecrackers, locksmiths, photographers, flap-and-seal experts? I thought I'd advanced past that. I speak six languages, Comrade Colonel. Is this a joke? Making me a supervisor for footpads and second-story men?"

Dort laughed, a wet gargle. "They're talking of early retirement for you if you don't come round. Look, someone's going to have to explain why Levitch didn't confess and implicate others."

"He was stubborn. A Zionist zealot."

"And he's got half the world screaming at us. The Pope, the Americans, even our Red brothers in the West. At least we could have come to an accommodation with him."

Karpov's face was enshadowed. "That was not the impression I was given. You said they wanted him put away for a long time. I delivered. I don't like this after-the-fact condemnation."

"Don't get upset, Major. Technical Support isn't a bad life."

"I'll resign."

"And do what? You've been a policeman all your life. You have no law degree. Look, we tend to take care of our own, but if you leave under a cloud, who knows? You could end up in command of a border post in Siberia. Overseeing customs in Vladivostok."

Karpov's eyes started to close. His head nodded.

"Andrei Borisovich, are you all right? Hey, stay awake."

"I'm tired."

"See? See what I mean? I have your interests at heart. You need a change of scenery. Take a vacation. That business of

opening your head stopped your fits, but I don't think you're
in any shape to work full-time. I'm having Zaitsev take over
the Zolkin file. It's top priority."

"I delivered Levitch. We plan to arrest Slesik this week."

"You won't be needed for that. We don't plan to try Slesik
for a long time. Let him sweat it out in Lubianka until he
gives us names and incriminates a lot of his friends."

"Who'll handle that?"

"Malik. This operation needs no fine tuning. After the way
we sewed Levitch up, the others will be guilty by implication."

Against his will, Karpov found his head falling again, his
eyes closing. He kept jerking his head up, clenching his fists,
battling the craving for sleep that washed over him.

"Go home and sleep, Major," Dort said. "Take a week off.
Two weeks. Think about where you'd like to be posted. The
organization could use some shaping up along the Chinese
border. We're short of intelligent leadership. You could take
six months off and learn Chinese."

"I see you're determined to destroy my career." Feeling as
if he were changing polarity, fading from positive to negative,
Karpov tried to express indignant anger. But his voice was
papery, remote.

"I'll discuss your case with the chairman later this week.
They know your record. But with this brain problem, and the
way you let Levitch defy you, maybe you need a rest, a
change of scenery. Give it thought."

Karpov could barely lift himself from the chair. His feet felt
unconnected to his body.

Flat muddy plains, groves of birches, nameless villages,
here and there the high wire fencing of a collective farm.
Everything was brown, tan, gray. All under a lowering iron-
gray sky. A steely cold day. Crows nattered and squabbled in
dead fields. Once Levitch saw a hawk circling high above a
grove of barren oaks, gliding on air currents, superior to all
that lived below its strong wings.

There were a hundred-odd men aboard the rattling Red
Army bus. Armed militia occupied the front row. They faced
the prisoners. They tore at chunks of black bread, took turns
sleeping, passed around a bottle of wine. *What kind of discipline is that?* Levitch thought. *Drinking on duty?* None of
the guards was an officer. An elderly corporal with a mal-

formed ear seemed to be in charge. At Lubianka, they had
assembled the prisoners before dawn in the courtyard. Two
thick slices of bread and a mug of tea were served to each
prisoner. Now, five hours later, deep into the plains of the
Tatar ASSR, they complained of hunger, thirst, the need to
urinate, defecate. The bus stank of sweat, farts, vomit. Behind Levitch a snowy-haired man kept moaning, asking for
someone named Grischa, making noises like a wounded dog.
Levitch could recall a story by Andreyev, *The Seven Who
Were Hanged,* in which a gypsy awaiting execution gets on
his knees in his cell and terrifies the other prisoners with
wolfish wailings.

Linked by handcuffs to a fellow jailbird, Levitch tried to
doze, control his bladder, inure himself to the stench, the
kidney-jolting passage of the bus. Foul fumes seeped through
the broken flooring; it seemed to Levitch that he was inhaling
slow poison, something that would kill him before they got to
Maridov. Didn't the SS use that technique to kill Jews?

His partner, Arkady Oren, a veteran of KGB jails, a raddled man in his sixties, assured Levitch that life at Maridov
was not too terrible. He, Oren, burglar, fence and forger,
had done time in four prisons and two camps. Hell, Maridov
was almost a resort compared to some he'd served in. For
one thing the weather wasn't too bad. Not like Siberia or
Turkestan where the wind never stopped howling, your ass
turned to a block of ice in the winter, sand clogged your ears
and nose, your feet became black from the frost and you lost
all sensation in your hands . . .

"Five years, Levitch?" Oren asked. He had jug ears. Gray
hair grew from his round skull and broad jaw, spikes of
silvery wire. His teeth were half steel, half rotting brown,
with gaps front and rear. He was from Odessa, Oren confided,
but he was no Ukrainian, no Yid, nothing but a deep-down
Great Russian, a veteran of Rostov and Stalingrad, a tough
old crook.

"Five in prison and fifteen in a work camp."

"Bad business, Levitch, I drew three and ten. I'll do it
standing up. Life in a KGB hotel isn't all bad. The guards
aren't as mean as they used to be. Younger guys, better
educated. Of course it's no secret that the KGB assigns the
shit and the scum to the camps. It's a lousy life. No chance of
promotion, yelling all day."

"Do we get work?"

"Work? Till your fingers fall off, your eyes look like pee-holes in the snow. Mail bags. Burlap sacks. The farm. Let's see your hands."

Levitch obliged, ashamed of his soft hands.

"No good. Try to bribe your way to the farm. It's outdoor work. You eat better; you can steal a potato or a turnip now and then. But with those hands it won't be easy. You're a Yid so they'll figure you have brains. If you're lucky you could end up in an office, or clerking in the factory. They don't like Yids." He leaned forward. "Look, if you were smuggling gold in, money, dollars, francs, then you'd stand a chance. They'll take bribes, the bastards. Or if you get a package—a cake, a jar of jam—maybe your wife or mother could smuggle in gold. You can buy yourself a soft job."

"How could I smuggle anything? We were searched."

"You have an asshole, don't you?"

Coarse laughter erupted around him. *Asshole* was repeated over and over. Men punched one another.

A blunt-headed giant with hands like wooden blocks leaned over the seat and bellowed in Levitch's ear.

"He means you could be boy hump. You look like boy hump to Oren. If anyone has a taste for Jew meat. Christ, look at him. Red hair, rosy cheeks. Ugly, but boy hump."

Levitch smiled weakly at Arkady Oren. "He's joking, I suppose. Besides, I'm married. I don't know about these things."

"I can see there's lots you don't know. Ah, the old days—you'd like them. The guards shot twenty, thirty of us one day for not delivering the norms. The *katorga* was something. Forced labor, no blankets or mattresses, working in chains. That was old Stalin's idea of a good time. Once I was with a bunch of guys who were selected to be shot. They packed us, fifty at a time, in a wooden shed. Ten below zero. So close we couldn't move our arms. Shitting and pissing on each other. They threw us chunks of ice instead of water. We had to catch the ice with our teeth. One guy, a Bashkir, started to eat the arm of the guy next to him."

Abram shivered. "How were you saved?"

Arkady Oren winked. "I was a section boss of the *urkas*, the criminals. The chief *urka*, he was a fat bum from Odessa, a smuggler. He got me out at the last minute. They shot the rest of them in a ditch, one bullet in the back of the neck. Pulled the bodies away on sledges. Filled an old mine shaft with stiffs."

The ogre in back of Levitch thrust his head between Arkady and Abram. "You'll learn about us *urkas*. We run the camps. Not the guards, not the KGB."

"These things, these shootings don't take place anymore, do they?" Levitch asked. "I mean, since Stalin . . ."

"Nah, it's like the Ukraina Hotel. A bathing resort on the Black Sea. You'll get used to it." Oren winked, jabbed Levitch in the short ribs. "You're a political, right? Most kikes are political. Besides, you don't know how to fight or kill or gouge. You're all teachers, doctors, smart guys. If you want to live, you get an *urka* friend. Like me, or Berzin back there. Get some murderer or robber to stick up for you. Can you offer anything?"

"I was a teacher. Mathematics."

Oren and Berzin roared with laughter. The giant wiped his scummy eyes. "Christ and Saint Peter, I've heard it all. A mathematics teacher. That's not bad, Jewboy. Maybe you could keep books for us. You think we don't run a business in Maridov? Arkady, I like this guy. He keeps the accounts for us, we might let him live."

Abram said nothing. There was a point, he imagined, where fear no longer registered. Like Chaim Slesik's cancer. After a while one accepted pain, suppressed fear, faced each day with a variety of courage. Counterfeit or real, it did not matter. Slesik survived by ignoring pain, stifling terror, trying to make sense of his life. Protest and honesty sustained Chaim. Levitch would have to do the same, never lose hope, never forget Sarah, pray that his friends would find a way to free him.

"Piss time," one of the guards called out. "Shitters and pissers, on your feet."

The bus lumbered to a halt on a narrow mud road. It was raining now. There was no one in sight for miles. Just the interminable furrowed earth, clumps of stunted trees. Levitch would have welcomed a flight of squawking crows. He longed for his hawk.

They were ordered out of the bus, two by two, joined at the wrists. In an open field, soaked by rain, they squatted, relieving themselves, joking, cursing, old-timers giving advice to newcomers, making deals, threatening, suggesting ways of beating the system.

"Enjoy it, Levitch," Arkady Oren said. "One of life's last pleasures in the camps is a good crap. They don't shoot you in the neck anymore for not filling norms. You even get mail now. You can send letters out. A visitor maybe once a year if you keep your nose clean. They have bookstores in the town of Maridov. You have extra money, some of the younger guards aren't bad guys—they'll buy books, or tobacco or chocolate for you. You'll be surprised how fast twenty years goes."

His trousers dropped, his behind bare, Levitch saw himself as an actor in an absurd play. One obscure half-Jew from a poor family, raised as a good little boy who did his homework, washed his face, went to party meetings, listened to music, gave his pupils a little extra effort, encouraged them to learn and to build the motherland. *What am I doing in a muddy field, squatting with eighty criminals and assorted wretches, trying to defecate?* His needs had reached the pit. To evacuate, to relieve his inner organs, seemed his greatest need.

A gaunt gray-bearded man was squatting next to him. He appeared to be in his seventies. He had serene blue eyes. He looked at Levitch quizzically.

"I know you. The refusenik. The one they had on trial."

"Yes. I suppose I was famous for a few days."

"Have courage, Levitch. I'm a Catholic priest. Father Ignatius. From Latvia."

"Why were you arrested?"

"Running a religious school without a permit. Levitch, I admire you. I know you protested for Christians as well as your own people. I've been in prison before. Be careful of the *urkas*. The KGB guards turn the work over to them and let them torture and beat up politicals, extort money, keep us in line. We have to form our own organization to survive. Don't cross an *urka*, but don't give in all the time. In Kolyma, long ago, the *urkas* murdered a Jewish doctor who refused to give them morphine from the infirmary. Slit his throat while he was sleeping. The nationalities—Poles, Ukrainians, Balts—we got together and killed the *urka* boss and his aide. They didn't bother us for a long time."

They were on their feet, buttoning trousers, fixing belts. The farmer's field lay under a patina of fresh night soil.

"How did you kill him?" Levitch asked it as casually as he would have asked Tony Parente what they were having for dinner.

"We buried him in mud."

Arkady Oren giggled. "Ah, a lousy priest. They're the worst. Don't listen to him, Levitch. Be smart—work with us."

They were ordered back to the bus. Levitch looked at the murky sky. The raucous crows of the plains appeared again, circling the field of excrement. Levitch envied them.

Karpov sat in his office, distressed by the lack of communication, the manner in which Dort was isolating him. Malik had assumed chieftainship of the Jewish Department. In the corridors lesser functionaries whispered and gossiped: Dort was getting ready to dump Andrei Karpov, bury him in Kamchatka, shove him back in uniform, dispatch him as far east as he could.

Dialing Malik's extension, Karpov got his secretary. She was a bewigged harridan, a cousin of Dort's. No, Captain Malik was not in. He was busy with new arrests.

What arrests? Karpov asked.

Hadn't Comrade Major heard? More refuseniks were being rounded up for questioning. Slesik, the young Jew Sokolov, an older man named Semonski.

Karpov asked why he had not been told.

"I'm sure I don't know, Major. Anyway, they're being held for questioning. Colonel Dort wanted them brought in. Levitch's testimony involved them. Not what he said in court, but in private sessions. Also his papers, his letters implicated them."

"I see. How long will they be held?"

"I don't know, sir. I'll ask Captain Malik to call you back."

The information barely imprinted itself on his mind. He lost images, the sense of what had happened. Three more troublesome refuseniks jailed. To what end? Slesik was a walking corpse, dead before entering the grave. Karpov could see him, bent at the waist, tentatively placing one foot after the other. Semonski was an older man, vague, submissive. A musician? And the new one—Sokolov. A young man, one of those mystic sectarians, wearing a round hat, fringes hanging from his waist. A vestige of the Middle Ages. Where did these people come from? What inspired them?

"I must see you," Karpov said to Irina. His voice was clotted.

"I suppose I have an obligation as your physician. Haven't you been checking in with Dr. Kolenko?" Kolenko was the neurologist Irina had assigned to Karpov.

"Once or twice. He's no help."

"Are you trying to do too much? Working too hard?"

He laughed once—it sounded more like a cough or bark. "Rest! I am asleep half the time. Irritable, off balance. No convulsions, but incapable of functioning. Can you help me?"

She breathed deeply. Yes, she might be able to help him. *And do a bit more for him than he imagined.* One ran risks. A Levitch, a Zolkin, took ultimate gambles, paid for them. Lev told her there was a report going around that Mikhail Zolkin was to be exiled to Siberia and kept under house arrest for the remainder of his life. He was ill with rheumatoid arthritis. He wouldn't last long in a land of forty-below temperatures. An icy hell where housewives carried their milk home in frozen discs.

"Come to the Institute tomorrow. Late afternoon, five o'clock. I have an operation scheduled, but I should be done by then."

"I'm grateful."

When he hung up, he tried reviewing his files on the dissident movements. Nodding, yawning, he did not notice that every time he looked at a letter from Dort, or from the KGB chairman, his left hand clutched the paper. Once it inadvertently tore a directive on the proper mode for interrogating refuseniks.

Tipped off by Olga Semonski, Parente went to Lubianka with a photographer. They waited in the rain in Parente's car—Olga, Schultze, the West German photographer, and Tony.

"How did you find out?" Tony asked.

"Someone from the police called. They said my husband would be released today."

"Go figure," Parente said. "They keep you guessing."

Olga sniffled into her handkerchief. Time was running out.

She was seventy, her husband seventy-one. Why this turmoil in their old age? Mikhail had survived twenty tank battles, earned his medals, his honors. Sergeant-Major Semonski of the 218th tank battalion. A hero of Rostov, Kharkov, Stalingrad, Kiev. And now this—a frightened old man, an unemployable piano teacher, a victim.

The side door of the prison building opened. Semonski and Slesik appeared—but not Sokolov.

Chaim walked with a cane, one side of his body bent, moving gingerly so as not to enrage the voracious cells that were devouring him. Mikhail, in workman's cap and leather jacket, seemed to have aged five years.

Olga got out of the car and went to her husband. Schultze took a photograph. A militiaman watched from the sentry post, but did nothing.

"What happened?" Tony asked. They had been held for a month. No letters. No communication with friends or relatives. As if the earth had opened, taken them in, rolled a stone over them.

"Not too bad," Slesik said. "They wanted confessions, but we had nothing to confess. We told them the truth."

"Sokolov?" Tony asked.

"I guess they're keeping him. Look, he succeeded Abram. He was in charge of the bulletins, our delegate to the Helsinki group."

"Did you see him?" Parente asked. He cursed silently— the police, the state, the spies, the jailers. A country dependent on thugs and informers. And where was Ivan Belus now?

"No. He's in solitary. One of the criminal types, a man named Vanak, got word to me." Slesik leaned on his cane, grimaced.

"What did he say?" Parente asked.

"They're turning the screws. Cold-water cell. No bed. They think he knows something special because he's so religious. They can't figure him out."

Parente gunned the motor. "Indeterminate sentence?"

"Until he talks," Slesik said.

The Semonskis were silent. They huddled in the back seat, held hands. She cried softly.

"Zalman Sokolov got word to me," Slesik said. "He wants somebody to get in touch with the Lubavitcher Rebbe in

New York. Tell him they should pray for him, and he's not afraid. The Rebbe is close to the President of the United States."

A big help, Parente thought. Nothing sounded promising. The worldwide publicity, the high-level protests erupting after Levitch's conviction were hardly slowing the KGB down. If anything, the policemen seemed enraged, blindly furious, striking out in all directions. Maybe the Levitch story had to be muted. He was at a loss. He wondered if perhaps someday in the near future they'd toss *him* out. Who had known Abram better, seen into his heart, loved him so much for his courage and his goodness?

"The problem remains," Irina said. "You exhibit distinct hemispheric duality in perception and motor tasks. Does it bother you? That your right hemisphere is tongue-tied? That your left won't supply words for tasks done with your left hand?"

"I'm hardly aware of it."

Karpov stared at the illuminated screen, shaded his right eye, squinted at a slide of a cat. But he could not say the word.

She tested him with other images. His left-eye–right-brain combination was as incapable of voicing a description as it had been six weeks ago. The precise word eluded him. The right hemisphere would struggle, make wild guesses, seek hints.

"You asked if I'm bothered by—what did you call it? —duality?" he asked.

"It happens with people who have commissurotomies. Do you sometimes sense a rivalry between the two sides?"

Karpov squinted at the blank screen. "Maybe I dreamed this, I don't know. I had an erotic dream some weeks ago. Carnal relations with a niece. I must have slept a long time, almost drugged. I must have dreamed that my right hand was slapping me. But I'm not sure it happened."

"It probably did."

He watched her graceful body move around the office. Why was she not his again? He would threaten Lev Tashenko. Warn her that if she did not bed down with him, Tashenko could be brought up on charges again, lose his cushy job, perhaps do a little time. His left hand locked itself into a fist

as he thought of the ways he could punish the spineless
editor. Then, as Irina arranged photographs on a table, his
right hand grasped the left, pried open the fingers.

"Sit here," she said. "Cover your right eye."

Karpov obeyed her. He felt childish, dependent. Always
he had possessed an awareness of command, a sense of his
power over others. Underlings obeyed him swiftly. Those
above him were wary of him.

There were four photographs on the table. Three were of
nondescript unidentifiable people, photos Irina had clipped
from magazines. The fourth was a photograph of Hitler.

"Point to any picture you recognize, using only your left
hand," she ordered.

Karpov's left eye studied the photographs. His left hand
went to the picture of Hitler, tapped at it. He frowned, made
a fist, hit it against the photo.

"Who is it?" she asked.

"Mmmm. The war . . . someone connected with the war."

With the index finger of his left hand, Karpov began trac-
ing letters on the back of his right hand.

"Stop that," Irina said. "No hints."

"Sorry. I don't know who he is."

"Do you know him personally? Historical figure? The enter-
tainment world?"

"Historical."

"Recent or past?"

"Past."

"USSR? Another country?"

"Ah . . . another country."

She studied his face. The duality was more marked than
ever. His mute right hemisphere, the emotional, spatial half
of the brain, was struggling. Language eluded it.

"Political figure? Like a president, a king?"

Karpov shook his head. "Something like that."

"Germany?"

He smiled. "Yes, Germany. Hitler."

She gathered up the photos. "You're still affected by the
split in your brain. I'm not sure why it is taking so long for
your right brain to learn."

"Why am I fatigued all the time? Why do I sleep so much?
I don't care if I have three brains or four—and I'm not sure I
believe any of that theorizing. I can't concentrate. I'm unable

to confront Dort, to fight for my rights. My will is not what it was. And the will is everything. I'll be damned if I'll let Dort ship me to Siberia. I won't live forever. I want decent food, good wine, tailored clothing. I'm sick of the motherland and its cold nights, dusty streets, unwashed bodies."

"And are you equally sick of the manner in which it persecutes and destroys innocent people?"

Karpov smiled. "Careful, Irina. I am still a man to be feared."

"I don't fear you. Answer me: Are you sick of the manner in which people like Levitch are tormented by you and your kind?" She was not certain what had emboldened her. Perhaps a sense of his weakness, his vulnerability.

"I'm not sure I care anymore."

"Ah. A small glimmer of conscience?"

"Boredom. Weariness."

"But no moral judgment? Andrei Borisovich, let your left brain range freely. Doesn't it have doubts, second thoughts about the life you've led, the way you've dealt out pain and death to so many?"

"I refuse to believe that there are different standards in the halves of my brain. Identifying a photograph or naming a pencil is one thing. No, Irina, I won't be baited. I'm not one of your rats."

"But you confess to being bored with your life as a KGB agent, an official trapper and torturer?"

"Bored, yes."

"This ennui, I suggest, may be the first part of a new decency in your mind. Would you admit to that? I'm looking for clues, Andrei Borisovich. You needn't be ashamed of admitting to a sense of remorse, or at least regret, over the way you destroyed Abram Levitch."

"Regret? Not at all." He sounded drained, wary.

"In Western countries, judges and policemen and prosecutors often admit that they don't have their heart in a certain case, that they sense pity and understanding for a convicted man. Can't you do the same?"

"You're confusing me. Irina Tashenko, you must know you're the only person in the world I'd let do this to me."

She saw a peculiar softness in his eyes. Had she touched something in the gentle, left hemisphere? She could not be certain. But clearly he was struggling, trying to come to terms with some remnant of sympathy, of human feeling.

"Irina, I trust you. I love you."

"These notions will not save you. I'm neither flattered nor insulted. You need help. You think I can help you. In your despair, you've come to me for salvation. But I'm not sure I can save you."

He got up and took her in his arms. She tried to move away, struggling against old passion. His cheeks gave off an aroma—an arch French cologne. His eyes were oddly gentle. The icy light had been diminished. Karpov at bay, Karpov frightened, needing someone to save him . . .

"You shared my bed. You took gifts from me. We gave each other our bodies. Don't tell me you didn't find pleasure in our affair. I know you did. No woman can hide that ecstasy."

"Against my will, I slept with you."

"No matter. Irina, I love you. I need your help. Perhaps, when I'm right again . . ."

Tenderly she disengaged his arms and walked away. "How badly do you want to be cured? How much risk are you prepared to take?"

"Almost any risk."

"All right. There is a procedure that may help. It involves implanting electrodes in the halves of your brain. Don't look appalled. It isn't painful or dangerous."

So. She had come this far, guiding him into a new phase of their relationship, an arena where he could not dominate. Not a police station or a court or a prison camp. The daring notion had been forming in her mind since the day she attended Levitch's trial. What was there to lose? Who could challenge her? She was concerned with Major Karpov's well-being, his mental health. What she planned for him now could be viewed as a patriotic gesture, an application of her surgical skills toward the healing of a trusted and valued high functionary of the KGB. And it would be something a great deal more, something the authorities, least of all Karpov, would never be aware of.

"Tell me about this procedure." The wig gave him the look of a cosmeticized corpse. He almost aroused her pity. She tried to be crisp and professional.

"The technique isn't new. It's been used to relieve

schizophrenia, aggression, depression and sexual disorders. I assure you the process is not irreversible. If there are no productive results, the electrodes can be removed painlessly."

"How will this help me?"

"The stimulation of certain parts of your brain may produce rewarding and pleasant sensations. They would tend to elevate your mood and relieve your fatigue and despair."

Karpov stroked his right cheek with his right hand. She watched him narrowly: almost a caress, a loving gesture. The affectionate right hand was reassuring him.

"Is it addictive?" he asked. He seemed amused.

"Not in the same way drugs are. We can control the electrical output to the brain. We can find an optimum level at which your mood and your attitudes are satisfactory, and not exceed it. Actually the level of pleasure is not nearly as high as that produced by drugs."

"I'm not sure I want metal wires stuck in my skull. Do I want to be like one of your white rats, jabbing a pedal until he collapses from exhaustion? I saw them in your laboratory. Rats who prefer to activate a wire in their brain rather than eat, drink or make love. Is that what you have in mind, Irina?"

"The human brain is far more complex than a rat's. The relief one gets is temporary and acceptable. People experiencing mental anguish report a generalized good feeling. They are able to go about their work, act cheerfully, accept their life. There has also been a marked enhancement of alertness in patients."

Karpov felt a numbness in his left side, a weakness of the left forearm and the left hand. Damn, damn his brain. He had to trust her. He could not imagine that she would harm him.

"What is involved?"

"It means another surgical procedure. Not nearly as extreme as the operation you had. You'll be hospitalized a few days. I'll have to keep testing you to see what the results are. I must warn you that while there is no danger involved, different subjects show different results. We know there are centers of pain and pleasure in the brain, centers of aggression and of beneficence, but they vary from person to person. So we may have to engage in a bit of trial and error."

Karpov buried his face in his hands. "I said I trust you and

I love you. I meant it. I'm your patient, your onetime lover. I saved your husband's career, perhaps his life. Let's get on with this . . . procedure."

She looked at a desk calendar. "At seven in the morning?"

He came to her, put his hands on her shoulders. "Tell me, Irina, is it possible I'll come out of this a man more to your liking?"

"I give no guarantees. But there is a chance you may emerge more at ease with yourself. That's all I want to happen. To give you some peace. It would be a grim joke if I cured you and enabled you to become more of a stalking beast. I won't try to change you too profoundly. But I am concerned about my patients. If the operation has made you miserable, I want to try to make amends."

"My poor brain. Can it take so much piercing, cutting and handling?"

"It's a resilient organ."

He put on his coat. "All right. Seven tomorrow morning."

She walked with him to the door. "Does anyone hear about Levitch anymore? What's happened to him?"

"He's in Maridov in the Tatar Administrative District. A maximum-security prison. After five years of that place he'll be begging to be allowed into a work camp."

"You don't regret what you did to him?"

Karpov shrugged. "He committed crimes. I'm afraid I can't express . . . what did you refer to? . . . remorse or regret."

She nodded. His cold-blooded account of Levitch convinced her she was right.

"May I invite you to dinner?" he asked.

"I think not."

"It's strange. I managed my loneliness until these unfortunate accidents. The convulsions, the torpor. I didn't mind being alone. Music, books, paintings, travel. Now, I'm depressed, despondent. I miss you terribly."

"That's why the implantations are a good idea. I promise nothing. But if they are nonproductive, they can be canceled. You'll be no worse for the experience."

She let him kiss her gently on the lips.

After he left she went to the operating room, refusing assistance from Dr. Skiba. She located the stereotaxic instrument. She checked all the parts, cleaned it with alcohol, placed it next to the operating chair. Then she found the plastic box containing the minuscule electrodes, the micro-computers, the transmitters.

"In the old days," Arkady Oren growled, "they'd never let you stick photographs on the wall. Christ, they've gone soft, running this place like a spa." He lay on his narrow bed, studying Levitch's array of photographs. Levitch had attached them to the gray concrete wall of the cell, using flour and water he'd filched from the kitchen. He was learning to be a modest thief.

"The one of my wife is my prize," Abram said. "She's beautiful, isn't she, Arkady?"

"Yeah. A dish. I always liked Jew women. Never slept with one, I admit, but I had some great wet dreams about them. Jacked off a lot, too. No offense, Levitch. In the black market in Odessa we had plenty of smart Jews. Not Zionist jerks like you, guys who get in trouble. For what? You'd been better off peddling jeans and watches."

"I did that also."

"You could fool me. You're like teacher's pet around here. Volunteered to work in the library after hours. Always on time, always trying to tidy up. It won't help, Levitch. You're a political. Worse. A political Jew. They'll bust your balls before you've done your five in Maridov. Then what? Fifteen in the gold fields?"

"You can't discourage me. Look, how bad can it be? They confiscated my photographs when I came here, but I got them back, didn't I? We get letters every other week. I asked the sergeant for my prayer book and phylacteries, and he gave them back. He said the only reason they stopped them in the mail was they didn't know what they were. They thought the prayer book was some kind of anti-Socialist tract. I told them it was a lot older than politics. So here it is. And if you don't mind, Arkady, I'll pray."

"Be my guest, Levitch. Sometimes I wish I could pray."

"You can join me. I know you're not a Jew. But you could repeat some of the words, stand here with me and keep me company."

"Jesus God, Levitch, don't I have enough troubles? Go on, pray your dumb head off."

Levitch donned his skullcap and a makeshift shawl fash-ioned from an old gray bed sheet. He turned pages in his *siddur.* He closed his eyes. Bone-weary, a great void in his gut. He'd joked with Arkady Oren, but he was dying of fear. A little death each day. *Twenty years of this? For what?*

He heard the steel window clatter open, the evening trays shoved in. Potato and cabbage soup, hard bread. It was astonishing how much energy one got from so miserable a fare. It had been worse, much worse in the time of Stalin, the old-timers told him. Now at least they kept you strong enough to work.

Haltingly, he stumbled over the unfamiliar Hebrew words. He regretted that he had been delinquent in learning the ancient tongue. He should have spent more time studying instead of floating around the streets, handing out bulletins, freeloading at the Parentes'. He'd have plenty of time now for learning Hebrew. Even with rising at four-thirty, working all day in the mail-pouch factory (scarring hands, ripping skin on the canvas, puncturing his fingers with the deadly needle) and his volunteer hours in the library, he would find time to study his Hebrew-Russian grammar.

Blessed art thou, Lord our God, sovereign of the universe, who causeth the lords of sleep to descend on mine eyes, and slumber on mine eyelids. May it be acceptable in Thy presence, O Lord, my God, and the God of my fathers . . . .

Arkady Oren was tempted to interrupt him with a rude joke or remind the Yid that his dinner was getting cold. But the look on Abram's face warned him off—happy, lost. There was something about the squirt that made it hard to tease him. The pickpockets, robbers, rapists and smugglers didn't pick on him. Maybe he was too easy, too poor, not worth the trouble. Or was it a kind of dumb honesty, an open and forgiving nature? Oren wasn't certain. It didn't matter. Levitch would be lucky if he survived the first five years of his sentence.

"Silver?" asked Karpov.

Irina said, "Stainless steel." She showed him the electrode, holding it with a sterile tweezers—seven centimeters of shiny needle-thin metal.

"It looks harmless." The small crown of fuzz on his head had been shaved. He sat upright in the surgical chair, wearing a green robe.

"It is. Only the tip is exposed. The rest is insulated with

silicone. The receiving apparatus is contained in the tiny disc at the top—a microcomputer. We have the Japanese to thank for it."

Karpov was hypnotized by the slender needle. He noticed that in the plastic box from which Irina had taken it, three identical needles rested on absorbent cotton.

"Four?"

"I shall implant only two."

"And these tiny mechanisms will cure me? Create a new Karpov?"

"I guarantee nothing. If it doesn't work, no harm will come of it."

He touched the back of her hand. "I know there is some residue of affection in you. You wouldn't hurt me."

She thought: *the charming villain*. Was it possible there were decent instincts buried deep in his psyche? Was there a chance that her daring experiment might arouse them, make him less of a heartless stalker?

She put him to sleep with sodium amytal, then a general anesthetic, and watched him carefully as he fell into snoring slumber. Quickly she moved the stereotaxic instrument into position. A metal frame enclosed either side of his head and held it rigid. Above the shaven pate, a metal crescent was put in place, its surface marked off in millimeters. Attached to the protractorlike metal arch was a vertical metal vise for gripping the electrode and forcing it into the brain.

She worked swiftly, professionally indifferent to the shaven skull and the figure in the chair. Deftly she removed a tiny bone button. It would be replaced with plastic cement once the electrode was in place. The slender steel electrode was inserted into the stereotaxic vise. Slowly, carefully, Irina lowered the metal vise a centimeter at a time. The sharp steel tip of the electrode pierced the dura easily, then moved through the other membranes of the brain, the pia and the arachnoid. Small amounts of blood oozed from the puncture. She turned the wheel on the vise. The electrode moved downward slowly, passing through the soft matter of Karpov's brain.

The naked metal tip came to rest in the septal area of his left hemisphere.

He slept soundly, dreaming multicolored, hard-edged dreams, unaware of the intrusion into his brain.

Irina moved the stereotaxic mechanism to the right hemisphere. She hesitated. One implant or two? Could his brain sustain the invasion? She sighed. Rats and dogs did. They survived unharmed after the experiments.

Once more she removed a bone button, placed a second electrode in the viselike mechanism, lowered the needlesharp metal into the brain. This time it came to rest in the hippocampus of the right hemisphere.

She removed the stereotaxic instrument, patched the tiny holes in Karpov's skull with flesh-colored plastic, wound a bandage around his head. He slept on.

With a warning to resign from the Helsinki group and the Jewish refusenik movement, Zalman Sokolov was released from jail on orders of Colonel Dort.

Andrei Malik, glorying in his potency as head of the Jewish Department, laid the law down to the Lubavitcher.

"Listen to me," Malik said. "You understand Russian?"

"Yes, sir."

"Get it into your thick skull. There must be a brain behind those whiskers. Why do you people wear all that hair? You got a bird's nest in there?"

"It is part of our tradition. The Lord asks these things of us."

"The Lord will like you better if you stop handing out bulletins and giving interviews. You're free now, so don't go making speeches about how cruel we are. Were you beaten?"

"No."

"Starved? Kept up at night? Tortured?"

"No."

"So don't tell lies about us. If I catch you making phone calls to the Americans, inciting your fellow Hebrews, organizing protests for Levitch, or in any way breaking the laws of the Soviet Union, you'll be back in jail as fast as I can arrest you. Go home. Pray. Look after your wife. If you stay out of trouble we might let you out. Meanwhile, if you want to make things easy for yourself, you'll tell us what those other Yids are doing—Slesik and that gang. And anything you know about Zolkin will be appreciated."

The youth stroked his beard, fingered his skullcap. "Sir, I can't. I am not Dr. Belus. I seek only to practice my faith, to love the Lord, blessed be He."

"Bless your luck that you've alive, Sokolov. Now get the hell out of here. If I get a report that you're going to meetings, or handing out papers, or slandering the Soviet Union, back you go to a cold, dark place where you can pray twenty-four hours a day."

Parente, Agnes Wardle and two other reporters caught up with the liberated Lubavitcher outside his apartment house, a few blocks from the synagogue. He was strolling with his wife. She was pushing a baby carriage. A four-year-old boy held her skirt. The four of them seemed to Parente the purest of victims. *Alongside these,* Tony thought, *Levitch was a tiger, a middle linebacker*.

"Good to see you, Zalman," Parente said. "You okay?"

"Please, gentlemen and Miss Wardle. I can't talk to you. It's all over for me. I am not a leader of the movement. I want to leave. I don't want to hurt my wife and children."

Under the awning of a food store, two of Malik's goons watched. Sokolov glanced toward them.

"You wish to be left alone?" Miss Wardle asked.

"I can't do what Abram Moiseivich did. I must trust in the Almighty."

Parente clucked. "You have no job. You can't go anywhere. How will you live?"

"The Almighty will provide. I believe in miracles. Come, Chana."

The couple, pushing the carriage, started away slowly so that the little boy could keep up. Malik's agents moved to follow them, *Hyenas*, Parente thought.

"Poor sucker," Parente said. "There goes the movement. Without Levitch, they're lost. Slesik's dying, the Semonskis are old, and the bastards are getting ready to shut Zolkin up."

"Can we help you?" Agnes Wardle called after them. "Mr. Sokolov, is there any way we can help?"

"It's all right," Sokolov replied. "I am going to pray. The Almighty will save us. Better I should not talk anymore to you."

They watched the little family walk off. An errant breeze fluttered Sokolov's beard.

Sad, sad, Parente thought. "Ah, maybe he's right," he said. "There's only one Levitch. Who can take that kind of heat?"

The journalists looked at each other helplessly.

* * *

"Are you in pain?" Irina asked.

"No. Just a little drowsy."

They were in a remote private room in the old wing of the hospital. Karpov sat in a comfortable chair. Once again his head was swathed in bandages. He smiled. He appeared relieved to have found the surgical procedure painless and quick, and with so few aftereffects.

Dr. Skiba wheeled in a slide projector and a screen, then left. Irina had warned her to be silent about the new work with the important patient.

On a metal table Irina placed two small black metal boxes. They were radio transmitters. One was marked R, the other L.

"What now?" Karpov asked.

"I want to see if the electrodes are properly positioned. I assure you that these tests will be pleasurable, for the most part."

"Most . . . ?"

"You may have some unpleasant sensations. But not nearly as bad as having one's fingernails torn off. Wasn't that what your colleagues did to the Hungarians in 1956?"

"I had no part in it." She watched his hands. They were steady, strong. "Irina, my dear, there are moments when I wonder if I did the right thing in permitting this assault on my aggrieved brain."

"You said you trusted me."

"And loved you. But are they related? I've known of lovers who couldn't trust one another for five minutes."

"We aren't lovers anymore."

"Ah, but there's hope, isn't there?"

She had to bolster his confidence, keep him from suspecting her. She was in treacherous waters, embarked on an uncharted course. Karpov was still dangerous, a police agent deep in his heart. She had joked about his R-complex, the reptilian brain that stalked, trapped and killed. She did not want it aroused, directing its primordial hatreds and energies at her, or Levitch or Zolkin. Thus far she had been lucky. So depressed and exhausted was Karpov that he had consented to the implantations. The trick now was to keep him pliant and agreeable. It would not be easy.

"Hope? For you?"

"For us."

Inhaling, arching her neck, Irina said, "Perhaps. My main concern is curing you." She paused, fingering the silvery buttons on the metal boxes marked R and L. "I must confess. I recall our intimacies with . . . joy. Call it what you will. An adventure, a fulfilling of animal desires. I'm not encouraging you, or promising anything. But you may change. Our lives may change."

All charm, he smiled warmly. Did she imagine it? Or was there a glimmer of humanity in his green eyes? She noticed that his right hand was dominant, resting on his right knee. He had all but buried his left hand between his thigh and the chair.

"What you've said convinces me I did the right thing in agreeing to this. I'm buoyant, energetic. Proceed, Madame Surgeon."

To her surprise, she found herself returning his smile. "Good, Andrei, very good. A cooperative subject is half the battle. Is there anything additional you wish to know about what I've done and where we have to go?"

"A bit more explanation."

"I've implanted two small thin electrodes in your brain. One is in the left hemisphere, in a so-called pleasure region. When activated by this radio transmitter it should induce euphoria, ease, a feeling of joy and warmth. The other is in the right hemisphere. When similarly activated, it should produce anxiety, fear and pain."

Karpov looked puzzled. "How will that cure me?"

"I hope to condition you to associating certain images, words and thoughts with both hemispheres. In time, it should not be necessary to buzz the electrode. Mere suggestion, a sighting, a thought should be able to induce pleasure or pain, accordingly."

He squinted at the transmitting mechanisms on the metal table.

"Radio signals to the microreceiver attached to the electrodes," she explained. "The Japanese refined a great deal of this. I'm lucky to have the equipment. A few years ago you'd have been heavily wired, attached to a control panel. It's all miniaturized now."

"Electronics are not my strong suit, Irina. Can you explain?"

"Stimulation will be at two milliangstroms, with reversible polarity at a pulse width of point-twenty-five milliseconds.

The stimulus current will be thirteen-point-eighty-six milli-angstroms per square centimeter, and so on. It all sounds complex but it isn't."

"All right. I'm ready. What must I do?"

"Close your eyes. Relax your muscles. Let your arms and hands rest heavily in your lap. Breathe deeply once, twice, and let your body go limp at the end of the exhalation. Good. Try it again."

She depressed the button on the L transmitter that was keyed to the electrode in Karpov's left brain. She held it for two seconds.

"What did you feel?"

Karpov shut his eyes. "I'm not sure. A . . . tremor? A *frisson.*"

She hit the button again, depressing it for three seconds.

He was smiling.

"Now?"

"Ah. Yes, more definable. A pleasing sensation. I can't describe it. A sense of being satisfied."

"Be more specific."

"Let me see. The rush of relief one gets from a pain-killer. Demerol or Percodan. That kind of warmth, security. Not nearly as strong. Do it again."

She depressed the button for five seconds.

"Good, good. I feel stronger. More alert. Very much at rest."

"Warmth?"

"Yes."

"Similar to what one feels on drinking good wine or brandy?"

"Possibly."

"Any sexual connotation?" She hit the button for five seconds again.

"Very faint. Not the real thing." He opened his eyes. "Your presence would confuse the nature of my reaction, Irina. A sense of sexual arousal? It's impossible for me to describe it precisely. But it is fine. May I experience it again?"

She struck the button. Eight seconds.

He grinned. It was the kind of broad smile she had never seen on Karpov's cold face. It suffused the lean features, spread his mouth, formed crow's-feet at the corners of his eyes.

"Quite good, quite good."

She brought the metal transmitter to him. It was a boxlike affair, aluminum painted black. The button was on its upper face.

"Try it yourself."

"Really? A reward?"

"Part of the training process. Fancy yourself one of the rats. You recall the way they kept depressing the lever to experience the good feeling it gives them."

He laughed. "This is marvelous. The great Karpov. The most feared man in the KGB, scourge of refuseniks and dissidents, reduced to the role of a laboratory animal." He winked at her. "Irina Tashenko, if I did not know that we're friends, and if I did not trust you completely, I might be wary of this contraption. Can one overdose oneself with this magical box? Can I become an addict?"

"Hardly."

Karpov's right index finger went for the button. As it did, his left hand pushed it away. The right hand moved again. The left hand slapped it.

Irina's eyes widened.

So soon. The brain divided against itself. The implants would intensify, enlarge enormously the capacities of the two separate brains. Hemispheric duality would become hemispheric antagonism, a contest of two wills in the same organism.

"That was clumsy," he said. He shifted in the stuffed chair, pushing his left arm and shoulder against the back of the seat, as if restraining that part of the body. The left hand reached again, then pulled back. With his right hand he hit the lever.

"It is good?" she asked.

"Floating, calm. I feel it all over me. Forgive me, Irina, but I . . . I . . . seem to need you. Want you quite badly. Most pleasurable, most pleasurable."

"Do it again."

He closed his eyes. Bliss smoothed the lines on his face. Karpov pressed the control button. He did not release it. His bandaged head rolled backward against the headrest. The left hand moved for the controlling right hand, then fell to his lap, clenched.

Someone else's hand, she thought.

"That's enough, Andrei. We can't let you indulge yourself. There'll come a time when you'll have to induce these sensations without benefit of the machine. If you gorge yourself on pleasure now, it will be difficult to wean you from it."

"My training session is ended?"

"Not entirely."

She took the black box from him. At the table, she placed her hand on the second transmitting apparatus. It was marked with an R to indicate the implant in the hippocampus of Karpov's right brain.

"Ah. The villain."

"I implanted you twice. This one is a control, a monitoring device for me. To see what your right hemisphere is up to, now that it has less communication with the verbal left. Are you ready for what may be a different experience?"

"I'm in your hands."

In many ways, she thought.

Irina hit the button on the second transmitter. She held it for four seconds.

Karpov frowned, pursed his lips. "Enough."

"Pain?"

"A kind of . . . imbalance. Loss of . . . something."

She held the button down for five seconds.

He was struggling, tensing his shoulders. The right hand was clutching the left. He leaned forward, eyes locked.

"What do you feel now?" She hit the button on the R transmitter again.

With a violent movement, Karpov's left arm shot forward as if delivering a blow. The fist was taut, the arm extended. It pawed the air, then drew back.

"Why did you do that?" she asked.

"What?"

"You struck out with your left hand. As if to hit someone. Weren't you aware that you did?"

"No. I'm uncomfortable."

She hit the button again. "Describe your feelings."

"Frustrated. Something threatening me. Not you. Others. I . . . I . . . I'm angry. Sense of being pursued. Enough, Irina."

She did not depress the button again. She came to him, took the pulse in his carotid artery. It was racing. His breathing was labored. A fine sweat covered his face.

Again she went to the machine and hit the R button. She

let him have a full ten seconds of voltage, activating the slender filament of steel in his right brain.

"Dammit, stop." He bared his teeth. "I said *stop*. Enough." Karpov jammed his hands to his temples, writhed in the seat. "No more. Irina, do you want to destroy me? You keep this up and I'll hurt you."

He got up. His arms dropped loosely to his side. Back bent, knees lowered, he lurched toward her. The left arm swung loosely. His eyes opened wide, stared with an insane light. She saw the flash of his white teeth.

She stopped the stimulation.

He straightened up. "Something I had to do, haven't done. They're taking things away from me." He halted, struggled to stand upright, wrapped the robe around his body.

"No one is taking anything from you."

"I'm angry about something. I don't know what."

"Are you afraid?"

His left hand raised itself, clawlike fingers attaching themselves to his left temple. "Afraid. I don't know why."

"The reactions are normal."

"Let me feel . . . the other. The left brain."

She picked up the transmitters. "Not now, Andrei. This was only a training session. I promise you less pain and more pleasure. You'll understand more fully in a few days."

"I beg you. Once more. I must feel that good sensation. Warmth . . . security . . . joy. Why deny it to me?"

She shook her head. "You must learn to be dependent on your own will. For the moment, rest. Enjoy your solitude. I'll bring you some books."

He moved to embrace her. She let him hold her, kiss her cheek.

"Don't deny me affection," he said. "I loved you. Perhaps I still do. When you were stimulating my . . . what shall I call it? . . . my good brain, I wanted you."

"A common phenomenon, Andrei Borisovich. Affection is often transferred to the attending physician."

She let him kiss her once on the lips—a long, probing kiss. He sighed, begged to kiss her again, but she refused.

10

LEAVING THE USIA Library on Tchaikovsky Street, Irina saw the burly man she knew as Anthony Parente. He seemed in a hurry, frowning, carrying a caramel-colored attaché case. She stopped him outside the gate.

"Mr. Parente?"

"Yeah, that's me."

"Do you know me?"

Parente looked at the handsome woman. Better-dressed, better-looking than the average Moscow housewife or office worker. She had serene eyes, clear skin, dark-brown hair brushed back to reveal a pair of delicate ears.

"You look familiar."

"I'm Dr. Tashenko."

"Oh, sure. The surgeon. The one who provided the papers that got Levitch convicted."

"That is not exactly correct. May we regard this conversation as confidential?"

"Why not?"

Parente's heart thumped, did the hundred-yard dash. Something was dropping into his lap. She had to be part of the intricate arrangement of lies that had sent Levitch away for twenty years. In the motherland these things did not happen by chance. Somehow the KGB had sucked her in on the deal. The Hanson interview. The nasty business of setting Levitch up by making him the go-between, handing medical papers to the innocent Hanson via the KGB informer Belus.

"We may be under surveillance," she said.

"It doesn't bother me. They have a tail on me all the time, and my phones are tapped. When I go to a restaurant with my wife or take my kid to the zoo, they have me followed. We might as well stroll down Tchaikovsky." He could not resist a gibe. "Of course the last American reporter you talked to got arrested and tossed out."

"I regret what happened to Hanson."

"Well, Hanson's free and working. Abram Levitch didn't end up in good shape. Did you help do him in?"

She looked at him piercingly. "I had no notion that would happen to him. I had no idea where those papers would end up. Please don't ask me to explain any further. Remember, this conversation is confidential. If you use any of this, if you quote me, even indirectly, I will be in trouble."

Parente laughed. "You? A heroine of the USSR? One of their hot-shot medical people? Prize winner, participant in international conferences? Dr. Tashenko, you're a member of the non-torturable class. They can't hurt you."

She let him take her elbow as they crossed the street. Thin sunlight spread faint yellow light on the gray streets. Flower vendors had appeared, carts selling ice cream, *kvass*, fruit.

"Mikhail Zolkin is a far more distinguished scientist than I am, and he has been hurt. They tell me it's a matter of time before he's exiled."

"Zolkin didn't play their game. He didn't help trap some miserable Jew trying to get out of this dump. He talked back to them. You haven't. Don't look upset. I don't blame you. The vast majority of your citizens, from street cleaners like that old babushka over there to brain surgeons like yourself, go along with the system. It's all you know."

"You make assumptions."

"All I know is I love Abram Levitch. It was wrong for one guy to have so much courage, be so honest, so willing to stand up. He's gone. He may never see a free day again. And

I can't help feeling you were part of the frame-up. Sorry, Dr. Tashenko, but that's my reading of it."

"You have a right to feel that way. You're an American. Things work differently here."

"Yeah, I keep hearing that. It doesn't make it easier for Abram, or his wife, or his friends."

They paused in front of a small park. Two men in mud-gray suits got out of a Volga sedan, looked them over, walked away. Local cops, probably. They didn't seem to recognize Parente or Tashenko. He wondered: *She is a national monument of sorts.* Besides, she'd played along with the entrapment of Levitch. They were probably not concerned with her. He, on the other hand, was hot. Too close to Levitch, too close to the refuseniks.

"I have a request," she said.

"From me?"

"I need a clear photograph of Levitch. One that can be reproduced."

"You've got a sense of humor, Dr. Tashenko."

"It's not a joke."

"Can't you dig one up? You could call up Malik at the KGB and get a hundred photographs of Abram. That's all they ever did, take pictures of him. Close-ups, medium close-ups, group shots. Smile, Levitch, you're framed."

"You're taunting me. I assure you I have no such entrée to the KGB, nor would I go to them." She breathed deeply. "You must know that my husband was jailed for a time. Lev Tashenko, the editor. He is not considered reliable. I'm not privy to KGB affairs."

"Right, right. The guy who recanted publicly. Said it was all a typographical error. Why do you want Levitch's photograph? Pinup boy? He's a head shorter than you are. You've never met him."

She bit her lower lip. A woman bred to authority and command, she found herself confused by this clownish Italian-American.

But she needed him. And she felt that he was trustworthy. "I can't tell you why. I'm not part of Zolkin's group. I'll sign no petitions. Nor am I an agent of the state. I am politically neutral, disinterested. I—"

"Your main concern is the human brain, I know. I read the handouts from Novosti."

"I can't explain my purpose. A clear photograph of Levitch, full face. And also photos of his associates—Slesik, the others."

"Lady, you are very strange."

She ignored his crudeness. "I was in the USIA Library looking through *Time* and other publications. They have pictures of Levitch and the others, but the magazines aren't allowed out of the building. And of course it's impossible to buy these magazines anywhere in the Soviet Union. I need an original glossy or, better yet, a negative. Can you help me?"

"If you tell me what they're for. More bad news for Levitch? Nail him with something worse than the twenty years he got?"

"I ask you to believe me. I am trying to help him."

Parente scratched his sideburns. "Beats me. You people send me up the wall. If you give me your word you won't hurt him, or Slesik, or any of the others, okay. I've got a file of photographs in my office. I'll see what I can dig up."

"I'll be grateful. And remember: silence."

After the arrest—and release—of Slesik, Sokolov and others, Colonel Dort was convinced that the back of the refusenik movement had been broken. But three weeks after they had been freed, the refuseniks coalesced again, made contact with one another, gathered each Saturday in front of the synagogue.

Parente, Agnes Wardle, Schultze, and the other journalists were surprised to see more younger Jews appearing—intelligent, determined people, ranging from the bearded Orthodox to couples with the look of athletes. No single leader had emerged. Zalman Sokolov, in spite of his earlier expressions of fear, was back, this time with three more black-clad Chassidim.

"I'm back in the Bronx," Parente said. "East Tremont Avenue on Friday night. I like those guys. I always did. The Irish kids used to toss bottles and rocks at them, but you couldn't keep them away from *shul*. I'm glad to say my own gang, the Italian-American Warriors and Handball Champs, left them alone. Most of the time, anyway."

"They are rather to be admired."

"Yeah, Agnes. Rather. I wish I knew what keeps them going."

Mikhail Semonski walked over to them. "A letter from Abram Levitch this week, Tony. He asks to be remembered to you. He wants to keep everyone's spirits up. He says it's not too bad. But his hands are bothering him. Stiff, almost paralyzed. They think he may have a neuromuscular disorder of some kind. He has trouble sewing."

"What else?" Parente asked.

"He misses Sarah. Asks about her all the time. He gets a letter a week from her. Letters from us are confiscated. Mine, Chaim's. Zolkin wrote to him. It got through, but heavily censored."

"What's the latest word on his getting out?"

"Not good. The American Jews are trying, but they fight so much among themselves they can't coordinate anything. And us? We're frightened. After the way Belus betrayed Abram, we're on guard. Who knows who the next informer will be?"

Agnes Wardle asked, "Where is Belus?"

"Gone. An un-person. They shipped him out. He writes to no one, explains nothing."

"You guys were too trusting."

The crowd shifted, formed eddies, currents. There were no more yellow bulletins given out. Malik's men ringed the square, taking photographs. Parente was tempted to ask one of them to take a few extra shots for Dr. Tashenko. What was she up to?

Irina negotiated with the photographer who worked in the Institute's laboratory preparing medical slides. His name was Ignatov, a white-skinned, starved man, who parted his black hair in the middle and squinted over rimless glasses. A relic, a survivor. She had been told once that Ignatov had spent twelve years in the gulag for the crime of having been captured by the Germans at the battle of Kiev. He was nineteen at the time, an explosives expert who had courageously helped set the mines that leveled Wehrmacht headquarters. Miraculously, he had survived three Nazi prisoner-of-war camps, only to be interned by Stalin's police.

Irina located him in his basement laboratory. She showed him the pictures Parente had given her.

His brow turned to a mass of ridges as he adjusted his spectacles. "These are not medical pictures, Comrade Doctor."

"Obviously. Can you make me a set of photographic slides?"

Ignatov cleared his throat. "I need authorization. You know

how it is. I have to account for all my work hours, all material used. I must keep a log of photographs. And these—"

"What about them?"

"Levitch? A jailbird?"

"I'm conducting experiments in cognition. Matching photos and verbal commands."

"*Levitch*," he repeated. "A spy? A traitor? And these others. They're the bunch around him. And why these shots outside the Jewish temple? My experience has been, dear lady, that matters concerning Jews are best left alone."

She adopted a sterner tone. "There is no political significance. Look at the other photos."

Ignatov thumbed through the glossies. "Flowers. Birds. Birch forest. Imported champagne? Fancy shoes. A sunset. A beach. France? Italy?"

"Go on."

"What is this? Gallows. Firing squad. Looks like scenes from the Great Patriotic War. Stalin? What is this? A picture of Stalin, the little father, may the devil eat his toenails. Who are these guys in uniforms? Cops, I can tell. KGB people."

The photographer was staring at photographs of Colonel Dort and Captain Malik. He recognized Dort's superior, Colonel Reshev of the Second Directorate.

"This one. With eyes like a shark. Dr. Tashenko, I don't want to go back to Gulag University. I have my degree already."

"I'll be responsible. Can I help you in any way? Do you need anything?"

Ignatov screwed up his bleached face. "You have influence. You know people. How to get things."

"What do you want?"

"Jeans. A pair for my son, a pair for my daughter. The real American stuff, with the metal buttons. Levi's. You get me them, I'll make fifty slides for you."

"I'll get them. Now please, give this work a priority. I'd like them in a week's time. And please, Ignatov, absolute secrecy about this. Do the work when no one else is around, and deliver the mounted slides to me personally."

"Are you joking? I'll call you when they're ready. The code word will be . . ." The shrunken, bleached man paused. "*Nerve cells*. That's it. Pictures of nerve cells. Fair enough?"

"Fair enough."

"And don't forget my jeans."

Before she left, he scrawled down his son's and daughter's sizes, stressing again that they had to be genuine Levi's.

Irina informed the Institute's director that she was conducting rehabilitation sessions with Major Karpov that required solitude, and after-hours access to the building. The work with him, she stressed, was as much experimentation for her as it was part of the healing process. The director agreed. She was a star of the medical constellation. She was allowed privileges.

Lev, busy translating East German criticism for his magazine, accepted her absences. She assured him that she was not having an affair with Karpov. He was convalescent, weak, his mind unfocused. The training sessions had to be done at night because of her busy operating schedule. Even her lab work was in abeyance. She'd turned the implanted white rats over to Dr. Skiba. They were making excellent progress on the explosive-detection program. After intensive conditioning, the rats were displaying markedly elevated brain and heart activities when they smelled TNT. No longer were they in need of the pleasurable electrical stimulation to excite them. A whiff alone did the trick.

Irina subjected Karpov to four days of training with the stimulating mechanisms. The box marked R, when its button was depressed, sent a charge into his right brain, activating the electrode in his hippocampus. Karpov hated and feared it. He cringed and screwed up his face. Yet it remained difficult for him to describe the sensation. He struggled for words. A right-brain phenomenon, she saw at once: something the left brain, with its verbal skills, would have had no trouble describing. "I want to run," Karpov said. "Someone's after me . . . not sure who. Something bad is about to happen. A problem I can't solve . . ."

She would alternate with the box marked L—giving him short shocks in the septal region of his left hemisphere. More and more he came to anticipate them with joy. She had merely to advise him that they would shift to the left brain for his face to brighten. He laughed, he joked. Then, with the administering of the shocks to the left brain, he grinned, hugged himself, relaxed. Once, undergoing a prolonged stimulation of the septal area of the left hemisphere, he experienced orgasm.

Irina was behind a screen, studying his reactions, varying the lengths of stimulation time. When she held the button down a full thirty seconds, she saw him start to thrust forward with his pelvis, rise in the chair, begin a series of breathy, soft gasps. Embarrassed, he let out an explosive discharge of breath and covered his face.

"I'm humiliated," he said.

"Don't be. It's a normal reaction."

After he had washed himself, changed his pajamas and returned, she explained that just prior to his orgasm he had been tense, filled with anxiety. "The stimulations were of an intense nature. I could see you recoiling, your hands gripping each other."

"That's right. The worst I've ever felt. What were you doing to me?"

"Prolonged stimulation. What did you feel?"

"Terror. When you switched to my left brain, the relief was transcending. I was soaring, liberated. May I experience it again?"

"In a moment. We're advancing to a somewhat more complex stage of your treatment." She wheeled the screen in front of him.

"Covering my eye? Identifying objects again?"

"You'll perceive images with both eyes. Both hemispheres will receive the message. Sit quietly for ten minutes, breathe deeply, let your body go limp on each exhalation. I want to relax your temporal muscles, your jaw, your eyes. I'll set up the projector."

He settled into the viewing chair. Yes, he felt better, wonderfully rested. When she had switched from deep stimulation of the hippocampal implant in his right brain, he had felt a satisfying sense of freedom. The rush of pleasure from the shift to his left brain's septal area had caught him by surprise, triggered his absurd sexual response. During the buildup of sexual sensations, he experienced brightly colored, hard-edged images of Irina, of boyhood fantasies, of his niece, of a prostitute he had patronized in Paris for several months, of an aunt he had once secretly loved. They had all been there: clear, welcoming, almost touchable. Then the gathering of sensation in his groin, the release.

"We're ready now," she said.

"May I request less right-brain activation? I don't like it. The sense I get is . . . one of imminent pain, loss, perhaps my death."

"We'll diminish its use. In time, the right-brain implant can be removed. All right. Look at the center of the screen. I'll flash photos onto it. No need to identify them. If you want to say something, do so."

She sat at the table. With her left hand she worked the projector. It had been specially modified for experiments in perception, with a fractionated exposure mechanism. A picture could be shown for a tenth of a second, a fifth of a second, a half-second. She used her right hand to depress the button on the L transmitter.

"Ready, Andrei?"

"Yes."

Irina hit the two buttons at once. On the screen she flashed a photo of a field of blue wild flowers. She kept it there for a full second, letting him receive, simultaneously, a charge in his left brain. He smiled.

She repeated the process, this time projecting a color photograph of a bottle of French champagne. Then the face of a beautiful German actress. She ran through a carrousel of slides—flowers, luxuries, women, sunsets. With each picture on the screen she let him experience a heightening of his pleasure potential with a jolt of electricity.

"This is most enjoyable," Karpov said. "I'm happy."

Without warning, using a second carrousel, she flashed Colonel Dort's bullish face on the screen and depressed the R transmitter button.

Karpov doubled over. "Stop it. He gives me enough pain. Why the extra jolt?"

She let him sustain a full two seconds of stimulation in his right brain. "What do you feel?"

"I want to get away. Strike back." Karpov shook his left fist at the screen. "Bastard."

"Calm down. He isn't here."

Karpov clutched his throat. What in God's name was she doing to him?

The photo on the screen changed: a gulag somewhere in the north. Barbed-wire fences, dogs, armed guards. Shadowy figures behind the wire.

Irina hit his right brain with an electric jolt. He squirmed, grimaced. "I don't want to see that. To hell with them."

"What do you feel? What is your mind filled with?"

"Fear. I'm not functioning too well. Change the picture. Show me the flowers . . . the birch forest. . . ."

She displayed a new photo. Stalin's face appeared. The thick mustache, the cold eyes of the murdering Georgian. She held the R button a full five seconds.

"Christ, stop it, Irina! I'm here to be cured, not tortured."

She let the screen go blank.

"Well?" she asked.

"I want to run. I can't place my fear. I don't know what it is that frightens me. I'm not a coward. But those last few . . . Was it what you showed me? Or the shocks?"

"Some of both."

"What now?"

"Stare at the screen."

He did so. "I beg of you. No more . . ."

She flashed the photograph of Dort again but did not depress a transmitter button.

"Get rid of him," Karpov snarled. "I don't want to see him."

She turned the screen off. "Did you have any sensations?"

"The same . . . less strong. Didn't want to confront him, wanted to get away . . ."

She flashed another photograph of the gulag on the screen. It was a closer view, of prisoners and booted guards.

"I don't want to see this either," he snarled.

She handed him the R transmitter. "Here. Hit the button. If it bothers you, release it."

Karpov depressed the button. He howled and pulled his hand away. "I'll be damned if I'll do that to myself. I understand now. Associating pictures with the right brain, getting me angry. Oh, no. Not again."

She flashed another scene of wild flowers—a field of yellow daisies. This time she gave him the left-brain transmitter. "Try it again."

He did. "Much better. No pain. Let me keep it on a bit longer." He smiled at her. "You can't keep me bobbing back and forth like a fish on a line. I feel rather good. Strong. Will you come closer? Stroke my head?"

"You're to cure yourself."

She continued the training process, associating the joyful photographs with the stimulation of his left hemisphere, occasionally switching to the right brain with something that would disgust or frighten him: Dort, Malik, Hitler, Stalin, the gulag.

Toward the end of the session she found that by merely flashing one of the negative photographs, *without any electrical stimulation,* she could induce feelings of dread and anger in him.

She interviewed him later, took notes. The right brain was irritable, angry, filling him with terrors, a sense of isolation, and vulnerability. Stimulation of the left hemisphere produced exhilarating, joyful sensations, erotic images, gratifying sequences.

"When you experienced orgasm," she asked, "what happened?"

"Visions. Images. Things out of my past."

"Quickly?"

"Yes. It built after a few stimulations. Then I shut my eyes, almost dreaming."

"Tell me exactly what you thought of."

"I'm ashamed. We don't go in for these . . . what—Freudian exposures?—of ourselves."

"Try."

"I had a memory of when I was ten, eleven. Struggling to climb a rope in a playground. The more I tensed my legs and thighs, the more I produced a curious sensation in my groin, a tingling. With each tensing of the muscles, new jabs of pleasure. Then I looked at the young girls in the playground. Long hair, braids, fair skin, bare legs. I must have experienced orgasm for the first time. It all was revived in my mind."

"Anything else?"

Karpov shut his eyes, stroked his nose. "Memories of an aunt. A beautiful dark woman. My mother's youngest sister. A round soft woman with liquid brown eyes, a full figure. I'm five or six. She's changing her dress in my mother's room. I'm peeking through a crack in the door. She sees me, doesn't mind. A pink corset, pink silken drawers, black stockings. I can see her roundness, the glow of her skin. She walked in front of me, teasing me. Combing her long black hair. I am very young, but I am having an intense sexual experience. It was clear to me—every detail. Even my dismay when she put her dress on."

"That brought you to orgasm, these fantasies of her? The playground incident?"

"No. They preceded it." He paused, touched his lips with a handkerchief. "I couldn't talk like this to anyone in the world except you. Our leaders are right when they forbid all that Freudian nonsense. It would reduce us all to slobbering fools."

Irina smiled. She sat on the edge of the metal table. "Yes, they're prudent. We prefer to jail our troubled citizens in so-called psychiatric hospitals, pump them full of sedatives until they approach the vegetable state. Why bother with seeking the truth—about either the state or oneself?"

"Lies can be useful."

"And ultimately corrupting. Sit in front of the screen again. We're advancing today. Your left brain is doing well. Your right remains a bit surly. Remember that our goal is to make you a more relaxed individual. We seek to eliminate fatigue, restore confidence, clarify your thought processes."

He settled into the chair. This time she attached electrodes to his temporal muscles in order to monitor the tension in his head. He seemed excessively interested in the procedure, joked with her, tried to stroke her hip. She did not dissuade him.

For ten minutes she led him through exercises—deep breathing, stretching, imagery—until his pulse was low. The temporal muscles relaxed, registering a low beep on a biofeedback machine.

"Cover your left eye," she said.

He obeyed.

She turned the projector's lamp onto the white screen. "Are you at rest? Feeling alert?"

"Yes, yes. I'm ready to respond."

"You won't have to identify objects or people. If you want to tell me how you feel, you may."

She went to the table with the projector and the transmitters. Only his left hemisphere would be stimulated.

She began the procedure, flashing pictures on the screen. With some, she activated the radio transmitter, with others she did not.

Karpov watched, smiling. A wondrous soothing sensation

overwhelmed him—warm, floating, utterly relaxed. Fields. Flowers. The facade of the Louvre. A Modigliani. Birches.

Then suddenly, for a fraction of a second, a face popped on the screen—a smiling face, a youngish man.

It happened so fast Karpov barely saw it.

He was puzzling over the intrusion when Irina flashed Levitch's face again. This time she held it for a second, depressed the button.

"Levitch," Karpov laughed.

"Levitch."

"Let me see him again. This is really odd, showing me that idiot among the flowers and the wine."

She projected Abram Levitch's features again. It was a black-and-white photograph, full-faced, very clear. Levitch was smiling, almost winking at the camera. Parente had taken the picture a year ago, when Levitch had first begun his appearances outside the synagogue. This time she kept the image on the screen three seconds, all the time letting Karpov feel the exquisite joy in the left septal area.

"Very clever, Irina," he said.

"No. Just routine training."

She switched photos again, sometimes buzzing his brain, sometimes flashing the scenes without benefit of the pleasure-giving charge.

On the monitor, she noted that his temporal muscles had relaxed completely. The beeping sound of the biofeedback machine had gradually diminished in register until now, with the muscles fully at rest, the audio signal vanished altogether.

In the midst of scenes of flowering meadows, a country brook, she projected for four seconds another of Parente's photographs. It was somewhat dimmer than the portrait of Levitch, but he was clearly recognizable, in a summer shirt, his arm around his fiancée, Sarah Varvansky. The woman was extremely pretty—fair, with lively dark eyes.

As she showed him the photo she activated the electrode.

"Levitch again. And the woman. His wife. Why?"

"To see how you're adjusting. Normally you'd be wary of them, would you not? The prey. Your victims."

"No, no. She's of no consequence. And he's nothing more than a convicted criminal. I never bore him any malice. He was in the way."

She flashed the photo again. They were standing in a

parklike setting. Bright sun. The lower branches of a maple
or an oak. Two smiling people. She struck the button, held
the photo on the screen for five seconds.

Karpov said, "I don't really understand what you're up to,
but I'll accept it. I think you're being naïve. Levitch is out
of my life. Gone. An un-person. Why do you insist I look at
him?"

"For your own good."

She switched to another photograph of Levitch. It was a
winter scene. The refusenik leader was wearing a fur hat, a
fur-collared coat.

She gave him five seconds of intense pleasure with the
radio transmitter, watched him smile, laugh softly. He was
stroking his right thigh with his right hand.

"You find this amusing?" she asked. "Pleasing?"

"Yes. But I'm not sure why I smiled. Levitch looks rather
ridiculous. The face of a tailor or a petty clerk—and decked
out in that outdoorsman's hat. He's a rather nice-looking
fellow. If he'd kept his nose out of other people's business, he
might have survived."

"What makes you think he's dead?"

She switched to the shot of Levitch and his fiancée. Sunlight,
flowers, young people in love.

"I spoke figuratively."

"Do you mean he's as good as dead?"

"I wouldn't want to be in his shoes. You understand,
there's not the slightest chance he'll be let free. He compromised himself unduly."

"You mean," she said, as she hit the L button, "*you* compromised him, trapped him with papers you forced me to
give Belus."

Karpov stretched, enjoying the flood of warmth, the sense
of *rightness. How explain it?* He had never been a user of
drugs, but he imagined that it was the kind of rush of joy, the
sense of utter abandonment, otherness, detachment from
pain, tension, worries, stress, that addicts received. But this
was so much more honest and simple. He felt no pain, no
sense of his brain being invaded or manipulated or unfairly
modified. But as he stared—for a full ten seconds—at Levitch
and the young woman, his mind was elevated, full of gentle
thoughts, a winging freedom, a peace he had not known in
years.

"It's all immaterial," Karpov said. "Levitch wrote his own ticket. He had to be punished and silenced."

She ran through a series of attractive photographs, withholding the stimulation. Then she projected a view of the synagogue, with the mass of Jews in front at the weekly exchange of information. For five seconds she stimulated him.

He laughed. "I understand the game. It's not a very subtle one. The sensation was a good one. But it didn't have to work too hard to master the image. I've told you before. I have no personal animus toward the Chosen People. If they break the law, I catch them. If they abide by the law, I ignore them."

She put her hand on the R transmitter and suddenly projected Dort's porcine face.

"I've had enough," he growled. "Don't subject me to that again." He wanted to run, hide, strike back.

His body tensed; his left fist clenched. Involuntarily, his left foot kicked at the screen.

To Karpov's surprise, Dort telephoned him at the hospital. He was curious about the progress he was making. Moreover, he needed leads on certain letters that had passed between the refuseniks and Zolkin's people.

Karpov was cautious and helpful. He assured his superior he was improving, slept less, ate better, had more energy. But as he listened to Dort's thick voice, he began to sweat. His throat grew taut and his left temporal muscle tensed.

"We picked up Arkangeli a few days ago," Dort said. "The file you had on him was helpful."

"The old soldier?"

"The old traitor."

Karpov looked at the blank screen, saw for a moment Dort's bleached face, the wide neck, the merciless eyes.

"What was he charged with?" Karpov asked.

"It wasn't a political arrest. It was for his own good. We sent him to the Serbsky Institute. They discovered he suffered from schizophrenia with paranoid tendencies."

"I see. How long will he be kept there?"

"Till he's cured. A warning to Zolkin. Arkangeli is to undergo forcible treatment." Dort chuckled. "To see if he can be cured of his schizophrenia. He's in the hands of the

ideological diagnostic team. The medical reports are not
encouraging. He isn't responding."

Karpov listened to Dort, giggling, delighted over the way
they'd pounced on the old hero of the USSR, the man who
had commanded an armored brigade outside Stalingrad and
effected the juncture that resulted in the surrounding of
Paulus's army. A tough old bird, Arkangeli, refusing to bend,
making his stand with Zolkin, showing up to demonstrate for
Jews. And now, buried alive.

"A full protocol to cure him." Dort was rumbling on. "The
diagnostic team tried talking to him, hypnosis, conditioning.
Not much help with a lunatic like Grigor Arkangeli. He's on a
course of *amazin* now. Maximum dosages. To see if that
stubborn peasant brain of his will come around. You know
about those treatments, Andrei Borisovich? Didn't you pre-
scribe them for your wife?"

"Of course."

Karpov congratulated Dort on his handling of Colonel
Arkangeli. As he did so, the words froze in his throat. His left
temple throbbed.

"You sound better, Andrei Borisovich," Dort said. "Even
when you're not here, you're a help. Malik and his people are
combing your files. Very thorough stuff, excellent material. It
helped us handle Arkangeli. He won't be demonstrating for a
long time. Give my regards to the beautiful doctor. And don't
be in a hurry to come back. We want you healthy and
happy."

Karpov cursed after he hung up.

When Irina came by to check his pulse and his blood
pressure, and to arrange for an EEG, he asked her what
amazin did.

"A KGB favorite," she said coldly. "Panacea in your KGB
hospitals. In small doses it's permissible. But the way your
people administer, it's a living hell. Why do you ask?"

"I thought it had a beneficial effect on schizophrenics."

"It causes depression, collapse, severe skin reactions, lack
of control of the muscular system, destruction of memory.
And in some cases it will induce malignant tumors."

He thought of Arkangeli, that eccentric ragged wraith. Half
mad, surely. Was it a loss to anyone to put him away, to
detach him from the body politic? Cut off like a wart, a corn.
He thought of his wife, shuddered.

She studied his drawn face. His eyes were staring out the window into the distance—ugly gray apartments, a clouded sky, distantly the spire of the Ukraina Hotel. He looked wistful, uncertain.

"Why do you ask about *amazin?*"

"Some of our hard cases were maintained on it. People I don't remember. Faces I've forgotten."

But you will never forget Abram Levitch's face, she thought.

Imagine, Levitch wrote to his wife, *the President of the United States spoke about me at his last meeting with the reporters. Don't ask me how, but Arkady, my cellmate, gets all kinds of information, and he says that the President is making an issue of my case, and that the United States may halt grain shipments if I'm not released. I can't believe it. Me? Levitch, a small-time teacher, with the luck to have a beautiful wife? I don't understand it. Maybe my knack for languages, the way the journalists could always come to me for a story. Is that good or bad? Bad, I suppose. They encouraged me to talk and I talked, and protested, and asked to leave, and encouraged others to do so. Enough about me. Tell me all about yourself, your friends, what our new home is like. You see, I call it our new home, since I know someday I'll be there with you. I won't lie. I'm not very vigorous, my head bothers me, and I'm short of breath. The prison hospital is sick of seeing me. They say it's in my head, but I don't believe it. The last thing I want is to go into one of their clinics, or hospitals or whatever they're called. We got word this week that old Arkangeli, the old war hero, is in a hospital. God knows where, for an indefinite term. . . . Meanwhile, I hope, pray, study and dream of you, Sarah my love. . . .*

Karpov was well enough to be sent home for a brief period, after a week's training with the stimulators and the implants in his right and left hemispheres. He felt more energetic, livelier, less depressed. He slept fitfully, often feeling his left arm and left leg thrashing about. His right side rested comfortably.

The morning after his temporary discharge he found himself wandering past the synagogue. It was a mild spring morning, with peasant women setting up stalls to sell fresh vegetables and flowers.

Good God, he thought. *Sixty-five years of Socialism, and all we have to show for it are these old babushkas taking the early morning trains and planes to Moscow from faraway provinces to sell illegally the fruits of their labors on private plots of earth.* Karpov bought some small sour apples and chewed on them. They were tart, but spicy, redolent of the earth and the countryside. It was treason to admit it, but maybe the capitalists knew a few things. Karpov had been in Hungary, the most prosperous of the Eastern bloc countries. There, farms produced magnificently—fruit, wheat, wine, pigs, chickens, eggs. And only because the government, in the mid-sixties, had retreated from collectivization, from the interference of the state in everything from seed packets to milk quotas, and let the industrious Hungarian farmers go into business for themselves. *Wonders!* Hungarians ate well, and Russians queued up for bread.

Never one to doubt the system, Karpov nonetheless felt the ground shaking a little. That's why Russia needed such a huge, efficient, multifunctional police force. It was this stubbornness, this addiction to Marxist doctrine that ensured his job, his eminence, his privileges, his access to special stores, imported luxuries, paid vacations.

Driven by some unknown desire, he wandered up the steps of the deserted synagogue. A crazy notion occurred to him: *I'm looking for Levitch.* Yes, that was it. He wanted to see him. The smiling face, the curling red-brown hair, the moist lips, the wide innocent eyes. All that nonsense about the hardness and cleverness of Jews. They were a soft, succumbing people. Brainy, resourceful, but unable to stand pain or hard work. Yet as soon as he thought that, he knew the stereotype was a lie. Jews had fought with valor and tenacity in the Great Patriotic War. Tens of thousands had died bravely. Others, driven out by the Nazis, had gone into hiding in the forests, forming "family camps," armed nomadic groups who lived off the land, hid, and struck back at their tormentors.

Karpov had seen suppressed documents, hidden in KGB files, about the Jewish resistance during the war. Today, it was not considered proper to discuss them. If Jews resisted, they resisted as Soviet citizens, not as Jews. And if they died—as they did at places like Babi Yar—by the hundreds of thousands, murdered in cold blood by the vilest killers the world had ever seen, their Jewish identity had to be obliterated. They died as Russians, and that was all there was to it. So went the official code, which he, Karpov of the KGB, had helped enforce.

He could recall going with Malik and a militia team to Kiev one day to observe Jews demonstrating at the Babi Yar monument. It seemed rather pointless to suppress them. But they had to be reminded that they had no special status. *Why all this blubbering and lamentation?* Karpov mused. *Haven't they had enough of weeping for two thousand years? Why don't they abandon their fossilized religion with its medieval nonsense, shave the beards, cut the earlocks, burn the sacred scrolls, and become citizens of the USSR?* Their intransigence both irritated him and evoked a curious admiration in him.

Inside, the synagogue was cool and musty. Old eroded benches, an odor of snuff, sweat, dust. Bronze chandeliers depended from the cracked ceiling. Toward the front of the temple was a high wooden cabinet—the ark in which the Torah was held, the five books of their Bible. Three old men sat in a front row, praying silently. Or were they statues, part of the ancient mildewed structure?

Here Levitch came to touch his past, Karpov thought. How had it affected him? What was the magic it had worked on him, that obscure half-Jew, mathematician, former party member, rationalist? Karpov looked at the empty pews, the stained and faded curtains, the red altar cloth embroidered in gold, Hebrew letters he could not read. Shafts of mote-laden sunlight slanted through high windows.

Karpov sat down. The oldest of the three worshipers stood up, stared at him curiously and asked him if he could help him. He spoke in Russian.

Karpov shook his head. They did not seem to recognize him. He said no, he was merely resting. He greeted the old man with his right hand, smiled gently.

"I see what you're trying to do to me," Karpov said to Irina. "Make me a philo-Semite, is that it? Rig my mind so that I look kindly upon the Chosen People? Nonsense, all of it."

"That's partially true."

She sat in front of the screen again, flashed Dort's face.

buzzed him with the R transmitter. He winced, doubled over.

"It's worse today. Release me. I can't take more than a few seconds."

She took her hand from the button. "Describe your sensations."

"I wanted to run. Someone was after me. I was anxious, fearful. Have you stopped?"

She held up her hand. "At least five seconds ago. And the feeling of terror stayed with you?"

"I still feel it. Don't do it again."

"I don't mean to make you suffer. It's part of your cure." She flashed a photograph of the gulag on the screen. Half-starved wretches lined up for inspection; wire fences, armed guards and dogs. Again she charged the electrode in his right brain.

"No more," he said. He gritted his teeth, rose in the chair. "Stop it at once."

She flashed wild flowers on the screen, then geese in flight, a woodland scene. Simultaneously she depressed the button that activated the electrode in his left septal area.

"Ah, that feels better," Karpov said. "It's astonishing. I'm free of pain. I don't feel pursued."

Levitch's smiling face, the innocent look of trust, faith, courage, peered at him from the screen. She kept the button depressed.

"Much better. You and your damned tricks. Yes, I'm my-self again. To think the sight of that Jew could do that to me. Ridiculous."

"It's not his picture. It's what you sense in the left brain."

She released the control. Karpov smiled, crossed his legs, laughed at a photograph of a circus scene, became voluble as she flashed a picture of a young woman pushing a baby in a stroller.

She flashed a photo of the synagogue, alternated it with a seaside scene, a sunny beach, Chaim Slesik's pained face. Without electrical stimulation, Karpov smiled again, stroked his left hand with his right, placed his right leg over his stiff left thigh to stop the kicking of his left foot.

* * *

She played a Mozart tape—the Jupiter Symphony. First Karpov listened with his left ear only, covering his right ear. He showed little reaction.

"Mozart," she said. "Does it please you?"

"Not especially. I'm not much on classical music. Wagner is all right. This lighter stuff bores me. It sounds scratchy."

She made him cover his left ear, listen to the same piece with his right ear.

"Now?"

"Delightful. Wonderfully calming. Why the difference?"

"Your left and right sides are growing apart. The left brain is more agreeable, happier. It reacts to music with more appreciation, even though it's the right brain that is more gifted musically. A paradox, but an explainable one."

She turned off the projector but kept the controlling transmitters plugged in. She hit the L transmitter for a long period, watched him shut his eyes, sink deep into the easy chair and begin to hum in time to the Mozart theme.

"Andrei Borisovich, you're now getting a deep continuing charge in the septal area. Let me ask you, was Abram Levitch guilty?"

He did not open his eyes. A faint smile lingered on his lips. "I have no knowledge of his guilt or innocence. I'm not aware . . . aware . . ."

She kept the implant activated, shooting current into his left brain. "Guilty or not?"

"I have no knowledge of his guilt . . . .He . . . he . . . means nothing . . . .He could not . . . did not . . ."

She gave him ten seconds without brain stimulation, let the Jupiter Symphony continue. Then she depressed the transmitter in his right brain.

"Andrei Borisovich, was Abram Levitch guilty?"

Karpov jerked upright in the chair, clenched his left fist, pounded it against the arm of the chair. "Yes. Yes. Damned meddling Jew. Damn him. Guilty as hell."

She released the button. "You're certain?"

"Yes, guilty." He paused. "Turn that music off. No. Let it play. Guilty? I don't know. I don't know what he did, what he was up to. What are you trying to do to me, Irina?"

"Open your eyes."

He did so.

On the screen she flashed a photograph taken at Babi Yar

by the SS. Jews lined up to be shot at the edge of the ditch. SS gunners, an officer.

She struck the L button.

Karpov stared at the screen. "Oh, God. God help them, they should not have been killed. The children. Thrown alive into the ditch. Tell me they were saved."

She flashed a photograph of the Star of David on the facade of the Synagogue of Prague, gave him a long, sustained charge in his septal area.

"Prague," he said. "A city of love. The old ghetto. The museum. With the paintings the Jews made in the camps. Will you go there with me someday?"

The six-pointed star stayed on the screen. Karpov, full of electrically induced pleasure, dominated by his sensitized left hemisphere, stared at it.

"How unique, how intriguing. Why do they persist? What is it they know?"

Chaim Slesik died in Nadya Burik's apartment. Death came as a kindly visitor to the gaunt man. He complained little, asked for little, coughed his way to a deep sleep.

A Dr. Mittelmann, an older man, not one of the refuseniks, a veteran of the Red Army who had made his peace with the party, attended him in his last hours.

During the early evening of a bright spring day Slesik became comatose, breathing deeply, sighing noisily.

Zalman Sokolov and his wife came. The Lubavitcher youth prayed for the agnostic Slesik. Others came to stay with him in his last hours.

"Only this morning he asked for a boiled egg, got off the couch, ate it, smiled, talked about when he was a boy in Poltava. He lived on a farm, he said, used to collect the eggs for his mother." Nadya dabbed at her eyes with her apron. "Poor Chaim. His wife is gone. His children are in Central Asia. God knows if they'll come back. They weren't happy when he became one of us."

Zalman Sokolov prayed in the corner of the room. Mirrors were turned to the wall at his behest. Slesik's desiccated body, as if divested of fiber and muscle, was placed on the floor and covered.

"Astonishing that he lived this long," Dr. Mittelmann said. "Belus told me he was ravaged. Pancreas, stomach, liver. But he kept smoking, talking, writing. A pity. With Levitch gone, and Slesik dead, what—" He stopped. "Don't tell me. I didn't ask. I respect you, but I'm not one of you. I'll call the authorities. We can arrange for burial. But please, don't make an occasion out of it."

More people came to visit: Tony and Martha Parente, Agnes Wardle, even Cardwell. They had all liked Slesik. No Levitch, but a kind, determined man. And brave. Prisoner of the Germans, prisoner of Stalin, prisoner of Brezhnev. He'd paid his dues. But he had died free, protesting, unrepentant.

Nadya Burik puffed on one of Tony's cigarettes, thinking of her dead husband, the murdered poet. *Why do they kill us?* she wondered. *And why is our will to live so strong?* An absurd thought occurred to her. Four hours before he died, Chaim had asked her to help him to the toilet. An arm's length from death, and he had to move his bowels! And did, and acted pleased with himself. How explain it?

We begin in slime and end in slime, the old woman thought. *But why can't the interim, the long years between dirty beginning and befouled ending, be happy, sunny, free of dirt and waste?*

Slesik was buried the following day. A surprisingly large group of mourners appeared. Levitch's imprisonment in Maridov and Slesik's death had not destroyed the movement. In some stubborn brave way, the dissidents drew strength from their losses. Sokolov, refusing leadership of the group—it had no spokesman now—came with a group of black-hatted, bearded men. So did other young people—modern, Russified, unable to utter a word of Hebrew, but determined to pay tribute to Slesik.

Mikhail Zolkin and his wife joined them. So did a handful of his supporters: unemployed writers, discredited scientists, out-of-favor intellectuals.

On a hilltop nearby, Karpov watched, chilled by the spring breeze, gripping his trembling left arm with his right hand.

Nearer to the grave site, Malik, Gorchakov and others from the Jewish Department surveyed the burial service. A feeble old rabbi did the honors for Slesik, who had professed no faith but had sensed—during the last six years of his life— that he was undeniably and forever a Jew. *If they hate us so much, want so badly to destroy us, he once told Levitch, we must be of value. It is in the nature of man to destroy the best in his world.*

"Look who's here," Malik said. He nudged the photographer Gorchakov, and pointed to Karpov. Why should the assistant head of the Second Directorate, currently on sick leave, be going to Jewish funerals? Dort had told him to take a prolonged rest, stay away from work, get his health back.

"Karpov," Gorchakov said. "I thought he was hospitalized."

"He should be. Crazy as a loon. The boss is trying to figure out a polite way to get rid of him. Trouble is, Karpov knows where bodies are buried, who bungled, who told lies, who slept with whom. Once Dort finds a quiet place far away, he'll ship him off."

The two of them—there were six other KGB plainclothesmen surrounding the grave site—stared at Karpov. He seemed thinner, holding one arm as if partially paralyzed.

"What was wrong with him?" Gorchakov asked.

"Brain all messed up. Fits. Then he had some kind of operation. Cut his head open. All he did was sleep and forget things. Dort sent him back to the hospital for repairs. From what I hear, by the time his girl friend Tashenko is through with him, he'll have a brain like a patched-up Studebaker engine. What's he doing here?"

Karpov, if asked, could not have explained his presence. He looked at the mourners and felt a rush of pity. Zolkin's seamed face loomed above the crowd. Karpov closed his left eye. The right eye fixed itself on Zolkin's visage, sent an impulse to his left hemisphere. Karpov smiled, sensed warmth, rightness, a feeling that so long as people like Mikhail Zolkin lived and spoke, the world was not utterly corrupted.

The chanting of Sokolov's colleagues drifted up to him. He turned so that his right ear caught the strange guttural sounds. He found them pleasing.

For another week Irina conditioned Karpov to associate shocks of pleasure with photographs of Levitch, Slesik, Zolkin, flowers, nature, and the good things of life he enjoyed. Every now and then, to tease him, she included a photograph of herself in a bathing suit. She varied the length of stimulation, sometimes only pretending to activate the electrode while showing him Levitch's face, and noting that his reaction, even without the stimulus, was pleasurable.

For an hour or so every day she also subjected him to photographs of Dort, Malik, other members of the KGB, Stalin, Hitler, scenes from the gulag, scenes of torture, death and destruction. These were always associated with the stimulation of the hippocampus of his right hemisphere. After a week he did not need a prolonged shock, or indeed *any* stimulation, to experience terror, a compulsion to run, hide or strike back.

Once, as she stimulated his right hemisphere for a few seconds and projected Colonel Dort in uniform accepting an award from Kosygin, he leaped from his chair and struck at the screen with his left fist.

After she ordered him back to his chair, she found him sitting on his left hand as if to squelch it. The next photograph was of a Torah scroll. She stimulated his left brain. He smiled, breathed deeply, let his errant left hand go free.

"I can't take much more of these unpleasant pictures," he said. His left hand was trembling.

"Even if I withhold stimulation?"

"Even so. Why is that? I don't harbor any fear of Dort. Stalin and Hitler are dead. What's the gulag to me? I'll never have to do forced labor. I won't go to the goldfields of Kolyma and die in the snow. Why should I react to them unless you condition me?"

"But you hate and fear Dort."

"I have contempt for him."

"Is it possible that deep in your left hemisphere there's a small voice that tells you that your way of life is essentially evil? And that you have a right to hate those who taught it to you?"

"Unlikely. I'm a product of history. We do what we must to preserve the system, to preserve the motherland."

"You believe that?"

Karpov nodded. "Of course. Greater good for greater numbers. Jews—at least people like Levitch—represent the lesser numbers. That goes for idiots like Arkangeli, traitors like Zolkin, and the mob of them. In the pay of the West, Zionists, Fascists . . ."

She hit the L button.

Karpov winced. "Don't do that. I'm not ready for it. Yes, we've killed and jailed people. What am I to do? Change things overnight?"

She flashed a scene from a kibbutz in the Galilee on the screen. Children held hands. A teacher stood in the center. In the background, Hebrew letters spelled the name of the community. It was a sun-splashed vibrant scene, full of warmth and life.

"More of their damned Zion."

"Damned Zion?" She knew that the terror he had felt from the previous experience lingered. She hit the stimulator that sparked the electrode in his left hemisphere.

"Full of joy," he said. "A pity I never had children. You and I, Irina, we might have had superior offspring. Show them the sea, a flowering garden. How does one achieve that?"

She turned off the projector, turned on the room light, and lit a cigarette.

"Our main concern is your recovery," she said. "Do you feel stronger? Less drowsy?"

"Considerably."

"Energetic? Able to do a day's work for Dort?"

"I think so. I'd be happier in a decent foreign post. I'm still after London, or Los Angeles. If Dort has it in for me, and I end up in Archangel or Kamchatka, I won't be amused."

She sat opposite him and crossed her legs. "I understand Levitch is having some kind of neurological trouble. His hands are weak. He's in pain all the time. It sounds like carpal tunnel syndrome."

"How do you know these things?"

"The refuseniks get information out. He is also emerging as one of the most popular prisoners at Maridov. Even the *urkas* let him alone. There's a pact among the common criminals to protect him. He teaches mathematics and runs the prison library. And never complains."

"Well." Karpov winked. "I seem to have done our criminals a favor by sending him there. Levitch, a savior among pickpockets and cutthroats. The stories are probably lies. He's got a knack for dramatizing himself. Why tell me this?"

"I'm wondering if you harbor guilt feelings over him."

"Ridiculous. I'm a policeman."

"And a human being. Somewhere in your brain resides a bit of honor and decency and kindness. You must surely have known Levitch was innocent. That he—"

"If we say he's guilty, he's guilty."

"You can't believe that, Andrei Borisovich."

"It makes no difference whether I believe it or not. Levitch got in the way. He upset the natural order of things."

"Natural?"

"Marxism-Leninism has its own imperatives. To a certain extent, Levitch was a useful idiot. He helped us rally a great many of our good Russian people against complainers, whiners and betrayers."

"The way Hitler used his Jews? To unite every anti-Semite in Europe?"

He pressed his right hand against his forehead, as if subduing pain. "No, not the same. But suppose it were? Life is hard. Building a society is no easy matter. The Soviet Union is always threatened, forever under attack. Why do you talk about Hitler to me?"

"We can talk about Stalin. You worked for him. As a young enforcer in the Baltic states, did you not?"

He shut his eyes and grimaced. "I'm having pain again. Sharp, deep. Stop telling me these things. Stop arguing with me. It's as if a switch turns on in my head. Are you sure you aren't using the stimulator?"

She held up her hands. "The current is off. You're having the experience on your own. Think of them, Andrei. Hitler, Stalin, Himmler, Beria—"

"Stop. Stop." His left fist pawed the air.

"There's no one near you. All right, that's enough. Breathe deeply. Lean back in the chair. Listen to me."

"I'm in pain. I want to run . . . to hide. . . ."

The stalking reptile, she thought. *Now stalked by memory.* "Listen to me, Andrei Borisovich."

"I'm not sure I trust you any longer."

"The Americans have gotten excellent results with a procedure called biofeedback. It has helped people conquer headaches, back pain, disorders of the digestive system. It consists of relaxing exercises, deep breathing and mental imagery, all of which induce a euphoric state. The patient is trained on a machine similar to the one we used to indicate the degree of tension in your temporal muscles. Simply stated, the headache victim is taught two methods of controlling his sympathetic nervous system. One is like the one we used— reducing muscle tension. The other consists of raising the temperature in the patient's hands and simultaneously lowering the temperature in the head. Cool head, warm hands, a relaxed feeling, drowsy state, and a resultant reduction of pain."

"But my training has been different."

"Yes, but we will use some of the techniques. Listen carefully."

Karpov put his feet up on the ottoman, leaned back in the soft chair. Astonishing how good it made him feel. He wondered if all the Freudian nonsense, the intimate revelations about oneself, had more to do with the old Viennese's couch than anything else.

"Whenever you feel these periods of anger, fear or tension coming on, or you sense an inability to cope with your life, sit down, breathe deeply for about forty-five seconds, and then tense each part of your body and relax it. Start with your feet—tense, relax. Work your way up to your facial muscles—tense, relax."

"Hardly a difficult procedure."

"Then work on mental images. Let a liquid warmth flow into your limbs, filling them with a gentle sensation. When you feel relief, summon up the images we have been working with. The ones that gave you pleasure. Name them."

Karpov laughed. "Oh, you trickster. I'm to get relief from thinking of Jews?"

"Not only Jews. There were other pictures."

Flowers. Beaches. Sunsets. The creature comforts I enjoy. Champagne, fine food, a window full of Gucci leather, another displaying English fabrics. Is that the idea?"

"They serve a purpose. But they hardly have the impact of the others. Think of Levitch. The Prague Synagogue. The children. All of these that you associate with your left brain."

He laughed again. "I have a better idea. Much simpler. Let me take the stimulator with me. Whenever I feel gloomy, or suicidal, or weak, I'll give myself a jolt of electricity. Why bother with Levitch's stupid face? Or the ghost of old Slesik? Who needs them?"

She shook her head.

"The use of electrical stimulation is only a temporary aid. Yes, it's been used on schizophrenics, violent patients, sex offenders. But its effect is temporary, and in some instances harmful. No person's brain is the same, and the brain changes. Stimulation of your left septal area today may induce pleasurable sensations, a sense of rightness. A month from now, who knows? It may make you morbid, angry and aggressive. That brings me back to the most effective biofeedback training in the United States."

"I do enjoy listening to your lecture. I am deeply fond of you. What can I do to induce you back to my bed, Irina?"

"I want a healthy patient. That's all." But she smiled and patted his hand.

"Those patients who have best succeeded in conquering pain have done so without the use of *any* mechanical apparatus. They are trained on the machines—mechanisms that give off an audio signal, a lowering in tone or a spacing of beeps—to be aware of their success in raising the temperature of their hands or relaxing facial muscles. Well and good. They have the machine to aid them, cue them, inform them when they're relaxing, and thus motivate them to improve. But the patients are not allowed to take the machines home with them. In their daily lives, at work or at home, they can do the exercises—in a matter of ten or fifteen minutes—and suppress a migraine headache or ease back pain, *without any electrical prodding*. In short, their brain alone conquers the ailment. I want you to do the same."

"The electrodes are still in my brain."

"They'll come out as soon as you've mastered the technique. When next you feel anxious, or experience terror or pain, do the exercises I outlined for you—I'll give them to you on a small card—and summon up images. In time you will focus on those mental images that relieve the tension and afford you a high level of pleasure."

"That idiotic Levitch again."

"Possibly." She shook a pencil at him, as if to underscore a point. "There is even a technique being developed in the United States in which biofeedback patients, people suffering severe migraine, can abort pain in six seconds."

"Six—?"

"We don't expect you to do that well. We'll continue with the training sessions another week. I know you're improving. Perhaps you can even return to work."

"Test me. I have the feeling I'm making progress. I'm not sure I like the therapy, but still . . ."

She flashed a photograph of Lavrenti Beria, murderer,

torturer, conniver, one of Stalin's worst thugs. Shot dead in a cellar one night after Stalin's death.

"Christ, not him."

Irina pushed the R button.

"Stop. The pain is killing me. I hate his guts."

Levitch beamed at him.

"Better," Karpov sighed. "Better. I'm not in pain." He drew her close, kissed her hands.

She had not stimulated his left hemisphere.

"So you're ready to work again?" Dort asked. "You look a little healthier, Andrei Borisovich. The lady surgeon must have worked miracles on you. Sure it wasn't all medical business? Maybe some bedroom therapy?"

"Nothing of the kind. Simple exercises to relax tensions. To reduce the aftereffects of surgery." He told him nothing of the implants, the electrical stimulation.

"I like your wig. Will you ever get your own hair back?"

"In time."

Dort's face seemed to harden. Karpov saw him dimly. Fangs protruded from his lips. His eyes turned to bird shot. The agony of the projection room tormented Karpov. Looking at the cruel face, he had a rush of fear, a desire to run or strike out. Sweat dribbled down his armpits. He pressed his right palm against the back of his quivering left hand.

"Anything wrong, Comrade Major?"

"Nothing."

"You're still on leave. So I'm not sure I can assign you to anything. Besides, you look pale. Didn't my office arrange to have special meals sent to you at the Institute?"

"I guess not. It doesn't matter. I don't eat much. Seem to have lost my taste for food and wine."

"A pity. So you want an assignment? Back in harness? A problem there. Zaitsev is doing a good job on refuseniks. He's got Malik toeing the mark. We intend to bring three more Jews to trial within the next month. Sabotage, espionage. The Levitch business caused a stink, but it hasn't hurt us. The United Nations thinks we've done the world a favor jailing him. It's marvelous. Pick on Jews and you get applause from all our cannibal and witch-doctor friends."

Hatred germinated in Karpov. A desire to crack his hand

across Dort's face, make his nose bleed, raise red welts on his cheeks.

"Getting bored? Like some work?" Dort asked.

"I think so, yes. I'm not sure Dr. Tashenko will let me work too hard. If Zaitsev is so efficient handling the Jewish Department, maybe there's another place for me." Karpov had never begged for anything in his life, never pleaded. He felt ashamed of himself.

"Good. There's a student group being formed at Moscow University. All kinds of Fascist shit is being disseminated, mostly support for the Poles. The leader is a kid named Lessin. He's no Yid. A real Russian, I'm sorry to say. Find him, get something on him. Then stick him in Serbsky for the full treatment."

"A schizophrenic type. Unable to act properly in society. Hospitalized for his own good . . ."

"That's the idea. You don't have to describe it to me. Hell, you wrote the book on that kind of treatment." Dort stared at him. "What are you twitching like that for? Your left eye is fluttering. Karpov, don't tell me you're going to throw one of those fits? I thought your girl friend cured you."

His left side tensed and shivered. It took a few seconds for him to control it. He thought of Levitch, the dead Slesik, the Prague ghetto, the Torahs he had once seen there. He breathed deeply, calmed his left arm and his left leg.

"What the hell was that?" asked Dort.

"Drug reaction. I'm fine."

11

ENTRAPPING AND ARRESTING the student Lessin was a minor effort for Karpov. He placed an informer within the ranks of the "Peace and Freedom" movement—she was an attractive musician whose guitar contained a tape recorder—and within five days of Karpov's entrance into the Lessin case, the youth was already on his way to becoming a state-nurtured vegetable.

Discussing the "protocol" of medication and other therapy with the director of the Serbsky Institute, Dr. Mtislav Fett, Karpov felt bored, unchallenged by what he had done. Lessin had been too easy. He was one of Irina's white mice.

"The psychiatric examination is incomplete," Dr. Fett said solemnly. "But already we see indications of instability, paranoia and schizophrenia."

"Astonishing the way these symptoms always surface in agitators and spies, isn't it?"

Dr. Fett nodded. "It's part of the pathological personality. An enemy of the state is by definition paranoid. And often schizophrenic."

Karpov reflected on Lessin. A string bean of a youth. Lank blond hair falling to his shoulders. Ratty sheepskin jacket, worn jeans, shagreen boots. For all his beggar's garb he was a hypnotic speaker. Karpov had watched him stir a crowd in the student cafeteria with an impassioned appeal for nuclear disarmament.

"Treatment?" Karpov asked. He yawned, touched the wig, patted the tiny protrusions of hard plastic covering the electrodes.

"Massive injections of sulfazin. Later, shock therapy. His hostile tendencies must be reduced before any improvement will be noted." Dr. Fett peered over rimless pince-nez at Major Karpov. *Queer duck, this elegant policeman.* There'd been rumors. A brain operation to stop convulsions, another rare procedure to calm him down. The director studied the fine reddish wig, the stitch marks on Karpov's high forehead. Some of the great Tashenko's handiwork?

"A long hospitalization is indicated?" Karpov asked.

"In all probability." Dr. Fett clasped his hands and leaned forward. "Surely the Major knows how these matters work. I mean, not just from his professional duties but on a personal level . . ."

Karpov's left eye fluttered. The left side of his face tightened. *Damn Fett. Nosy bastard, pen-pushing fumbler.* Hinting, without fear or shame, at the matter of Karpov's wife.

"You're talking about Mme. Karpov."

"Of course. I recall the day you brought her to us. A tragedy, a pity."

"How is she?" Again the left eye flickered.

"I'm sorry to say, Comrade Major, she is stabilized, but that's all. She's maintained on drugs. I don't see any hope for her."

Karpov rubbed his left temple, trying to massage away darts of pain. The damnable right brain was at work, reacting to unpleasant news, sordid memories, traces of guilt.

"I'd like to see her."

"I'm not sure that's wise. For you or for her."

"You think so?" Karpov closed his left eye and shuddered.

"I must be frank. You know how these patients deteriorate. In appearance, in behavior . . ."

"Can I look at her through the viewing glass?"

Dr. Fett nodded. "Of course. It would be easier for both of you."

Karpov lit a cigarette. Since undergoing the experiments,

he had resumed smoking. He locked his left hand against his hip. "Tell me, Dr. Fett, are you using the old criteria to determine if a patient is schizophrenic?"

"Old . . . ?"

"Yes, the tests. The ones that were given to my wife some years ago. Testing them for opinions, coordination, motor skills?"

Fett nodded. What the hell was eating him? The great Karpov. The ultimate schemer and trapper. What was he after? Fett pursed his lips. "We look for personality failings. Anti-Soviet statements, sympathy for the enemies of the USSR. Treasonous attitudes. The usual."

"Ah," Karpov said. He exhaled. "Political views." His left eye remained locked.

"One could say that. As the Major knows, at our KGB sanatoria we have discovered a remarkable variant, an isotope, as it were, of schizophrenia. There are no clear definable symptoms as in classical schizophrenia. What the stricken person manifests are political and social views of a negative and destructive nature."

Karpov smiled. *Crazy,* thought Fett. *He's smiling with half his mouth. The right side of his face is smiling; the left is somber.*

"With all due respect to the efficacy of our mental hospitals," Karpov was saying loudly, "isn't schizophrenia a disease with clearly defined characteristics? How can you and your colleagues decide that anti-Soviet opinions alone are signs of schizophrenia?"

Bastard, Fett thought. *He wants it both ways. Sent his wife here to get rid of her, so he could fornicate his way around the world, enjoy affairs, mistresses, the good life. Harpooned her because she didn't care for some aspects of the police state, having her phone tapped, her mail read. And now this same Karpov, with Lessin his latest victim, stewing in a soup of mind killers and sleep inducers, he dares to bait me!*

"Major, Major, why bother? Why fool around with all this psychological babble?" Fett giggled. "When we say a man is schizophrenic and has to be put away for his own good and for the good of society, he's schizophrenic, and that's the end of it. Just as if I say that the chair you're sitting on is schizophrenic, it's schizophrenic."

Karpov got up. "I should like to see Mme. Karpov."

*   *   *

She had aged, yet she had not aged.

Marfa's hair was still golden and lustrous, but it seemed the hair of a very young girl, perhaps a retarded woman. Her broad Slavic face had been arrested in mid-life. The features were bland, unformed. Yet there were hard lines etched in the wide forehead, the firm chin.

She wore a wrinkled gray nightdress and a gray robe. Her feet were in ragged scuffs. An attendant had opened the door and let her enter the room. She moved hesitantly, like an injured animal. Karpov and Dr. Fett sat in easy chairs and viewed her through a one-way glass.

"A terrible tragedy," Fett said. "So young when she was stricken. To lose a mind that way."

An old agony clutched at Karpov's heart. He did not know why he had insisted on seeing Marfa. God alone—and perhaps Irina—could explain it. Wrenching visions flitted through his divided mind. A meadow, a stream, willows. She, with skirts pulled high over smooth round thighs as they waded across. He was in his cadet's uniform—smart gray uniform with red tabs, the shoulder boards of an elite unit. And laughing, chasing her up a hillside, intoxicated by the musty smell of her hips, her female secrets.

Karpov closed his eyes. He savored the old memory briefly, felt it turn into a sour essence of the past.

"She is authentically insane, Doctor?"

"I believe so, Major."

"But how does one distinguish between someone like my wife and a Lessin, a politically unreliable and dangerous type?"

"You know how it works, Major," Fett said slyly. "They're one and the same. A man who preaches disarmament or supports the Polish Fascists must be as insane as a woman who can't think clearly any longer."

Karpov said nothing. He stared at his wife in the room below. She was resting against a blank wall, pressing her hands against her cheeks.

What in Christ's name was he doing? Dr. Fett wondered. Karpov was clenching and unclenching his left fist, twisting in the chair. Fett, ill at ease, ordered tea on the intercom. Maybe something to drink would calm him.

"Is she under medication?" asked Karpov.

"Yes. The full dosage of sulfazin."

"That aimless behavior we are seeing," Karpov said. His voice shook. "Is it a result of the drugs? Or of her illness?"

"Both."

Shapeless and ungainly under the layers of gray cloth, Marfa wandered around the room. She touched the walls, ran her fingers over cracks, windowsills. She sat heavily on the cot, felt the mattress, ran her hands around the edges of the gray blanket. Then she rose, leaned against a wall again, took a dozen slow steps to the center of the room and stopped, as if lost. Again she returned to the cot, sat, rose, walked the perimeter of the room liked a caged jungle cat.

"This trancelike behavior," Karpov said. "Is it typical?"

"I'm afraid so. And the unsteady gait. Body movements can be painful. She was overdosed last week and is still recovering. Sulfazin can shoot body temperatures up to a hundred and four degrees. She's normal now, but the use of muscles and joints remains painful. The wandering is an attempt to find a comfortable place to light. Rather like laboratory rats."

"And of course it affects the mind."

"We aren't sure how. Such patients come to us already damaged. Oh, we do autopsies from time to time . . . ."

"What do you find?"

"Additional brain damage. From the biological condition but also from the drugs."

Karpov shut his right eye. The seeing left eye sent a message to his right hemisphere. He saw the torture of his wife, of Lessin, in all its horror. The evil imprinted itself in his right brain, which absorbed it and feared it. The right brain knew. It understood evil, wickedness, pain.

"Your tea will get cold, Comrade Major."

Karpov picked up the teacup with his left hand and hurled it at Dr. Fett's face.

Back in the Institute, Karpov reported the incident to Irina. It had caused a storm at Dzerzhinsky. Reports to Dort, to the chairman. Karpov was clearly crazy, perhaps in need of the same kind of treatment they gave to agitators like the student Lessin.

Irina asked him to explain his actions. He had difficulty articulating what had happened. A compulsion to hurt Dr. Fett, yes. A profound, almost personal, understanding of his wife's misery, of Lessin's fate. And something forcing him to act, to take sides.

"When I viewed her with both eyes," Karpov said hoarsely, "I saw nothing bad about her situation. A woman in hospital garb, wandering around a room."

"And with your left eye alone?"

"It was evil. The people punishing her were monsters. I had to act."

She gave him a sleeping pill. As he began to doze, two men from Dort's office appeared in the hallway and stopped her.

"We're to stand guard outside Karpov's room," one told her. They flashed badges. "Colonel Dort wants him watched for the next forty-eight hours."

"There's nothing seriously wrong with him," Irina said. "I guarantee that he'll be tranquilized for a long time."

They shook their heads. Irina argued with them. She knew about Karpov's mad attack on Dr. Fett. A faceful of tea? A broken china cup? On a colleague of Dr. Tashenko's?

She left them as they settled into chairs, one inside Karpov's room, one in the hallway.

Her phone rang at two in the morning. Lev Tashenko answered it. His voice quavered. He would never get used to middle-of-the-night calls. That was how they'd arrested him four years ago. No warning, no finesse. A call, then escorted to Lubianka for twelve hours of questioning. No lawyer, no family, no friends. They isolate you, wear you down, inject fear into you like serum. He'd heard of the Lessin case. Miserable, misguided wretch. What were the Poles to him and his ragbag collection of students?

"For you, Irina."

She took the phone, listened, nodded, hung up.

"Karpov," she said. "He's attacked his guards."

She found Karpov straitjacketed. He was awake, his eyes staring coldly at the ceiling. His speech was unaffected. "Get me out of this," he said. "This is lunacy."

The KGB man who had been inside the room had a white patch on his forehead. One eye had turned into a purple lump. He explained angrily to Dr. Tashenko: Comrade Major had awakened, picked up a bronze lamp and come at him, howling. He had struck the guard—his name was Belayev—with the lamp, kicked him, then suddenly stopped. Belayev and his partner had no difficulty subduing the patient.

"Do you recall which hand he used?" Irina asked.

Belayev patted his bruised temple. "Left. He hit me with his left hand, used that heavy lamp. Kicked me with his left foot in the guts. As soon as I was down, he stopped and he pulled back. As if he was ashamed of what he'd done. Or scared."

"Can you recall the position of his body? What exactly he did?"

Belayev frowned. "Hell, I was half out. But he was crouching in the corner, sort of showing us the right side of his body, hiding his left arm."

She prevailed upon Dort to call off his guards. He refused. They were to stay on. Karpov was not getting better; he was getting worse. One more such outburst and he'd be sent to the Serbsky Institute. They would pump him full of sulfazin and turn him into the same variety of vegetable Lessin had become. He could join his crazy wife, Dort taunted.

Toward morning, over tea, Irina asked Karpov to recall the attack on Sergeant Belayev.

"I woke up. Saw him sitting there. Recognized him. One of Dort's favorites. Can't explain it. I wanted to brain him. But as soon as he was down, I stopped."

"Your right hand grabbed your left hand, didn't it? Forced the lamp out of it?"

"How did you know?"

"The hemispheres were fighting each other. The right hand, directed by the left hemisphere, ordered the right brain to stop its murderous signals."

"I have no recollection of that. But it must have happened. I was conscious all the time. Part of me wanting to kill Belayev. Just as part of me wanted to throw something at Fett. Something else . . . someone else . . . in me . . . wanted to stop me. How can that be?"

"There's a struggle going on." She stared at him. "What can I do to make you feel better? More at ease?"

He smiled. "The slides? The stimulation? Can't we have another training session?"

*   *   *

Later she persuaded the guards to leave them alone in the projection room. Again, she flashed Levitch, Slesik, the synagogue, scenes of Israel, kibbutz children, the tablets of the law, mingling these with more neutral photographs. With each picture, she activated the electrode in his left septal region. He breathed deeply, thanked her. He smiled, laughed. Once he suggested they have sex.

"You'll have to settle for Levitch's face," she said. "And ten more seconds of stimulation."

He stretched, rubbed his temples. Soon she stopped the stimulation, but kept projecting photos. She watched him fall into a blissful semi-trance simply by staring at the photographs. He said he felt marvelous, fulfilled.

Like the TNT-sensitive rats, she thought. They did not need the electric prod to feel pleasure, a satisfaction deeper than the sexual urge, the need for food, water, the presence of their young. A sniff of explosive and they reacted joyfully.

" 'My hands and arms are stiff, full of pain all the time,' " Parente read.

Levitch's neat handwriting, the cursive script of a mathematician, stared at him from the flimsy blue paper. The letter had come to Mikhail Semonski. It had not been censored. Apparently the prison administration did not care whether he informed the world about his ailments or not.

Parente sat in a dingy cafeteria near the Leningradsky Railway Station with Mikhail and Olga. They had given up on getting visas. Tarred by their association with Levitch, they were now listed as agitators, potential criminals.

Parente read on. Levitch was pleading for help, asking that everything humanly possible be done to get him released. It was not like him. Uncomplaining, stoic, making jokes about his condition. His tone had changed. He'd developed—so the prison doctor said—a condition called carpal tunnel syndrome, affecting the wrists and hands. It was extremely painful, limiting his actions, a constant source of suffering. He couldn't handle sewing, so they'd moved him to the kitchen. He worked in clouds of steam, amid dampness, garbage, fetid water, rat droppings.

" 'Whatever I write now,' " Parente read, " 'must not reach Sarah's ears. Do not publicize this letter. I write to her and I tell her all is well. I tell her that I get books, writing paper, work in the library, and am in good health. The truth is I have a growing feeling of paralysis, some kind of neurological malaise that is overtaking me. A fatigue I can't describe. Headaches. And these damnable pains in my arms, wrists and hands. They keep telling me I'm getting special medical care. Would you believe I have trouble handling the pencil right now? That it keeps falling from my fingers?'"

Parente folded the letter and gave it to Semonski.

"So?" the music teacher asked. "What now?"

"I don't know. The President of the United States couldn't get him sprung. Not even a trade-off for a Russky spy. Protest meetings, petitions, appeals. Even the Pope is getting in on the act. But the way I read it, he's in for a long time. Still, you never know. Someday the KGB chairman may wake up feeling terrific and let Levitch out."

"And perhaps send Olga and me to jail?"

"One never knows in this madhouse. Let me see the letter again. What does he mean by special medical care?"

Semonski shrugged. "They may be drugging him. You know what our jailers do to recalcitrants. Tony, for all of Abram's bravado, he's a soft man. They may kill him."

"Dear lady, dear Comrade Surgeon, you're a famous medical person, and what am I?" Dr. Belus whined. "Not much more than an orderly now. Yes, I'm on the staff of the Charta Sanatorium of Sochi, our famed mineral spa. But what does it mean? Prescribing hydrosulphide waters, mineral beverages rich in bromium, sodium and potassium. I even have a different name. I'm Dr. Bogasch from Magnitogorsk. Why do you seek me out? I can't help you."

"I'm not sure."

Irina looked out at a vista of the Black Sea, the swarming hot beaches with their multicolored umbrellas, the bordering cypresses, oleanders and mimosas. It reminded her of Rapallo, where some years ago she had attended an international conference at the behest of the University of Genoa. It was an altogether pleasing place, Sochi, even with the crush of vacationers, people taking the cure. The KGB must have been satisfied with Ivan Belus's services. The informer could just as easily have been shipped to some icy outpost.

"I'm sorry about Levitch . . . ." Ivan Belus paused, ran his freckled hand through his curling hair. "I . . . can't say more. I don't know who you're working for or what you want."

"I want to get Abram Levitch out of prison and out of the country."

"And you come to me? The man who helped convict him?"

"I was thinking, perhaps, if you and I issued a statement. Said it was a misunderstanding, a series of foolish errors. That you had no idea what was in the papers I gave you—"

"My testimony was that I stole them."

"All right. I'd say that they were of no importance. That Levitch had no idea what he was giving Hanson."

Belus was smiling, moving his head from side to side. "My dear Dr. Tashenko, how innocent you are. They own us. They control us. They would have both of us in prison in a matter of days. I should not even be discussing this with you."

"You were an informer. You betrayed your friends."

"Please, please. I'm a Soviet citizen. I have to survive. What are Levitch's friends kicking about? You can manage in this country if you walk a straight path. Why do *you* have to get involved in this Levitch mess? I know it's an international issue, but why do you have to get in trouble? You're famous. You have a superb reputation, a career. And me, I'm content. Besides, Levitch was guilty."

On the beach below, children shouted and cried. A mother dragged a howling little boy out of the water. Two teenagers kicked a soft ball. Hugely fat women paraded their bloated bellies. Muscular men admired them, flexed browned muscles.

"It was Karpov who arranged the whole affair, wasn't it?" she asked.

"Why must you know?"

"He's my patient now."

"Really? Who would think the major would ever need medical help? The most frightening man I ever knew. I suppose it's no secret. But I can't discuss it with you. I have no apologies for what I did. Levitch and his crowd made it worse for the rest of us. Medieval nonsense. That atavistic return to Judaism! All that sentimental trash about Zion. I wanted no part of it."

She studied his face. A bit furtive, too ready to please, to accommodate. Good-natured, talkative, but essentially corrupt.

"Suppose you and I—anonymously—with a guarantee that

our names could not be disclosed, revealed the true nature of
the Levitch case to a journalist."

"You must be joking."

"I'm not. We don't put it in writing, but we vouch for the
truth of what we say. That Karpov and others—we need not
name them—ordered us to transmit papers to Levitch, and
requested he pass them on to Floyd Hanson. Would you
agree to that?"

Dr. Belus sipped lemonade. He looked out at the gentle
surf of the Black Sea. Sailboats scudded in the distance. A
loudspeaker announced a ballet performance that evening at
the Summer Theater.

"Why this interest in Levitch?" he asked. "Why all this
fuss over him?"

"He's innocent. We helped destroy him."

"I don't accept that. He was guilty of many things. He got
mixed up in matters that didn't concern him. Listen, esteemed doctor, what makes you think we wouldn't be severely punished if we let that information out to Anthony
Parente? You might get away with it. Me, I'd be joining
Levitch in prison. No, thank you. I'll keep my job here as a
medical assistant. In fact, I intend to get married soon. All I
need is to be arrested and jailed."

"I promise you secrecy."

"No, no, *no*. They're probably watching us right now. One
thing you should understand, especially after what they did
to your husband: We can't beat them. They give us just
enough to keep us in line. Levitch wanted too much. I'm not
even sure I'm sorry for him anymore."

On her return to Moscow, Irina found two new guards
outside Karpov's room. She telephoned Colonel Dort to protest.
Dort's secretary would not let her speak to him.

One of the men explained that since the nocturnal attack
on Sergeant Belayev, Karpov could not be trusted. She argued with them, got them to agree that whenever Karpov
was undergoing therapy they would leave the room.

"If he is to be cured," she said firmly, "you can't be
around. I'll take personal responsibility for him."

They took up positions in the hallway. Crude louts, low-
level watchdogs, they flirted with the nurses, read the sports
news, took turns sleeping.

In the room, Irina subjected Karpov to more intense stimulation. He awaited the sessions eagerly. Like a child in a dentist's chair who senses vast relief when the drill is set aside, Karpov smiled when she announced that she was halting right-brain stimulations, that he would receive no more unpleasant sensations, no more exposures to his superiors, to faces and scenes that, in association with the right hippocampal electrode, induced sensations of terror and pain.

She concentrated on left-hemisphere stimulations. He viewed pictures of fields, flowers, wine, fine clothing—and always, more than any other scene, more than any other face—Abram Levitch.

Toward the end of the day she turned off the power in the transmitter, flashed Levitch's face, and watched Karpov smile, lean back and ask to hold her hand.

Later he insisted on helping with patients in need of inhalation therapy. He volunteered to wheel amputees and aged patients through the corridors, distributed mail and flowers to other patients, smiled a great deal, joked with his guard.

It was a common phenomenon, she knew. A desire to please, to follow the benevolent impulses of the left brain.

The guards followed him from room to room, puzzled by the curious way in which the fearsome Karpov had become a beaming volunteer, a fellow who went around adjusting pillows and blankets, comforting the aged and infirm. It was almost comic, a farce.

"Crazy as a cross-eyed donkey," one of them said. "What do we tell Dort?"

"The truth. The major is nuts. He thinks he's an orderly, a floor nurse."

But at night Karpov tossed, howled, kicked off his sheets. Once he rose from the bed, looking for the transmitter. He tugged at locked drawers, threw open closets, searched in corners and under the bed.

The guards attempted to comfort him, finally had to beat him into submission. Insensible to their blows, he bit and kicked at them. Left foot, left hand, half his body battled them, resisted violently. Curses burst from his throat, the words garbled and thickened by the temporary failure of the left brain.

Drugged with a massive dose of sedative administered by Dr. Skiba, Karpov dropped into a vivid, terrifying nightmare.

He was strapped to a chair. Malik was shaving his head. Dort was looking on, grinning, commenting cruelly on the scars and patches on Karpov's pate. *She did a great job on you, Comrade Major,* Dort was mocking, *carved your head up like it was a roast pig.*

He tried to respond to Dort but his tongue was locked. The words became clots in his throat, choked him. In prison garb, he was being dragged down a dark corridor by guards, Malik and Dort following him, laughing, joking about his shuffling gait, his bent body.

He awakened bathed in sweat, craving the rest-giving, comforting sensations that only the electrode in his left brain could supply.

"Irina," he called. "Irina."

But he saw only Skiba's flattened yellow features, the cold faces of his guards.

Once more he snarled, started to rise from the bed, swung at them with his left arm. Subdued, he struggled and fainted.

Skiba noted that he slept with his right hand gripping his left wrist.

The following afternoon Irina ran a series of neurological tests on Karpov. Apart from a slight acceleration of his heartbeat, he appeared to be in good health. His reflexes were sharp, his responses good.

As she listened to his heartbeat and examined his extremities, she noticed that he was touching her with more than casual warmth. At length, while she was examining his eyes, he embraced her hips and drew her close.

"Andrei, stop."

"I love you."

"Patient and physician, that's all. I told you so."

"I must have you again. Don't deny you experienced great pleasure during our affair. I don't care how you interpret it now. You liked our evenings together. You craved them. I feel strong now. Full of affection. Lock the door. Consider this part of my training."

She tried to disengage his arms, but he was strong. Now he was on his knees, kissing her thighs, her abdomen, gripping her buttocks with hard strong hands, muttering about his love.

It was impossible for her to lie to herself. Hating him, she had found him to be an exciting lover. But her goal had never been a replay of their abandoned nights, the passionate afternoons in hotels in London, Stockholm and Paris.

"I must have you," Karpov said hoarsely. She could feel his lips through her dress and underclothing. Probing, seeking, determined.

"Andrei, this will delay your recovery. It will be an impediment."

"No, no. I know what you're after. I'm no fool. You have some notion you can condition me. Deflect me from my policeman's duty and embark me on a lunatic scheme to save Levitch. Appeal to someone, work on Dort, try to reverse the sentence. That's impossible. You must understand that. No matter how intense my feelings may become about Levitch, I could never change the course of events. He's guilty, he's gone, he must pay the price—if you will, fulfill the role he chose. I'm sorry, Irina, but that's the way of the world. What I seek is my own sanity. If the little game you've concocted involves Levitch, I don't care. It won't succeed. But if you truly seek my recovery, why not give me what I want, what I need? You. Your body. Your spirit."

"If I don't?"

"I'll leave. You can't force me to continue with these electrical wires in my skull. I'll order them removed, check out, go back to Dort and see what he has in store for me."

She sat on the edge of his bed. "You'll hurt yourself. Besides, Dort thinks you're totally unreliable. He'll discharge you or send you to the East. Your professional life will end."

"I'm not so sure. I have resources." Karpov came toward her. He was tall and strong, a handsome, cold man. Yet did she see in his eyes a glimmer, a spark of something that transcended his life as agent, spy, informer, the distillation of the merciless state? She had sensed it now and then: a suggestion of a human heart, a faint capacity for compassion, no matter how minute or how buried.

"You're serious? You'll quit halfway through your cure?"

"I'm not sure if it's a cure or a curse. But you know me well enough, Irina. If I make my mind up, I'll leave today, put an end to these shocks, these manipulations of my mind. I beg of you."

She thought of Levitch. Alone, ill. Perhaps never to see his wife or friends again.

"Very well," she said. "Lock the door."

Irina began to remove her dress.

Two days later he seemed remarkably calm, in total control of himself. Irina came to the room, brisk and formal, in her starched white coat, clipboard in hand. She had shared the hospital bed with him twice, was forced to admit that on the lowest of levels, the basic animal gratification—release of tension, discharge of fluids, spasms and contractions—she had experienced profound pleasure.

Now she would put the experience to use. Karpov, convinced he had mastered her, had no idea of the surprise she had in store for him.

"My love," he said. "Come to me."

"Not yet. Remember. What we did together was in the nature of a reward. Like my laboratory rats, who are fed when they perform well. We call it reinforcing."

"Is that all it was?"

She lied. "Yes. I'm a scientist, Andrei. My body was temporarily enlisted in the experiment. Your reward for good behavior, for learning quickly. Close your eyes."

She went to the transmitters. For a few minutes she had him breathe deeply, recline in the easy chair, summon up mental images of fields and flowers, magnums of champagne, bolts of fine silk and wool, the window at Fauchon, full of unearthly delicacies, foods whose combined price would equal the budget of several West African republics. He smiled, kept his eyes shut.

Then she began to stimulate his left brain—long jolts of electricity, reaching deep into the septal area, plunging him into Elysian fields, honey-sweet sensations, freeing him from pain, anxiety, guilt.

"Very good, very good," Karpov gasped. "Oh, my love, it's better than anything, the best thing in the world."

She thought of the eager rats who would rather spark the electrode in their brains than eat, drink, or copulate. The time had come to present Karpov with the ultimate decision.

Once more she hit the transmitter, evoking a dry laugh and a series of breathy gasps from him. She came close to him and took his hand.

"Andrei?"

"Yes, beloved."

"Shall we make love?"

"Now?"

"Of course." Once more she stimulated the left brain.

"Ah . . . ah . . . perhaps. I don't know." He opened his eyes. Bliss coated them like an oily film. "Not yet, my love. Not yet. I'm quite satisfied to rest here, to know you're with me, to experience these wonderful sensations. May I feel the pleasure again? Once more?"

You are ready, she thought. *Like the white rat.*

No sooner had Karpov sat down in Dort's office, face-to-face with his superior, than the terror began.

Five weeks had passed. Irina had pronounced him cured, or as cured as he could be. He no longer showed signs of violence. He was far more energetic than he had been after the split-brain operation. He did not convulse, fall asleep without warning, find himself adrift mentally.

But the terror surfaced from time to time.

Karpov had improved in appearance. His hair had grown back, covering the deep cut of the commissurotomy and the burr holes. Tanned, his eyes alert and knowing, he had put on muscular pounds, worked out at the KGB gymnasium.

But something deep in his consciousness, some recollection of the dread he had experienced when his isolated right brain was stimulated, lingered. It frightened him.

Once more he saw Dort's animal teeth, the porcine head, and he felt his bowels shiver, his heart pump faster. The old fears froze his hands and feet. He tried the six-second relaxation response Irina had taught him—deep breathing, an amused inward look at oneself, eyes slowly shutting and opening. It did not help. Dort horrified him. In his mind's eye he saw not only the colonel but Stalin, Beria, Yagoda, Yezhov, all the killers and torturers. He saw the wired fence of the gulag, the dogs, the guards, the ragged prisoners. And the memory of the jolt in his right brain was revived.

"We thought he was faking at first." Dort's voice roused Karpov, heightened the terror, jerked him to full awareness of the doughy face.

"Who?"

"Your friend Levitch. Sick call every day, whining, claiming he's in pain. He's got a neurological disorder of the limbs. Numbness and pain in his hands and feet." He glanced at the medical report. " 'Entrapment neuropathy. Neuromuscular disorders.' The doctors confirmed it. He's in pain all the time, has trouble using his hands, can't walk far. He may need surgery to correct the conditions. Christ, what a weakling, a fairy."

"I gather he won't last his sentence. Is there any chance of an early release?"

"No chance. He shit in his own kitchen. Someone tried to bring him up at the United Nations last week, some Swede or Dane, and he got laughed out of the General Assembly. Our cannibal friends made short work of it. Levitch may end up in a prison hospital for the rest of his life."

Karpov looked blank. "My understanding was that he was a model prisoner."

"A coward. Like all of them."

"That wasn't my reading of him. It took courage to say what he did in court."

Dort turned sideways. "Courage? The Jew had an audience. He lacks real courage. The murderers and robbers at Maridov know what courage is. They'll take pain, starvation, beatings, and come back for more. That kike puts in three months stitching mail sacks, and he's bedridden. Anyway, he may still be of use to us."

"How?"

"Zolkin."

Karpov had a desire to hide, to shield himself. It was as if Zolkin had crept into his consciousness. Karpov was no longer the stalking reptile Irina had described, the primitive hunter. *He was the prey.* The screen impinged on his mind: Levitch's smiling face, Zolkin's, now his own. Each time Dort spoke, something fluttered inside his chest.

"We're going to shut Zolkin up once and for all. Make him sweat. Like most of those traitors, he's sick in the body and the head. Ever think of that, Karpov? They're physically ill, most of them. Like that tramp Slesik who just croaked. Now Levitch with his nerve problems. Zolkin's got a bone disease. That's what makes him nuts."

He wanted to say: *But maybe it's the other way around, Comrade Colonel. Maybe the torments we inflict on them, the horrors we commit in the name of the motherland, make them ill in their minds, and that in turn produces physical disease . . . . Maybe we are the true spreaders of sickness, the infectors, the carriers. And maybe,* Karpov thought, *we are the ones who are deeply diseased, worm-eaten, corrupted, rotting. . . .*

"You look queasy, Andrei Borisovich. Are you sure you're well enough to be out of the hospital?"

"Yes, yes." He sucked his breath in. "What about Zolkin?"

"We're putting the screws to him. One more yap from him about prisoners of conscience, and he'll be arrested. Enough of this special treatment. He's no different from any of those loonies."

"But you said Levitch—"

"Levitch is going to implicate him. Evidence. Testimony."

"How?" The cold spread from his groin downward to his knees, upward into his chest, like a jagged chunk of ice.

"Levitch is going into solitary."

"And then?"

"We'll get him to talk about Zolkin. New documents will turn up. Taped phone calls. Levitch will no longer be a hero—he'll be an informer. He'll be the next Ivan Belus, giving us the goods on his great benefactor Zolkin."

"Don't be so sure Levitch will become another Belus."

Dort got up, hefted his sagging gut, paced the room. "Andrei Borisovich, you've gone soft. I could overlook that business of jumping your escort at the hospital. You've had all kinds of things happening in your brain. But at least I thought you'd still have your heart in your work."

Karpov had a vision: his left hand gripping Dort's throat. Left knee nailing the fat man to the floor. Choking him with one hand.

"Zaitsev has been doing one hell of a job in your absence. I told him to take your files. All your material on Zolkin's crowd. We're going to do a job on him, with Levitch's help, that'll send him away for a long time."

"Does the Politburo dare? A man like Zolkin?"

"Dare? They ordered it."

"Zolkin's not an obscure Jew. He's one of the great scientists of our time. He's—"

"A miserable troublemaker. A spy. A Fascist deep in his heart. We'll work on Levitch. Freeze him, put him on a cockroach-soup diet, take his shoes away. By the time we've handled him, it won't be his wrists and his knees that bother

him. He'll be begging to be shot. If he thinks he'll ever see
that wife of his again, he's mistaken."

Karpov remembered the photograph. The smiling, pretty
woman standing in the sunlight. A cinder-block house, palm
trees, chíldren.

"Why not offer him his wife as a reward? Tell him if he
talks about Zolkin, he can go free."

"We tried it already. He said that as much as he loved his
wife, he would not betray his friend. So, we'll have to let
Zaitsev handle him. All that international publicity has gone
to Levitch's head. He thinks he's a hero."

Schemes, plans, avenues of escape formed circuits in
Karpov's mind. He sensed that only half of his brain was at
work. Or was it autosuggestion, the concepts that Irina had
fed him? He thought of exits and entrances, modes of escape,
excuses, alibis, complex plans, arrangements. . . .

"I should like to be present when Zaitsev does his prelimi-
nary interrogation. I put Levitch away. I smashed the
movement."

"Smashed? The bastards breed like pissants. They're back
in force, handing out their goddam yellow sheets, defaming
the USSR. Major, there are times when we must concede
that Hitler was right. Christ knows I'm no fan of Ukrainian
nationalists, but maybe they had the right idea when they
volunteered to shoot Yids. Or our Byelorussian friends who
worked the same game, shooting Jews to save their skins.
Lithuanians, Latvians. Assholes, to be certain. But they must
have known what it was all about when they joined the SS
and shot kikes."

"It sounds as if there are moments when you envy Hitler."

"Oh, he was a murderous crank. But he called the turn on
Jews. Well, that's all past. We've got our present problems to
deal with. I'm glad you're feeling better."

"You haven't answered my request."

"Request?"

"To interrogate Levitch."

Dort ran his hand up the back of his neck, over the shiny
pate. He squinted, took off his rimless spectacles and cleaned
them with his tie.

"Sorry, Karpov. That's out. You're unreliable. A pity. One
of our best men, once. But the big shots aren't buying it.
You're off the Levitch case and the Zolkin case also."

"Then what's my future? A uniformed job in Archangel? Colonel Dort, I must protest this—"

Dort halted him with a raised hand. "You might as well know, Andrei Borisovich. You're finished. You're being given early retirement. There was some thought about sending you to Mexico again, in view of the marvelous work you did training students in Guadalajara. I even suggested it. I recalled how you made me look silly when I wanted to spread Marxism among workers. Dumb Indian shit-heads didn't know what I was talking about. But you showed our superiors the right way. Students! Middle-class adolescents! That's where the revolution will come from, you said. You taught me a lesson, Karpov. Well, I tried to save your skin, but it's a lost cause."

From the bitterness with which Dort recalled the Mexican campaign, Karpov knew it still rankled with him. Oh yes, he'd tried to save Karpov's job. The truth was—and Karpov could smell a lie the way Irina's rats sniffed TNT—Dort had ticketed him for firing. The nocturnal assault on Belayev was the last straw. But how could Karpov explain that his right brain alone had acted, that only half of him had wanted to kill the guard?

"I'm grateful, Colonel. What now?"

"You might as well clear out."

"Out?"

"That's what I said. We've emptied your files. Zaitsev has all your documents locked up. The works. Going back to your first assignment in the Baltic states. I must say you've been an ornament to the service. That job you did on De Gaulle's people is an object lesson for field operatives. I've always admired the way you sneaked a half-dozen people into the Quai d'Orsay—agents who rewrote speeches, made policy, fed the Big Asparagus exactly what we wanted. Don't think Reshev and the others aren't appreciative. But times change. And let's be honest, Karpov. You're a sick man. Dr. Tashenko isn't that hopeful."

"I feel fine." His voice was distant.

"Maybe you do. But who knows what's brewing inside your skull? You've got needles in there, something to stabilize your personality. Sure, your fits stopped. You look alert, ready for action. But it's no deal, Karpov."

"My retirement is effective immediately?"

"Actually as of two days ago. We left your personal effects in your office. Some of that French cologne, a case of champagne, English shirts. I must say, the Second Director-ate will never have so elegant a subchief. So long, Karpov."

They shook hands. Insanely, Karpov felt warmth and friend-liness in the grasp of right hands. His right eye crinkled in a minuscule smile.

As they embraced, Karpov's left hand became a claw. He started to dig hard fingers into the space between Dort's shoulder blades, caught himself, stopped. He had tensed his left knee and was about to jerk it upward into Dort's gut when the phone rang.

"Cleaned me out," Karpov said. "Everything."

Irina looked at the wreckage of his apartment. The West German stereo had been torn apart. So had the Japanese shortwave radio, the English record player, the American clock radio. All his tapes and discs had been stolen. Every document and all his personal correspondence were missing.

"Worse at my office," he said. "Every file I had. But they didn't find this."

He placed a 9 mm pistol on the Florentine mosaic coffee table. There were three extra magazines for the weapon.

"Surely you were searched," she said.

"The concierge is an old friend. I hid it with her. She stored it in the toilet tank of her basement flat. It never occurred to Dort's hounds that I'd be friendly with an old babushka with half her teeth missing."

"Now what?" She felt dimly sorry for him. Lev had pleaded with her not to see him when he had called. Was the invita-tion an intricate scheme to trap her? She did not think so. What had she done, except cure him of convulsions and his half-alive state? Unafraid, she agreed to come to Karpov's flat. Then, almost as if arming herself, she had gone to her office and picked up the transmitters, carrying them in a small leather case.

Karpov dumped the contents of a tan envelope on the table. "I salvaged these. Hid them with the fellow who runs the stationery store around the corner. An old Jew, scared out of his wits. I always had the feeling I might need them."

She looked at his cache, realized at once it represented a

safety net, items that might rescue him, give him leverage, protection.

Sorting the items, he identified them. "Official KGB stationery. Dort's letterhead. Transportation orders. Assignment sheet. Blank ID cards. Blank KGB passbooks. Seals, stamps, a paper embosser with top-priority seals. Necessary inks and envelopes."

"And what do you intend to do with them?" she asked.

"I'm not sure."

She studied his face. She was amazed. One could see the division. Someone who knew him well would understand at once. His left eye squinted; the left side of his forehead was scored with creases. The right eye was open and calm, the right side of his mouth relaxed.

She stared at him: *two Karpovs.*

"I spoke to the journalist Parente before I came here," Irina said. "It's true that Levitch is ill. He isn't faking. He's bedridden a good deal of the time. His mind is wandering."

Karpov shut his eyes, stretched his legs. He told her of Dort's plans. Punishment for Levitch. Solitary confinement, until he cooperated in the scheme to smear Zolkin, became another Belus, helped concoct a poisoned case against the dissident leader.

"He won't go along," Irina said. "He'll die first."

"We—they—have means of keeping him alive. He may wish he were dead, but in the long run he'll give in."

Dread enveloped him, a cold fog. "I'm chilly. You must sleep with me, comfort me."

"No. That's past. But maybe I can help you." She removed the twin transmitters from the carrying case.

Irina had gotten from Parente an American magazine cover with Levitch's face on it—the innocent, rather childish expression. So full of trust, so lacking in guile. A man who would hurt no one, harbored no mean thoughts, wanted nothing more than to be with his wife.

The right side of Karpov's face smiled. "Sometimes I don't believe it. I look at him and I feel warmth, a hopefulness, an optimism. Odd that a weakling like Levitch should do that to me."

Suddenly he scowled and bent forward. His left eye was an angry slit. He reached for the magazine with his left hand.

"I'll finish the bastard off, once and for all. Let them kill him. Let him rot forever—"

As he wrenched the words from his mouth, she pressed the button on the L transmitter. His right hemisphere was excluded; the electrode sang its song of wonder and goodness in the left brain.

Karpov pulled his left hand away. "Christ, you did it to me again. That's better. I'm feeling it now. Let me see the picture of him. And Slesik. Where is he? And the old ones, the men praying . . ."

She halted the stimulation.

"I can do it to myself," Karpov said, pleased as a child. "Like your biofeedback. Lowering the tension in a facial muscle. Raising the temperature of my right hand. Control over my own nervous system. I can see our friend, the traitor, the troublemaker. He's smiling at me, the fool. And I am smiling back. Damn you, Irina."

"Andrei Borisovich," she said softly. "We are going to free Abram Levitch."

There were a dozen beds in the prison hospital. They were always filled, although the authorities did not like to keep prisoners under medical care too long. It spoiled them; it encouraged goldbricking.

Levitch sat on the edge of his bed, trying to restore sensation and motility to his hands and fingers. They were either in pain or numb, and he could grip nothing, not a newspaper, not a pencil.

The camp physician was a woman, a Dr. Anisenko. She was squat, walleyed, with a face broader than it was high, wheat-colored hair braided and tied in a topknot.

"You're to be discharged," she said curtly. "You have no fever. Your tests are negative."

"I can't use my hands. Joints ache. My knees are like water."

There were two *urkas*, leaders of the criminal clique, lounging on the adjacent bed. They were playing cards. They often joked about their schemes for fooling the camp administration, how they faked symptoms. "Swallow soap, Levitch," one of them had advised. "Run the thermometer under the hot water." The other would giggle, scratch his belly, marvel at Levitch's dumb honesty. "Your problem, Levitch, is you're really sick. You look like hell." But in the presence of the doctor they were silent, secretive. Levitch admired them, had tried to talk to them about Israel, his wife, his friendship with Zolkin. Subterranean creatures, they had no interest in anything beyond crime, deceit, the tricks of survival.

"I was diagnosed as having an entrapment neuropathy," Levitch told the doctor. "The pain is unbearable. The drugs didn't help."

She shook her head. "A minor muscular condition. The median nerve in your arms is being compressed by the volar carpal ligament. But there are no objective neurologic signs, and the nerve conduction tests I performed were negative. Are you sure you aren't faking?"

Levitch picked up a glass. His fingers had trouble holding it. He watched it slide from his tormented hand to the coarse blanket. "What can be done to help me?" he asked.

"We will give you corticosteroid injections in the wrists and splint your wrists at night. But you aren't a hospital case. Get dressed."

Levitch rose, started to take off his hospital pajamas. He winced, shook his head. "I can't move. My arms and shoulders hurt. It's gotten worse."

"Nonsense. You're exaggerating. Go on, dress yourself."

He was ashamed of his pain, his exhaustion. Martyrdom was not for him. Craving warmth, comfort, affection, he decided he could not long keep his sanity. At least they did not want to kill him or put him in solitary.

"What's my prognosis, Doctor?"

"You're not ill. Minor neurological complaints. If it gets worse, we can operate."

His fingers clutched at his prison shirt. The rough texture did not register. When he reached for his heavy shoes, he could tell only by sight if they were in his hand.

Light-headed, pain radiating up his hands, arms and shoulders, he was pushed away from the bed by a uniformed guard.

Back in his cell he noticed that his books had been removed. Without his Hebrew-Russian dictionary and grammar, his history books, his guide to Israel, his mathematics books, he felt denuded, defenseless.

A half hour later the guard came for him. He imagined he was being taken to the bag factory. He protested that he was unable to hold the rough fabric, incapable of pushing the needles.

But he was escorted to the office of the commandant. Through the window he could see a man in the uniform of a KGB officer. It wasn't Karpov or Malik. A younger man, dark-haired and hatchet-faced.

12

BELOW THE TWO-ENGINED plane, the Volga River snaked its way past Kazan. They could see the vast blocklike outlines of the Kuibyshev dam, the great metallic lake, the mammoth enbankments that protected the city.

"How far is the prison?" Irina asked.

Karpov said it was a half-hour ride. He would hire a taxi.

"I'll leave you at the airport," she said. "This is something you must do by yourself."

Twice during the flight she had showed him Levitch's photograph. The first time—running the risk that the radio frequency might be picked up by the jet's communications system—she stimulated his left brain. He smiled, took her hand, shut his eyes in childlike bliss. Twenty minutes later she showed him Levitch's face again, after stimulation of his right brain associated with pictures of Lubianka, Lefortovo and the gulag. He grimaced, breathed deeply.

"I don't need the prod," he laughed. He was looking at Levitch's blurred face, feeling an indescribable sense of comfort and joy. Like one of Irina's TNT-sensitive rats, he did not need to be electrically stimulated to feel pleasure.

"Are you confident?" she asked.

"Yes, yes. The ID papers were in order. The guard at Moscow didn't even bother studying the booklet. He saw KGB and he waved me on. These rural types will be even more trusting."

His confidence astonished her. Yet he could not be all that sure of himself. He had insisted she accompany him to Kazan to reinforce his left-brain feelings about Levitch. Without her presence, he said, he found himself succumbing to right-brain contempt for the refusenik, regarding him as trash, a criminal not worth saving. But when she was near him, rewarding him with the joy-giving jolt, he felt differently about Levitch.

She wasn't sure what he had in mind. He had been secretive, smiling knowingly, assuring her that he could succeed. He had resources, documents, official papers and orders, uniforms, a weapon, and a blind cocksurety.

He'd come to the hospital once after they had met in his ransacked apartment. Like a puppy seeking affection, he'd asked for intense stimulation. She'd refused. He would have to master the technique himself. If pictures and photographs failed to move him, he would have to find Levitch in the flesh—the living, breathing embodiment of his pleasure.

"How stupid, how irrational," Karpov said. "A joke, an awful joke. And yet I sense something in me. What? It goes beyond that rush of warmth and joy. It has to do with rightness and wrongness. Who have I been fooling? I know Levitch is innocent. But never until this past week did I for a minute sense remorse or regret or the need to undo some wickedness."

She took his hand. They were in the screening room. Levitch beamed at them from the screen, four times life-size. Something new was stirring in Karpov. Moral values? Standards of behavior superimposed on the conditioned response, the good feelings that the pictures induced? Perhaps he was advancing to a stage beyond that of the implanted rats. Irina thought: *He is, after all, human.*

In the airport—they were whisked through security, the guard nodding at the forged KGB pass—Karpov went to a public phone and called the office of the commandant at Maridov prison.

News traveled slowly in the vast, clunking organization. It was unlikely that his discharge from the service was known to the head of a prison in the Tatar Autonomous Region.

Karpov waited, looking through the glass at Irina. She was seated, reading a magazine, smoking. He wondered for a moment about what she had done to him—splitting his brain, implanting metal inside the soft tissue. He could not resent her actions. How could he deny that he felt healthier, more human, more alive? Gone was the convulsing, headache-prone neurotic. He laughed to himself; he might get his head blown off looking for Abram Levitch, but he would die with a smile, a surge of joy. . . .

He identified himself to the commandant.

"Major Karpov? In Kazan? We weren't notified. Your colleague is here. Got here this morning."

"Colleague?"

The commandant had a moist voice. *Probably not too bright*, Karpov thought, *terrified of the KGB*.

"Major Zaitsev. He's with Levitch now. He said he's going to spend a few hours with him, stay overnight."

Karpov shivered. A narrow escape. Too narrow. He could not believe his bad luck—and his good luck. Had he gone directly to Maridov and asked for Levitch, he'd have walked into Zaitsev's arms. Now he was forewarned.

"Shall I tell Major Zaitsev you're on your way out?"

"No, no. I assume he's staying in Kazan? I wanted to check a few details before helping him interrogate Levitch. The case was originally mine, you know. I got the arrest and the conviction."

"So I'm told. Thank God for men like you, Major, keeping an eye on those traitors. Shall I—?"

"Where did you say Zaitsev was staying?"

The commandant hesitated. "The Intourist Hotel."

Karpov thought a moment. "Don't bother him. No messages. I'll meet him later. Thank you."

Irina had a few hours before her return flight to Moscow. They went into a flyblown airport cafe and ordered coffee. Karpov took her hands.

"I feel liberated," he said. "Euphoric, unafraid."

"You're doing the right thing."

"Did you plan this? Rearranging neurons in my brain,

reconstructing my nervous system so that Levitch would benefit?"

She shook her head. "It was accidental. The commissurotomy was medically indicated. It helped you but it produced other symptoms. The electrodes—I don't know. I went ahead. I wasn't sure what I was doing. Andrei, I hated you. I wanted revenge for Lev Tashenko, for Levitch, for all those you have hurt, ruined, consigned to torment. But something unique has happened. You aren't merely in the grip of a mechanical device, an electrical technology. A spread effect has set in, a bonus to your soul."

"You believe in souls?"

"I don't know. Call it soul, spirit, an essence that makes man better than clay. I saw it in you. Keep it alive. Nurture it. You're courageous to try to free Levitch. I know it may not work. But I hope you succeed. I hope you will be safe and secure somewhere."

"And will you come to live with me?"

She moved her head slowly. "I don't love you. But you'll have my respect."

He stroked her folded hands with his right hand. His left hand lay clenched in his lap. When he raised it to pick up his coffee cup, it shook and sent the coffee spilling.

They dabbed at the puddles of coffee with soiled napkins. Irina summoned the waitress. Karpov paid her, found his left hand trembling almost uncontrollably.

They walked toward the gate.

"Are you all right?" she asked.

"Yes. Confident, unworried."

"I admire what you're doing. It's strange. I always sensed something else in you. Long before the operations. What is the expression the Americans have? A thin man trying to wriggle out of every fat man? In your case I suspected a good man was trying to get out of a bad one."

"Bad? I obeyed orders. I . . ."

"You need not make excuses."

He held his left hand to his left temple. He was swaying slightly, averting his face from the late afternoon sun. "I . . . I . . . really have no knowledge of anything bad . . . prisons . . . interrogations in cellars . . . Someone else was involved, responsible. . . ."

The duality was complete. Deeper, more dominating than

ever. His brain had been split. The two hemispheres, goaded
into independent thought and action, each with its separate
compartment of ideas and emotions, were competing. The
left hemisphere had no knowledge of evil acts. It was innocent,
beneficent. *A bit of a hypocrite,* Irina thought. The right
brain understood evil, accepted it, accommodated itself to it.

"I wish you good luck, Andrei Borisovich."

"I want to see Levitch clearly and plainly. I always wondered about him. Where did the courage come from? How
did he manage to smile, to joke, to insist on his innocence? It
wasn't the kind of behavior I expected from a meaningless
Jew."

"No one is meaningless."

"Yes. Quite right. Part of me acknowledges that. Even
though the *other* Karpov, the old reptile you once told me
about, would argue against such a thesis. He'd claim that only
the state has meaning, only the police possess the ultimate
truth."

"You know that isn't true."

The right eye smiled, the right hand touched her arm. "It
isn't. Goodbye, Irina."

"Goodbye, Andrei."

She kissed his cheek. Passing through the gate, showing
her boarding pass, she saw a tall man in a KGB uniform
approaching Karpov.

"What a pleasant surprise, Major," Zaitsev said. "To find
you in Kazan. You're looking better. You must be feeling well
to make the trip from Moscow. But Dort told me you were
going to take a long rest. I'm puzzled."

Karpov smiled, a twisted half-face smile. "This is part of
my program of rehabilitation."

"The message I got was that you came in connection with
some matter relating to Levitch. But my understanding was
that Colonel Dort relieved you of all duties. Levitch is my
responsibility, as you surely know."

"I thought I might be useful to you. The Zolkin business. I
wanted to warn you that Levitch won't talk. Not to anyone
except me. He and I have a special relationship. He's dependent on me. It isn't just fear. The fellow doesn't have any
fear. He relishes playing the martyr. So I indulge him, and

he responds. I knew of the agency's profound interest in the Zolkin matter, so I came here to see if I could help."

They walked through the dusty terminal. Tatars, Buryats and Bashkirs walked past them. *How Asian we are,* Karpov thought; *there are more of these yellow-skinned, slant-eyed people in our ranks than Caucasians. No wonder Europe is wary of us.*

"Frankly, I'm at a loss," Zaitsev said. He had narrow liver-colored eyes, hollow cheeks, sable hair. His nose was bladelike, wide-nostriled. One of the young breed of enforcers. An expert in Indian policies, Zaitsev was said to have subverted several ministers in New Delhi, compromised them, secured crucial papers from them. He had been politely asked to leave, but there had been no protest. The trusting Indians adored their Soviet friends, even when they betrayed Indian officials. Not a word had issued from New Delhi, not a squeal over Zaitsev's bribes, threats and thefts.

"Puzzled?"

"Why this interest in me, your successor? Or in Levitch?"

"I'm trying to get back into Dort's good graces. He thinks I'm burned out because of the neurological problems I've had. I know it's irregular, but if I can assist you in getting Levitch to furnish us with a confession about Zolkin's treason, Dort may reinstate me."

Major Zaitsev was shaking his head. Karpov studied the red tabs on his gray uniform, the sparkling medals on his chest. "I will have to inform Dzerzhinsky about this. It really isn't permissible. You're out of service, Karpov. You have no standing. I appreciate your offer to help, but it won't pass muster."

"Give me fifteen minutes to explain how I can get Levitch to cooperate."

They were outside the terminal. A black Zhiguli pulled up. A militiaman was at the wheel.

Zaitsev held the door open for Karpov, as if acknowledging his seniority. The car sped off for the city.

"I'm having a bit of trouble with this," Zaitsev said. "You're retired. You're ill. And I find you here."

Patiently, full of smiles and winks, his voice oily and reassuring, Karpov explained again. How easy it was to lie! He wondered: *Which brain is lying?* Surely the right brain, the dissembler, the gloomy one, seeking to hurt, to destroy.

But it is the left brain that craves Levitch's freedom. Karpov, persuasive, logical, laughed inwardly. The left brain was using the right. Lies in the service of truth.

"When we get to my room, Comrade Major," Zaitsev said, "we must put in a call to Colonel Dort and see if we can't straighten this thing out."

"Of course. I'll be happy to talk to him."

Karpov turned his head away. He felt the frown wrinkle his left eye. His left hand tensed against the flat bulk of the automatic strapped in his belt.

"A minute to bleed the lizard," Zaitsev said. "I couldn't tolerate that stinking lavatory at the prison. A stench that could curdle your stomach. Why can't these louts learn sanitation?"

"A good project for the State Scientific Committee. Maybe we can get Dort's staff to work on cleaner toilets."

Zaitsev unbuttoned his collar and his tunic. He told Karpov to order drinks from room service—a double vodka and Narzan water for himself—and went into the bathroom.

Karpov pretended to call room service. He kept the bar depressed, listened to his own voice. No waiter would come to the door.

His left hand riffled the clothing in Zaitsev's opened valise. No weapon was in evidence. But Zaitsev was wearing one—a small pistol.

Karpov wondered what would happen. He doubted Zaitsev would buy his story. Still, Zaitsev was ambitious, conniving and not quite as intelligent as he seemed. He had not yet called Dort.

Karpov sat opposite the bathroom door. He touched the 9 mm automatic but did not withdraw it. He gauged the distance to the door. Six feet. A good leap and he could gain the advantage.

A toilet flushed; water gurgled in a sink. Karpov, and the inevitable pictures of Lenin on the wall, waited. Lenin at the Finland Station, borne aloft by the cheering crowd. He studied Lenin's bald head, stared at the Red Star and shuddered. The stimulus of the images was enough to flood him with terror, an urgent desire to run, to strike.

"Put your hands up, Karpov. You are under arrest."

Zaitsev had opened the door. He was pointing the pistol at

Karpov. His jacket was off. Wide suspenders, white shirt
open at the throat, gray riding breeches, black boots. He
looked frightened.

"Comrade Major, this is foolish. I came to help you."

"Pick up the phone and get Dort."

"That was my intention. You can put the gun away. I'm a
threat to no one, with my carved-up head."

"Get on the phone. We're going to straighten this idiotic
thing out."

Karpov got up. He stopped halfway to the phone. "Why
not take a chance on me, Zaitsev? What can you lose?"

"Do as I say."

Karpov's left eye narrowed, squinted at his adversary. His
left fist clenched. But he did not move. "Major, this is crazy.
We're on the same side. I'm here to make sure that Levitch
doesn't trick you. Let's the two of us go back and interview
him. I know the way his mind works. I can twist him around
my little finger."

"Pick up the phone. I order you. Karpov, you have no
standing in the organization any longer. Your brilliant record
means nothing. You're finished, severed from the team."

The stalking reptile, Karpov thought. *Irina's analogy of the
two hunting lizards in the terrarium. The defender bobbing
his triangular head, fanning our his throat, doing pushups.
The invader mimicking him.* A quote Irina had read to him:
"In the lizard world, the one who does the most pushups
is the one who survives." Deep in man's brain rested the
neural circuitry for violence, pursuit, stalking, ritual, deceit,
killing. . . .

"Move, Karpov."

The right brain was taking over. The knowledge of evil and
pain, of violence and anger . . .

Zaitsev gestured with the pistol. As he waved his hand in a
short arc, the barrel pointed away from Karpov. Karpov
lunged at him, hurling the left side of his body at the reed-
thin figure.

The gun exploded, a subdued popping sound. Karpov's left
hand locked on Zaitsev's wrist. His left leg kicked at Zaitsev's
middle. The left knee jerked into his groin.

Zaitsev wheezed. The gun dropped under the forceful twist
of Karpov's left hand. He bent double in pain.

"Damned fool, you're insane," Zaitsev grunted. "Dort warned me. You bastard."

Karpov kicked him in the head with his left foot, kicked him again. Zaitsev twitched, lay still.

In the taxicab Karpov smoked and offered a cigarette to the terrified driver. He was yellow-skinned and pan-faced, and he had balked vociferously at driving out to Maridov prison. Then Karpov, his green eyes glinting, had shown him the KGB card. The Asian face paled. The driver gulped. He was all apologies. "Anything you want. Comrade Major," he'd stammered. "Of course, whatever you wish."

Karpov thought: *I wish your cab had wings. And was armor-plated.*

He'd stripped Zaitsev, gagged and bound him, dumped him in an air shaft. They'd find him sooner or later. But it would be hours before Zaitsev would work free of the bonds and be able to shout for help. The air shaft was ideal: a place never cleaned or swept, covered with a heavy wooden lid. The hotel room he'd left in disorder, taking Zaitsev's pistol. Only one shot had been fired. Neither of them had been struck.

Appropriate, Karpov thought. *He and I, members of different generations of stalkers, interrogators, jailers—but we don't kill. We let others do it.* Lesser men pulled triggers, injected drugs, destroyed minds and bodies. Let Zaitsev twitch and struggle in his rat-tracked air shaft.

Levitch's face appeared before him—innocent of evil, posing unasked questions with the arched eyebrows, the accepting eyes.

There was a shivering moment in Karpov's mind. He saw Levitch as if reflected in the vehicle's windshield. And he thought: *Kill him.*

Warmth and joy were not infusing his body. His limbs were not experiencing the blessed release, the sense of relaxation, ease, goodness.

Kill him, something said.

The taxi turned onto a mud-bordered road, bounced past wretched wooden houses, a clutch of miserable shops. Karpov saw none of it. The glories of the Tatar Autonomous Region eluded him.

Instead he saw Levitch again. This time the face was

bloodied, mashed. The eyes stared but seemed sightless. The mouth, so often smiling with its secret knowledge, was dribbling blood.

The left side of Karpov's body tensed. Muscles in his left arm tightened. The arm rose, hardening the shoulder muscles and the left side of his neck. He had an urge to release the dammed strength, smash Levitch, knock him down, kick him the way he had kicked Zaitsev.

No, no, the other Karpov told him.

This is Levitch. Your friend. See him, and feel the warmth, the pleasure, the joy.

His right hand—warmth infusing the fingers—patted the tensing left hand. His right foot, feeling as if it had been massaged and oiled, rested itself on the instep of the taut left foot and subdued the kicking.

Again Levitch's mangled face appeared to him.

The dirty windshield became a screen, a mirror of his mind. *Yes, yes,* one of the Karpovs thought. *Kill him. Destroy him.*

There was a moment when he saw Irina, brushing back a strand of brown hair, gazing at him with her cool eyes, measuring him.

Now stare at the screen. What do you see?

Levitch.

What are your thoughts about him?

Another troublemaker. No more, no less.

What else?

Agitator. Spy. Zionist conspirator. Fascist.

Then the stimulation, the spreading warmth, the indefinable joy.

Levitch, beaten and dying, stared at him from the windshield. The eyes appealed for help.

"Lousy kike," Karpov said. "You'll get what you deserve."

Another Karpov said, "Gently, gently."

The left hand thrust the calming right hand away. "Go to hell. When I finish with him, I'll finish Irina also. All of them."

"You asked me something, Comrade Major?" the driver interrupted.

"No. Keep driving."

The voice snarled, threatened. The right-brain Karpov had responded. It was dominant.

* * *

The commandant shuffled the papers nervously. He looked at the seals, the embossed marks, the dating. Rarely did he see such high-level stuff.

In the suffocating office Karpov crossed his legs. His eyes were calm and hard. He let the bumpkin read the papers a second time, study the forged orders.

"This is irregular, to say the least," the commandant said. "First time it's ever happened. A release order for a political prisoner on such short notice? And only this morning Major Zaitsev was here interrogating Levitch."

"I know. As you can see, these papers are signed by Colonel Dort and Colonel Reshev. There isn't any higher priority. So get it moving, Captain. Levitch is to be released to my custody at once."

As he pronounced Levitch's name, a rush of anger shivered his left side. The old reptile, the creature dominated by the R-complex. The lizards in the terrarium.

"At once?"

"At once. I'm taking over the case. He's in my care as of now."

The commandant's fingers tapped the papers, rubbed the KGB seal a few times.

"I will take the prisoner Levitch, I said. I want him dressed and discharged and brought to me."

"A new one on me," the commandant said. "Really a new one. I assume Major Zaitsev has been notified?"

"He's aware of this change of plans. No need to notify him. We'll rendezvous in a half hour. Now bring me Abram Levitch."

He seemed to have shrunk, turned paler. His skin appeared to be covered with a waxy substance.

They get that way, Karpov knew. Outwardly the same, yet the sickly sheen of their flesh betraying what has been done to them, the inner torment, the pain, the dread, the surrender.

Levitch, in a baggy gray suit, tieless, wearing scuffed brown shoes, stood facing him. He was making a brave effort to stand erect, displaying the knowing smile on his sensuous mouth. The eyes were forgiving, wise.

"Prisoner Levitch," Karpov said. "You're under orders to accompany me."

"I am free?"

"No. You are not to ask questions."

Karpov stared at the doughy face. Smiling at him. *Damn Levitch.* He was smiling at him.

He envisioned him dead, bloodied, trampled in the mud.

And in a fraction of a second, he saw him grinning, opening his arms to a woman. The woman smiling in the sunlight, framed by flowers.

Karpov blinked.

The commandant and the two guards who had brought Levitch to the office stared at Karpov. He was swaying, inhaling deeply.

"Are you ill, Comrade Major?" the commandant asked.

"No. Give me the papers to sign."

"These orders are all that's necessary. I've never seen such a priority."

"All that fuss over me?" Levitch asked. "I remember, Major Karpov. You once sent eight of your best men to follow me around. My cage."

The commandant crossed from behind his desk and slapped Levitch on the mouth. "Silence. You heard the Major."

The slap awakened Karpov. He took handcuffs from his coat pocket and walked to Levitch. The refusenik's unjudging eyes looked at him.

Damn him, Karpov thought. *Damn his innocence, his goodness. He is not even aware of what he is, what he means.*

He clamped the gyves on Levitch's wrists, made sure they were fast. Arms in front of him, Levitch looked more vulnerable than ever.

"All is in order, Major?" the commandant asked.

"Everything. He's in the custody of the Fifth Chief Directorate. Interrogation and examination. He'll be returned to custody when Zaitsev and I have finished with him."

Levitch's knees sagged. A guard helped him upright. "Sorry," Levitch said. "I'm in pain."

"Where shall I say you have taken him?" asked the commandant.

"To the Intourist Hotel. He will be with us a few days."

"Ah, a vacation," Levitch said. "Major, I know I'm not supposed to talk, but could I telephone my wife? My mother? Just a few minutes of talk. Talk never hurt anyone—"

The guard moved to hit Levitch with the butt of his rifle.

Karpov's powerful right hand grabbed the butt, pushed the weapon away. "He's under my authority, Sergeant. Leave him alone."

In the taxi, Levitch, hiding the handcuffs with the sleeves of his oversize suit, hunched in a corner and stared at Karpov.

"Why?" he asked. "Is this the end for me?"

Karpov put a finger to his lips.

"The hotel, Comrade Major?" the driver asked.

"The airport."

Saying this, Karpov had an urge to hurt Levitch. His right brain jerked the left arm, the left knee. Half his body twitched, tensed, sought to turn away from the seat, move toward Levitch. The refusenik looked puzzled but unafraid.

"You seem upset, Major," Levitch said. And smiled again.

The warmth began to germinate in Karpov's left brain. It was as if Irina were depressing the button on the transmitter. The aura of utter relaxation, the satisfying glow, the sense of things being right with the world, of problems solved, pain eased, anxiety suppressed, began to suffuse his being.

Karpov smiled back at Levitch. "Follow orders, Levitch. Listen to what I tell you. Don't argue with me."

At the flaking terminal, Karpov dismissed the driver, paid him double, warned him to lose himself, say nothing about any of the trips he had made.

"No one knows you took me to Maridov or here," Karpov said. One fearsome green eye pinned the man. "Silence. Don't volunteer information. You'll regret it."

"Of course, Comrade Major. We Tatars know how to keep our mouths shut."

Karpov took his suitcase from the luggage compartment and nodded at Levitch.

There was an abandoned storage shed with a rusting corrugated roof and slanting faded walls at the edge of the terminal building. A ruined chain-link fence had been broken. Theft was endemic. Anything not nailed down or under armed guard was looted by the grateful workers.

"In there," Karpov said.

"You will kill me?" Levitch asked. His voice was plaintive. "This isn't proper, Major. You and I, we have almost become partners in this sad business. I—"

A sudden urge to murder him seized Karpov. *Damn Irina!*

Without her, without the stimulation of the filaments in his divided brain, the struggle was constant. No sooner had he suppressed his right brain with sunny images of Levitch, with waves of good feeling, of exquisite pleasure, than it reasserted itself. It infected him with a craving for death and brutalization.

"Move, Levitch."

Kill him, kill him, the right brain whispered.

Let him go, the left brain said.

The left brain is verbal, rational and affective, Irina had said. *There is poetry and music in the right brain, but also a Nazi hidden in it. . . .*

They entered the storage shed. Nothing of value had been left—rotting boards, old crates, paper bags that had contained cement.

Karpov unlocked the valise. Inside was a uniform of a captain in the KGB—red tabs, insignia, shoulder boards. Peaked cap, boots, riding breeches, a smart tunic.

"Get dressed. Quickly."

"Levitch in the KGB? It's a joke."

"It is no joke." The warmth drowned him, a wondrous sense of fulfillment.

"My hands are locked. My arms hurt. I have this disease. . . ."

For a moment, as he unlocked the handcuffs, Karpov felt a rush of hot anger, of blind hate. It was a compulsion, a need to smash the metal bracelets against Levitch's nose, rip gashes in the waxy skin. He held his breath, waited for the left brain to assert itself.

There was a battery-operated shaver in the suitcase. Karpov had bought it in London. "Here," he ordered Levitch. "As soon as you are dressed, shave off all your hair. Then put on these smoked glasses and this mustache."

"It's a game," Levitch said. "Why are you doing this to me? Do you have some motive? If you want to arrest Mikhail Zolkin you can do it anytime you want. I know that's what you're after. Zaitsev told me this morning. If I don't implicate Zolkin they'll add ten years to my sentence. That's crazy. I won't last another two years. And if I do, fifteen more at labor in the camps? Do what you want with me, but please, Major, no more of these games."

Karpov's voice was comforting. "Dress, Levitch. Shave your head. Paste the mustache on. I am letting you go free."

In tattered underwear, Levitch seemed the ultimate victim, a paradigm of all the victims of the state. He pulled on the gray trousers, struggled with the polished boots, wincing, fumbling, grunting.

"I don't understand you," Levitch said. "I don't think I ever did. A man of your breeding and intelligence, to do what you did. This is all a prank."

A soft cloud, a gentle haze surrounded Karpov. Sunlight slanted through the rotting boards of the shed. He saw motes of dust agitating in shafts of golden light. Outside, a jet blasted its engines, another responded in a different key. It sounded to him like the music of the spheres.

"What now?" Levitch asked.

"Shave your head."

"I don't understand this."

The electric shaver buzzed, hummed, removed the last of Levitch's prison fuzz. Clots of red-brown hair tumbled on his shoulders. Solicitously, like a concerned mother, Karpov dusted clumps of hair from his prisoner, helped him finish the job.

The tunic was an almost perfect fit.

"Stand up straight," Karpov said brusquely. "Try to look like a soldier. Keep the sunglasses on at all times. Smoke a great deal. Don't look anyone in the eye."

"I have no cigarettes."

Karpov took a carton of cigarettes from the valise. He also removed a leather folder, a stack of papers. He spread the documents, fanlike, on a wooden crate.

"Passport. KGB identity booklet. Travel orders. Other relevant documents. Air tickets."

"I still don't understand."

"You are Captain Yuri Belkin of the First Chief Directorate. Third Department, which covers KGB operations in Scandinavia. These papers confirm that you are on an official mission to Stockholm to investigate irregularities in the timber trade between the Soviet Union and Sweden. Study them on the plane."

"Plane?"

Karpov checked his watch. In an hour there was a flight to Moscow.

"That's right. You'll be aboard the flight. At Sheremetevo Airport, you will make yourself as invisible as possible for two hours. Then you will board the night flight to Stockholm. You will be free."

With difficulty, Levitch buttoned the tunic. He moved like a man in a trance. "I'm at a loss, Comrade Major. What is this all about? You'll probably have me arrested in Moscow. Why?"

Inexplicably, Karpov was covering his left eye. His right eye was smiling at Levitch.

"Really, Major, this is silly." Levitch ran his hand over his shaved pate, patted the idiotic red mustache. *A new Levitch? Levitch reborn?* What in God's name was Karpov grinning about?

Karpov knew. As Irina had told him many times, it was the left brain that got the point of jokes. And he was looking at a sublime, Olympian, monumental joke. Levitch, whose childish face made him simmer with good feeling, was touching off unearthly delights in his heart, in his bisected brain.

"I see you clearly," Karpov said. His left hand covered his left eye. "I am amused. I find you droll and damn near lovable in your uniform, Levitch. Does it fit properly?"

"The boots are a bit stiff. I told you, my joints ache terribly."

Karpov exploded in laughter. He laughed until he had to hold his left side. "Let's test the theory."

"What theory? What are you talking about?"

Karpov covered his right eye. The left eye alone saw Levitch. It sent signals to the right brain. The right brain recoiled. "Damn you. Disgusting. An impostor." The old terror shivered his legs. He felt sweat forming in his armpits.

For a moment, as Levitch saw the snarl twist Karpov's lips, noted the cold anger in his eyes, he feared the worst. The man was insane. Karpov would toy with him, then end the charade, turn him over to the authorities. Karpov would invent some wild tale, make a hero of himself, consign Levitch to interminable life in prison, perhaps to execution.

"Look, if you've made a mistake, we can unmake it," Levitch said cheerfully. "This is lunacy. An airplane flight to Moscow in this costume? And then, without a farewell

I go on to Stockholm and I'm free? Please, Major, end the joke."

His right eye covered, Karpov experienced a desire to smash the forgiving face. *Damn them!* Why were they so vulnerable, innocent, incapable of fight? They deserved to be tormented, jailed, shot.

Baring his teeth, Karpov grunted. He reached for his automatic.

Levitch saw the move and backed away. "So. That's it. All right. I should have known. I ask only you inform my wife that I died bravely."

Karpov's left hand locked on the weapon. The right hand grasped the left, dug in its nails. Karpov dropped his left hand from the gun and smiled again.

"Major, I'm sorry. You are in need of help. I beg of you, stop playing with me."

Studying Levitch with both eyes, Karpov smiled. It was laughable—the bleached prison face, the unconquerable brown eyes, the gentle features, now camouflaged with a shaved head, a ratty mustache, the rumpled uniform. It was comical, sad, poignant and, to Karpov, pleasing.

"I must ask for an explanation," Levitch said. "I was never aware that humor was given a high priority in the KGB."

"But this is marvelously funny, Levitch. I haven't felt so gratified in years. I'm not one for carnivals or masquerades, but this is surely one of the best."

Levitch opened his palms to Karpov. "At your service, Major. I can't help feeling someone will present me with the bill in Moscow. But why the fuss? I'm no threat to anyone."

"Stop babbling," Karpov said. "You Jews are your own worst enemy with your endless blubbering."

"We prefer the word *lamentation*."

"Whatever you call it." Karpov circled him, admiring his creation. Each time he studied Levitch's stumpy form, concealed in the uniform, he could not suppress a chuckle, a sense of gratification.

The electrode was not needed. He was supplying his own left-brain stimulus.

"So? What now?" Levitch tugged at his collar tabs. He had a mad memory of a superb Italian film he had seen at a student center years ago. He'd gone with Sarah. An Italian drifter, a thief and pimp, is planted in a prison by the SS and told to pose as a resistance hero in order to ferret information from political prisoners. In time, the shabby impostor comes to believe in his new identity. Confusing his lowly self with the courageous soldier, he begins to live the soldier's life. He resists torture, refuses to inform on his prison mates, and is ultimately executed.

But he was only Captain Belkin of the First Directorate. An utter fraud. The uniform fit but not the new identity. What did it mean? What kind of depraved farce was Karpov inventing?

"Sit down and relax, Levitch."

Levitch squatted on a pile of lumber. Karpov sat opposite him, smiling his self-satisfied smile. He offered Levitch an American cigarette, inquired if his health was good, assured him that in Stockholm he could find decent medical care.

"As a matter of fact, I feel dreadful. Didn't you see the trouble I had getting into this costume?"

"You'll be fine, Levitch. I may even come to visit you in Sweden. Or Israel. Or wherever it is you wind up."

"With sincere thanks for whatever it is you're doing for me now, Major Karpov, I'd just as soon not see you for a long time."

Karpov, sitting on a crate, dragging on his cigarette, enveloped himself in smoke. He laughed softly, stared at the unlikely figure in the gray uniform. A softness surrounded him; he felt the warmth ooze through his limbs, caress his chest, ease his mind. The left brain was ascendant.

The documents and the authenticated ticket got Levitch aboard the Moscow flight without a hitch. The uniform alone worked to whisk him through unsearched. No questions were asked. Not of a KGB captain.

From a slit in the walls of the shed, Karpov watched him vanish into the terminal. A half hour later he saw the four-engine plane rising, nosing toward Moscow.

At once his mood changed. Without Levitch's presence his left brain was desolate, lethargic. Right-brain terrors began to work. In his mind's eye he saw prison camps, dogs, the faces of Dort and Reshev, the jailers, torturers, schemers and murderers.

Dozing, lulled by the late afternoon sun, alone in the abandoned shed, he slept. In slumber, left and right brain battled for his mind inconclusively. Images of brutes and savages alternated with scenes of peace, flowery meadows, a house by a sunlit sea.

They came with dogs.

Karpov heard them yapping, howling, sniffing. Zaitsev must have been found. The prison commandant had told his wild story. Karpov checked his watch. *Good God!* He'd been asleep for six hours. With luck, Levitch (he smiled as he said the name to himself) was on the SAS night plane, safe in his uniform, armed with his forged passes, his faked documents. A bald-headed bespectacled captain of the First Directorate . . .

The dogs were screaming, coming closer, wild with insane energy.

The flimsy metal door to the shed, rusted and askew, came loose. Cones of light illumined the interior.

Finished, Karpov thought. He got to his feet. Ever the dandy, he dusted dirt and straw from his coat, adjusted his tie.

"Who's in there?" a voice called.

He saw uniformed men. Three, four, five bulky shapes.

The dogs picked up his scent, lunged toward him, turning the leashes into taut lines.

"Who's there, dammit?" a voice called. "Hands up and come on out."

"It's him," someone said.

He could not be sure whether it was Zaitsev or someone else. There were a half dozen of them in uniform. They would not kill him. They would want to interrogate him, pry information from him, track down Levitch.

Karpov saw the uniforms, the slavering maws of the dogs, the muzzles of sidearms, a shotgun, AK rifles.

He stood at attention. His right eye closed.

With his left hand he found the automatic in his belt. The right hand went to it, tried to restrain the left. The fingers of his right hand dug into the left, drawing blood.

"Drop your weapon, Karpov," Zaitsev called. "Come forward."

Karpov yanked his right hand away. It did not know violence. It would be innocent.

The left hand, directed by the angry right brain, turned the barrel of the handgun into his abdomen. Twice it pumped the trigger. The gun made barely a sound, buried as it was in flesh and clothing.

"What the hell is he doing?" Zaitsev called. "Jesus, get him."

Karpov, his face locked in a half-smile, half-scowl, fell slowly. His eyes were open, outraged and pleased.

13

TONY PARENTE TOOK the call in the vestibule of his apartment.

"Tony, my friend. This is Abram."

Parente gulped, felt his legs go weak, sank into a chair. "I don't believe you. Prove it."

"Is Jimmy there?"

"Yes. What do you want?"

"Put him on the phone."

Jimmy Parente was summoned from his math homework. He listened to the voice. His eyes were like dinner plates. "It sounds like Abram, Pop." The boy grinned. "He says he beat me at Monopoly twice in a row. Knocked me off with hotels on Tennessee and Boardwalk. It's got to be him, Pop. Only Abram would know it."

Parente took the phone. Martha entered the vestibule and listened, tears in her eyes. She anticipated something dreadful.

"Stockholm?" Parente asked.

"Don't ask me how or why, Tony. I'm here. I'm alive. I'm safe. I'm at the Israeli Embassy. Tomorrow they fly me to Israel. I'll see Sarah, all my friends."

Parente said, "You know, Abram, this line is tapped. Double tapped. Doesn't it bother you?"

"I'm free. I can't explain how or why. It happened, that's all. They'll have a version, I'm sure. So will I. Listen, my friend. I can't talk much longer. Next year in Jerusalem. What am I saying? This year, Tony, this year!"

Parente wished him well and hung up. He looked at his wife. "Crazier things have happened in this loony bin. But I can't remember when."

Through the Moscow grapevine—nothing appeared in the newspapers—Irina Tashenko learned two months later that Karpov was dead. A suicide, the rumor said.

She never got details. But word from the *urka* "messengers" at Maridov leaked out. An old thief named Oren sent Nadya Burik a letter one day. The paper smelled soapy, and Nadya knew it had been secreted in a dollop of wet soap, pasted to a sink or toilet, and smuggled out by a civilian workman. It was a common practice in prisons. Her murdered husband had used the same device twenty years ago.

The letter told of a strange event in the prison. Levitch had been summoned one day from the bag factory, interrogated by a KGB officer in civilian dress, then spirited out of the prison and never seen again. Of course the prisoners had gotten word of Levitch's surfacing in Israel. Oren thought Mme. Burik, an old friend of Levitch, might want to know. All his friends were happy. Little Levitch, the criminal wrote, was one hell of a guy. . . .

Parente heard the story from Nadya, made a copy of the letter, and on a hunch sent it to Dr. Tashenko. He was not sure why. But he suspected her involvement.

She read it but never said anything to him. Andrei Karpov was dead. *A final orgy of self-stimulation*, she mused, the implanted subject indulging his need to look clearly at Levitch, to experience that rush of ultimate inexplicable joy.

It had killed him. She felt drained, sorrowful. He had served her the way the twitching white rats served her. Like the rat who would depress the lever thirty times a second—*850,000 times in a twenty-day period*—until he collapsed of exhaustion. Karpov had gone the limit, a cooperative subject.

She wondered idly what they had done with his body. And at last she afforded herself the luxury of tears. Yes, he had to have been something better than a laboratory animal. There had been glimmers, hints of a lost humanity in him.

As she prepared for surgery, smoking a last cigarette before going to the scrub room, she had a vagrant wish that perhaps both of them might have been saved.

But the experiment was over. Levitch free, Karpov dead. On balance, it seemed a fair trade.

ABOUT THE AUTHOR

Gerald Green is the author of twenty-three books including *The Last Angry Man, Holocaust, To Brooklyn with Love* and *The Lotus Eaters*. He wrote the television drama *Holocaust*, which was seen worldwide by 500 million people and resulted directly in a change of West German laws, making it possible to prosecute Nazi war criminals in perpetuity. He received the Dag Hammarskjöld International Peace Prize for *Holocaust*.

Mr. Green has lived in France, Italy and Mexico, and currently makes his home in Connecticut. He was associated with NBC Television News for many years and produced such programs as *Today, The JFK Reports,* and the *Toscanini Centennial*.

A novel of terror from the bestselling author of
THE GOD PROJECT

NATHANIEL

by John Saul

Some thought him no more than legend, a folktale
created by the townsfolk of Prairie Bend to frighten
their children on cold winter nights. Others believed
him a restless spirit, returned to avenge the past.
But for eleven-year-old Michael Hall, Nathaniel is
the voice that calls him across the prairie night, the
voice that beckons him to follow . . . and do the
unthinkable.

NATHANIEL will be available July 1, 1984, wherever
Bantam Books are sold, or you may use the handy
coupon below for ordering.

"Not since SHOGUN has a western novelist so succeeded in capturing the essence of Asia."
—*The New York Times Book Review*

THE WARLORD

BY MALCOLM BOSSE

Ever so rarely, a novel emerges that propels us from our time and place and sets before us a vanished world, made as vividly real as our own. THE WARLORD is such a novel.

China in 1927 is a world of opportunity, of war, of adventure. Caught up in the storm of events are Phillip Embree, American missionary-turned-soldier; Vera Rogacheva, a beautiful Czarist emigree; Erich Luckner, a German arms dealer; and Kovalik, a Russian Bolshevik determined to bring the Revolution to China.

And standing in the eye of the hurricane is General Tang Shan-Teh, both a firm believer in the ancient Confucian values—and in the need for a truly progressive China. He is a man whose power and vision will forever change the face of an ancient, timeless world.

He is the Warlord.

Don't miss THE WARLORD, on sale May 23, 1984, wherever Bantam Books are sold, or use this handy coupon for ordering:

Here are the Books that Explore the Jewish Heritage-Past and Present.

Fiction

☐	24352	**Karpov's Brain** Gerald Green	$3.95
☐	24160	**Mila 18** Leon Uris	$4.50
☐	22536	**Dawn** Elie Wiesel	$2.95
☐	20807	**Night** Elie Wiesel	$2.95

Non-Fiction

☐	23653	**The Last Jews in Berlin** Leonard Gross	$3.95
☐	01418	**The First Step: Guide for the New Jewish Spirit** Zalman Schachter	$5.95
☐	34003	**The Jewish Almanac** Siegel & Rheins, eds.	$10.95
☐	01369	**Seasons of Our Joy** Arthur Waskow	$8.95
☐	22500	**Children of the Holocaust** Helen Epstein	$3.95
☐	13810	**World of Our Fathers** Irving Howe	$3.95
☐	23477	**The War Against the Jews** Lucy S. Dawidowicz	$4.95

Prices and availability subject to change without notice.

Buy them at your local bookstore or use this handy coupon for ordering:
